W9-CDW-245

**Brynne Stood Stock Still
and Glared Up at Him.
"All Right. Have Your Way with Me
and Get It Over!"**

Joshua's response was a shout of laughter that rendered him temporarily helpless. He let go of her wrists and doubled over.

Any other girl of his experience would have run away, but this one stood still, her hands on her hips, one foot tapping furiously up and down.

"What," she demanded loftily, "is so funny?"

With great effort, Joshua swallowed yet another fit of mirth.

"All right," Joshua conceded wickedly, approaching her. "I'll be happy to have my way with you."

Dear Reader,

We, the editors of Tapestry Romances, are committed to bringing you two outstanding original romantic historical novels each and every month.

From Kentucky in the 1850s to the court of Louis XIII, from the deck of a pirate ship within sight of Gibraltar to a mining camp high in the Sierra Nevadas, our heroines experience life and love, romance and adventure.

Our aim is to give you the kind of historical romances that you want to read. We would enjoy hearing your thoughts about this book and all future Tapestry Romances. Please write to us at the address below.

The Editors
Tapestry Romances
POCKET BOOKS
1230 Avenue of the Americas
Box TAP
New York, N.Y. 10020

Most Tapestry Books are available at special quantity discounts for bulk purchases for sales promotions, premiums or fund raising. Special books or book excerpts can also be created to fit specific needs.

For details write the office of the Vice President of Special Markets, Pocket Books, 1230 Avenue of the Americas, New York, New York 10020.

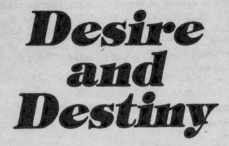

Desire
and
Destiny

Linda Lael Miller

A TAPESTRY BOOK
PUBLISHED BY POCKET BOOKS NEW YORK

Books by Linda Lael Miller

Desire and Destiny
Fletcher's Woman

Published by TAPESTRY BOOKS

This novel is a work of historical fiction. Names, characters, places and incidents relating to non-historical figures are either the product of the author's imagination or are used fictitiously. Any resemblance of such non-historical incidents, places or figures to actual events or locales or persons, living or dead, is entirely coincidental.

An *Original* publication of TAPESTRY BOOKS

A Tapestry Book published by
POCKET BOOKS, a division of Simon & Schuster, Inc.
1230 Avenue of the Americas, New York, N.Y. 10020

Copyright © 1983 by Linda Lael Miller

All rights reserved, including the right to reproduce this book or portions thereof in any form whatsoever. For information address Tapestry Books, 1230 Avenue of the Americas, New York, N.Y. 10020

ISBN: 0-671-49866-5

First Tapestry Books printing December, 1983

10 9 8 7 6 5 4 3 2 1

POCKET and colophon are registered trademarks of Simon & Schuster, Inc.

TAPESTRY is a trademark of Simon & Schuster, Inc.

Printed in the U.S.A.

For Wendy Diane Miller

*If a beloved child has many
names, you surely have a thousand*

Prologue

Washington Territory
July 3, 1885

BRYNNE MCFARREN KNELT BESIDE THE NEW GRAVE ON the grassy hillside, determined not to cry. Gently, she traced the words she herself had laboriously burned into the wooden marker with an iron poker. JOHN MCFARREN, BELOVED FATHER, APRIL 2, 1837–JUNE 3, 1885. MAY THE ANGELS GUARD HIM.

The warm July breeze lifted a tendril of Brynne's free flowing, golden-brown hair, and she shifted her eyes to the snowy flocks bleating at the base of the hill. They had been shorn just after the lambing in April, those two hundred sheep, but they were already sporting new white fleece.

Brynne swallowed. The sheep belonged to Tanner Enterprises now, just as the small farm did—the sturdy, stone house, the shearing shed, the barns, the vegetable garden, the wildflower-strewn hillsides and lush meadows—all of it belonged to them.

A cry of helpless rage rose in Brynne's aching throat, but she suppressed it. She sat down, spreading her worn poplin skirts around her like a gaily printed banner, and frowned pensively at the rough-hewn pine marker.

Perhaps she'd been wrong, working so many hours to

1

make it. Hadn't her father told her often enough that he wanted no stones or monuments when he passed on to join her mother? Brynne sighed. She supposed John McFarren's odd behavior over the past few years would remain a mystery forever.

They had come to the sheep farm near Tacoma, Brynne and her father, very suddenly, two years before, when Brynne was barely sixteen. Her recently widowed parent had not only dropped the proud McFarren name, he had forbidden his daughter to use it in the bargain. In the valley at the base of the snowy mountains, they had been known as the McFarlands.

Bewildered and still in the tearing claws of her own grief for her lost mother, Brynne had not thought to wonder about her father's actions. Once the pain had been blunted by time, however, a thousand questions had loomed in her mind.

Despite the fact that Brynne plagued him constantly, John McFarren would not say why they had fled Port Propensity, the small, booming town on Puget Sound's Hood Canal, when they had only recently settled there. Nor could he be persuaded to explain abandoning the practice of medicine or using a false name.

Brynne had been forced to assume that the loss of his cherished wife accounted for his aberrations.

Even now, however, as she prepared to leave the home she had dearly loved, Brynne McFarren was puzzled by other elements of the mystery, elements that did not quite knit together into a sensible pattern.

Her father's sudden fondness for strong drink was understandable, she supposed, in light of his shattering loss. He'd consumed frightening amounts of whiskey in the days following his Maggie's tragic death.

What bothered Brynne was that the drinking had never abated—even after they had started new lives on the farm, where whiskey and rum were not readily available, John McFarren had managed to keep himself in a constant state of congenial intoxication by swilling *no moi ju,* the rice brandy brewed by his Chinese workers.

Raising smarting gray eyes to the polished, pastel-blue sky, Brynne sighed again. Would that the liquor had been all, but the dreams had to be considered, too.

How many times had she been awakened in the night by her father's unearthly shrieks? How many times in the last two bittersweet years had she rushed to his bedside, the stone floors cold beneath her bare feet, to find John McFarren wild-eyed and sweating with terror?

"The bairn!" he would gasp, lapsing into the Scottish brogue of his childhood. "Mother of God, Daughter, it was the *bairn!*"

And Brynne would comfort him as best she could, wondering about the baby that haunted his rest and knowing, all the while, that it was useless to question him.

"Brynne?"

The name broke gently into her thoughts, and a clean hand, unmarked by hard physical labor, came to rest on her right shoulder. She looked up at the figure framed in sunlight and smiled shakily. "Time to leave?" she asked.

Evan Pierpont, the middle-aged, itinerant photographer who had stopped often at the "McFarland" farm during the past two years, and thus become a trusted friend, squatted beside Brynne to frown at the humble grave marker. "McFarren?" he mused. "But I understood that—"

Brynne thrust out her chin, rose gracefully to her feet, and drew a deep, preparative breath. "That was his real name, Mr. Pierpont," she said quietly. "Please don't ask me about it now."

Still frowning, Evan stood again, to face Brynne. His kind blue eyes were dark with sympathy and shared sorrow, but there was something else there, too—a sort of grim, dawning suspicion. "Brynne—"

Brynne looked away and folded her arms across the bodice of her dress. "I suppose we'd better hurry, Evan. After all, you've got to be in Port Propensity tomorrow to take photographs at the picnic."

Evan would not be deflected. "Port Propensity is no place for you, Brynne. Let me take you to Olympia, please—you could room with my sister, Lorraine, and—"

At last, Brynne met his gaze. *"No.* There is a job waiting for me in Port Propensity—my aunt said so in her letter—and I want to make my own way."

Temporarily thwarted, Evan shook his head and then offered one coatless, gartered arm in a gentlemanly fashion. "We'd-best be leaving then," he said. "I've loaded your things."

Brynne took Evan's arm and swallowed scalding tears as she glanced once again at the marker on her father's grave. *Good-bye, Papa.*

It was, mercifully, the last farewell. She had already said good-bye to the Chinese families who tended the sheep, to the cozy house, to the garden and the countryside.

Now, bravely, her hand clasping the crook of Evan Pierpont's elbow, she descended the verdant hillside and fixed her eyes on the bright red, enclosed wagon marked, in flowing, gilded script, E. PIERPONT, DAGUERREOTYPIST. LIKENESSES TAKEN.

The two horses hitched to the wagon were impatient; they neighed and tossed their enormous heads and made the harnesses squeak.

Brynne dared not look back, even once more, at the small house behind them—if she did, her dearly won composure would be shattered. She lifted her chin and climbed, without Evan's help, onto the high, hard seat of the garish wagon.

Evan joined her in silence, taking up the reins, urging the faithful old bay horses easily into motion.

Between Evan and Brynne, on the worn seat, was a small satchel. It contained Brynne's brush and comb,

4

her two spare dresses, a change of underthings, and dim daguerreotypes of her father and mother. Pressed between those portraits were the foreclosure papers delivered only hours before her father's death, by the minions of Tanner Enterprises, along with her Aunt Eloise's last letter.

Hot color burned in Brynne's cheeks as she remembered that letter. John McFarren would surely burn in hell, his sister had written, for the mortal sin of taking his own life. All the same, Aunt Eloise had gone on to say, there was plenty of work for a strong girl to undertake in a growing town like Port Propensity, and Brynne could be assured of something to turn her hand to.

There was no warmth in the brief missive, and no invitation to share the spacious white house behind her aunt and uncle's prosperous, respectable hotel, but she told herself she didn't care.

Brynne shifted her mind to the foreclosure papers. *Tanner Enterprises.* The very name pierced the inside of her battered heart like a metal point and made rage churn in her stomach. She reached out for the worn satchel and balanced it on her knees.

The wagon pitched and rolled over the rutted dirt road leading away from home.

Surreptitiously, Evan Pierpont studied the beautiful, half-defeated girl beside him. Despite the warmth of the day, he shivered.

What had it been like for the child, finding her own father hanging dead from a beam in the shearing shed roof? Dear God, it must have been a frightful shock, and coming right on the heels of the foreclosure, too.

Trees rose, thick and fragrant, on both sides of the narrow road—cedars, Douglas fir, the red-barked Madrona. The ground itself was invisible under a carpet of ferns, blackberry vines, leaves, and fallen pine needles. Since the horses knew their business, Evan concentrated on the foliage.

Brynne was eighteen now, and as fetching a sight as he'd ever laid eyes on, so he needn't worry, Evan assured himself. Some fine young man would marry her, quicker than you could say Paul Bunyan, and she would have a happy life. No need to worry, no sir.

But Evan *was* worried. For one thing, he knew Brynne's aunt and uncle, and they weren't the kind to offer a warm welcome to a poor relation—he'd known that even before the girl had shyly shown him their letter. For another thing, he was taking her to Port Propensity, and that was where the all-powerful Tanner Enterprises had its base.

Because he traveled so widely, Evan knew the secrets of every town on the rocky shores of Puget Sound. He also knew the name McFarren and, as the team and wagon navigated that sun-dappled country road, he suddenly had all the answers to all the puzzles that Brynne's father had presented.

He thought of Joshua Tanner—the Half-Breed—and shivered again.

Brynne turned wide gray eyes to him—they were thickly, darkly lashed, those eyes, and the pupils were rimmed with a darker gray—and managed a slight smile. "Are you cold?" she asked, obviously poised to scramble back into the wagonbed in search of his discarded suitcoat.

Distractedly, Evan shook his head. McFarren, McFarren, McFarren—the name echoed in his mind, along with the beat of the horses' hooves. *Oh, God,* he thought miserably, *God Almighty.*

At noon, they stopped to rest the horses and eat the food Brynne had brought along—thick slices of buttered bread, sheep cheese and apple cider.

Evan had deliberately selected a site with a view of Puget Sound and the majestic Olympic Mountains, hoping that Brynne would be comforted.

He waited until she had absorbed some of the natural splendor around them, until she had eaten. Then, still sitting cross-legged on the moist, quack-grass covered

6

ground, he said cautiously, "Brynne, you mustn't go to Port Propensity."

She stared at him, her hands nervously smoothing her poplin dress. "There isn't anywhere else to go," she replied evenly.

Evan searched his mind and heart for the words to warn her about the misdirected vengeance she might encounter in that rambunctious harbor town, but he could not find them. Silently, he cursed himself for a coward. "It's a rough place, what with the timber mills and the shipyard and the crimping . . ."

For the first time since they'd left the farm behind, Brynne smiled. "Crimping, Evan? I'd hardly be shanghaied to work on a lumber ship, now would I?"

Evan flung his smooth, plump hands out in affectionate annoyance. "You know that isn't what I mean—the town is full of unsavory types. Crimps. Brawling sailors and lumberjacks. Wh—bad women."

Brynne laughed, though it was a raw and humorless sound, lacking the ingenuous merriment of other days. "And I suppose that Olympia has none of those things?"

Evan sighed. Why couldn't he bring himself to tell her what her father had done in Port Propensity? Or even warn her about Joshua Tanner? "Lorraine would look after you," he said lamely. "And Olympia is a lot more civilized."

Brynne had plucked a tiny wildflower, resembling a daisy, from the lush grass rising, spiky and fragrant and green, around her skirts. She studied it in pensive silence.

Not for the first time, Evan Pierpont wished that he were thirty years younger. "If you're counting on that aunt of yours for any help, you're bound to be disappointed. God knows what kind of job she's gotten for you."

Reluctantly, Brynne laid the flower aside, and, from her bearing, it looked as though she'd laid all her hopes aside, too. "We have the same blood running in our veins, Aunt Eloise and I. She was a McFarren before she married—she was my father's sister—"

Evan made a rude sound. Eloise Jennings was a screaming shrew, from what he'd seen, and blood wouldn't mean sheep pellets to her. She was more likely to draw it than respect it. Before he could say as much, however, Brynne was standing up again, smoothing her skirts, searching the sky. "When will we reach Port Propensity?"

The dreadful things that Evan knew hammered at the back of his throat, but he could not bring himself to voice them. "Sometime tomorrow morning," he admitted gruffly, gathering the cups and the cider jug and leaving crumbs of bread and cheese for the chattering birds.

At nightfall, they stopped again, and Evan built a campfire to warm them. Later, as he lay beneath the wagon, listening to the night sounds and watching the fire die, he prayed that the girl slumbering above him, inside the equipment-cluttered wagon, would find her way in the world and have a happy life.

All the while, he knew she wouldn't. The Half-Breed would see to that.

Chapter One

Port Propensity, Washington Territory
July 4, 1885

DREW TANNER PAUSED IN THE GAPING DOORWAY OF THE
study, his eyes fixed on his half-brother's wide, impervious back, his throat scalding with contempt. Sweat
beaded beneath his collarbone and in the space between his shoulder blades.

Lord, how he hated being summoned to this room,
like an errant schoolboy, whenever Joshua deigned to
come home from his travels.

Drew hooked his thumbs in the pockets of his gray
silk vest and glowered at Joshua, who was working at
the massive oak desk, his dark head bent in concentration. The man had no respect for propriety—the collar
of his white linen shirt was open, his sleeves were rolled
up, and he'd tossed his suitcoat and black string tie
aside.

Drew would have sighed if he hadn't known the
sound would betray him—he wasn't ready to give an
accounting for any of his actions yet, though he'd had
over a week to assemble a convincing story or two.

Irritated, the young man tossed a scathing look in the
direction of Caleb Tanner's portrait, which hung, huge
and dark and imposing, over the fieldstone fireplace at

the far end of the room. *Damn you, old man,* he thought, hoping that his father would hear him, even from the deepest reaches of hell, and writhe. *Damn you for ever siring that half-breed bastard in the first place.*

The windows facing Joshua's desk were open, in concession to the heat, and the slightest breeze billowed the white lace curtains. Even the elements, it seemed, catered to the Half-Breed.

Drew watched as his half-brother lifted his eyes from the account journals spread out before him and tilted his head back.

"Are you coming in or not?" he demanded, in a surly undertone, without even looking in Drew's direction.

Drew started slightly; it was unnerving, the way Joshua could sense someone else's presence no matter how hard one tried not to attract his attention. "You're busy," he said, hating himself for the obsequious tremor in his voice and the chill in the pit of his stomach.

Joshua's wooden chair creaked loudly as he swiveled to glare at Drew. His sun-browned jawline was hard and edged with white, and his fierce violet eyes narrowed slightly. "Sit down," he said, biting off the words.

"Damn it," Drew snapped, finally withdrawing his thumbs from his vest pockets and allowing his finely tailored, dove-gray suitcoat to fall back into place. "Don't order me around! I'm nineteen years old, for God's sake, and I'll sit down when and if the mood strikes me!"

Joshua sat back in his chair and kicked his expensively booted feet up onto the surface of his desk in a fluid, ominous motion. He interlaced his fingers and studied Drew thoughtfully before replying, "The mood had better strike you before I do."

To his eternal chagrin, Drew colored. Then, scowling, he made his way to the dreaded leather chair facing his half-brother's desk and sat down.

Joshua smiled, took a cheroot from the pocket of his

shirt and a wooden match from a crystal box on his desk. The light of the match flared crimson, hardening his chiseled, arrogant features as he lit the thin cigar.

All the while, Drew stared at his half-brother in stubborn silence, hating him, hating himself because he didn't dare express the terrible rage he felt. Joshua was a bastard and a savage and a host of other unsavory things, but he was also thirteen years older than Drew, a good eight inches taller and at least fifty pounds heavier.

Finally, Joshua broke the silence with a sigh. "Shall we start with the outraged husbands, Drew? Or would you feel more comfortable explaining why you forged my name on that bank draft?"

Drew swallowed hard and lifted his eyes to the high ceiling. God, the air was so hot and heavy—why didn't it rain? "The Tanner money is as much mine as yours," he said, after a long interval of preparation.

There was another silence, and when Drew dared to look at his brother again, he was drawing on the cheroot and the smoke was wreathing his head like a blue-gray mist. "I don't think we need to go over the terms of our dear father's will again, do we?"

"I needed the money, Joshua."

Joshua raised one dark eyebrow, and the ebony hair on his muscle-corded forearms glistened as he gestured. "Your allowance is already four times what the average working man makes in a week, Drew—or, at least, it was."

A kind of reckless bravado swept through Drew, and he leaned forward slightly, gripping the chair arms and glaring. "What the hell do you mean by that?"

"I mean you're covering the bank draft. My guess is it will take you about three months."

Drew spat out an ugly word and jumped to his feet in outrage, but Joshua maintained his relaxed position in the desk chair. "Three months!" Drew shouted, in a fury-strangled voice, "Goddamn it, Josh, you can't do this to me! Christ, it's summer and—"

11

"And your lady friends are expensive, aren't they? Which leads us to the other subject."

His color high, Drew sank despondently back into his chair. Three months without money, and the goddamned Independence Day picnic was today. He shot another look of sheer hatred at the portrait of Caleb Tanner and swallowed again. "It's all a lie—about the women, I mean."

Joshua sighed, drew several letters from his inside vest pocket, and tossed them onto the desk as damning evidence. "These caught up with me in Tacoma," he said evenly, but his dark orchid eyes were fierce upon his brother's face. "There are plenty of whores in this town, Drew. Why in hell do you insist on taking your pleasures with married women?"

Drew clenched the smooth, cool arms of his chair so hard that his knuckles whitened and the muscles in his neck and shoulders ached. It was a question he'd asked himself, many times, and he didn't have an answer. Still, he was going to have to throw out something, or Joshua would be on his back until the crack of doom.

Nervously, he ran one hand through his straight, sandy hair and tried to summon a repentant look to his face. "I was in love," he offered guilelessly.

Joshua's answer was a hoot of disdainful amusement. "Four times in six weeks? You're going to have to do one hell of a lot better than that, Drew."

At a loss, Drew shrugged miserably. "What can I tell you? The opportunity presented itself and I took advantage. Can't we just forget it?"

Idly, Joshua took up the letters in one powerful, sun-browned hand. His brow furrowed as he read the handwritten addresses. "I would like nothing better than to 'forget it,'" he said. "However, Harry Randall and Pete Arlington—to name just two people—are ready to rearrange your vital organs." The hard, handsome face tightened. "Damn it all, Drew, I don't blame them. A man's wife is sacred!"

12

Drew wanted to laugh aloud. "Sacred" was hardly a word he would use to describe Flossie Randall or Maude Arlington. Alas, wives were a touchy subject with Joshua, a subject it was always wise to avoid. "I'm sorry," he lied.

Joshua's wide shoulders moved in a stiff shrug. "You will be, by the time the summer is over. And I assure you, you'll have a profound respect for the working man."

Drew grimaced. He didn't like the turn this conversation was taking, he didn't like it at all. "What are you getting at?"

The surly giant brought his feet to the floor with a soul-numbing crash and rose to his full, frightening height of six feet, four inches. "I think you know," he answered, in tones as rough as oyster shells. "But just in case you don't, I'll leave no doubt in your mind. Be at the shipyard first thing Monday morning. For once in your life, you're going to work for your money."

Drew was dumbfounded, and all he could manage was a stricken, "But—"

"But nothing," Joshua snapped. "You'll get the same wages as everyone else, and if you do one of your famous vanishing acts, just remember that you won't be half as attractive to the ladies with nothing but lint in your pockets!"

A raw lump twisted in Drew's throat and, for the life of him, he couldn't get a word past it.

Joshua sat down at his desk again, dismissed his brother with a curt wave of one hand, and began reading the ledger open before him. It was as though Drew didn't exist anymore.

The scent of Joshua's cheroot stinging his nostrils, Drew Tanner turned and stormed out of the large room, with its brass lamp fittings, redwood paneling, and richly woven oriental rugs.

Slamming the heavy front door assuaged some of his frustration and outrage, but he hurried down the stone

13

steps to the lawn, all the same, on the off-chance that Joshua might take issue with his behavior and come after him.

Drew glanced only briefly at the splendid vista fronting the house—the canal, the mountains and the town itself were all too familiar for him to take note of their singular beauty. He mumbled a curse and strode around the western corner of the massive, gray stone house, his spirit smarting as if it had been wrenched out of him and soundly slapped.

In the sideyard, his sister, Miranda, sat reading in a wicker chair, dressed in gingham for the picnic ahead, her dark hair dancing around her face in the slight breeze coming up from the canal. Drew knew by the almost imperceptible tensing of her elegant shoulders that she was aware of his presence but, since she didn't speak to him, he didn't speak to her.

Pushing back the sides of his coat to cram his fists into the pockets of his trousers, Drew kept walking until he reached the lawn behind the house. There, carefully pulling dresses and camisoles and lace-edged drawers from the clothesline, was How Ling, Miranda's Chinese maid. The girl was about seventeen, he guessed, and sweetly, exotically nubile.

Drew smiled at the fear in her slanted eyes and held out one hand.

How Ling swallowed visibly and shook her head. Her glossy black hair shimmered like polished ebony in the sunshine, reaching well past her waist to the seat of her odd, blue cotton trousers, which matched the shapeless shirt she wore.

"No," she protested.

"Yes," countered Drew Tanner briskly, as he took her arm and propelled her toward the small, stone springhouse near his late mother's cherry tree. At the door, he looked back at the colorful trail of laundry she'd dropped on the lush green grass and grinned.

"No," pleaded How Ling, once again.

Drew opened the springhouse door and thrust the girl inside.

Brynne had forgotten what a pretty town Port Propensity was, for all its bustle and clamor. It faced the Hood Canal and the towering Olympic mountains, for one thing, and if one didn't look too far afield, one wouldn't even see the squalor of Little Canton, the Chinese community.

The town proper was set apart from that awful place by a crooked, rutted road and a sparkling freshwater pond spanned by an arching wooden bridge.

As Evan's wagon and team rattled over the planking of the bridge, Brynne stared at everything, refreshing her memory. Straight ahead was the Orion Hotel, an imposing brick structure owned, these past ten years, by her aunt and uncle. Adjoining it was a saloon patronized only by those who expected no fleshly pleasures in addition to their "blue ruin" whiskey.

There were a number of shops lining the planked streets, along with a bank and a two-story business building. Further to the right, under trees with wild ivy growing up their trunks and whispering willows, rolled the velvety green grass of the town's pride—the public park.

Already, though it was still quite early in the day, celebrants were gathering there in preparation for the Independence Day festivities. Ladies in brightly colored dresses strolled along the banks of the glimmering pond, turning ruffled parasols over their heads. Some wore bonnets, while others boasted magnificent, sweeping feathered hats secured with broad ribbons. Children played chase and rolled hoops and their laughter rang in Brynne's ears like music, easing her dread.

She looked again at the richly dressed ladies and then down at her own gritty, oft mended poplin dress. How she wished she had something fine to wear, but her pink and white gingham, neatly folded in the satchel, would have to do. She would, however, present herself at the Jennings' and boldly prevail upon Aunt Eloise to let her take a bath.

Evan agreed to the plan with gruff reluctance and made Brynne promise to meet him at the wagon before wandering off to mingle with the picnickers. From the porch of the gingerbread trimmed white house facing the water, she waved at him in reassurance.

It appeared, after Brynne knocked at the sturdy door and was greeted by Kwon Su, her aunt and uncle's Chinese cook, that fortune was with her. Aunt Eloise wasn't even at home, and Kwon Su, a small, squat woman with a toothy smile, happily provided the hot water, soap and towels for a bath.

Not wanting to take the time to dry it fully, Brynne did not wash her hair. Instead, once her bath was finished, she brushed the golden-brown mane until it glistened and wound it into a loose chignon at the back of her head. Peering into the one mirror the tiny dressing room boasted, she saw that her slate-gray eyes were dancing in anticipation of the day ahead, and that one would have to look very close indeed to see the grief trembling there, too.

She drew a deep breath and smoothed the skirts of her pink and white gingham dress with graceful, work-reddened hands. The dress was very simple, but it had full sleeves, a suggestion of a bustle, and lace trim edging the modest neckline.

Brynne sighed philosophically. She wouldn't hold a candle to those elegantly dressed women she'd seen in the park, but she guessed she looked pretty enough.

Humming, Brynne helped Kwon Su remove the bathtub and empty it, and then she said a hasty thank-you and hurried off toward the picnic grounds.

If she had but one good day before the realities of her life set in, she meant to make the most of it.

* * *

How Ling lay still on the cool, moss-scented floor of the springhouse for a long time after Drew Tanner was gone. She would not let him hear her cry.

After a while, though, the time for crying came, and How Ling shed bitter tears and wailed softly in her shame. She was bad. Evil. It was all her fault that this dishonorable thing had happened.

She raised herself to her sandaled feet, dried her eyes and drew a deep breath. Then, calmly, How Ling went outside and gathered up Missy Tanner's beautiful garments from the grass.

Evan's wagon was parked near the pond, and he was already setting up all his mysterious gear when Brynne reached him. A burly lumberjack, his severe-looking wife, and four children were waiting anxiously to be immortalized on magic paper.

Evan's hands kept right on working, but his eyes moved to Brynne and smiled independently of his mouth. "Aren't you a sight, Miss Brynne McFarren! The gents will be falling face first into their potato salad after a look at you."

Brynne blushed, all too aware of the lumberjack's silly grin and his wife's glare. "Evan," she scolded.

He laughed and slid a developing plate into his enormous box camera. But then, in only an instant, his face sobered. "If it isn't your own dear aunt," he said sourly, draping a black cloth over both his head and the camera.

There was a loud pop, a puff of sulphurous smoke, and a flash as he recorded the images of the lumberjack's family for posterity.

Eloise Jennings appeared at Brynne's side simultaneously with the flash, and, for a moment, it seemed as though this grim, glaring woman had been conjured from the bowels of hell. Her plain face was rigid as she surveyed her niece, and her black sateen dress crackled as she drew herself up in outraged disapproval. "Brynne," she said bitterly, in greeting.

17

Brynne squared her shoulders, thinking that Aunt Eloise might have been a very pretty woman, with her wispy blonde hair and wide blue eyes, had it not been for her sullen and querulous nature. "Hello, Aunt Eloise," she replied.

The hateful azure eyes swept over Brynne's gingham dress. "My brother is dead a month and you're not in mourning?"

Brynne lifted her chin. "Papa didn't believe in wearing mourning clothes," she said evenly. "He said that grief itself was bad enough, without black garments to make it more dismal."

Eloise's jawline hardened. "I've arranged a position for you," she informed her brother's daughter. "You'll start Monday, since Letitia insists that you spend one night in our home. The work pays two dollars a week and includes your bed and board."

Brynne was smiling, not because of the position, but because of the mention of her cousin's name. She loved Letitia, and hadn't even dared hope that the girl, two years her junior and impossibly loyal, had returned from her Eastern finishing school. "Letitia is home?"

It was a stupid question, and Brynne didn't need the expression on her aunt's face to tell her so.

"No doubt she'll find you soon," Aunt Eloise replied stiffly, her eyes again assessing Brynne's dress with horror. "I'll be wanting to introduce you to your employer sometime today, so kindly don't venture away before I get the opportunity."

Brynne drew a deep breath and drummed up a polite smile. "I'm very grateful that you've made arrangements for me to work. . . ."

A smirk played in Aunt Eloise's features, and she tossed her head in brusque dismissal. Then, without another word, she turned and walked away, her somber mourning dress rustling as she moved.

Brynne sighed and searched the growing crowd for Letitia's sweet face and cylindrical figure. There was no sign of her, but that was all right for the moment—she had something important to do before she sought out her cousin anyway.

Not daring to glance at Evan, who would no doubt be steaming over her reception from Aunt Eloise, she began wending her way through the mobs of laughing celebrants. There was a path leading up a small, tree-dense hillside, and Brynne followed it, silently preparing herself.

The graveyard sprawled atop a green knoll, and its many stones and statues and markers were bordered by a neatly painted white picket fence. The sun was bright and warm, and it danced on the blue waters below in blinding flashes of silver.

Brynne let herself in through one of four gates and walked purposefully, head held high, toward a small, simple marker in a far corner. The words on the stone slab were hidden by the dazzling glare of the sun, but that didn't matter—Maggie McFarren's daughter knew them by heart. MARGARET BRYNNE MCFARREN, CRUELLY TAKEN FROM US ON THE 14TH DAY OF JUNE, 1883.

Brynne's throat ached, and she knelt beside the grave and folded trembling hands in her lap. "Hello, Mama," she said softly, in an unsteady voice.

There was no answer, certainly, but the passing of a summer-scented breeze, whispering in the leaves of the adolescent elm trees planted on the inland side of the cemetery served much the same purpose. Brynne did not feel alone.

"I hope Papa is with you now," she went on, brushing tender fingers over the bright yellow, spiky faces of the dandelions growing where her mother rested. "I—I know you'll plead his cause with God, Mama. He didn't mean to take his own life—I know he didn't mean to."

Behind Brynne, and beyond the wooded hillside, the boisterous noise of the Independence Day picnic rose on the warm summer air, blending peacefully with the buzzing of bees and the lapping of the nearby waters.

19

Brynne swallowed hard as despair swelled in her heart and closed off her throat. *Please, God,* she pleaded. *You mustn't send my papa to hell. He was a good man. But after Mama died and there was that strange trouble here and then we lost the sheep, his mind just wasn't right.*

No voice spoke in response to Brynne's prayer, but there was an answer, all the same. A certain warmth folded itself over her heart, like a sheltering garment, and she knew that God had forgiven John McFarren and received him.

She stood slowly and turned away from her mother's grave, lifting her face to the blue, blue sky. "Thank you," she said, and then she started back toward the gate, ready to enjoy the picnic.

At the edge of the woods, she encountered the giant.

He was an enormous man, with muscular arms and legs, and he wore dark, lightweight trousers, a white linen shirt open to reveal a hint of shimmering ebony down, and a black vest. His hair was as dark as a moonless night, and his eyes were the most incredible shade of lavender Brynne had ever seen. His proud, arrogantly handsome face was grim, but, as he looked at her, it broke into a stunning white smile.

Brynne was oddly taken aback. *Is this him,* she wondered wildly, knowing she was gaping at the stranger in a shameful fashion and that there was no way she could stop herself.

Her mother had told her many times that she would feel a gentle tug in her heart when she met the man chosen for her, but this was no tug. It was a jarring wrench that weakened her knees and made the pit of her stomach spin, unanchored, within her.

"Hello," he said cordially.

Brynne's lips moved, but no sound would pass them.

He laughed, but it wasn't a joyous sound, not really. It was edged with a peculiar, fathomless grief as deep as Brynne's own, perhaps deeper. "I startled you," he said, "I'm sorry."

Brynne felt breathless, as though she'd gone swimming in the pond at home and stayed under the water too long. "No. I just wasn't expecting . . ."

He lifted powerful, sun-browned hands to his hips and tilted his magnificent head to one side, studying Brynne with no evidence of the wild confusion she was feeling. "You're new in Port Propensity, aren't you?" he asked, in tones that changed the meter of her heartbeat.

"I lived here two years ago," Brynne said, wanting this harmless conversation to go on forever.

But his face changed the instant she'd spoken—his fine features hardened visibly, and he lifted the orchid eyes to the treetops. After a moment, without so much as a word of dismissal, he strode around Brynne as though she were no more than a stump blocking his way.

Feeling injured, Brynne lifted both her chin and her gingham skirts and made her way through the lush woods and onto the picnic grounds.

Her thoughts remained on the stranger in the cemetery only briefly—there were so many things to do and see and taste and touch. And once she found Letitia, she would feel truly welcome.

Dazzled by the circuslike spectacles taking place all around her, Brynne undid one of her shoes and dumped the five-dollar gold piece she'd received at Christmas out into her palm. A delicious sense of unbridled extravagance swept over her as she tried to decide whether to buy refreshments first or have her fortune told by the gypsies.

She was still deliberating—not because she tended to be indecisive but because it was such a pleasurable dilemma—when a well-dressed young man carrying two plates heaping with fried chicken and potato salad hurried by. He glanced briefly at Brynne, who was still holding her shoe in one hand and her gold piece in the other, and then stopped and looked back again.

He had hair the color of butterscotch taffy, and his

eyes danced with hazel mischief. One corner of his humorous mouth tilted upward in a fetching grin. "Hello, there," he drawled.

Brynne thought him quite forward, but she laughed all the same. "Hello."

Still balancing the dinner plates, he appeared to give the objects in Brynne's hands ponderous consideration. "The money is the best choice," he observed, after a moment. "I really don't think any of these merchants will want the shoe."

Brynne laughed again and bent to pull her shoe back on and lace it. When she straightened, she knew by the color in the young man's cheekbones that she had revealed rather too much bosom. Responding pink rose in her own face.

"Let's get married," said the young man.

Brynne pretended outrage and failed miserably. "I don't even know your name," she reminded him, choking on a giggle.

"Drew," he answered, with a slight shrug and a speculative frown. "Now can we get married?"

"You're insufferable."

Drew smiled and tilted his head to one side. "Yes, but charming. What, future wife, is your name?"

She hesitated only for a moment. "Brynne. Brynne McFarren."

Something moved in his face, displacing some of the humor and mischief. "McFarren?" he breathed, nearly dropping the plates of fragrant food. "You're a McFarren?"

Suddenly nettled and wildly hungry, Brynne nodded. "Is there something wrong with that?"

He beamed. "Certainly not. Tell me, Brynne McFarren, will you help me eat this food?"

Brynne sighed. "You were planning to share it with someone else, obviously," she said.

His right shoulder lifted in an affable shrug. "Only my sister. She knows I'm hopelessly irresponsible."

"Are you?"

"Oh, yes. But I have every intention of being a stalwart and admirable citizen from this day forward. I want our children to respect me."

Thinking him delightfully brazen, Brynne could only shake her head. Five minutes later, she and her new friend were comfortably seated in the lush grass beneath the flagpole. As they ate, they talked and watched a group of grown men try to catch a greased pig.

After that, when their empty plates had been consigned to one of the enormous tin tubs set out on a rough-hewn table, Drew turned to face Brynne and grinned. "What now?"

Brynne cast an eye in the direction of the gypsy wagon. It was even more garishly decorated than Evan's, with its bright blue wheels, red and gold sides and dark scrollwork.

"I believe I'll have my fortune told," she said.

Drew laughed. "I've already told your fortune, my love, and for free. You're going to be my wife."

"I'd like another opinion, if you don't mind," Brynne retorted. And then she lifted her skirts and marched, with haughty resolution and a thrill of mystery, toward the outlandish wagon.

Drew followed, grumbling.

The inside of Madame Fortuna's wagon smelled of candlewax, sweat, rancid oil and several pungent spices. Once she had collected Brynne's gold piece and returned change, this last following one swift and discerning glance at Drew, the flamboyantly turbaned woman bid her client to sit.

Awed by the woman's jewels and colorful clothing—she wore bright purple skirts of some shiny, rustling fabric and a shawl with metallic threads glistening in its folds—Brynne sat. There was a table between herself and Madame Fortuna, draped in worn black velvet and graced with a slightly scuffed crystal ball.

Madame Fortuna began to make an eerie, crooning sound, her head lolling on her bare brown shoulders, her gold loop earrings nearly catching in the dingy white ruffles of her strapless blouse.

Drew sighed impatiently.

Suddenly, the gypsy woman started violently, as though someone had prodded her with a sharp stick, and stared into the crystal ball with wide, glazed eyes.

"You have suffered a great tragedy," droned the gypsy, in a voice that made Brynne's spine tingle deliciously. "But there will be a great and all-consuming love in your life very soon." Madame Fortuna's shrewd dark eyes lifted to Drew's face, sparkling with hostility. "This is not the man I see in your future. The man I see is swarthy and very tall. Beware your heart, little one, for he is driven by a black passion that tortures him without ceasing."

Brynne remembered the startlingly handsome man she'd encountered near the cemetery and trembled, despite the warmth of that July Fourth. "Is there anything else?" she asked, in a small voice.

"You will have many enemies here, but you will have friends, too. Good friends. You are new in this community, no?"

"I came with the photographer," answered Brynne, still bedazzled by the mystery of this woman and her words and her strange wagon.

"Beware the one who lives between two worlds," finished Madame Fortuna, a note of dismissal ringing in her voice. "Once he has taken your heart, no power in heaven or on earth can cause him to return it." She looked again at Drew. "Your fortune, sir?"

Drew's jaw tightened, but, after a moment, he brought a coin from his trouser pocket and laid it on the velvet-covered table with an angry motion.

When Brynne had stood up and moved aside, he sat down in her place. "Well?" he challenged.

Madame Fortuna reached for his hand, ignoring the crystal ball this time, and searched the palm. "You will one day be an important man," she imparted, almost petulantly.

"How discerning of you," remarked Drew, in tones of sweet acid.

Madame glared, her eyes flashing like polished onyx beads in the gloom of the wagon. "As I said, one day you will be very important. That day, however, is far off."

Drew looked up at Brynne and grinned before facing the gypsy again. "Tell me, madame—who will I marry?"

She peered into his palm, tracing the smooth, uncalloused flesh with a practiced thumb as though she might be following a map. "One who deserves far better than you, as this young lady does," Madame answered, glancing up at Brynne. "You will not find love in her—before the stars were flung into the heavens, she was chosen for someone else."

Drew muttered something and bolted from his chair, and, when he lifted Brynne over the wagon's three steps and into the sunshine, there was an odd strain in his face.

Chapter Two

LETITIA'S VOICE RANG THROUGH THE MUGGY AIR LIKE THE chime of a sheep's bell. "Brynne! Brynne McFarren!"

Brynne turned her attention from the disturbing expression on Drew's face to see her cousin approaching. Still plump but prettier than ever, Letitia was wearing a striped blue pinafore over a lacy, full-sleeved white blouse, and her light brown hair was done up in a fetching arrangement of ringlets that framed her face and glistened on her shoulders.

Beaming, the girl flung herself at Brynne and embraced her with a warmth that brought back the joy and peace of other, less troubled days.

Letitia sniffled when the hug ended. "I've been searching for you all morning. I should have known Drew Tanner would find you before I did!"

Brynne felt as though someone had just flung a bucketful of icy water all over her. She turned and cast a stunned and angry look into the face of the man beside her. "*Tanner?* You're a Tanner?"

Drew's features tightened, and all the boyish light faded from his eyes. "Yes."

Brynne swallowed hard and closed her eyes against

the shock of it. She might have guessed who this man was, by his fine clothes and smooth hands, but she had been too charmed to think about such things. Now it was too late—she liked him, and there was no changing that, grudge or no grudge.

"Brynne?" Letitia faltered, tugging worriedly at her cousin's sleeve and frowning.

Brynne's smile trembled a little, but she turned it on Drew as well as Letitia. "I've just had my fortune read," she announced, feeling a need to get the conversation off in some other direction.

Letitia's eyes widened. "Who are you going to marry?" she wanted to know.

Drew rolled his eyes. Apparently he knew as well as Brynne did that marriage was uppermost in Letitia's mind. The subject positively fascinated her.

"Someone dark and handsome and possessed by a tragic passion," Brynne answered, embellishing the tale just a bit. Now that she was outside the gypsy wagon again, bathed in sunshine and reality, she wondered at her earlier awe.

"You forgot 'tall,'" scoffed Drew, annoyed again. "Aren't they always tall, dark and handsome?"

Letitia's bright blue gaze had found the pond. "Look —rowboats! Oh, Brynne, let's go rowing!"

His recalcitrant mood gone as quickly as it had appeared, Drew gestured grandly toward the pond's edge, where small rowboats were being rented for the sum of fifteen cents. "Allow me, ladies," he said.

Letitia giggled in delight, and then frowned. "It just occurred to me that I might be intruding . . ."

Brynne shot a warning look in Drew's direction and noted with relief that it was well understood.

"Nonsense," he said expansively. "We wouldn't think of leaving you behind."

On the sparkling water, Drew rowed without complaint while Letitia chattered on and on about her school in Boston and the train trip home. Wishing that

27

the day would never end, Brynne drew all the sweet magic of the Independence Day picnic into her heart and held it there, to save.

After the boat ride, Letitia suggested that she and Brynne have their pictures taken. Wanting a chance to reassure Evan that things were going well, Brynne agreed.

It was the custom of the day to look circumspect and sober when one had one's image taken, and Brynne honestly tried. The problem was that Drew was standing behind Evan and his huge camera, making faces, clasping his throat, falling unceremoniously onto the grass.

Both Brynne and Letitia were laughing when the flash powder exploded, and Brynne was glad she'd forgiven Drew for being a Tanner.

The next few hours were exhausting ones. There were foot races of all sorts, and Brynne participated in several with abandon, to Letitia's mortification and Drew's delight.

Once or twice, Brynne caught sight of the darkly handsome man she'd met on the hilltop, after leaving her mother's gravesite, but she was careful not to look too closely. For all she knew, he might turn out to be a Tanner, too, and she couldn't find it in her heart to forgive two of them in one day.

By mid-afternoon, the heat and exertion and glaring sunlight were beginning to tell. Brynne and Letitia took temporary refuge under a willow tree near the pond, glad to rest for a little while.

Letitia fanned herself with one hand. "Mercy, this heat will turn our complexions to parchment."

Brynne sighed, sat back against the trunk of the cooling, sheltering tree, and closed her eyes. "I suppose," she said sleepily, wishing that she could take a nap without missing any of the glorious day.

"Do you like Drew Tanner?" Letitia wanted to know, and there was a slight tremor in her voice.

Brynne smiled and opened her eyes, saw that Drew

was approaching even then and carrying three small bowls. "He's nice," she said, "For a Tanner."

Letitia's lower lip was trembling. "I love him, Brynne," she whispered miserably. "I've always loved Drew Tanner and if he doesn't marry me, I'll just perish."

Brynne patted her cousin's hand, understanding. "Please don't worry."

Letitia's face brightened. "He doesn't match the gypsy woman's description of your great love, does he?" she whispered. "And fate must be considered."

"Oh, indeed," agreed Brynne, suppressing a smile.

Letitia bounded to her feet, her face flushed with determination. "I'm going to have *my* fortune read," she announced, and then she was hurrying away toward Madame Fortuna's wagon.

Drew watched her pass with amusement and sat down on the grass, beside Brynne. "I suppose it's too much to hope that she's on her way home?"

Brynne frowned. "I don't want her to go home. She's a treasure and I love her dearly."

"Truce," said Drew, shoving one of the three bowls he had been juggling into her hands and setting a third aside.

Brynne studied the fluffy, pudding-like stuff mounded in the bowl. "What . . ."

Drew laughed with delight. "You've never had ice cream?"

She shook her head.

He nodded toward the spoon protruding from the crystalline concoction. "Try it. But be careful not to get it behind your front teeth—it's cold."

Brynne nibbled suspiciously at the smidgeon of vanilla ice cream clinging to the end of her spoon. It *was* cold, and at once sweet and salty. Marveling, she took another, larger bite—and regretted it instantly.

The roof of her mouth throbbed in aching protest, as did the bridge of her nose and the rounding of her skull. She frowned and set the bowl aside.

Unruffled, Drew consumed his own ice cream and then Brynne's. He was just starting on Letitia's when she returned, beaming, her arms swinging at her sides.

"The gypsy says I'll have bosoms before Christmas," she whispered to Brynne, as she sat down beside her in the cool grass. Then, patting her beaded handbag, she added, "I've a potion for it, right here."

Drew fell backward into the grass, roaring with laughter, and spilled ice cream all over his gray silk vest.

Letitia blushed, bit her lower lip, and then laughed, too. Brynne thought her a dandy sport.

At nightfall, the first rockets shot into the air, leaving glistening trails of gold and silver to shimmer in their wakes. Boys and men lit firecrackers, scaring the horses and the women in about equal proportions.

The women retaliated with true frontier spirit—by stripping the watermelons brought from east of the Cascade mountain range of their hard, green rinds and flinging the pulpy fruit at their tormentors.

The fight was on, and Brynne joined in with relish, laughing as she pelted Drew with the sweet, seedy stuff. He returned the favor, and Letitia fled, squealing, to take refuge behind a pine tree.

Within minutes, everyone seemed to be embroiled in the battle, and the Great Watermelon War raged unchecked for over half an hour. It was nearing its end, due to waning supplies of ammunition, when Brynne laid claim to a huge, juicy handful and hid behind Evan's wagon to launch a surprise attack. She would *fix* Drew Tanner.

There was a rustle of footsteps in the fragrant grass, and Brynne braced herself, brimming with delicious terror. When the moment seemed right, she stepped out from her hiding place and hurled the watermelon pulp with all her might.

And it struck the tall, mysterious man from the cemetery dead in the center of his chest.

Horrified by her mistake, Brynne gasped and stepped back so quickly that she fell over the wagon tongue and landed hard on her bottom. Gulping, she looked up at him. "I'm s—sorry," she whispered "I thought you were Drew—I—"

He gazed down at her in apparent shock, without bothering to wipe the sticky, red mess from his shirt and vest, a giant framed in shadow. His purple eyes glittered in the flickering light from the pitch torches burning along the pond's edge, and his jawline looked hard.

Brynne was terrified. When he thrust back his magnificent head suddenly and shouted with laughter, she was too awed to move.

"What is your name?" he asked, after his mirth had subsided to less alarming proportions. He offered a hand, but Brynne stubbornly ignored the gesture and got to her feet on her own.

Some primary instinct warned her not to answer his question, though she certainly felt no shame for a proud name such as McFarren. "What's yours?" she countered.

Before he could reply, Aunt Eloise was on the scene, the very picture of moral outrage. "Brynne McFarren, you shameless hoyden!" she shrilled, ignoring the shadow man and glaring murderously at her niece. "God in heaven, look at you! And you about to meet your employer!"

Brynne swallowed, all too conscious, suddenly, of her spoiled, seed-speckled dress, her hair falling from its pins, her smudged and sticky face. She cast one look in the shadow man's direction and saw, with unaccountable disappointment, that he had gone.

Since there wasn't anything she could say in her own defense, Brynne staunchly followed her furious aunt to the torch-lit center of the picnic grounds. She was only mildly comforted to notice that Drew Tanner fell silently into step beside her.

* * *

Minnie Blode watched the approach of Eloise Jennings and the girl with cultivated asperity. It was damnably hard not to smile.

The child was pretty—even in the light of the pitch torches and the fireworks, any fool could see it. No wonder Eloise was so anxious to foist the girl off on just about anybody—she didn't want this little imp drawing attention away from her own daughter.

Minnie folded calloused, work-reddened hands on her lap and sat back in her folding wooden chair. She pretended an interest in the fabric of her skirts—drat, she'd had this dress so long and washed it so often that she couldn't begin to recall what color it had been—and waited.

"Mrs. Minnie Blode, this is Brynne McFarren," Eloise announced, in that tooth-jarring voice of hers.

Minnie's wise, benign eyes shot up from her skirts to the girl's face in open surprise. McFarren, was it? *McFarren?* "Hello," she said, in a gruff voice.

"Hello," Miss McFarren replied, and she looked neither right nor left, but straight at Minnie.

Minnie liked that. "You John McFarren's girl?" she asked bluntly.

The small, smudged chin lifted. "Yes, ma'am," replied the child.

Lord, thought Minnie, *there'll be trouble now.* She glanced at Drew Tanner—so she'd drawn that one, had she—and then Eloise Jennings. To Minnie's delight, they both looked as uncomfortable as hell.

"Two dollars a week, bed and vittles," the old woman said briskly, liking John McFarren's kid. "The work is hard, but, from them hands of yours, I'd say you're no stranger to that."

"I've shorn sheep," the girl responded, in a proud, if slightly unsteady, voice. "I've helped with the lambing, too, and cooked and scrubbed and—"

Minnie laughed. "No sheep at Minnie Blode's Dininghall," she broke in. "But there'll be cookin' and scrubbin' and servin' table, too. We open at five

32

Monday mornin's and work through Saturday, though there ain't many customers that night."

"Yes, ma'm."

"I'll be lookin' for you tomorrow night, then." Minnie's eyes sliced piercingly to Eloise's face. "Don't want to drag you away from the bosom of your family afore they've had time to make you welcome."

Eloise flinched at the barb—Minnie had intended it to smart—and folded her skinny arms. "I'll apologize, Mrs. Blode, for Brynne's appearance. It seems that she doesn't have a great deal of respect for her poor father's memory. Why, it was shock enough, I declare, to find her wearing *gingham* so soon after her loss—"

"Shut up, Mrs. Jennings," Drew Tanner broke in sharply. In that moment, he rose a bit in Minnie Blode's estimation.

"Odd that you never said you was related to John McFarren," pressed Minnie, watching Eloise Jennings with eyes that had seen a lot in forty years of cooking for lumbermen and sailors and just generally making her own way.

It was another hit, and dead center, too. Eloise bridled, gripped Brynne McFarren's hand, and stormed away, dragging the girl behind her.

Drew moved to protest, but Minnie Blode stopped him. There was trouble enough coming, sure as winter, what with this young rascal wearing his heart in his eyes and the Half-Breed bound on vengeance.

Releasing Drew's arm from a grip as strong as any man's, Minnie stood up. Nobody was going to trifle with that girl while Minnie Blode had a breath in her lungs, and if that meant rough dealings with the Half-Breed and his kin, so be it. They didn't scare her.

Drew was mad as hops. "Why the hell did you grab me like that, Minnie? I was just—"

Suddenly, Minnie felt every one of her sixty-seven years. "I know what you was doin'," she snapped. "You leave that girl alone, Drew Tanner, or I'll lay your middle open with a meat saw. She ain't one of your playthings."

The boy's mouth moved like he was going to argue, but he must have thought better of it, because he didn't say one word. Minnie took a look at his face, lit up by a Fourth of July rocket bursting in the night sky, and shivered clear down to her soul.

Then, after draping her bulky frame in a shawl as colorless and shabby as her dress, Minnie Blode started home.

Brynne lay still in the bed beside Letitia's, too weary to sleep. Her thoughts were racing about in her head like ants on a rotten stump, and she couldn't seem to catch them.

It was late, and the room was silvery with the light of the moon and stars. Over the soft sound of Letitia's snoring, Brynne could hear the endless celebration of liberty filling the night. A piano tinkled, at some distance, and men shouted and laughed and occasionally fired pistols. Chinese rockets still whistled into the sky.

Brynne sighed and burrowed deeper under the light covers on her bed. Doubtless, the saloon adjoining the nearby hotel was doing a very brisk business indeed. She hoped that Minnie Blode's establishment was situated in a quieter part of town.

Minnie Blode. Now there was someone she dared think about. The woman had looked rough and unkempt, but her eyes were kind and Brynne liked her.

Still skittish, Brynne's tired mind moved to Drew Tanner. Heavens, but he was handsome, and his humorous charm was something a girl could get used to in short order. If there was no tug inside her heart when she looked at him, what did that matter? Such things were more fancy than fact anyway.

And what of that incredible man she'd met at the edge of the cemetery and then assaulted with watermelon? Brynne felt a strange heat in her loins, and her

34

heart hammered furiously against her rib cage. She imagined surrendering herself to him and, though she had only vague ideas of what that would be like, she suddenly felt as though all the Independence Day rockets had found their way into her bloodstream, spewing gold and silver fire as they went.

Brynne drew a deep breath, closed her eyes, and slipped suddenly into a fathomless, welcome sleep.

"Wake up, Brynne!"

Brynne reluctantly opened her eyes. For a moment, upon realizing where she was, she felt a wrench of terrible homesickness.

But Letitia was smiling at her, kneeling on the end of the bed next to Brynne's. The warmth in her cousin's ingenuous face did much to soothe her.

"Today is the day!" cried Letitia, her blue eyes bright, her plump cheeks flushed.

Brynne yawned. "Today is Sunday," she said flatly.

"And there's *church!* Maybe Drew will be there. He comes sometimes, with Miss Miranda."

"Miss Miranda?" Brynne sat up and stretched her arms above her head.

"That's his sister," Letitia rushed on. It seemed to Brynne that the moment the girl's eyes opened in the morning, her mouth did, too. A pretty frown moved in the round face. "Joshua *never* comes to church. He's a pagan, Mama says."

Brynne sighed and fussed with her covers. "Who is Joshua, pray tell?"

Letitia's face brightened again, with what appeared to be much relished scandal. "He's the head of the Tanner family, Brynne. Have you been living on Venus or something? He was born on the wrong side of the blanket, you know, and his mother was an *Indian,* for mercy sakes!"

Brynne shook her head, but she felt some of the strange sensations she'd felt the night before, too. It was odd, she thought, that that peculiar grinding in her groin should come back in the full light of day. "His mother was an Indian?" she echoed stupidly.

Letitia's freckled, turned-up nose crinkled. "Oh, not like the Indians around *here*—they groom their hair with dogfish oil and urine and aren't in the least noble. Joshua's mother was a Sioux—she was his father's woman."

"Didn't he have a wife?"

"Of course he had a wife. Why do you think Drew hates Joshua the way he does? After all, he and Miranda were both legitimate."

Brynne frowned. It hadn't seemed to her that Drew Tanner was the kind to hate anybody—especially a half-brother.

Letitia's eyes grew very wide, and her face was suddenly pallid and pinched.

Alarmed by this abrupt change in demeanor, Brynne stiffened. "Letitia, what is it?" she whispered.

"The Half-Breed. Oh, my goodness, you're a *McFarren!*"

"So?" demanded Brynne, even more alarmed.

But Letitia was turning away, scrambling off the bed, rummaging through the clutter of atomizers and powder boxes and jars on her vanity table. "You'll find out soon enough," she answered, in a hollow voice.

After that, no matter how Brynne plagued her, Letitia wouldn't say another word about the Half-Breed or the reason why the name McFarren should inspire such horror.

Brynne picked at her breakfast and agreed to attend church services only because she didn't want to be left at home alone.

Aunt Eloise and Uncle Walter were prosperous, and they owned a fringed, glistening surrey with two padded leather seats and a matched team of white horses. Sitting in the rear seat, beside Letitia, her hands folded in her lap, Brynne looked about in delight, forgetting the Half-Breed and all her other worries in the wonder of riding in such grand style. The clatter of the horses' hooves was a merry sound, and even the stiff countenances of Eloise and Walter didn't spoil the joy of it all.

Deftly, the reins light in his gloved hands, Walter Jennings guided the team and surrey onto the planked street that passed in front of the Orion Hotel.

Brynne's eyes swept the sloping front lawn of that august structure, idly at first, and then were wrenched back by sheer horror.

There were dead men lying in front of the part of the building where the saloon was housed—twenty or thirty of them, at least. A strangled cry escaped Brynne, and she clasped her uncle's shoulder in desperation, startling him so badly that he immediately reined in the two white horses pulling the surrey.

Aunt Eloise whirled in her seat, as did her husband, to fix Brynne in a steely glare. "For heaven's sake, Brynne, what is it?"

What is it? Were her aunt and uncle blind? Did they see dead men sprawled about their property on such a regular basis that they didn't even take note anymore? Brynne's throat was tight and dry, and her eyes were bolted to the neat rows of corpses aligned on the hotel lawn. "Those men," she managed at last. "Won't they be buried?"

"Buried!" hooted Walter Jennings contemptuously. And then he exchanged a sour look with his wife and the surrey was moving again. They were going on!

Brynne was on the verge of forcing Uncle Walter to stop the surrey again when Letitia's hand closed over hers and tightened. There was a sparkle in her cousin's cornflower blue eyes. "Brynne, those men would be very annoyed if we buried them. They're not dead, you see—they're drunk."

Brynne swayed a little, her throat still constricted, her stomach spinning. "Oh, Letitia, I thought—"

"I know," said Letitia softly. "Papa and the bartenders put them out when they carry on too much and let the night air sober them up."

Embarrassment pounded in Brynne's cheeks. "Oh."

"Of course, some of them come to and go on to the Shore House, where there are—bad women."

"The Shore House?"

Letitia bent closer, lowered her voice to a whisper. "It's the best bar in the West, save Erickson's in Portland. Mr. Darnell patterned it after that place. Of course, it's at a discreet distance from town."

"Of course," said Brynne, who couldn't have cared less.

In her usual mercurial way, Letitia was ready to move on to another subject. "Brynne," she whispered thoughtfully, gazing at the bodice of her cousin's freshened blue calico dress. "Did your bosoms just grow that way, or did you do something to make them—well—sprout?"

Before Brynne could think of a reasonable reply, Aunt Eloise twisted in the surrey's front seat and swept both girls up in a stern look. "This is Sunday," she reminded them acidly, mortification raging in her face. "Must you talk like tarts?"

They arrived at the white frame church facing the canal just as Brynne swallowed the last of her laughter.

For all she'd suffered, Brynne McFarren was on relatively good terms with God. She expected little of Him, beyond the sweet warmth that often draped itself over her heart like a soft blanket when she talked to Him, and she was looking forward to Sunday services.

The inside of that tiny church, with its rough pine pews and sealed windows, was close and hot, however, and the rank smell of too many bodies sweating under Sunday finery was pungent indeed. Brynne was already regretting her hasty decision to attend when the preacher appeared, a fierce, homely, pock-marked little man with hellfire and damnation burning in his eyes.

The Reverend Bradshaw did not deliver a sermon that sweltering Sunday, but a violent harangue. He shouted and raged and even smashed a perfectly good ladder-back chair to splinters.

If I saw God the way he does, Brynne mused, *I'd devote myself to a life of sin.*

As if he'd read her thoughts, the reverend leveled his maniacal gaze at Brynne and shouted for another five minutes without looking away once. She wasn't sure exactly what his topic was, but it seemed to boil down to the duty of Christian men and women to purge themselves of all lust.

Brynne squirmed on the hard pew and nearly shouted for joy when the service finally ended. She was drawing in great gulps of fresh summer air, beneath a whispering maple tree, when Drew Tanner appeared, looking cool and handsome in his dashing, fawn-colored suit.

After a polite nod in Letitia's direction, he let one corner of his mouth rise in a quirky grin. "You do stir a man's mind to thoughts of sin, Brynne McFarren," he said.

Brynne blushed, embarrassed for herself and for her cousin, too. But before she could come up with a suitably sharp retort, a beautiful, dark-haired woman materialized at Drew's side looking equally cool in her pink summer dress and turning a matching ruffled parasol on one shoulder. "So you're the lady who ate my chicken and potato salad yesterday," she said, and there were little crinkles around her wide, dark eyes when she smiled. She extended one kid-gloved hand in gracious greeting. "I'm Miranda Tanner."

Brynne didn't know whether to be charmed or to feel chagrined because Drew had given her this woman's dinner at the picnic. Since she had problems enough to think about as it was, she decided to be charmed. "My name is Brynne—Brynne McFarren."

Miranda Tanner stiffened almost imperceptibly, but the handshake she exchanged with Brynne was steady and firm. She smiled again, and though she was close to forty, she must have been the most enchanting, self-assured creature ever turned from God's hand. "I'm so happy to meet you, Brynne." The dark eyes shifted

39

smoothly to Letitia, including her in their warm perusal. "And Letitia! My, my, how very grown up you are. Did you like Boston?"

Letitia was clearly as awed as Brynne, but she managed to stammer a polite answer.

"I hope you'll both come to call," Miranda said, in parting, and, though there was no display of force, it did seem that she was somehow dragging Drew away in her wake. They got into a very smart carriage, complete with driver, and rattled away.

Letitia sighed dreamily. "She's wonderful, isn't she? Too bad we can't accept her invitation."

Brynne had her own reasons for never wanting to call at the Tanner house, but something small and rebellious within her was pricked by Letitia's remark. "Why can't we?" she asked.

"Mama would positively foam at the mouth!" Letitia imparted. "You see, Miranda Tanner is d-i-v-o-r-c-e-d."

"What man in his right mind would divorce *her?*" Brynne demanded, shading her eyes with one hand and staring after the Tanner carriage.

Letitia did love a scandal, it appeared. Her face was flushed and her eyes were twinkling. "She divorced *him,* silly. He was a gambler and he already had two wives, it turned out, so Miss Tanner went to Olympia and appealed to the territorial legislature and they unmarried her by a unanimous vote."

"Mercy," breathed Brynne. Such goings on. Port Propensity was certainly a far cry from the sheep farm.

The carriage shifted and rolled and stirred up all sorts of nasty July dust. Miranda Tanner sighed in irritation, took a cheroot from her handbag, and glared at Drew until he took the wooden match she held out and lit it.

He coughed contemptuously as she drew on the cheroot and then he slid over on the carriage seat to be near the other window. "Damn it, Miranda, that thing stinks."

Miranda leaned toward her brother and summarily blew smoke in his face.

In spite of himself, Drew laughed. "Wretch!"

Miranda's playful mood evaporated. "Brynne McFarren," she mused, drawing again on her cheroot and gazing up at the tufted leather roof of the carriage. *"The* McFarren?"

Drew was stubbornly silent.

"Damn it, Drew, she *is,* isn't she? She's John McFarren's daughter."

Still refusing to meet his sister's eyes, Drew nodded. His throat worked, but he said nothing.

"Joshua will rage like a tiger!"

At last, Drew looked at Miranda. The usual mischievous glint was conspicuously absent from his hazel eyes. "Let him. She's not to blame for what her father did, for God's sake."

"Of course she isn't. But I wonder if Joshua will see it that way."

Drew undid his string tie with a vicious motion of his right hand. "I don't care how Joshua sees it."

"He's bound to meet her, Drew. Hear her name. Port Propensity isn't very big, you know."

Slow color seeped up Drew's face from beneath his starched collar. "You're the one who invited her to our house."

Miranda lifted her chin. "She won't come, though. More's the pity. I think she's lovely, and I'd like to know her better."

"If I have anything to say about it, you will."

"Meaning what, Drew?"

It was interesting the way Drew's jaw tightened into knotted muscle. "Meaning that I intend to marry her."

Miranda studied her cheroot, careful not to look at her brother. A puff of dry dust blew in through the window, mingling with the acrid smell of confined smoke.

"Isn't that a bit rash? You've known the girl all of one day."

"And I want her."

"That's different from loving, Drew. Very different."

"I do love her."

"Spare me."

"I do," Drew insisted coldly, and he looked so serious that Miranda wondered if he hadn't succumbed at last.

Chapter Three

JOSHUA TANNER SAT BACK IN HIS DESK CHAIR, WATCHING the breeze-billowed curtains at the study windows. After all these hours, his stomach was still churning.

McFarren. The hotelkeeper's wife had said the girl's name was Brynne McFarren.

He lifted one booted foot, and then the other, to the surface of his desk. McFarren wasn't a common name, but it could be coincidental, all the same. Young girls didn't travel unattended, and Dr. John McFarren wouldn't dare show his face in Port Propensity—

Or would he?

The debate had been tormenting Joshua all night, and even whiskey hadn't assuaged it. Coincidence or no coincidence, the girl had told him herself, at the edge of the cemetery, that she'd lived in Port Propensity two years ago.

Scowling, Joshua raised one hand to his chin. There was a rough stubble of a beard growing there—despite the Sioux portion of his mixed blood. His hair felt gritty and he was still wearing yesterday's clothes, watermelon stains and all.

In spite of himself, Joshua had to laugh. As long as he lived, he would never forget the look on that saucy little nymph's face when she realized she had bombarded the wrong person with watermelon. And the way she'd fallen backward over the tongue of the photographer's wagon—well, in some inexplicable way, it had made him want her.

His sigh was a harsh sound in the otherwise quiet room. In all honesty, he'd wanted her even before that. He had wanted her when he first laid eyes on her, in fact, even though he'd been on his way to pay his respects to Rosalie at the time. And he'd gone on wanting her, all through the day, while he'd watched her cavorting with Drew.

Dollars to flapjacks, she was John McFarren's daughter.

Joshua's head began to ache fiercely. The ironies of life being what they were, the consuming attraction he felt for Brynne McFarren would probably grow instead of lessen.

He imagined himself courting her and laughed bitterly. *Oh, but there is one thing, Sweetheart,* he would confide, no doubt on bended knee. *I plan to kill your father with my bare hands. I do hope it doesn't spoil the honeymoon for you.*

Joshua brought himself up short. What the hell was he even thinking such things for? He'd never loved any woman but Rosalie, and he never would. Drew could *have* the bright-eyed, disheveled little wretch.

Joshua stood up and stretched his aching muscles. *Be rational,* he ordered himself, but, somehow, he couldn't. Not when it came to John McFarren or, for that matter, his imp of a daughter.

He strode out of the study and up the carpeted stairs to the second floor. At the end of the hall was his room, a large, sparsely furnished chamber boasting little more than a brass bed and a bureau. And, of course, the portrait of Rosalie.

Joshua stood beneath it, staring at the gentle, familiar face and searching his heart for the feelings that had been there only one day before. He found them all, one by one, in the dusty corners of his spirit, but they were dulled, somehow, and not so solid.

He turned away and, with one sweeping motion of his right arm, cleared the top of his bureau. Watches, cufflinks, pocket change—even the fading, framed daguerreotype of his mother—all clattered to the polished wooden floor. The sound echoed into the very core of Joshua Tanner's battered soul.

Though it was something Brynne would have rebelled against under other circumstances, the prospect of a Sunday afternoon nap appealed to her that day. While Letitia was still arguing petulantly with her mother, maintaining that she and Brynne weren't children and shouldn't be ordered off to bed as though they were, Brynne was climbing the stairs.

The ordeal of Reverend Bradshaw's two-hour sermon had left her exhausted and, because of that, Aunt Eloise's dictum, however shrill and high-handed, was welcome.

There was a cool, salty breeze coming in through the open windows of Letitia's room, wafting pleasantly over the beds. Brynne took off her shoes and dress and lay down on top of the covers in only her drawers and camisole. With a small sigh, she closed her eyes.

When she awakened, perhaps an hour later, she was scandalized to see Letitia kneeling on the bed opposite her own, smearing something from a jar onto her flat breasts.

At first, she thought she was dreaming, but that misconception soon passed. Brynne swallowed hard, but a giggle escaped her all the same.

Letitia blushed furiously and covered her breasts with one arm.

"What are you doing?" Brynne demanded, sitting up and wrapping her arms around her knees.

Letitia's chin lifted proudly. "I'm using the potion I bought yesterday," she imparted, her eyes daring Brynne to comment.

Brynne held out one hand. "Let me see that stuff," she said.

Grudgingly, Letitia, still shielding her bosom, extended the sizable jar.

Brynne sniffed it—it had a pleasant, lavender scent—and frowned at the label. *Mother Godeen's Breast Food Cream,* it read. *For a more womanly bustline.*

"Don't you *dare* laugh, Brynne McFarren!" hissed her cousin defensively.

Brynne shrugged and bit the inside of her lower lip to keep from bursting with unrestrained glee. "It's only cream," she said. "Harmless enough, I suppose."

"Harmless?" choked Letitia, coloring again. "Madame Fortuna swore it would make my bosoms grow, and look at the label! It's guaranteed!"

Brynne handed the cream back and let her forehead drop to her raised knees, in an effort at hiding her smile. "Yes, it's guaranteed—to make Madame Fortuna richer and you poorer. You might as well cover yourself with lard as that stuff."

"You think it's funny, Brynne!" cried Letitia, her voice metered with small sobs. *"You* have busts, you don't have to worry! And Drew T—Tanner likes you."

Sobered by her cousin's obvious pain, Brynne lifted her chin and met Letitia's gaze. The girl's chin was trembling, and there were tears sparkling in her wide eyes. "Everything will be all right," Brynne said gently. "You'll develop naturally, without any help from Mother Godeen's scented lard."

Letitia was pulling her lacy camisole back on and her motions were jerky and quick. "What about Drew?" she demanded. "I want him to like me."

Brynne sighed. "If big bosoms are all Drew Tanner cares about, he's not worth a sheep pellet anyway."

Letitia was not mollified. "He's smitten with you," she accused. "Just you wait, Brynne McFarren, just you wait until *I* have bosoms, too!"

After that, Letitia was so testy that it was almost a

46

relief when Evan Pierpont came to take Brynne to Minnie Blode's dining hall in his wagon.

Minnie was standing in the doorway of her establishment, wiping her big, rough hands on a shabby but spotless apron, when the photographer's wagon drew to a stop. She nodded cordially in his direction. "Evan," she said.

He smiled broadly. "Minnie," he returned.

Brynne was a little hurt by Evan's calm demeanor—he'd been so upset that she planned to stay in Port Propensity, but now he was almost jovial about it. Perhaps he was glad to be rid of her.

"Got biscuits and fried oysters in here, Evan," the sturdy woman sang out.

"Now that sounds tasty, Minnie," Evan said, as he rounded the wagon to lift out the two crates of books that Brynne had purloined from her father's well-stocked shelves. "Trouble is, I'm due in Olympia in less time than I've got. Thank you all the same."

During this exchange, Brynne stood awkwardly beside the wagon, the handle of her carpet satchel clasped in both hands. Minnie Blode's business was housed in a weathered frame building, quite apart from the rest of the town. However, the water was nearby, and the tide made an elemental, reassuring sound as it came in and out. Over the roof of the dining hall, Brynne could see the framework of several schooners rising against the stunning backdrop of mountains and sky.

Suddenly, Evan caught Brynne's arm. "Come, come," he whispered. "Let's get you settled."

Brynne was miffed, but she was careful not to reveal her feelings. After all, Evan had been good to her, and if he was eager to be shut of her, she couldn't very well be nasty about it.

Minnie left the doorway when they reached it, so that Evan and Brynne could enter the long, narrow structure. There were shadows inside, but Brynne could make out the shapes of a dozen or so wooden tables

47

and benches. It was the floor that gave her pause—it was oddly spongy and, even in the dim light, it looked as though it had been chewed to a splintery mash by some fearsome beast.

Minnie Blode's laugh was boisterous and warm. "You like my fancy floor, Miss Brynne? Them calked boots the men wear do tear it up some. Have to replace it twice a year, and that's a fact."

"That must cost a lot," remarked Brynne, because she couldn't think of anything else to say.

Again, Minnie laughed. "It do for a fact. But them ship rats and timber jumpers is payin' a penny toward it every time they buy a meal—they just don't know it."

"Where shall I put these books, Minnie?" Evan asked, hoisting one of the heavy crates up into his arms again.

Minnie gestured toward an inside door, barely visible in the gloom. "Back there," she said, watching Brynne. When Evan was gone, she spoke again. "Don't you be lookin' so scairt, girl. You'll work hard here, but you'll be looked after, too. Ain't a sane man in a hundred miles that'd tangle with me."

"D—Do the men from the lumber camps eat here?"

Minnie shook her head. "Not often. Most of my customers is millhands, and them what works in the shipyard over here. The men in the camps got their own cooks."

Nervously, Brynne shifted her old satchel from one hand to the other and then back again. "Oh," she said, looking down at the demolished floor and frowning.

"They all wears them damnable boots," observed Minnie, the soul of long-suffering good humor.

Evan was coming back now, and his smile was broad, if a little wan, as the sunlight from the open door touched his face. "I'll be back in about a month, Brynne, to give out the portraits I took yesterday. You mind what Minnie says, now, and you'll be all right."

There was a hard lump in Brynne's throat. "G—Good-bye, Evan. And thank you."

Two minutes later, after a brief and, for the most part, inaudible conference with Minnie Blode, Evan was gone. Brynne fought back tears of desolation as she listened to the retreating beat of his horses' hooves and the clatter of the wagon wheels.

"I'll show you where you sleep," said Minnie, turning her barrel-like figure with surprising agility. "I already put up a cot for you, 'longside mine and Bessie's. Bess be Chinese, but I can't for the life of me twist my tongue 'round her name, so I calls her Bess. Old China Joe works here, too, but o'course he don't sleep over."

There was sunlight in the plain room at the back of the dining hall, at least, and it was clean. The plank floors here were solid, if a bit splintery-looking, and there were three cots jutting out from a wall that had never been finished. A washstand faced the beds, and it was equipped with a pitcher and bowl and a big, misshapen bar of harsh yellow soap. In one corner, there was a battered old screen to change clothes behind, and a series of wall pegs on the other side of the door would do as a wardrobe.

"It's nice," said Brynne, who was not in a position to be choosy. Then, bravely, she marched to the cot at the far end. The other two beds were unmade, and Evan had set the two crates of books at the foot of the neat one. "Is this mine?" she asked politely.

Minnie nodded, watching her with benevolent puzzlement. "You can do what you like for the rest of the day, but I'd advise sleepin'. Four o'clock comes 'round early."

Brynne swallowed and turned away, ostensibly to unpack her two spare dresses. Both of them needed washing, especially the one she'd worn to the picnic, and she'd had all the sleep she needed at her aunt's.

"Girl?"

Brynne turned again, and met Minnie's eyes. "Yes?"

"I oughtta be shot for sayin' this to a sweet thing like you, but I'm always more comforted to get things right out. My man comes acallin' of a time. Mind you don't bat them stormy-sky eyes of yours at Sam Prigg and you and me'll get on just fine."

"I promise not to," replied Brynne, with dignity. And then, when Minnie had left her alone, she collapsed onto her narrow, lumpy cot and laughed until she cried. The last part came easy.

By nightfall, Brynne had washed her dresses and underthings and dried them in the sun, draping them over the wild tangle of blackberry bushes behind the dining hall. She'd scrubbed her hair and toweled it and even managed a bath of sorts by standing behind the changing screen and dabbing at herself with a rough cloth dampened in a chipped enamel basin.

At seven-thirty, she and Minnie sat down to warmed-over oysters and biscuits, in the big dining hall, and ate by the light of a kerosene lantern.

"All them books yours?" Minnie asked, nodding toward the other room.

"They were my father's," said Brynne, aching a little as she remembered him touching those favored books with reverent hands, reading passages from them aloud of an evening, quoting their wisdom when it applied.

But that had all been before. Before Maggie McFarren's death, before they'd gone away from Port Propensity like thieves skulking in the night, before the drinking.

"You read 'em?"

"Some of them. A couple are in Latin."

"Your papa must have been a bright-minded man."

Brynne smiled fondly. "He was. He was a doctor, and he studied in Edinburgh."

"Figure you could read some of them words out loud to me? I do favor readin' out loud."

"I would be happy to," said Brynne, in all sincerity. "What would you like to hear?"

"Somethin' Biblish, I reckon."

Twenty minutes later, after the briefest of evening

ablutions, Minnie Blode settled herself in the cot beside Brynne's and folded her square, work-scarred hands over her middle. The kerosene lamp on the upended apple crate between the two beds flickered, blue-gold, in the warm night air.

Sitting cross-legged on her own cot and wearing her flannel nightgown, Brynne McFarren opened her mother's musty, much read Bible and peered at the tiny print. "The Lord is my shepherd," she began, in a soft voice. "I shall not want . . ."

By the time she reached "my cup runneth over," Minnie was snoring amiably. Brynne closed the Bible, blew out the lamp, and snuggled down in bed, sorely reminded of the sheep resting in a faraway, night-shrouded meadow. Her sheep.

Just before she closed her eyes, Brynne sternly corrected herself. They were Tanner sheep now.

The thought brought her wide awake.

There were nine men gathered in a back room at Walter Jennings's hotel—Drew Tanner and eight others. The place was hot and close and the air was blue-gray with the smoke of cigar, cheroots and pipes.

Drew went casually to a window and tried, without success, to open it. Behind him, the group argued in terse, furtive undertones.

The Committee of Nine, they called themselves, and this alliance, only one of many gathering all over the West, had been spawned by yet another committee. Each member had been enjoined to recruit nine other men, and everyone in the room, with the notable exception of Drew Tanner, had met the stipulation.

Drew smiled to himself, though the smoke was burning his eyes and chafing his throat. All his friends were women, and their husbands and beaus certainly weren't inclined to join this group or any other on his say-so. Still, because he nearly always knew what the Half-Breed was up to at any given time, these men were willing to overlook his failure to recruit.

51

Though Drew was largely uninterested in most political subjects, he wholeheartedly concurred with the aims of this particular association—they wanted to drive the Chinamen out of the community, by force if necessary, and Drew Tanner was all for that.

Besides, this was august company. The mayor was there, along with Reverend Bradshaw and two city councilmen. Even the sheriff had joined up, though he always looked a little disgruntled when somebody suggested burning Little Canton to the ground or simply shooting every last one of the yellow-skinned, rat-eating bastards.

Here, the division was drawn. While half the committee wanted to accomplish the purpose with terror, the other half leaned toward peaceful persuasion.

Persuasion, Drew thought bitterly. What did those opium-sotted sons of bitches know about logic or reason? Besides, they knew they weren't wanted and they still stayed. As far as Drew was concerned that left no other course of action but eloquent violence.

Something inside him craved that.

Suddenly, though, Brynne McFarren edged past the wall of hatred guarding Drew's heart and her image frolicked inside him, dispelling all other thoughts and feelings. His groin ached.

It was Walter Jennings's even voice that brought him back to the business at hand. "We're gonna have one hell of a time with the Half-Breed if we trouble his workers," he said, to the group at large.

Alf Gunderson, the sheriff, made a disdainful sound —it was almost as though he'd spat. "Just think of payin' them yellow devils the same wages as a white man gets!"

Drew smiled, folding his arms.

"Injuns, too!" marveled Charlie Ryan, the blacksmith. Charlie liked to tell how his whole family, save him, of course, had been massacred along the Oregon Trail, back in the fifties.

Walter Jennings's beady eyes swept to Drew. "You

think that's right?" he demanded, even though he well knew the answer.

"Hell, no," growled Drew defensively.

"Then why don't you do something about it?" grumbled Charlie Ryan.

Drew felt hot color surge into his face. Before he could come up with any kind of answer, the blacksmith burst out in roaring laughter.

"The Half-Breed'd cut out his gizzard, that's why!" boomed the burly smith, between guffaws.

It was then that the door of the hotel room smashed resoundingly against the inside wall. Drew swallowed hard as his half-brother filled the opening like some kind of living mountain.

"Jesus," breathed the sheriff.

Joshua's jawline looked rock-hard, and his big, powerful hands clenched and unclenched at his sides. His fierce eyes took in the men in that room, one by one, in a savage, searing sweep. Finally, they came to a stop on Drew's face.

"Go home," the Half-Breed said, in a deep, raspy voice.

"Now just a—"

"Now," added Joshua, and his massive chest moved up and down beneath his shirt in an ominously regulated rhythm.

The other men in the room were too awed to smirk as Drew stormed out, forced to squeeze past his brother at the door. In a semblance of rebellion, he waited in the hallway, leaning against the high wainscotting, his arms folded across his chest.

Damn it, he'd never live this down. Never. By morning, the story would have grown to embarrassing proportions—people would probably be saying that Joshua had taken a strap to him, right there in that room.

I'm ruined, he thought.

Joshua was still facing off with the Committee, and his voice was low, dangerous and oddly hollow. "You listen to me, you milk-livered, night-prowling sons of bitches, because I'm not going to repeat myself. If you've got complaints about my workers, you'd damned well better come to me with them."

"Now, Joshua, w—we weren't plottin' against you or none of your Chinaboys, neither," stammered the sheriff.

"I know what you were doing, Gunderson. The thing that turns my stomach is that you actually believe it's right. Just bear one fact in mind: any one of you bothers one of my men and I'll stuff your knees down your throat."

Walter Jennings finally worked up the guts to speak out, and the tremor in his voice made Drew smile in spite of his own precarious position. "This is a territory of the United States, Tanner, and we've got the right to assemble peaceably and talk about whatever we want!"

From his station in the hallway, Drew saw his brother's dark head move in a crisp nod. "You can talk from now till doomsday, for all I care. That's about all you're good for anyway. Just remember what I told you."

There was a placating, obsequious note in the blacksmith's voice. "Damn it, Joshua, simmer down. We're all your friends."

Joshua's reply was a disdainful hiss. "Sure you are, Charlie. That's why you included my brother in the harmless little gathering, isn't it? That way, you could always know firsthand that I was in good health!"

There was a silence, pulsing and ominous, and Drew would have laughed at the Committee's fear if he hadn't been so cussed scared himself.

It was the visible relaxation in Joshua's broad shoulders that broke Drew's paralysis. Sensing that the Half-Breed's seething rage was about to be turned on him, he whirled and ran like hell.

Joshua caught up to him at the base of the hotel stairway, grasped him by the back of his collar, and thrust him across the lobby and out into the night. When he released his hold, Drew plunged unceremoniously onto the planked street.

"Get up," growled the Half-Breed.

Throat working painfully, Drew rose with as much dignity as possible. The night was quiet, since it was Sunday, and the kerosene-fed flames in the streetlamps flickered eerily behind their glass panels.

Joshua put his hands on his hips and tilted his head back, ostensibly to study the star-strewn sky. After a moment, his gaze dropped, once more, to Drew's face. "If I ever catch you selling me out again, Drew, I'll turn you inside out."

Drew tugged nonchalantly at the sleeves of his shirt—like Joshua, he wore no suitcoat. "What makes you think I was doing anything like that?"

The Half-Breed turned his head and spat. When he spoke, his voice was like gravel. "You're swimming in deep water, boy," he warned. "Those bastards in there couldn't care less about fair wages—they're looking for a way to vent hatred. So before you get out any further, maybe you'd better make sure you can still touch bottom."

"We don't need the Chinese anymore!" Drew burst out.

Joshua was untying his blue-black, blooded stallion, Chinook, from the hitching rail. "So we just throw them out, like yesterday's bathwater?"

"Yes."

Joshua swung onto Chinook's bare back, and the beast nickered and danced under the weight of its master, anxious to be gone. "You're a fool," said the Half-Breed. He turned the horse and rode away.

It was as though both animal and man had become a part of the night.

Drew stood still, ignoring his own pinto gelding, for almost a minute. He wished he dared rejoin the meeting upstairs, in the hotel, but he didn't. Joshua

55

could be pushed only so far, and that point had already been reached.

Grinding his teeth, Drew untied his horse and mounted it. Then, at a deliberate pace, he rode home.

In the darkened study, always his favorite refuge, Joshua Tanner did not bother lighting a lamp. He sat down in a leather chair facing the fireplace, pulled the knoblike lid from the decanter of aged brandy that had awaited him on the occasional table, and poured a generous dose into a crystal glass. "Here's to you, you lecherous old reprobate," he growled, raising the glass to the portrait of his father over the fireplace. The painted face was hidden in shadow, of course, but Joshua glared up at it anyhow.

After a moment or two of reflection, he downed the brandy in one gulp and calmly refilled his glass. Then, letting his head rest against the high, cushioned back of the chair, he closed his eyes and consciously tried to unclench his jaws, the taut muscles in his shoulders and his mid-section.

He'd been stupid to leave Tacoma, to come back here. So much better to lose himself in Corrine Temple's gifted attentions—never mind that he was tiring of her—than to grapple with Drew and all the others. So damned much better.

"Joshua?"

He tensed at the sound of his sister's voice. She was the best friend he had, but he was in no mood to make idle conversation with her or anyone else. "Go to bed," he said briskly. "I'm all right."

Miranda's lemony scent came to him through the darkness, and her skirts rustled as she sat down in the chair next to his. "Don't order me around, Injun," she said calmly. "I'm six years older than you are, remember? That gives me a certain authority."

The brandy mingling with the blood in his veins now and easing the misery inside him, Joshua laughed hoarsely. "I thought ladies guarded their age for a

56

precious secret. Thirty-eight. Remind me to order you a cane and wooden teeth."

"Have you got a cheroot?"

Shaking his head, Joshua drew the requested item from his vest pocket, along with a match. He struck the match on the sole of one boot, lit the cheroot, and extended it to his sister. "Have you no morals?" he teased.

"Shut up, you sanctimonious bastard," she replied pleasantly.

Behind them, the front door slammed eloquently, and the sound was followed by the irritated report of boots hammering up the stairs.

"Dearest Drew," said Miranda, in a caustic croon, when another door closed sharply in the distance. "What's he done now?"

Joshua swallowed more brandy. "He's joined up with those idiots."

"What idiots, dear? We have a variety around here, you know."

Joshua brought his right foot to rest on his left knee. "The ones who plan to drive out the Chinese."

Miranda sighed. "Oh, them. You know, I've always wondered where they expect those poor people to go."

"The Great Somewhere Else," said Joshua.

"There is going to be trouble, isn't there?"

Now it was Joshua who sighed, and the sound was ragged and bitter. "Of course."

"Why don't you go to Europe or something? You could just forget Drew and Tanner Enterprises and the Chinese problem and—"

"And John McFarren."

Miranda stiffened. Joshua sensed the motion, rather than saw it. "John McFarren?" she croaked, in a miserable attempt at subtlety and confusion.

"Yes. John McFarren. It's a good thing you didn't turn to the stage in your hour of need, Miranda. You would have been pelted with rotten fruit at every performance."

Her hand moved unsteadily toward the liquor decanter on the table between them. "All right, all right," she muttered. "The man is dead, Joshua."

Everything within Joshua Tanner stiffened in reaction. "What?"

"Drew has met his daughter, and he overheard Eloise Jennings say that McFarren was dead."

"He can't be dead!"

"Why, Joshua? Because you wanted to kill him yourself?"

Yes, screamed the dark forces gathering inside him. *Yes, yes, yes!*

He bolted to his feet and flung the glass he held with indiscriminate fury. It shattered musically against the fieldstone fireplace.

"Joshua!" cried Miranda, in fear more than protest, leaping to her feet and rummaging through the darkness for matches to light the nearest lamp.

To his own amazement and Miranda's, too, a bellow of primitive rage escaped Joshua Tanner, echoing in the confines of that gracious, well-appointed room.

The weak light of the hastily lit lamp illuminated Miranda's face, revealing her shock. *"Joshua,"* she pleaded.

But he felt possessed, demonic. Some scurrilous entity had taken him over and, though he wanted to heed his sister's plea for reason, he couldn't.

"Where is she?" he demanded.

Miranda trembled and lifted her chin. "Brynne? I'll die before I'll tell you, Joshua Tanner!"

"I'll find her myself," he vowed, in a vicious rasp. And then he stormed out of the study and into the dark hallway.

"Joshua!" Miranda cried.

The front door shuddered on its sturdy hinges as he slammed it behind him.

Chapter Four

JOSHUA'S STRIDES WERE LONG AS HE ROUNDED THE shadow-draped house and approached the stables. The pungent, clean scent of summer grass, bruised beneath the soles of his boots, rose to his nostrils and calmed him slightly.

Inside the stable, despite the gloom, he found Chinook's stall easily and bridled the horse with deft, practiced motions. There was no need for a saddle—he swung onto the animal's glistening, muscled back and rode out.

The night was still and warm and star-laden, and it spoke soothingly to that part of Joshua that thought and functioned as a Sioux. By the time he'd ridden down the long, steep roadway that separated the Tanner property from Port Propensity proper, he was, for the most part, in control of his emotions.

Still, there were times when a roof and walls were intolerably confining, and this was one of them. He couldn't find John McFarren's bewitching daughter and confront her—that would change nothing—but he wasn't about to go back to that sumptuous house on the hill and suffocate, either. Tonight, the elements themselves would lend him comfort.

He skirted the town, certain that if he ventured inside its borders he would be drawn to Brynne McFarren, wherever she was.

What was it about the wench that pulled at him, that stirred thoughts and feelings he'd been sure he would never know again? Whatever it was, and it was far more than a desire to strike out at John McFarren through her, it was not bound by the normal rules of reason and logic.

Joshua Tanner muttered a curse.

Suddenly, memories rose around him like barking dogs, demanding his attention, and he prodded Chinook into a canter and then a full run. The bright, silvery moon guided them both, man and beast.

Rosalie, he thought, trying to summon her image in his mind. But she eluded him; the disparate features he recalled would not solidify into anything familiar.

Joshua was both outraged and frightened. For two years, he'd been conjuring Rosalie whenever he needed her, and now she would not or could not come to him.

Traveling along the road that rimmed the sleeping town like the crook of a mother's arm, Joshua rode hard until he reached the graveyard. There, he swung one leg over Chinook's powerful neck and slid to the ground. The balls of his feet ached in protest as he landed, but his eyes were fixed on the spectral, moonlit stones covering a quarter acre or so on the crown of a high knoll.

They were all here, except for Snowbird, his mother. God only knew what part of the Montana Territory served as her resting place.

Crisply, his heart rising raw and thick into his throat, Joshua tied his horse to the white picket fence and vaulted over the barrier to approach the section of the cemetery reserved for members of the Tanner family.

He paused before Caleb's impressive, stonework monument, but only for a moment. The next grave was

60

Etta's, and it, too, was marked by a fancy marble memorial, complete with a trumpeting angel.

Joshua was suddenly a child again, as he stood there in the glow of the moon, almost expecting Etta Tanner, his father's legal wife, to rise from her grave and berate him in her shrill, soul-piercing voice.

Dear God, how she'd hated him, though he'd tried, at first, to establish some sort of peace with her. It hadn't taken him long to realize, however, that she would forever see him as the living, breathing evidence of her husband's betrayal.

His jaw clenched, Joshua tilted his head back and gazed up at the stars. Even from the mysterious beyond, it seemed, he could feel her vicious hatred grasping at him.

I'm Miranda's mother, he heard her say again, just as clearly as if the infinite distance of death itself did not separate them. *Your mother was a filthy Indian.*

The words still stung, though Etta had been gone for years. "I guess I was a nasty surprise," Joshua said aloud, by way of concession.

A sea breeze whispered in the tops of the dark, brooding pines, as if in answer. Joshua resisted the other memories, but they came anyway, piercing the secret, reserved grounds of his heart.

His mother had been Caleb Tanner's woman, as far as the whites were concerned, but Joshua knew that, in her mind, she had been a true wife. She'd loved Caleb enough to leave her tribe after meeting him in the Montana Territory, to venture where his eastern wife wouldn't go—to the wilds of Puget Sound.

While Etta Tanner flourished in her richly furnished Boston house, the story went, Snowbird had labored beside Caleb, helping him to found the tiny lumber mill that would one day become part of an empire.

They had been together, these ill-guided lovers, until Joshua was two years old. It was then that the world turned upside down—Etta suddenly arrived, having scorned wagon trains and stagecoaches for a ship sailing around Cape Horn, with her eight-year-old daughter in tow.

Probably overwhelmed, Snowbird had left her man and her son to return to her people. Word of her death came promptly, by way of an intertribal grapevine, and even though he'd been very young at the time, Joshua remembered the loss of her. The other details, of course, had been sketched in, years later, by his father.

The days and months and years to follow would have been unbearable if it hadn't been for Miranda, his half-sister. For some reason, this mischievous, gypsy-eyed girl had befriended him from the very first.

Caleb Tanner had loved his son, but he was an empire-builder, after all, and as his small milling operation expanded to include untold acres of timberland, hop fields, two shipyards, two banks and a multitude of other interests, he had little time to spare for his wife, his daughter or his bastard son.

Surfacing momentarily from the ocean of memories swirling around him, Joshua turned his head briefly in the direction of the Tanner house. It was hidden by trees and darkness and distance, of course, but that didn't matter—sometimes it seemed that the structure followed him wherever he went, closed itself around him, squeezed until he couldn't breathe.

Had it not been for Miranda's staunch friendship, living there would have been so void of human warmth that Joshua would have had to leave. Etta's rancor had been like a snarling, cunning beast, always awaiting him, always stalking him.

It had been a relief, except for leaving Miranda, to go away to England at twelve and attend school.

At least his absence had engendered some sort of tenuous peace between Caleb and his embittered wife—a year after Joshua had gone away, Drew was born.

Raising his face again to the watching sky, Joshua permitted himself to remember being pleased at this news. He had shown Miranda's letter to every friend he had and looked forward to knowing his brother.

Drew had been seven years old when Joshua returned from England, at twenty, and the child's resemblance to Etta hadn't stopped with the color of his hair and eyes. He'd already been taught to hate with keen and uncanny skill.

For a long time, especially after both Caleb and Etta died, within the space of a single year, Joshua had tried to reach Drew.

Even now, after more than a decade of failed efforts, he still hadn't completely given up, though the whole idea seemed more hopeless every time he attempted any kind of understanding with his half-brother.

Determinedly, Joshua broke away from the foot of Etta Tanner's resting place and moved on to Rosalie's.

Hers was a simple stone—he hadn't wanted to put her here, with the others, but somewhere high in the mountains instead. He'd been insane with grief, though, and Miranda had prevailed with sensible, calmly stated arguments. Rosalie was a Tanner, the reasoning went, and she belonged in the family plot.

The moment Joshua laid his hand on Rosalie's cool, marble headstone, he remembered her face, her shape, her scent. The need of her ached in every fiber of his being, and he closed his eyes against the knowledge that he would never see her again.

She'd been gone two years, but sometimes it seemed that she walked beside him again, that her small, gentle hands rested on his shoulders, that she spoke just beyond his hearing.

He stood still for a long time, in that full yet empty place, hating John McFarren. How dare that bastard die before he could close killing hands around his throat, before he could avenge his murdered wife?

Anguished, Joshua shouted a curse, and the sound echoed off the gravestones rising all around him like silent and disapproving witnesses.

"Excuse me?"

The voice made Joshua jump half out of his skin.

"Are you all right?" it chimed again, in tremulous, wary concern.

Joshua whirled, staring. Just behind him, like a wraith clad in moon-kissed calico, stood Brynne McFarren.

Her eyes widened as she looked at him, and she retreated a step. "I didn't mean to intrude," she said bravely.

At last, Joshua found his voice. "What in God's name are you doing out here in the middle of the night?" he rasped, still wondering how she could possibly be real.

Her chin rose in spritely rebellion. "I might ask the same question of you, mightn't I? But I won't. I'll simply tell you the truth." She gestured, with one hand, toward an area in another part of the cemetery. "I came to see my mother."

Joshua closed his eyes against the indescribable emotions warring inside him. "This is no time, no place for a young girl to be wandering around—"

"I beg your pardon," she broke in crisply. "I'm a grown woman of eighteen, thank you very much, and self-supporting in the bargain, so kindly don't tell me where I may or may not go!"

He laughed. In spite of the situation and the bizarre surroundings, he laughed. The feeling it gave him was amazingly medicinal.

Brynne moved back another step. "If you're all right . . ." she faltered, watching him with the eyes of a stricken pixie.

Joshua laughed harder. "If *I'm* all right?" he shouted, in a spate of roaring mirth. And then he bowed the sweeping, master-of-the-manor bow he'd learned in England and never, until this moment, had occasion to use. "Thank you, my protectoress."

Even in the darkness, the color suffusing her elfin face was clearly visible. "Good night, sir," she snapped, turning on one heel and promptly tripping over a low, grass-covered marker to sprawl, in a calico heap, on the ground.

Joshua lifted her easily to her feet, with as much consideration for her dignity as possible, and then ruined it all by laughing again.

She raised one hand and slapped him smartly across the face.

The blow stung, and it brought Joshua's churning emotions immediately back into focus. "You little wretch!" he hissed, gripping both her wrists in his hands and glaring down into her proud, terror-stricken face.

She kicked him, hard, in the right shin, and his howl of stunned pain seemed to echo all the way to the ghostly mountains beyond the water and back again.

"Let go of me!" she shrieked.

Joshua swore roundly. It seemed, in that moment, that every word with more than four letters had fled his vocabulary. And the more she writhed and struggled in his grasp, the more determinedly he held her.

Suddenly, she stood stock still, probably realizing the hopelessness of her situation, and glared up at him, her breath coming in loud gasps. "All right," she said, with consummate dignity. "Have your way with me and get it over!"

Joshua's response was a shout of laughter. It came from a place deep within him and it flooded his mind, his heart, and his muscles, rendering him temporarily helpless. He let go of her wrists and doubled over.

Any other girl of his experience would have run away, and with sound reason, but this one stood still, her hands on her hips, one foot tapping furiously up and down.

When Joshua recovered enough composure to look at her face, she was glowering at him.

"What," she demanded loftily, "is so funny?"

With great effort, Joshua swallowed yet another fit of

maniacal mirth. *God, I must seem like a madman,* he thought. *And instead of being sensibly frightened, she stands here challenging me.*

"Well?" she pressed.

"All right," Joshua conceded wickedly, approaching her. "I'll be happy to have my way with you."

She screamed and whirled away, but Joshua caught her arm and held on.

"Wait," he said patiently, evenly, trying to sound sane. "I'm sorry—please don't be frightened."

And the miracle was that she *wasn't* frightened. She lifted her splendid chin and the moonlight played on her beautiful face and sparkled in her eyes. "What is your name?" she asked, in a reasonable voice, as though they'd encountered each other at an ice cream social or a dance, rather than in a graveyard.

The answer rose to Joshua's throat and lodged there, stopped by forces he didn't begin to understand. "Let me see you home," he said, finally, and ushered her toward the fence, where Chinook was tied.

"I don't know—we haven't met—"

"Sure we have," replied Joshua, lifting her onto Chinook's back, where she sat, in a tenuous, sidesaddle fashion, gripping the animal's black mane with both hands. "First, we met here, if you'll remember, and then you assaulted me with a hunk of watermelon."

She said nothing until he had mounted behind her, one arm curving around her small waist to grip the reins.

"I guess I should apologize for that. I thought you were someone else, you see."

"Oh," said Joshua mildly, careful to keep Chinook to a pace that wouldn't alarm the girl riding so scandalously with him through the darkness. The nearness of her was doing strange things to him, and it was all he could do not to bend his head and kiss the sweet, moon-whitened nape of her neck.

"I thought you were Drew Tanner," she went on, blissfully unaware, it seemed, that she was riding alone

66

with a man who would like nothing better than to introduce her to the singular pleasures flesh is heir to.

"Do you like Drew?" he asked evenly.

Brynne laughed, and the sound etched itself, forever, on the walls of Joshua's reeling spirit. "Yes. He's funny. Why, before he even knew my name, he asked me to marry him."

"Did he? What did you say?"

The teasing tone in his voice made her turn, beaming, to look up into his face. "Why, I said he was insufferable."

Before reason and honor could overtake him again, Joshua reined in the horse, with an almost imperceptible movement of his hand, bent his head, and kissed Brynne McFarren.

She stiffened at first, but then she was suddenly, sweetly cooperative. He wanted her so fiercely that it was almost impossible to keep from sliding to the ground, pulling her with him, taking her in the lush, scented grass.

Brynne drew back from his kiss, finally, and stared at him with innocent color pulsing in her face. Joshua closed his eyes and silently recited the litany that would be her salvation as well as his own. *This is a virgin. This is not some practiced whore, this is a virgin.*

But, God, how he ached to take her. How he ached to really kiss her, to bare her sweet, ripe breasts, to carry her skyward in a mingling of his passion and the wild, untried fire he sensed within her.

"My aunt will skin me alive if she ever finds out about this!" she breathed, at last, finally breaking both the silence and the spell of that strange summer night. "And Mrs. Blode would shoot you dead."

Joshua laughed and urged the stallion into an even walk again. "Mrs. Blode, is it? How do you happen to know Minnie?"

"I work for her," she answered. "She's a rough sort, but nice enough."

He nodded.

"She'd never understand this, though."

Joshua chuckled hoarsely. "No. She'd shoot me, all right."

"I wouldn't let her do that."

"Why not?"

Brynne turned to look up at him again, and the scent of her hair came at him in a sweet, inescapable rush. "I like you," she replied, matter-of-factly, "Though you are very mysterious."

"Am I?"

"Yes," she said, still watching him, still driving him to the very edges of his integrity. "For instance, you won't tell me your name."

"My name isn't important."

"I think it probably is, though."

"Why?"

Her shoulders moved in a fetching little shrug. "You aren't—well—you aren't *ordinary*."

"Thank you, I think."

The pixie smiled. "Oh, it was a compliment. You have presence, you know. I imagine that people listen when you talk, though you don't talk much, do you?"

With his free hand, he touched her face. "When I get the chance," he teased. "Promise me something, Pippin—that you won't go wandering around in the dark again. It really isn't safe."

Surprisingly, she did not draw away from his touch. "I know. I just tend to do things first and then think about them later."

"You could have lost more than a kiss tonight, you know."

She smiled, somewhat wistfully, and lowered her head. "Yes," she replied. "I know."

Joshua wondered if she could feel his need rising, hard, against her soft, slender hip. *Oh, to have no conscience,* he thought.

"What's a 'pippin'?" she asked, a pretty frown moving in her features.

They were nearing the town now, and Joshua was

careful, even though it was late, to keep the horse to the shadows at the side of the road. No need to ruin the girl's reputation. It would seem that she could manage that dubious task all on her own. "A pippin is an apple," he answered.

"I remind you of an apple?"

He laughed. "Yes. You're crisp and tart and very delicious."

She went gloriously red and didn't say another word until he'd seen her safely to Minnie Blode's door.

There, a creature composed of moonlight and saucy mischief, she smiled up at Joshua, her head tilted slightly to one side, and said, "Good night, Mr.—"

Joshua returned her smile, but he still wasn't willing to reveal his name, though he couldn't have explained the decision. "Good night, Pippin," he replied briskly, and then he left her to mount Chinook and ride away.

It was only as he reached the stables behind his own house that Joshua remembered that he'd wanted to question Brynne McFarren about her father's death. The thought hadn't once crossed his mind, all during their highly improper encounter, and, as he settled the stallion for the night, Joshua Tanner marveled at the effect she'd had on him.

Heart hammering, Brynne made her way cautiously through the dark dining hall and into the sleeping room beyond. No doubt she would regret her impetuous night sojourn when morning came, she reflected, as she quietly undressed and slipped back into her cot, but there were no regrets to spoil the adventure now.

Within moments, she was asleep, and dreaming of the man who would not tell his name.

It was still dark, but a strong hand was shaking Brynne's shoulder. "Wake up, child," said a voice that might have belonged to either a man or a woman, for all its deep timbre.

Brynne's vision focused and she saw Mrs. Blode's

face looming above her. A feeling of wretched loneliness churned in her spirit as she realized that she was no longer the daughter of a gentleman, but a woman essentially on her own. The picnic was over.

Somewhere outside, a rooster crowed.

"You awake now?" quizzed Mrs. Blode, turning away to pull on her colorless clothes.

"Yes, ma'am," said Brynne, bravely. And then, with resolution, she got out of bed, washed swiftly at the basin, and slipped behind the changing screen to put on a dress. Within five minutes, she'd made up her cot neatly, brushed her hair and pinned it up beneath a bandanna provided by Minnie, and presented herself in the cool, kerosene-lit dining hall, ready for work.

Bessie and China Joe—Minnie did not introduce them but Brynne remembered their names from the conversation the day before—were already working at the massive iron cookstove at the far end of the building. Two huge pots were bubbling over the heat, their contents carefully overseen by Bessie, and China Joe, his queue twisting down his back like a glistening black snake, was busily putting bacon on to fry.

"Set them tables," Minnie said, pushing up her sleeves and then pumping water into the biggest coffeepot Brynne had ever seen. "The dishes and forks is in that cabinet over there."

Brynne hurried across the room to open the indicated cabinet. "How many places shall I set?"

Mrs. Blode laughed gruffly, dispelling some of the anxiety Brynne felt. "Just keep settin' until all the plates is on the tables."

Mercy, thought Brynne, taking only a moment to estimate the number of plates and bowls and cups tucked away in that cupboard. *I'll be at this all day.*

Though she worked fast, it took almost twenty-five minutes to line the twelve long tables with the implements for eating. Brynne was just setting the last fork in place when Minnie grumbled, "Shake a leg, girl, or them workin' men'll be here afore you get a bite to eat."

Brynne was hungry, and she hurried to join China Joe and Bessie and Mrs. Blode at their table near the stove. A dish of oatmeal and three strips of bacon awaited her.

There was no table conversation as there would have been at home, on the farm. Time, as Mrs. Blode might have said, was a-wastin'.

The first workers arrived with the light of dawn. They were boisterous, burly men and, had Brynne had a moment to consider, she would have been afraid of them. However, the task of carrying platters of bacon and pots of coffee to the rapidly filling tables took every ounce of her concentration.

"That's a pretty piece," one man shouted out, his mouth full, his eyes sliding over Brynne's calico-clad figure as she refilled his coffee cup. "Where'd you find this one, Minnie?"

"Never you mind, Jack Clemmons," snapped Minnie, who was busy dishing out oatmeal at another table. "You bother that girl and I'll gut-shoot you for the pawin' grizzly you are."

Shouts of laughter rose all over the room.

"You mean we can't come a-courtin', Minnie?" called out another man.

"It's my shotgun you'll be courtin', you timber louse!" bellowed Minnie, who appeared to be enjoying the exchange for all her blustering disapproval.

Brynne went quickly about her business, her eyes averted. Surely, the room was full now, she thought frantically, even as a dozen more men came through the door and took places at the long tables.

As she moved, she caught snatches of conversation here and there.

"No more slackin' for you, Simpson, 'cause now the Half-Breed's back—"

"Why ain't there no damned biscuits?"

71

"No, sir, we's better off just like we are, as a territory. We got statehood, we got trouble—"

Brynne rushed on. Just when she'd filled all the coffee cups, the workers were shouting for more. She scurried back to the giant cookstove for another pot, and the thing was so heavy that she had to grip the handle with both hands.

There must have been a hundred men in that room, and all of them seemed to be holding up their cups. And, except for scattered groups of Indians and Chinese, who kept their attention carefully on the meal at hand, they all seemed to be competing for Brynne's time.

This, too, shall pass, she told herself, as she emptied the last of the coffee into an extended cup and scrambled back to the stove for another pot.

She was just turning around, the weight of a blue enamel pot trembling in her hands, when a sudden and unnerving hush fell over that rowdy group of shipyard and mill workers. It was as though everybody there had drawn in their breath and now feared to exhale.

Brynne followed the communal gaze to the doorway and felt her heart rise into her throat. There, clad in the rough clothes of a working man, stood the handsome, violet-eyed giant she'd encountered in the graveyard the night before.

He shrugged, his fierce eyes sweeping the room. "Eat," he said, and, at this off-hand command, the place came to life again, like a daguerreotype touched by a magician's wand.

In that moment, Brynne knew who this man was, and all her instincts were screaming his name.

Joshua Tanner strode across the room and took the enormous coffeepot from her hands just as she would have dropped it.

Brynne reeled inwardly and, suddenly, the room faded away, with all its noise, and became the shearing shed at home. It was dark, and the air was still scented with the singular odor of sheep's wool. There was an odd, creaking sound, and Brynne lifted her eyes to see her father's boots swinging in a gruesome back-and-forth pattern, just above her head.

She wanted to scream, but her throat closed over the sound.

"Brynne!"

Mrs. Blode's voice came through the pounding fog surrounding Brynne. "Get back, damn you. Yes, that means you, too, Joshua Tanner. Give the girl a breath."

Brynne opened her eyes and was stricken and embarrassed to realize that she was lying on the spongy floor and everyone was staring at her.

She sat up quickly, keeping her eyes on Mrs. Blode's concerned face because she dared not look further. "I—I'm all right," she said.

With a nod, Minnie helped Brynne to her feet. "All the same, you'd best lie low for a while, girl."

Color pulsing in her face, Brynne shook her head. "There is work to be done," she said, and she went about her tasks with grim determination, taking great care not to notice any of the men around her.

At last, a steam whistle blew in the distance, and, at this signal, the workers left their food to trail out into the waiting day.

Only then did Brynne dare to scan the room and make certain that Joshua Tanner was gone.

"You're sure you're all right?" Mrs. Blode ventured, with gruff kindness, as they gathered up the plates and cups and bowls and scraped the leavings into pails for China Joe's pigs.

Brynne thrust out her chin. She couldn't have Minnie thinking that this job was too hard for her—she'd starve without it. "I'm fine, ma'am," she said.

As she scrubbed dishes and flatwear that would immediately be set out again, for the noon meal, Brynne did her best not to think about Joshua Tanner.

When he continually invaded her determined mind, she set about hating him. After all, her father had died because of that man—

73

A hard lump ached in Brynne's throat. To think she'd let him bring her home in the night, let him kiss her, granted him sinful liberties in her dreams. And the worst thing of all was that she wanted him still.

Brynne was almost grateful when it came time to serve the next meal—the frantic, hectic rush of it gave her no chance to think or feel. And the moment dinner had been accomplished, supper had to be started.

In between all this, every fork, spoon, knife, plate and cup had to be thoroughly washed.

The men, full of boisterous mischief that morning, were as subdued at supper as they had been at noonday. There were no jokes exchanged with Minnie, and even the white men didn't so much as glance in Brynne's direction.

She was exhausted by the time the last of the supper dishes had been washed and dried, but something within her dared not rest. What if she did, and the dreams came again?

Telling herself that she would save precious minutes in the morning, Brynne set the long tables for the fourth time that day before slumping into a chair to stare uninterestedly at the cold leftovers that constituted her supper.

Since Minnie was out walking with Sam Prigg and China Joe had gone home and Bessie was on the step, haggling with one of her countrymen, who was selling fresh cod, Brynne was alone. She was hungry, and she ate what she could, but she was so tired that the food had no taste.

It was still light outside when Brynne McFarren washed the dishes she'd used and stumbled off to collapse on her cot without even bothering to unpin her hair or wash her face or take off her dress.

She slept instantly, and without dreams.

Chapter Five

MORNING CAME ALL TOO SOON, AS FAR AS BRYNNE McFarren was concerned. Since there was no point in complaining, she didn't. She simply washed her face and hands, dressed, and pinned up her hair.

"You could've slept a mite longer," Minnie said, with gruff approval in her voice, as she surveyed the tables so carefully set the night before.

Brynne shook her bandanna-covered head and began to eat hungrily of the toasted bread and scrambled eggs Bessie put in front of her. She smiled at the Chinese woman and then looked across the table, at Minnie. "You didn't hire me to be a layabed, did you?"

Minnie laughed. "You're one for workin', I'll say that. I've seen plenty of men who could do with as much gumption."

"I don't have much choice," Brynne replied honestly, between bites of scrambled egg. "I can't afford *not* to have gumption."

"It ain't easy keepin' up with that pack of hungry dogs," Minnie said, lifting her speckled, blue enamel coffee cup. "Lord, some days I'd just as leave roll over and forget earnin' a livin' myself. I've been at it forty years, but it won't be that long for a pretty gal like you."

"Forty years?" Brynne echoed, appalled at the thought.

"Started when I was widowed—Homer Blode didn't leave me a nickel—but I've worked with the best of 'em, I'll tell you that. I cooked for Big Mike Fletcher, up Providence way, and, at one time or another, I've put grub in the belly of every timber baron from here to the Willamette."

"But you work for yourself, now, don't you?" prodded Brynne, one ear trained for the dreaded sound of the workers' arrival.

Minnie nodded. "I'm getting pretty old for this, though. I declare, if Sam Prigg would just speak up, I'd be sellin' this place afore you could whistle."

Brynne had met Sam briefly, the day before—he was a nice, grizzled man with one wandering eye and a shy manner—and she smiled at the thought of Minnie setting up housekeeping and calling herself Mrs. Prigg. She hoped the dream would happen. "How long has Sam been courting you?"

Minnie surveyed the high, shadowed ceiling as she reckoned, her lips moving. "Must be twenty years," she said, at last.

Before Brynne could reply to that, the door opened and the workers were ambling in, grumbling among themselves.

Their surly mood held, and it turned out to be almost universal. It wasn't fair, one after another of them complained, to no one in particular and everyone in general, that a white man should get the same wages as a Chink or an Injun.

It was Sam Prigg who dared to interject a contrary opinion. "Quit your bellyachin'," he said, through a mouthful of China Joe's flapjacks. "You got it good."

"Good?!" bellowed a man two tables away. "Any time I'm breakin' my back for the same money as a rat-eater or a war-hoop gets, I don't figure I got it good!"

The Chinese men, sitting at their separate table, looked as though they'd like to fold in on themselves, like the delicate paper fans of their country, and disappear, while the Indians, also gathered at a table of their own, seemed ready to hit the warpath.

"The Half-Breed's an Injun hisself!" put in a burly man with a bushy red beard and brown teeth.

Slowly, and with consummate dignity, Sam Prigg stood up. His wandering eye glistened ominously in the dim light. "Why don't you tell us somethin' we don't know, Burns? Mr. Tanner's a fair man."

"Fair!" scoffed Burns, looking around to make sure his coworkers were of a mind with him.

"Yes, fair!" Sam Prigg shot back. "He could just lay off the lot of you grousers and replace you with Chinamen and Injuns. And he don't pay in scrip like most bosses—no, sir, a man can go and get his wages in federal money any time he wants 'em. And you ain't settin' choke on the mountain anymore, are you, Pete? You ain't settin' choke because Josh Tanner gave you easy work after you was hurt in the woods last fall."

Pete Burns had the good grace to look sheepish, however briefly.

And Sam Prigg went ruthlessly on. "You people can jaw till the cows come home, but it ain't gonna do nobody no good, 'cause bellyachin' don't move the Half-Breed. If you don't like workin' with Injuns and Chinese, head on outta here!"

An Indian, his dark hair braided, his tall frame clad in buckskin trousers and a coarse-woven shirt, rose slowly to his feet. "Mr. Tanner is *kloish tillicum*—good friend," he imparted somberly.

"Well, I say Injuns and Chinks is takin' food from white men's mouths!" challenged Burns, obstinately, standing up. "The railroads is built now, and there just ain't no place for yeller dogs and redskins!"

A muscle moved ominously in the Indian's coppery jaw, but, before he could reply, Mrs. Blode interceded eloquently. She'd gotten a double-barrel shotgun from some convenient place, and, standing protectively beside Brynne, she cocked it.

Instantly, all eyes were on Minnie Blode. "There'll be no trouble in my place," she said. "Sit down and shut up, every last one of ya."

Sam Prigg, the Indian and Pete Burns all sat down.

"They gets testy once in a while," confided Minnie, in a hoarse whisper, nudging Brynne with her elbow.

Brynne realized that her mouth was hanging open and closed it. Then, stoically, she resumed her eternal rounds with the coffeepot.

And the last man at the last table was Drew Tanner.

He grinned at her and raised one hand to his forehead, as though to tip an elegant hat. "Brynne," he said cordially.

Brynne surveyed his clothing as she casually filled his cup. He was dressed for work, there was no doubt of that, but his clothes were made of fine fabric and they were tailored. "What are you doing here?" she demanded, suddenly ashamed of the bandanna covering her hair and her ancient calico dress.

Drew ignored her question and presented one of his own. "You don't work on Sunday, do you?"

All too conscious that she was dawdling, a sin Mrs. Blode could not be expected to overlook, Brynne shook her head and started to retreat. The coffeepot was empty, and she had to get another.

But Drew stood, as though there weren't almost a hundred people looking on, and caught hold of her arm. "We'll take a carriage ride at two o'clock, then," he said, straight out.

Brynne swallowed. She liked Drew, but he was a Tanner, after all, and there was no sense in getting too thick with that bunch. Again, she shook her head.

Undaunted, Drew released her arm and wedged his

hands into the pockets of his trousers. "Two o'clock," he repeated.

Brynne blushed and fled back to the stove.

"You're drivin' your ducks to a poor pond if you take up with that one," Mrs. Blode informed her, tossing her head toward the opposite side of the room.

Brynne pretended not to hear. Tanner or none, Drew was a pleasure to be around, and the prospect of a carriage ride was appealing indeed. She was still dreaming of fresh air and sunshine when the steam whistle blew somewhere in the mill yard and the workers straggled out.

As she cleared the tables and scraped plates, Brynne considered Drew Tanner. Was he courting her?

Surely he wasn't, she reasoned, her mind as busy as her hands. Men of his station in life didn't take up with serving girls, unless they wanted a bit of fun and adventure.

Brynne was blushing furiously as she filled the dishpans with scalding hot water and began to scrub cups and plates, forks and knives. If Drew Tanner thought she was cheap, she'd tell him a thing or two, thank you very much.

Mrs. Blode, armed with a dish towel, came to pluck utensils out of the steaming rinse water and dry them. "Sam says there's a crew workin' through dinner over in the shipyard," she said, without looking at Brynne. "Bessie and me'll pack up some vittles for you to take over there. We oughtta have it ready by the time you're done with your chores."

Brynne was delighted at the prospect of escaping the dining hall, if only for a few minutes. In fact, she could have kissed Minnie Blode's rough, weathered old cheek.

"I'll be happy to go," she said, with prim honesty.

Minnie laughed. "I thought so. Mind you don't dawdle, though, 'cause we'll have a herd here next meal, same as always."

"I'll hurry," Brynne promised.

Two hours later, she was leaving the dining hall with an enormous basket over one arm and Minnie's instructions clear in her mind. The crew was working onboard the schooner *Rosalie,* refurbishing her decks. Brynne was to deliver the food and come straight back, minding that she didn't dally along the way.

The day was as bright as polished brass, and Brynne hummed as she hurried along the rutted dirt road to the Tanner shipyard. The salty scent of the Sound and the raucous cries of seagulls were welcome changes from the sounds and smells inside that ill-lit, airless dining hall.

She reached the wide gateway of the shipyard all too soon, for it was less than half a mile from Minnie Blode's, and ventured inside. Here, there were new sounds—the pounding of hammers, the squeaking of saws, men shouting back and forth. There were six ships, in various stages of construction—some on scaffolding on the rocky shore, and some moored along half a dozen creaking wooden wharves.

Brynne was pleased by the sight of the new vessels, with their fresh, fragrant, lumber bones exposed. Who knew where they might go when they were seaworthy—China? The Barbary Coast? Boston or even London, England or Paris, France?

The romance of it all buoyed Brynne's tired spirits on a swell of delight.

The *Rosalie* was easy to spot—she was the only ship bearing a name on her bow, and the only one with masts and sails. The canvas triangles snapped noisily in the wind as Brynne made her way down the wharf to the boarding ramp.

She paused a moment—despite Minnie's edict that she not dally—before going further. After all, one didn't set foot on the decks of a real ship every day of the week, and the memory would have to last a long time. She closed her eyes to savor it.

"Ahoy, there," said an amused masculine voice, from above.

Brynne opened her eyes and looked up and there, silhouetted against the schooner's sails and the pearly blue sky, stood Joshua Tanner.

It seemed that the sturdy wharf buckled beneath her feet, and she might have turned tail and run if it hadn't been for the eloquent weight of the dinner basket she carried.

Joshua looked like a magnificent savage, his shirtless torso bronzed and muscled in the summer sun. He'd tied a red bandanna around his forehead, Indian-style, and his trousers, worn as they were, seemed molded to his powerful thighs. His smile flashed, blindingly white, and his violet eyes chafed Brynne's very soul with an impudence that should have been offensive but wasn't. After only the briefest pause, he came down the boarding ramp and stood facing her, his hands on his hips.

Dapples of sunlight reflected from the water danced on his copper-brown, sweat-polished chest and, for a moment, Brynne could hear nothing but the sounds of her own heartbeat and the rhythmic grating of the *Rosalie's* side against the wharf.

She retreated a step, stricken by the sight of him, by his very nearness. Her throat worked painfully, but no words would come out.

Joshua caught her forearms in strong, work-hardened hands. "Don't step back, Pippin. Not unless you can swim."

Brynne blushed hard, just at the thought of falling into the Sound, in full view of this disturbing man, with all Minnie's carefully prepared sandwiches. "I can swim," she said, with foolish pride.

Joshua Tanner's smile flashed again, dazzling her. When he released his hold on her arms, a hollow feeling seized her. "If you say so," he said. "But you're really not dressed for it, are you?"

Setting her jaw against the wicked needs she was feeling, Brynne reminded herself that her father would probably not be dead if it weren't for this man. She thrust out the heavy basket. "I've brought your dinner," she said.

He smiled and took the basket easily in one hand, as though it were light as the passing breeze. His right hand rose, in a motion that set Brynne's insides to spinning, to rest on the shabby bandanna she wore to cover her hair.

"You shouldn't hide that splendid mane under a rag, Pippin," he informed her in a low voice.

"It would get in the food if I didn't," Brynne retorted tersely, realizing that she was, alas, dallying. "Good day, Mr. Tanner."

"Fare thee well, Miss McFarren," he replied, with a mocking salute and a note of profound amusement.

Brynne turned and walked away with as much dignity and composure as she could muster. It was God's own wonder that she didn't walk right off the wharf and into the sparkling water, with his eyes pulling at her the way they were.

On the shoreline, Brynne dared to look back. She'd been right to think Joshua Tanner was watching her—he was still standing at the base of the boarding ramp, his splendid head tilted to one side, his gaze searing Brynne even from a distance. A glistening sheen of sweat covered his naked torso and inspired all sorts of shameful reactions inside her.

Brynne turned and fled, at a dead run, and the sound of his laughter rang out over the cacophony of hammers and saws and seagulls and the shrill whine of the machinery in the adjoining lumbermill.

She was breathless and flushed when she bounded into the dining hall, and her heart hammered as though she'd been pursued.

China Joe and Bessie and Mrs. Blode all stopped what they were doing to stare at her. Typically, Minnie spoke first. "What the devil's chasin' you?" she wanted to know.

Brynne began to laugh. She'd been running, not from the devil, but from a part of herself—the part that wanted to throw itself at Joshua Tanner's feet and surrender shamelessly to his hands, his lips, his—

"I'm all right," Brynne said quickly, swallowing the strange, mad, helpless laughter that was rising from some deep and untouched part of her.

That afternoon, she worked harder than she ever had before, hoping to exhaust herself.

From a physical standpoint, the tactic was successful; after a sponge bath and other ablutions, Brynne tumbled into bed and her eyes closed of their own accord.

This night, however, she dreamed. And in her dreams, Joshua Tanner was doing strange, sensuous, achingly beautiful things to her.

Every muscle in Drew Tanner's body protested as he sat down in his chair at the family table, and he gritted his teeth. In a sidelong glance, he noted that Joshua was watching him with undisguised amusement.

Damn the half-breed bastard anyway, he sat easily in his chair at the head of the table, looking as cool and rested as if he'd spent the day lounging around with a book.

Crockery rattled as How Ling set a china tureen in the middle of the table and began ladling out soup. Her eyes did not meet Drew's, though she spared a smile for Miranda, as she served her, and actually spoke to Joshua.

Another time, Drew might have been annoyed, but tonight he was only amused. For the first time since he'd achieved manhood, there was just one woman he wanted—Brynne McFarren.

"How do you like the working life, Andrew?" Miranda asked, when How Ling had gone.

Drew stiffened at the use of his full name and glared

at his sister. "It has its redeeming qualities," he snapped.

Miranda's dark eyes sparkled with amusement. "Does it really?"

"Yes," he said tartly, dipping a spoon into the potato soup before him. Just then, he imagined bedding Brynne McFarren in such vivid scenes that he felt himself harden. It was embarrassing the way thoughts of her crept up on him at the damnedest moments—if he didn't have the little nymph, and soon, he would surely die of the wanting.

"You weren't here for breakfast," Miranda said, dispelling the sweet anguish engendered by Drew's imaginings. "We missed you."

"I'll bet," he retorted, not looking at his sister. Sometimes she could read him too well, and there was much he didn't want her to know. "I ate at Mrs. Blode's."

A glance in Joshua's direction revealed that his broad shoulders had stiffened ominously. Drew could feel his half-brother's eyes scraping his face even after he'd returned his attention to the soup.

"My, my," trilled Miranda, enjoying herself. "Mrs. Blode's. Next you'll be consorting with all manner of commoners, won't you?"

Drew sliced a menacing look in his sister's direction, then turned his eyes to his half-brother. "There's going to be trouble, Joshua," he reported off-handedly, careful not to reveal his delight. "Some of the workers are complaining because your cherished Chinese and Indians are getting the same wages as the white men."

Joshua wasn't even pretending an interest in his soup. He hadn't lifted a spoon to it. "That's nothing new," he said, then added, in a razor-sharp tone, "What's the attraction at Minnie's?"

Drew smiled broadly, for all the world like an adoring brother revealing good news. "Brynne McFarren," he replied. "I mean to marry her."

84

Joshua's throat corded into a column of coppery muscle and then relaxed again. "I see."

So it was true, then, Drew marveled. On some instinctive level, he'd suspected that Joshua had not only noticed Brynne, but found himself drawn to her in the bargain. Here, at last, was a mode of sweet revenge.

"She's going out with me on Sunday," Drew said pleasantly. "I'll be using the carriage, if you don't mind."

Joshua pushed his soup bowl away and scowled. "I don't mind," he lied. And then he slid back his chair, rose to his feet, and strode, without another word, out of the dining room.

Miranda watched him go in open surprise, Drew in singular amusement.

Suddenly, Drew's fatigue-dulled appetite was keen again. He ate hungrily of the roast beef, boiled potatoes and wild asparagus that How Ling carried in from the kitchen. Then, sated, he excused himself with uncommon politeness, climbed the stairs, and strode down the darkened hallway to the door of his room.

The rim of light under Joshua's door made him smile. Dollars to cow chips, the Half-Breed wouldn't sleep tonight.

While she dressed for yet another day of hard work, Brynne McFarren wondered if she could be sent to hell for her dreams. They had been so vivid—her breasts still tingled, as though Joshua had really caressed them, and the nipples were hard and distended. Even the secret place remembered, and it ached just as though it would soon receive him.

"Stop it!" Brynne cried, out loud, startling poor Bessie, who was just coming out from behind the changing screen.

The Chinese woman looked at her in open puzzlement. "Stop?" she mumbled.

"I was talking to myself," confessed Brynne, taking up her brush and grooming her sleep-tangled hair with brisk, furious strokes.

Bessie looked sedately alarmed and scurried out to join the industrious Minnie, who was already helping China Joe at the cookstove.

Brynne pinned up her hair, donned the ugly bandanna, and marched out to face the morning. Blessedly, she was entirely too busy to think about Joshua Tanner or anyone else.

Drew appeared again for breakfast, standing out among the rough workers around him without the slightest effort, and he spoke to Brynne only once. "Sunday?" he asked, as she filled his coffee cup.

Without meeting his eyes, Brynne nodded.

At noon, Minnie again sent her to the shipyard with a dinner basket, but, this time, Brynne did not encounter Joshua. She was both relieved and disappointed when Sam Prigg met her at the end of the dock to claim the crew's carefully assembled meal.

When Sam came to supper, he returned the empty basket, just as he had the night before.

All during the rest of that week, Brynne worked like a madwoman, always pursued by the savage yearnings of the night. She began to smile at Drew every morning —he never appeared at dinner or supper, for some reason—and even spoke to him.

Though she carried the basket of sandwiches and bottled coffee to the boarding ramp of the *Rosalie* each day, she didn't catch so much as a glimpse of Joshua.

She told herself that that was good, given the sinful dreams he inspired to plague her nights, but, even so, she was always crestfallen as she hurried back to work.

On Saturday evening, after the handful of men who weren't off drinking their supper at the Orion Hotel or the nefarious Shore House had gone, Minnie Blode dropped three shiny silver dollars into Brynne's palm.

"You've made a mistake—"

Minnie laughed at the expression on Brynne's face. "No mistake, child. I told you two dollars, but you're worth every cent of three."

Brynne gaped at the money, feeling rich. Why, with this and that other five-dollar gold piece, she had seven dollars and fifty cents! She twisted her head to consult the old clock on Minnie's plain board wall. It was five minutes after six—too late to hurry to the mercantile and buy a new dress.

Sadly, she sat down on one of the worn benches. Given her working hours, she would *never* get a chance to shop. She would just have to wash and press her pink and white gingham and wear that to ride in Drew Tanner's grand carriage.

"Miss Ada is usually in her shop at least till seven," said Minnie, with that uncanny, coarse insight of hers. "Anyhow, she's such a pinch-penny that she'd probably open the place up if you knocked like you meant to do business."

Brynne had seen Miss Ada Tuppin's dress shop the day she arrived with Evan, and she remembered exactly where it was. Beaming, she rushed into the sleeping room, ferreted out the money left over from the Independence Day picnic, and ran unceremoniously into the street.

Miss Tuppin was just pulling down her shade when Brynne reached the shop, her heart pounding, her breath burning in her lungs.

The dressmaker's severe little face brightened, and she unlocked the door and swung it wide open. Minnie had been right—the woman was eager to make a sale.

Trying to be considerate of the lady's time, Brynne explained quickly that she needed something ready-made, if possible.

Miss Tuppin carried a small line of clothes imported all the way from San Francisco, as it happened, and Brynne gleefully bought a skirt in soft gray cotton, a pink blouse made of gossamer lawn and a broad-brimmed straw hat with a cluster of artificial, rose-colored daisies affixed to its pink band. She left the shop impoverished but happy.

Everyone was gone when she reached the dining hall again, so Brynne rummaged around until she found the community washtub. Then, singing, she heated water for a bath. The few dirty dishes, which she'd expected to find awaiting her, had already been done up and put away.

Ever fearing invasion, Brynne had placed the tub in the sleeping room, behind the screen, and now she carried pot after pot of hot water to fill it. When, at last, all was ready, she stripped off her clothes and sank into the water with a sigh of contentment. No matter that she must sit cross-legged, like an Indian, because the tub was so small—the bathwater felt wonderful against her skin.

Finally, as the bath began to grow tepid, she soaked and scrubbed her hair. When it was clean, she wrapped it in a rough towel and scoured the rest of her body until her flesh stung.

She was just rising out of the tub when she heard the knock—it was quite forceful enough to be masculine, and it came not from the front door, but from the closed door of the sleeping room.

Quickly, Brynne unwrapped her hair and covered herself with the damp towel. "Who's there?" she asked tremulously.

"Letitia!" sang her cousin, in a cheery voice. "May I please come in before I'm accosted by some millhand?"

Relieved, Brynne laughed. "Of course. Come in," she called.

Letitia opened the door and came to peer around the changing screen, an enamel coffee mug in her hand. "I had to use *this* to knock," she said, holding up the cup. "I pounded on the front door until my knuckles were raw!" Frowning, Brynne's cousin curled the fingers of her right hand and studied them as though she expected to find bones and sinew exposed.

Since she didn't own a wrapper, Brynne pulled her flannel nightgown over her head and stepped around Letitia to fetch her brush and begin working at the squeaky-clean tangle of her hair.

Letitia ceased the critical inspection of her delicate knuckles to look at Brynne. Wearing a pretty, sprigged cambric dress, she thrust out her flat chest and demanded, "Do you think my bosoms are growing, Brynne? I've been using that cream for almost a week!"

Brynne suppressed a grin and pretended to observe Letitia's charms from all angles. "I do believe they are just a bit bigger."

The lie brought a glorious light to Letitia's face. "I *told* Mama I was developing, but she just laughed and said I'm built like the women in Papa's family."

Brynne sat down on the edge of her cot to tug at her wet hair with her brush. "You look so pretty in that dress," she said, this time speaking honestly. "Are you going somewhere?"

Letitia nodded. "Strolling with Howard Macumber," she said glumly. "He's just back from Harvard."

"I thought you were taken with Drew," Brynne ventured cautiously, thinking of her promise to go carriage riding with him the next day and wondering if Letitia would feel betrayed if she knew about the plan.

"Drew never notices me," admitted Letitia petulantly. And then her blue eyes widened and she lowered her voice to a confiding whisper. "Howard says I'm womanly."

Brynne smiled. "Discerning fellow."

Letitia sat down on Minnie's cot, facing Brynne. "He's handsome, too—except for his nose. He has the Macumber nose, I'm afraid. Merciful heaven, between their noses and the Jennings bosoms, our children would be frightful, if we had any."

Again, Brynne suppressed amusement and tried to look solemn. "Children? Letitia, you're not thinking of marrying Harold—"

"Howard," said Letitia crisply, examining her fingernails. She consulted the watch pinned to her nonexistent bosom, a moment later, and added, "I've got to go. Mama asked me to tell you that we'll come for you at ten o'clock tomorrow morning, so you can go to church with us."

Brynne stiffened. "Tell Aunt Eloise, if you please, that I will not be attending church from now on."

Letitia's mouth dropped open. "Mama will be—"

"I don't care."

"Brynne McFarren!"

"I said I don't care! I support myself and your mother has absolutely no say about what I do. Besides, I will not sit for two hours listening to that odious man rant on and on about sins of the flesh!"

Letitia blushed, but there was a mischievous light dancing in her eyes. "He was staring at you, wasn't he? I think Reverend Bradshaw likes you, Brynne."

Brynne trembled with theatric disgust.

"He used to pick on Miranda Tanner," Letitia went on. "I think she came to church just to spite him."

Despite her angry feelings, Brynne giggled.

"Personally, I rather favor sins of the flesh," Letitia went on thoughtfully. "Brynne, have you ever—"

Brynne reddened. "Letitia Jennings! I have *not,* and I certainly hope you haven't either!"

"I would, though," said Letitia firmly. "If Drew Tanner asked me, I would in a minute."

Bending forward, the task of brushing her hair forgotten, Brynne breathed, in all sincerity, "Don't you think it takes more than a minute?"

"I hope so," replied Letitia, looking at her bodice watch again. "I'll tell Mama that you aren't going to church."

"Thank you."

At that, Letitia said good-bye and hurried out to meet Howard Macumber of the Macumber noses.

Once she'd gotten the tangles out of her hair and cleaned her teeth with baking soda, Brynne took her new clothes from their boxes and hung them carefully, so that they would look nice the next day.

Then, with a yawn, she rummaged through the crates she'd brought from the farm until she found a promising book to read. Against her better judgment, she chose a saucy adventure novel and read until her eyes wouldn't stay open.

When she slept, at last, a great many new elements were added to her dreams about Joshua Tanner.

Chapter Six

"KILL THE HALF-BREED?" GUNDERSON RASPED, BEFORE
he thought. He was immediately grateful for the din
of the Shore House, grateful that the tinny piano music,
the laughter at the bar and the calls of invitation from
the girls up on the mezzanine had covered his words.
"Jesus," he breathed, as an afterthought.

His companion smiled, his green eyes catching with
bright irony on Alf Gunderson's badge. "You'll never
be rid of the Yellow Menace," he observed, in his low,
cultured voice, "until you're rid of the Half-Breed."

Alf Gunderson was all for running off the Chinks,
and by any means necessary—short of murder. God in
heaven, he *was* the sheriff, after all. "Now you listen to
me, Darnell. Joshua Tanner ain't too popular in this
town, but he's got friends in high places, make no
mistake about that. 'Sides, I'd rather tangle with the
Devil himself than that Injun—a man'd stand a better
chance."

Austin Darnell sat back in his chair, still smiling that
high-born smile of his. With his neatly trimmed,
caramel-colored hair and aristocratic features and dan-
dified clothes, he looked like anything but the dangerous filth he was. With a gentlemanly hand, he raised his
glass to his lips. "There are ways. A few drops of

chloral hydrate in a man's whiskey and he's as easy to control as a child."

Alf shuddered. "You ain't talkin' about no regular man," he argued. "You ever seen that crazy Injun fight?"

The well-bred, choirboy face tightened a little, and Alf had occasion to regret his question. Everybody in Port Propensity knew that it had taken Darnell months to recover from his own confrontation with the Half-Breed. A man didn't like to be reminded that he'd had his ass kicked, and this particular man was nobody to shame.

Darnell set his glass down, drummed the felt-covered table with genteel fingers, and let the remark pass. "I have my own reasons, as you know, for wanting Joshua Tanner's blood. If he—er—disappears—well, it seems to me that we'd both benefit."

Alf drew a deep breath and released it slowly. It was a good thing his Myrna wasn't alive to see him sitting here in this glorified whorehouse, drinking with the likes of Austin Darnell. He'd been a good sheriff, Alf had, when he'd had her to account to, but now he was alone and it seemed to get easier every day to look the other way when there was wrongdoing going on. "No, by God," he said, gathering the last shreds of his integrity. "I've let you get away with more than I should have as it is. You're nothin' but slug bait, Darnell, and I can't say I blame the Half-Breed for callin' you out that night. Been me, I'd have killed you." He paused, knowing that his life wasn't worth a scraped-out oyster shell now and not caring. When he got home, Myrna wouldn't be there. "Joshua Tanner is an honest man, and if he turns up dead or missin', I'm gonna be all over you like flab on an old whore."

"As you wish," said Austin Darnell, in an even voice, and the only outward indication of his rage was the small, brief twitch at the corner of his mouth. "Good evening, Sheriff."

Alf lumbered to his feet and cast one glance upward, at the girls lining the railing of the mezzanine. Not tonight. He felt too damned old and tired tonight.

Tossing a coin onto the table to cover the cost of his drink, Sheriff Alf Gunderson squared his weary shoulders and walked toward the door. It was a long ride back to town, but the night was balmy and the stars were out and it was easy to pretend that Myrna would have a lamp burning in the window and coffee simmering on the stove when he reached home.

Only Alf Gunderson never got home.

Brynne awakened promptly at four, out of habit, she supposed, and could not go back to sleep no matter how hard she tried.

In the cool darkness, she got out of bed and dressed quietly, to avoid waking Bessie and Mrs. Blode, who were no doubt hoping to sleep late. In the empty dining room, she lit one lamp and then brushed her hair and pinned it into a loose chignon. It was nice not to have to wear the bandanna.

Still taking pains to be quiet, Brynne built a fire in the big stove and put water on to boil for coffee. Then she found a loaf of fresh bread and sliced off a heel, which she ate without butter or jam. When the coffee was ready, she filled a cup and went to the window to watch pink and gold light spill over the mountains and dispel the darkness.

She was totally unprepared for Joshua Tanner's appearance and, when he suddenly loomed just on the other side of the window, she started so that some of her coffee spilled and made a brown stain on her pink and white gingham dress.

When she looked up, shaken and furious, he was grinning at her, Ivanhoe framed in the light of dawn.

"Open the door," he mouthed.

Brynne considered. She wanted so to rebel, to turn away and ignore him, but she knew instinctively that he would only knock and rouse Bessie and Mrs. Blode.

Irritated, she unbolted the door.

Joshua Tanner entered the deserted dining hall with surprising stealth for a man of his size—Brynne supposed it was his Indian blood that permitted him to move so quietly. She wondered if Mrs. Blode and Bessie wouldn't feel his presence the way she did—as some sort of charged jolt.

"Be quiet!" she whispered sharply, not wanting to seem the slightest bit friendly.

Though his aristocratic lips were still, his eyes were dancing with laughter. It seemed to shake the room, that silent mirth, and Brynne was braced for the rattling of tables and benches and dishes.

Calmly, he moved around her to help himself to coffee at the stove.

Alarmed and annoyed and, at the same time, almost desperately excited, Brynne sat down at a distant table, in the shadows, and hoped devoutly that Joshua Tanner would go away.

Her stomach leaped as, instead, he crossed the room in long, soundless strides, and sat down at the opposite side of the table. Cupping his coffee mug in sun-browned, powerful hands, he met her stricken gaze and winked.

Light was shafting in through the windows now and glistening with tiny speckles of dust. At last, Brynne found her voice.

"What do you want?" she whispered.

Again, the violet eyes danced. They moved almost imperceptibly to her full, gingham-garbed breasts and left hot color in their wake as they traveled back to her throat, her lips, her face. "Coffee," he said gruffly, lifting his cup in a gesture that was at once conciliatory and mocking. "Just coffee."

"You could have gotten coffee at your house!" Brynne whispered furiously, resisting a fundamental need to squirm on the hard wooden bench.

Joshua regarded her somberly now, and she sensed a peculiar sort of pain within him, a pain she doubted she could have borne had it been her own. "Why did you faint the other day, when I came in here?"

Brynne swallowed. She wanted to avert her eyes, but she could not tear her gaze from his. She should tell him, she knew, but somehow she couldn't bring herself to add to that indefinable thing that writhed, shadowlike, in his eyes. "I was tired," she said.

"And recently bereaved," he prodded, at last releasing her from the odd grip of his gaze by looking down at his coffee mug.

So he did know that her father was dead! Did he also know that he was the major cause of John McFarren's final collapse? Surely, he must. He was a man of business, after all, and the fact that he had foreclosed the mortgage on a sheep farm couldn't have escaped him, however humble that property might be. Brynne lifted her chin. "Yes. My father died."

"I'm sorry," he said, with such sincerity that Brynne was immediately confused again. There should have been at least a flicker of guilt in the strong face or the tormented eyes, but there wasn't.

Perhaps, Brynne thought, Mr. Tanner was not only a very successful businessman, but an accomplished actor, too. She decided to find out. "He hanged himself," she said, with dignity and deliberate bluntness.

"My God," breathed Joshua Tanner, his eyes widening in what appeared to be honest horror. "Why?"

"We lost our farm."

"I'm sorry," he said again, and one of his hands crossed the table to close soothingly over Brynne's.

She longed to wrench free, but she couldn't. The motion of his thumb against her palm was sending liquid fire through her bloodstream and she wondered frantically if he could see the throbbing pulsepoint at the base of her throat. "Why did you come here?" she asked, desperate to distract him, to cause him to release her hand.

His thumb shifted, stroked the fragile inside of her

wrist. "To see you," he replied, in a low voice that made Brynne's heart flip like a circus acrobat. And then, to her amazement, his grip tightened slightly and he drew her to her feet and closed the small distance between them.

Brynne's ingrained sense of propriety screamed in protest, but the adventurous, sensuous side of her nature won out. She reveled in the hard press of his body against hers and made no move to resist when he lifted her chin and covered her lips with the warm, compelling command of his own. This kiss was different from the one they'd shared that night they'd met in the graveyard, and it jarred Brynne's soul.

The yearning ache in her midsection intensified to almost unbearable proportions, and, when his hands rose to the place under her arms, where her breasts rounded, she moaned softly.

The sound stirred a responding one in him, and the kiss deepened. Treacherous needs raged through Brynne's system to harden her nipples and cause the secret place to expand in preparation for his conquering.

It was Joshua who broke the kiss and stepped back. "I think we'd better take a walk," he said, his words broken by the hard rasping of his breath.

Brynne blushed to the roots of her hair. "I think you're right," she responded.

In the dazzle of the rapidly rising sun, Joshua took Brynne's hand and half-dragged her down the empty street. His massive shoulders moved rhythmically as he tried to breathe normally, and Brynne found herself enthralled by the way his ebony hair curled at the nape of his neck.

They were entering the shipyard, now void of all sounds but the lapping of the tide and the cries of gulls, before Brynne McFarren had managed to regulate her own breathing.

The *Rosalie* rolled on the calm water, her port side grinding against the end of the long wharf, and her sails were snow-white against the sky. Wonder filled Brynne at the sight of her.

When, at last, she looked away from the schooner, she saw that Joshua was smiling down at her, reading the dreams of far-flung adventure in her face. His hand was warm and strong and calloused around hers.

He laughed and executed a sudden, elegant bow. "Allow me, Pippin, to squire you aboard."

"Aboard?" echoed Brynne, in delight.

He answered by pulling her swiftly down the wharf and, at the base of the *Rosalie*'s boarding ramp, sweeping her up into his arms.

She frowned.

"Don't get proper on me now." He grinned, and, in spite of herself, Brynne was laughing as he carried her to the waiting deck of the ship.

There, he set her carefully on her feet and surveyed the rolling decks and sturdy masts with pride.

Brynne was thrilled to be standing on the deck of a real, sea-going ship. "Have you ever taken an ocean voyage?" she breathed, gaping about in wonder, trying to see everything.

He waited for her to look at him again before he answered, and, for a fraction of a second, his eyes were fixed on her mouth. Then he smiled, revealing perfect, incredibly white teeth. "Yes—a few."

"Where did you go?" demanded Brynne, wondering if all the people in his tribe had teeth like that and whether or not they chewed roots to accomplish it.

Joshua's shoulders moved, in an easy shrug, beneath the straining fabric of his white shirt. "The East. San Francisco. Europe."

Brynne made a mental note of his clothing—plain black trousers, a lightweight vest, the white shirt. It was amazing that she hadn't noticed what he was wearing until he shrugged. "Europe!" she choked out, trying to keep her imagination in check.

He shrugged again, but his beautiful, darkly lashed

eyes belied the nonchalance of the motion. They were, in fact, scraping the outer boundaries of Brynne McFarren's very soul. "I went to school in England," he said. "We'd better go."

Brynne rebelled. She'd never been on a real ship in her life and she wasn't about to leave without seeing more of it. "I want to see the wheel," she said stubbornly. "And the galley and the captain's cabin."

"Brynne."

Brynne folded her arms and lifted her chin in silent challenge.

Joshua shook his dark, splendid head. "I'll be damned if you aren't the *stubbornest*—"

"How do you steer this vessel?" she demanded.

He laughed again and took her hand and led her to the wheelhouse, where the great, knobbed, wooden wheel waited. He watched her with an unsettling mixture of amusement and desire as she pretended to be a brave captain battling a storm-tossed and dangerous sea.

The moment Brynne abandoned the wheel, Joshua caught her elbow in a warm, insistent grasp and started back toward the boarding ramp.

Brynne used all her strength to resist. "The galley!" she reminded him, scowling.

He turned to face her, his hands resting on his hips, his eyes snapping with lavender fire. "The galley is below deck!" he snapped, oddly nettled.

Brynne glared up at him. "I don't care if it's in the crow's nest. I want to see it!"

"Damn it all to hell and creation!" he thundered. "If Minnie Blode shoots me for a rounder, let it be on your conscience, provided you have one!"

Brynne tried to convince herself that she didn't know what could happen if she ventured below the decks of an empty ship with this particular man and, to a certain degree, she succeeded.

The galley was simply a long room with tables and

benches bolted to the floor. Bits of silver light danced on the varnished walls, cast through the high portholes by the water rocking the ship.

"There," Joshua said tersely, his eyes scorching Brynne as they moved over her face and then, unwillingly, to her rounded breasts. "You've seen the damned galley!"

Some of Brynne's bravado deserted her. Asking to see the captain's quarters, where there would undoubtedly be a bed, was out of the question. She was in over her head as it was, and, so she suspected, was Joshua.

"Thank you," she said, with cool dignity.

Joshua's jaw tightened ominously and it seemed, for a moment, that he was about to roar some horrid curse. Instead, he made an odd, strangled sound, deep in his throat, and closed the crackling space between them in two strides. His lips were at once searching and fierce as they moved on Brynne's.

And Brynne's normally practical mind spun like a bit of flotsam on the swell of her wild, inexplicable desire. A wanton ache tormented her as Joshua trailed his mouth to the sensitive place beneath her ear and then to the hollow of her throat. When he lifted her into his arms, it didn't even occur to her to protest.

The captain's cabin was nearby and, after a brief walk down a narrow hallway, they entered it, Joshua opening the door with a swift motion of one booted foot.

Almost angrily, he tossed Brynne onto the narrow, quilted bed affixed to the wall of the cabin. His eyes seemed to divest her of her crumpled gingham dress as they swept ominously from her face to her shoes, and water-light from yet another porthole shimmered on his broad chest.

Brynne shivered. She'd never been wanton before, but it was certainly delicious. "Well?" she said.

He rolled his eyes. "I don't believe this," he rumbled, in angry wonder, his hands once again resting on his hips. "Brynne, have you ever been alone with a man?"

She blushed and shook her head.

Joshua swore hoarsely and, for one wretched moment, Brynne felt sure that he would turn away and storm out, leaving her alone. Instead, he sat down on the edge of the bed and drew her into a sitting position.

"You're sure you want this to happen?" he asked, in a rough, almost despondent whisper.

Brynne wasn't sure at all, but her body was, and she nodded, closing her eyes in delight as his hands deftly undid the buttons at the back of her dress. Slowly, gently, he slid the garment down over her shoulders, the sides of his thumbs leaving a trail of fire along the length of her arms.

She sat now in a pool of pink and white gingham, naked, except for her thin muslin camisole, from the waist up. It was like actually living one of the sweet, scandalous dreams she'd had about this man—wickedly delicious. She made a soft, hungry sound as he slid the straps of her camisole down to reveal her ripe and waiting breasts.

A long, ragged sigh escaped him as he studied the rose-tipped, golden-white globes that were his to claim and conquer. He pressed her backward onto the captain's thick down pillows and she stretched her arms above her head in preparation for surrender and in contentment.

Joshua groaned and caught both her wrists in one hand, holding her in that scrumptiously vulnerable position. Then, with agonizing slowness, he lowered his face to the warm valley between Brynne's breasts.

The sensations tingling on her flesh were exquisite, and she waited, in wonder, for him to unfold the mysteries, one by one. A primitive, throaty gasp of pleasure escaped her as his lips encircled one nipple. He then charted the same fiery course with his tongue.

Brynne cried out as he nibbled at the hardened

nubbin and then feasted upon it, his hand still holding both her arms in gentle restraint. Without releasing her, he lifted his head.

"Do you want me to stop, Brynne?"

Hot, crimson color throbbed in Brynne's face, and she shook her head. "No," she pleaded. "Oh, no. The other, Joshua, the other . . ."

He licked and nibbled at the opposite, pulsing button until it was hard and protruding, until Brynne begged for its capture. Only then did he suckle with all the fierce hunger he'd been restraining.

Just when Brynne was certain that she could bear the sweet torment no longer, he drew back, released her wrists, pulled her dress and her camisole and her muslin drawers down, almost in a single motion. With one hand, he flung the garments aside.

Then, gently parting her legs, he knelt between her knees and began undoing his shirt. Stripped of that, he paused, at the very height of Brynne's curiosity and rioting desire, bared her secret, velvet-clothed place with his fingers, and began, lazily, to stroke it.

"Ooooo," Brynne groaned, arching her back as a new and incredibly fierce pleasure shot through her surrendering body. And just when she was certain that there could be no greater pleasure than this, he introduced her, with the warm motion of his mouth, to sensations that caused her spirit to soar. As his hands pressed her knees further and further apart, to make her still more vulnerable to the ministrations of his marauding tongue, Brynne's entire body tensed reflexively and then there was a sweet, warm explosion within her, an explosion that left her shuddering and sated.

But he drew her knees up and parted them again and once again he was sampling her sweetness, driving her on to new desire. He kissed and nibbled and explored until Brynne was wild with the need of complete fulfillment.

"Take me," she pleaded. "Oh, please."

But he would not. He kissed the warm, flat surface of her belly, her rib cage, and then her breasts. Again, he suckled freely, hungrily and at his leisure.

This time, her hands were free, and Brynne sought the pulsing shaft of his manhood, bulging at the fabric of his trousers, with desperate fingers. He moaned and rolled onto his back, turning Brynne with him, so that she was above him. He caught one suspended breast between gentle teeth and then closed his lips around the nipple and tugged at it until Brynne was certain she would die of the pleasure.

Finally, Joshua released her and lowered her again onto her back. His hands paused at the buttons of his trousers, and his eyes were gentle on her face. "Are you sure?" he whispered.

Brynne nodded quickly.

An instant later, he was gloriously naked. He parted her legs and poised above her, searching her face for any sign of reluctance. When there was none to see, he entered her with a slow, tender caution that was obviously costly to him.

There was a brief, prickling pain, followed by a wonderful sensation of being filled with him, of being one with him. Instinctively, Brynne moved her hips in rhythm with his, her breath coming in quick, feverish gasps underlaid by a continuous and pleading moan.

The motion of their joined bodies increased, by degrees, until they were both rising and falling in a fury of sweet desperation. Brynne's release was so violent that she cried out in the soul-sundering throes of it, her hands clasping the corded muscles of Joshua's back.

He was still moving inside her, still plunging deep and more intensely when Brynne was finally able to open her eyes. She watched in tender wonder as his magnificent features grew taut, as his eyes closed. His hard frame stiffened, suddenly, and then he shuddered in the force of his pleasure and a loud groan echoed through the tiny cabin.

Brynne smiled as he fell to her, exhausted, his breath

seeming to tear its way in and out of his lungs. His flesh was moist beneath her palms.

After a time, he lifted his head, kissed her gently. "Are you all right?"

Too moved to speak, Brynne simply nodded. Later, she knew, she would feel terrible regrets, but right then, being close to Joshua Tanner, pleasing him, was all that mattered.

They lay still on the narrow bed for a long time, lulled by their mutual satisfaction and by the gentle rocking of the *Rosalie,* their arms and legs entwined.

Eventually, Joshua put on his trousers and went off somewhere. When he returned, he had water and soft clothes, and, tenderly, without speaking, he washed her.

That done, they knelt, facing each other, on the bed. Brynne ran one hand over the bronzed, ebony-matted expanse of his broad chest and circled one dusky nipple with an exploring finger.

Swiftly, Joshua caught both her hands in his and halted the expedition. Brynne smiled mischievously, unashamed of her total nakedness. "Minnie Blode is surely going to shoot you," she said.

"My life is in your hands," he replied, with mock pathos.

Brynne did not want the scandalous adventure to be over—when it was, the regrets would begin and the world would be terribly empty.

"Love me again, Joshua," she whispered, her palms circling, free again, on his chest.

"Brynne."

"Please?" The plea was uttered with a proud lift of her chin, but it was a plea all the same.

Joshua sighed, releasing her hands only to grasp her bare, tingling shoulders. "Pippin, I already feel like a monster. You're so young—"

"I'm a woman grown!"

He laughed, and his eyes moved to her breasts. He

was clearly remembering pleasures taken there. "You can say that again," he admitted gruffly.

Then, gently, Joshua Tanner lowered Brynne to the rumpled bed and the magic began all over again.

Miranda watched her half-brother dismount and stride angrily into the stables. It was half past one and he'd left the house early in the morning. Where on earth had he been?

"Joshua?" she ventured, from the wide doorway of the stable.

She could barely make him out in the gloom, and the effort made her sun-dazzled eyes ache.

"What?" he snapped, and the motions of his shadow-draped arms were swift and violently angry.

Miranda's eyes were adjusting to the change now, and she walked inside the stable to stand at the open door of Chinook's stall. "Joshua Tanner, stop fiddling with that horse and listen to me!"

Miraculously, he stopped. In the half light, she saw that his magnificent features were taut with some deadly annoyance. "I'm listening!" he growled.

"Alf Gunderson is dead."

Chinook's bridle dropped to the straw-covered floor with a melodic clink. "How?"

"His body washed ashore in Little Canton this morning," Miranda answered evenly. "Joshua, they're blaming the Chinese. There's been a lot of talk about lynch mobs—"

"Christ!" Joshua spat. "Did anybody see anything? Was he with anyone in particular last night?"

Miranda drew a deep breath. "Nobody saw the murder, and the last time he was seen alive was out at the Shore House. He talked with Austin Darnell and then he left."

There was a silence. Miranda used it to brace herself for the inevitable explosion.

It didn't come until Joshua had closed the stall door

behind him and dragged his sister out into the glaring midday sun. The pallor in his face was frightening to see.

"Austin Darnell?!" he roared, so loudly that How Ling and her mother, who was the Tanner cook, ceased their labors in the vegetable garden a hundred yards away and stared. "When did he get back?"

Miranda pulled free of her brother's painful grip and rubbed her throbbing elbow. "For heaven's sake, Joshua, how would I know? He's back, that's all."

Joshua swore roundly and some of the color came back into his ravaged face. He turned and started back toward the stables, but Miranda caught his arm and held on tenaciously.

"Joshua, wait. Stay out of this."

He drew a deep breath and searched the brassy blue sky in an obvious attempt at patience. "Miranda," he warned, in a voice that would have chilled anyone but his sister.

"I'm begging you to take a few minutes to think, Joshua," she said reasonably. "Please, come inside. Have one drink. We'll talk."

Something terrible moved in his face—perhaps the memory of the night Austin Darnell had nearly raped Rosalie. Miranda remembered, too, and shuddered despite the balmy warmth of the day.

"Joshua," she pleaded, in a whisper.

He sighed, and some of the rigid fury in his shoulders drained away. It was then that Miranda noticed that his clothes were rumpled and his hair was mussed.

She smiled, tugging him in the direction of the house. "For shame, Joshua Tanner," she teased, to lighten the mood. "You've broken your hard and fast rule and condescended to . . ."

Instantly, he was immovable again, and his face was stony with warning. A muscle flexed and unflexed in his arrogantly chiseled jaw, and his eyes were like dark orchid fires.

Miranda met his gaze fearlessly. He might intimidate

everybody else in the territory, but she wasn't afraid of him. To her, he was still the little boy who had borne her mother's cruelty in staunch silence and then hidden in the springhouse to cry.

For an endless moment, they stood there, brother and sister, glaring at each other. Finally, Joshua conceded defeat with a hoarse, reluctant chuckle that seemed to be torn from some vital part of him.

"Who is she?" dared Miranda, always one to make the most of any advantage.

"That," replied Joshua crisply, folding his arms, "is none of your damned business."

With that, he strode imperiously toward the house, probably intent on changing his clothes and consuming the drink he obviously needed. One thing was clear: there was absolutely no point in trying to talk to him.

Miranda waited until the door of the kitchen had closed before she followed. She would surely go insane with curiosity if she didn't find out who Joshua had been with.

He hadn't had time to visit his mistress. As far as she knew, Corrine Temple, the current recipient of his passions, lived in Tacoma, and he'd made no secret of his decision not to enjoy romantic forays with local women. Joshua was a man to keep his vows, but someone had gotten past his formidable determination this time.

In the kitchen, Miranda's eyes fell on the picnic basket Drew had meant to take along on his carriage ride and, typically, forgotten.

An inexplicable chill moved up and down her spine, a thing of instinct and of thoroughly knowing her brothers. Brynne McFarren. Was the woman who had swayed the unswayable Joshua Brynne McFarren?

Miranda pulled back a chair and sank into it, unsteady. She tried to tell herself that she was wrong, that she was being fanciful, that there was no solid reason to think what she was thinking. The effort failed.

Drew and Joshua were already at dangerous odds with each other and, now, sure as the tide would ebb and flow, they both wanted the same woman.

Chapter Seven

ONCE THE CARRIAGE WAS MOVING, ABLY DRIVEN BY THE man who cleaned the Tanner stables and cared for the horses, Drew surveyed Brynne covertly and pondered.

She resembled a sweet confection in her pink blouse, broad-brimmed straw hat, and trim gray skirt, and Drew doubted that she knew what a singular and sweeping power she wielded.

"Brynne?"

She turned slightly, on the leather carriage seat beside him, but her eyes did not quite meet his. There was a glow about her, the glow of a woman who has just been roundly and thoroughly loved.

"Yes?" she asked.

Drew pulled in a ragged breath. He wanted her so badly that he was imagining things. Good Lord, it was two o'clock on a Sunday afternoon. Who could have gotten past her virginal defenses and Minnie Blode to caress all those inviting curves?

"You look lovely."

Brynne smiled, but her eyes were still averted. No doubt, she was shy. "Thank you."

Drew stayed a savage need to touch her and smiled in response. He felt a sudden and magnanimous urge to put her at ease. "Please relax. I'm not planning to make advances."

Apparently, he'd spoken the magic words. The tension in her small, straight shoulders faded away, and her eyes came warily to his. "D—Do you know who I am, Drew?" she asked.

God, how he wanted to slide his arm around that small waist! If she'd been any other woman in his circle of friends, they would have been having fun by now.

"You're Brynne McFarren," he said, lifting one corner of his mouth in the teasing grin that had so often stood him in good stead.

She'd been clutching a batch of folded papers in her lap and, now, she suddenly thrust them at him.

Perusing lofty documents was not Drew's forte, but he recognized this one for what it was. Tanner Enterprises had foreclosed on the farm of someone named John McFarland—

Drew fought down a shout of triumph. "McFarland —McFarren?" he mused gently, raising one eyebrow.

The carriage rolled and shifted over the rutted dirt road, and Brynne gripped his arm to steady herself. Silver fire shot through Drew's system and set his loins aflame with the need of her. Her eyes were slate-gray and full of pain as they searched his face. "Papa told everyone that our name was McFarland, including your family's bank, it would seem."

Drew had to look away. He couldn't be certain what he might do if he didn't. He pretended an interest in the passing countryside, purposely taking note of the trees and the sparkling, silver-blue mirror that was the Sound. When he felt safe in looking at her again, and that was after an uncomfortably long interval, he did.

"Brynne, I'm sorry."

Anxiety colored her face a fetching pink, and her eyes widened as her hand came impulsively to his. "No. It was Papa's fault. He didn't pay the mortgage."

"Still," Drew said, with exaggerated concern. Secretly, he was glad that some fool—the signature on the bottom of the document was a proxy for Joshua's—had overridden company policy to reclaim the McFarland sheep farm. If he hadn't, he wouldn't have met Brynne.

"I shouldn't have told you," she said, in a wretched whisper. "It serves no purpose and—"

Drew caught his hand under her chin before he had a chance to think about it. "You were just trying to be honest, weren't you? I admire that, Brynne."

God, if Flossie and Maude could see him now, they'd stand up and cheer.

The reward for his grand performance was a faltering, gut-wrenching smile. "We can be friends, then?"

Drew wanted to shout, this time in frustration, but he smiled instead. "Friends," he concurred. "Besides, Brynne, it's only fair to tell you that I don't have any say in matters like this, anyway. Joshua makes all the company decisions."

There was a disturbing response in the delightful, animated face. Brynne's eyes suddenly had a hollow look, and her inviting lips were pressed together in consternation. She seemed to be remembering something terrible.

Again, Drew lifted her chin. "Brynne?"

To Drew's utter amazement, one tear slid, glistening, down her cheek. Her eyes were fixed on the papers in his other hand. "That was more than Papa could take," she said, in a faraway voice that tore at some part of Drew like the teeth of a wild animal. "H—He went out to the shearing shed and he hanged himself."

"And you found him?" Drew whispered, stricken at the thought.

She nodded and made no move to resist when he drew her into a consoling embrace.

The carriage came to a lurching stop beside a small, sun-glimmered pond, and Brynne, her composure regained, allowed Drew to help her out of the luxurious vehicle to stand before him on the grass-carpeted ground.

"I forgot the picnic basket!" he grumbled, but his mischievous hazel eyes were shining and his hands lingered, just for a moment, on Brynne's waist.

Her stomach was churning, and the last thing she wanted was food. She'd been so wanton with Joshua, and they'd had a terrible argument—he'd been furious to learn that she meant to take a carriage ride with Drew after all that had happened and refused to understand that she'd promised. And then, for a reason she would never understand, she had felt compelled to show at least one Tanner those foreclosure papers. "I'm not hungry," she said, at last.

The beginnings of a headache were gnawing at the nape of Brynne's neck when Drew suddenly took her hand in a warm grip and pulled her away from the carriage. As if at some unspoken signal, the driver brought the reins down over the backs of the four bay horses harnessed to the vehicle and it rumbled away.

"He's leaving us!" Brynne cried, realizing, too late, that for all his charm, Drew Tanner might not be a gentleman.

Drew laughed, and the sound was warmly reassuring. "Brynne, it's all right. I promise to mind my manners."

Brynne's throat ached, and she gazed up into the affable, rakishly handsome face of her escort, hoping that he could indeed be trusted. She'd already given herself to one man that day, and she had no intention of making the same disastrous mistake all over again.

"What are we going to do?" she asked, in weak tones.

"Walk," Drew replied calmly.

And walk they did. They rounded the shimmering pond, climbed to the top of a grassy hillside that afforded a wondrous view of the mountains, gathered wildflowers in a hidden meadow rimmed with madrona trees.

Once, Drew picked a wild tiger lily and placed it gently behind Brynne's ear and, for one wretched moment, she thought he might kiss her. In the end, however, he simply traced the outline of her jaw with a newly calloused thumb and smiled.

"You've been working," Brynne said, somewhat stupidly, her memory sparked by the roughness of his hand.

Drew sighed expansively and held out both his hands, palms up. "Alas," he confessed. "I guess my brother decided that I've been a waster long enough."

Brynne might have laughed if it hadn't been for the mention, however indirect, of Joshua Tanner. A cold shadow draped itself over her heart and she shivered. Dear heaven, what had she done?

"I wondered why you were taking meals at Mrs. Blode's," she said distractedly.

"Did you?" he asked, in a soft voice, his tone giving the words a shade of extra meaning, his eyes steady and full of hunger as they rested on Brynne's face.

There was a short silence, broken only by the buzzing of the bees and the songs of the birds and the whisper of a summer wind passing high in the treetops.

Drew retreated a step; he appeared to be waging some desperate struggle within himself. When his eyes met Brynne's again, they told her things she didn't want to know.

"Brynne, the work at Minnie's is too hard for you. I can't stand to see you racing about like some kind of servant—"

Brynne broke in proudly, but politely. "I *am* a servant, Drew."

He shook his head in a disagreement that was almost feverish. "No, you're too fine to be fetching and carrying for that lot of flea-bitten rounders. I won't have it!"

Brynne flushed with anger. "You won't have it?" she demanded. "You won't *have* it? Who do you think you

113

are, Drew Tanner? Unlike you, I'm not the cherished darling of a rich family. I have to earn my living—"

Drew stopped her by laying calming hands on her shoulders. "I didn't mean it that way, Brynne," he said evenly, but his eyes were hard and sharp and completely void of their usual merry mischief. "I want to take care of you."

Baffled, Brynne simply stared at him from under the brim of her picture hat.

Drew had left his suitcoat in the carriage and, now, as he turned away, Brynne saw that the muscles in his back were taut beneath his shirt and silken vest. "My sister has a house in town," he began, in a gruff, reluctant voice. "I want you to live there until we can be married."

Brynne's mouth fell open. Married? She'd known Drew Tanner for one week and he wanted to *marry* her? She blushed. She hadn't known Joshua any longer, but he'd already been as intimate with her as any husband could ever be. "Drew," she said, at last, in broken tones, "we can't be married."

He whirled to face her. "Why not?" he rasped.

Honest, he'd called her earlier. Well, Brynne couldn't bring herself to be honest now, at least not completely. How could she stand here and say that she'd shamelessly bared herself to the very man who had driven her father to suicide? How could she tell him that, however misguided her actions had been, she didn't regret a single kiss or caress? "I'm—I'm not pure," she said, miserably.

His face looked murderous, and it was almost entirely void of color. "Who?" he bit out.

Brynne thrust out her chin. "That isn't important. Furthermore, it isn't any of your business, Drew Tanner!"

"It is, damn it!" he roared, flinging his arms out wide. "I love you!"

Now it was Brynne who retreated—one step, two.

114

She longed to run, but they were miles from town and Drew would catch her easily. "Don't say that," she pleaded, "I just told you, Drew, that I'm—"

"I don't care!"

"But . . ."

His eyes were fierce on Brynne's face, her throat, her bodice. "When, Brynne?" he whispered.

Brynne averted her eyes. *This morning.* No, she simply couldn't say that, she had already hurt Drew too much as it was. "Years ago," she lied, surprised at the steadiness of her voice.

Drew's jaw knotted momentarily. Clearly, he didn't believe her. His words confirmed the fact. "Years ago," he mocked, in a low, deadly voice. "How old are you now, Brynne? Seventeen? Eighteen? Were you eleven when you lost your virginity? Twelve?"

"Stop it!" Brynne shrieked, her heart pounding with shame and fear, her stomach turning flips. "Drew Tanner, you wicked—"

He came to her, caught her shoulders, gave her a hard shake. "I'm sorry!" he bellowed furiously. "Brynne, for God's sake, will you listen to me? I'm *sorry!*"

This day had been too much. Tears streamed down Brynne's face and she sniffled, unable to speak.

Drew brought a clean handkerchief from one of his trouser pockets and dabbed gently at her tears. "It doesn't matter, Brynne," he said softly. "God help me, I love you so much that nothing matters."

A sob of despair escaped Brynne. *"No,"* she pleaded.

But he drew her close and held her. The press of his lean, agile body seemed wrong, like a garment that didn't fit. His scent was wrong, the timbre of his voice was wrong, everything was wrong.

Brynne wrenched herself out of Drew's arms and glared at him. "You promised to be a gentleman!" she accused, in a hoarse whisper.

Drew put his hands on his hips and tilted his head to one side to study her soberly. "This man—he was someone you couldn't have, wasn't he?"

How true, Brynne thought, with dismal resignation. *How horribly, inescapably true.* Joshua Tanner was and always would be the man who had pushed her father beyond the reaches of sanity. And even if that fact could be overlooked, Joshua wasn't very likely to come courting Minnie Blode's waitress, was he? By nightfall, he would no doubt be laughing about his conquest over a glass of fine brandy, perhaps even boasting to his friends. "Yes," Brynne admitted finally. "He is someone I can't have."

"Then let me help you forget him. Move into Miranda's house. Brynne, I swear I can change your mind. . . ."

Move into Miranda's house. The words echoed into the dark chambers of Brynne's heart and, for the first time since this insane conversation had begun, the full weight of their significance came crashing down on her. "You want to *keep* me, like some—some prostitute? Well, I won't be your mistress, Drew Tanner!"

With that, Brynne turned to run away, without any destination in mind. As she'd feared, Drew overtook her easily, caught both her elbows in his hands, and forced her to face him.

"I'm not asking you to be my mistress!" he hissed, his face betraying all the fury he was trying so hard to conceal. "I want you to be my wife!"

Before Brynne could dredge up an adequate reply, the carriage came rumbling along the narrow, little used road and it was time to leave. Drew cursed, opened the vehicle's gleaming door, and fairly thrust Brynne inside.

He was in a nasty mood all the way home, and Brynne made no attempt to coax him out of it. It would be better if they didn't talk.

Half an hour later, at Minnie Blode's door, Drew

116

said a terse good-bye and strode back to his carriage, his shoulders stiff, his sandy hair glistening in the sun.

Brynne swallowed hard and went inside.

The dining hall was deserted, it seemed, and cloaked in shadow. "Minnie?" Brynne queried, feeling uneasy.

The answer was a rhythmic, creaking sound.

"Minnie?" she repeated, and, outside, she heard boots approaching angrily on the wooden walk.

"Brynne," began Drew, from behind her, as he shoved the door all the way open and thus admitted a stream of bright sunlight. "Jesus God," he breathed.

Brynne looked up, just then, and saw that China Joe was dangling, lifeless and staring, from the end of a rope tied in the rafters.

She screamed and screamed again, and then there was nothing but darkness and the strength of Drew Tanner's arms beneath her.

Reeling inwardly, the inert Brynne in his arms, Drew stumbled out of the dining hall and into the dazzling sunshine. He couldn't see for a moment, couldn't think.

It was the sound of hoofbeats that cleared his vision and drove the shifting fog of confusion out of his mind. Joshua, Sam Prigg and two Indians were riding up, probably drawn by Brynne's screams.

Joshua was off his horse and towering before Drew in an instant, it seemed, and the look in his eyes intensified the churning nausea in the pit of his stomach.

"What happened?" the Half-Breed demanded, looking now, with an unreadable expression, at the unconscious Brynne.

Drew was sick. He thrust Brynne into his brother's arms and ran around the side of the plain board building to gag convulsively and then vomit. When he had finally recovered himself, he stumbled back to the sidewalk in time to see Joshua grimly dispatching the carriage and driver.

Drew followed as his elder brother joined Sam Prigg and the Indians inside the dining hall and caught sight of the Chinaman hanging from the rope like a limp doll at the end of a string.

"Cut him down," the Half-Breed said, and then he turned and went outside again.

Drew was right on his heels. "Where's Brynne?" he demanded, in a rasp, his throat still sore and burning from the bout of sickness.

There was no expression at all in the lavender eyes as they lifted to the distant, snowy mountains rising beyond the water. "Her father—"

"I know," breathed Drew. "Joshua, where is she?"

"On her way to our house, for now," Joshua said, in a toneless voice, his gaze still fixed on the mountains. "Miranda can look after her until we decide what to do."

Just then, from deep within the dining hall, there came a sudden and piteous howl of grief.

Joshua swore and bounded inside, Drew following warily in his wake. "Sam!" the Half-Breed shouted, sparing only a glance for the two Indians who were wrapping the Chinaman's corpse in a blanket.

"In here," Prigg choked out.

"Stop your infernal fussin', Sam," Minnie Blode was saying, as her stricken swain helped her up from the board floor. "I be all *right!*"

"I thought you was dead!" wailed Sam, chafing Minnie's thick wrists with a tenderness that touched even Drew.

"Never reckoned you'd notice I wasn't," Minnie retorted gruffly, her eyes moving to Joshua and bypassing Drew completely.

"What happened?" snapped the Half-Breed.

Minnie looked ashamed. "I don't rightly know that, Josh. I heared a ruckus out in the dining hall and I was just goin' for a look-see when some polecat tried to split my head open. Next thing I knowed, Sam here was a-cryin' and fawnin' like as if I was done for."

Sam looked embarrassed, but he didn't say anything.

Minnie was watching the Half-Breed as though she could read the bad news in his face. "China Joe?" she whispered, her thin lower lip quivering.

Joshua nodded.

"Damn them hateful, murderin' bastards. I'll see 'em in hell!" Minnie's coarse features contorted. "What about Brynne? W—What about the girl—"

"She wasn't here, Minnie," Joshua said quickly, and his eyes touched Drew and then returned to Mrs. Blode. "I think she'll be all right."

"You *think?*" demanded Minnie.

"She found the Chinaman," choked Drew, and then he remembered the way Brynne had screamed and crumpled to the floor and he felt sick all over again. He stumbled past Joshua, one hand over his mouth, just as Sam Prigg gruffly proposed marriage to Minnie Blode.

Drew was gasping for air, his throat raw, when Joshua came around the side of the building and handed him a cup of cold water. Leaning against Minnie's wall, Drew filled his mouth, spat and then drank thirstily.

"Thanks," he said, when he could manage the word.

Joshua's eyes seemed to be looking right inside him and seeing things that were better left hidden. "That kind of prejudice is a grand sight to behold, isn't it, Drew?" he drawled sardonically, and then he turned and walked away.

Though something within him wanted to call out to Joshua, or even to run after him, Drew stood fast until he heard the horses' hooves hammering on the dirt road. It was too late to reach out to his brother now. It had always been too late.

Remembering that the carriage was gone and he had no horse, Drew swore and started the long, hot walk home.

Satisfied that Brynne was resting comfortably, Miranda let herself out of the room adjoining her own and

119

closed the door softly. The upstairs hallway was dimly lit and very quiet, and yet the air seemed charged somehow, as though a horrendous racket might break out at any moment.

Miranda descended the staircase slowly, her hand sliding along the bannister. Both her brothers, she knew, would be waiting in the study for an accounting of Brynne McFarren's state of health.

Entering the austere room that was, in reality, the center of an ever growing empire, Miranda lifted her chin and paused just over the threshold. At the windows, the light was fading, and someone had lit the lamps placed at strategic points around the room.

Joshua was seated at his desk, pretending to work, and Drew was unabashedly pacing. Neither brother seemed aware of the other, but Miranda knew they were both wondering about things that had already been settled in her mind.

"Well?" asked Joshua, in a gruff tone, without even looking up from the papers and journals spread out over his desk.

Drew's gaze swept to his sister, fierce in the gathering twilight and the flicker of the lamps. "Is she awake? Miranda, it's been hours since the doctor left."

Miranda drew a deep breath and interlaced her fingers. "How can I answer you, Drew, if you won't let me speak? Brynne was very upset and I didn't want to leave her."

"The doctor said she was sleeping," grumbled Joshua, still not turning around to face Miranda. The muscles in his wide shoulders were taut beneath his shirt, and he kept tapping the surface of his desk with the end of a pencil.

"He gave her laudanum," Miranda admitted evenly. "But she kept thrashing about and crying and I was afraid she would wake up and be frightened. She seems to be resting now."

"My God," Drew breathed, pausing at a side table to

pour himself a drink. "If you could have heard her . . . seen her . . ."

Miranda closed her eyes for a moment. Even so, she was totally aware of Joshua rising out of his chair. When she looked at him, he was leaning against the desk, his powerful arms folded across his chest, his eyes reading her face.

"Brynne McFarren cannot stay under this roof," she said, bracing herself for the inevitable explosion. "Why didn't you take her to her aunt and uncle?"

Before Joshua could speak, Drew's lip curled in furious dislike and he glared at Miranda. "To Eloise Jennings? My God, Miranda, the woman despises Brynne!"

Miranda had been holding her own with both Drew and Joshua for years, and she was undaunted now. "I don't think I need to tell you what the gossips will make of this, do I? And don't assume that they'll deal kindly with her because I'm here. A divorced woman is hardly the ideal chaperone."

Drew swore and turned away, draining the contents of his glass, and, in this brief interim, Miranda and Joshua exchanged a look that needed no words.

Miranda almost swore herself. She'd been right. She could see by the expression in Joshua's eyes, by the set of his shoulders, by the way his hands clenched into fists even though his arms were folded, that she'd been right. The great, impervious, recalcitrant Half-Breed had fallen at last.

And for none other than Brynne McFarren, daughter of the man he had cause to hate above all other enemies. Miranda felt a vast need for a drink and edged Drew aside to help herself.

In a sidelong glance, she studied her younger brother. He was upset, and his color was high, but Miranda knew that he didn't know yet who his competitor was. It probably hadn't even occurred to him, vain as he was, that he had one.

Oh, Lord, thought Miranda wearily. *They'll kill each other.*

"I want to marry Brynne," Drew said flatly, a fresh drink poised inches from his lips, without looking at either his brother or his sister.

There was a dangerous silence, during which Miranda could manage no other action than a furtive, warning glance in Joshua's direction.

Please, she pleaded silently, after averting her eyes again. *Please, Joshua, don't challenge him. Not here, not now.*

It was Drew who whirled, in the tense silence, and glared first at Miranda and then at a grim, taut-lipped Joshua. "Well?" he demanded, in a sharp, furious undertone. "Isn't anybody going to say anything? Miranda, your line is, 'You're too young to be married, Drew'!" He paused, then went on, with a reflexive, angry gesture of one hand. "And Joshua, dear brother, you're supposed to say, 'By God, nobody named McFarren is going to live under *my* roof!'"

"Shut up, Drew," said Joshua, in level, ominous tones. "Right now."

But Drew laughed, and the sound was tinged with madness. "John McFarren's daughter! Life is ironic, isn't it, Big Brother?"

Joshua's lips thinned into a horrid parody of a smile. "More ironic than you think," he muttered.

The remark went directly over Drew's head, to Miranda's profound relief. "I think we're a little off the subject here," she put in calmly. "I won't have that poor young girl's reputation ruined and that is final—don't interrupt me, Drew. She is not your wife, whatever plans you might have for the future. I'm going to call on Eloise Jennings right now."

"No!" snapped Drew.

"She'd be better off at Minnie's," put in Joshua, and the look in his eyes belied the easy meter of his words.

"Do either of you seriously expect that child to go back to Mrs. Blode's after what happened?" demanded

Miranda, glaring at one brother and then the other. "The shock must have been dreadful!"

"I won't let you turn her over to that Jennings witch!" Drew raged. "She *hates* Brynne!"

Miranda sank into a chair and closed her eyes. A steady ache pounded beneath her temples and at the nape of her neck.

"There are two unmarried men in this house," she pointed out, paying a high price for her patience. "Neither of whom, I might add, have reputations for celibacy or even discretion. And, as I have already said, I myself am not exactly considered a shining beacon of womanhood. Therefore, we have only one choice— Brynne's family."

"There is another option," Drew put in, and this time, his tones were eager, rather than fierce. "She can live in your house, Miranda. The house you lived in with your husband."

Miranda's eyes flew open. "Alone?"

"With you," said Joshua, obviously taken with the idea. Or had these born adversaries been discussing possibilities all afternoon?

"Good God," Miranda marveled acerbically, "are your skulls made of oyster shells? I just finished saying that I—"

"That you're a scarlet woman," interrupted Drew, with buoyant enthusiasm. "Come now, Miranda. You know that you aren't really the problem, Joshua and I are. She could be your companion or something."

"My companion!"

"Why not?" asked Joshua, shrugging. "Rich women always have companions, don't they?"

"Yes, if they're ninety-five and blind as bats!" snapped Miranda.

"Then you'll do it?" pressed Drew, beaming.

"I most certainly will not!"

"Miranda," sighed Joshua.

"Damn it, *no!* N—O, no!"

"In that case," began Joshua, with studied and rather noble reluctance, "I have something to say—"

"We'll move in the morning!" cried Miranda, in desperation, before he could go on.

He grinned.

"Excellent," said Drew, raising his glass in an appreciative toast to his sister and then draining its contents. "And good night."

Neither Miranda nor Joshua spoke until they had heard the sound of Drew's bedroom door closing in the distance.

"It was Brynne," breathed Miranda. "You were with Brynne McFarren, weren't you?"

"Do you really expect me to admit to anything like that, Miranda?" her half-brother countered, raising one eyebrow. "And you so concerned with her reputation!"

"Damn you, Joshua!"

His shoulders slumped a little, and he averted his eyes. "I didn't plan it," he said.

"Drew loves her!"

"So he says."

"So help me God, Joshua, if you're using Brynne to hurt him—"

Joshua approached the sidetable, towering beside Miranda like a human mountain, and poured brandy into a glass. "Here's to blood," he said, in a raspy, scathing whisper, his eyes slicing into Miranda's gentle heart like swords, his glass held high in a savage salute. "It being, alas, thicker than water."

Tears smarted in Miranda's eyes and her lower lip trembled. Then, in her pain, she raised her hand and slapped Joshua's face as hard as she could.

"Damn you!" she hissed.

Joshua's head turned slightly, but, beyond that, he did not react to the blow. "Don't lose any sleep, Miranda—Miss Tanner. Papa's bastard son has no intention of hurting your baby brother."

Miranda stomped one foot. God, she hated it when he threw that between them, used it as a defense. "Joshua!"

But he was putting down the glass he'd held, turning, striding away. A moment later, he was gone, and the slamming of the front door underlined his passing.

Chapter Eight

Austin Darnell stood at the window of his bedroom, looking out. He'd missed the sun-dappled waters of Puget Sound, missed the mountains, missed his very lucrative business.

Outside the door, he could hear the clink of glassware and the rhythmic whisk of a broom. It was early—just past sunup—and the girls up on the mezzanine probably weren't even stirring. He sighed. Stirring? Hell, it would be noon before any of those lazy sluts opened their eyes.

There was an anxious knock at the door, and then it creaked on its hinges. "Mr. Darnell? You up and around?"

Austin turned, fully dressed, to look at his bartender —Peterson, Pedderson, Peters? The name eluded Austin, as did the names of the trollops who turned such tidy profits in the rooms upstairs. "It's obvious that I am," he said coolly.

The rebuff drifted, unnoticed, over the barkeep's balding head. He cleared his throat and averted his eyes.

"What is it?" snapped Austin impatiently.

"Mr. Darnell, sir, it's the Half-Breed. You know he's back in Port Propensity now?"

Austin had known—he made a point of knowing where Joshua Tanner was at any given time. "Yes," he said, grateful that the tremor in the pit of his stomach wasn't audible in his voice. "I'm sure we can expect a social call at any time."

"I could say you're not here," volunteered the barkeep, a little uncertainly.

"Don't bother," retorted Austin, turning back to the window. The view had faded away now, and all he could see was Rosalie. Rosalie Meredith Tanner. "I can't avoid him forever," he added.

"But, Mr. Darnell, last time—"

"That will be all," said Austin, in a clipped voice. When he heard the door close, he let his forehead rest against the cool glass of the window. *Rosalie,* he mourned.

She'd belonged to him first, Rosalie had. Dear God, she'd come west to marry him, Austin Darnell.

The arguments had begun shortly after her arrival. Rosalie Meredith had assumed that her husband-to-be ran a staid hotel, and she was not pleased to learn that the Shore House, however elegantly appointed and profitable, was really a thriving saloon and brothel.

Even now, after more than three years, the memory made Austin Darnell ache to the core of his soul. He'd been prepared to give in to Rosalie's demands and sell his business when she came to him and announced that she'd fallen in love with Joshua Tanner and meant to marry him.

And she'd done just that, his beautiful, dark-haired, blue-eyed Rosalie. She'd married the Half-Breed and, worse still, she'd been happy with him.

The glow in her face, the gentle, subtle rounding of her tiny figure, had driven Austin half mad. One night, he'd caught her alone, during a strawberry social in Port Propensity's public park, and his need and his passion had suddenly been too much to bear.

127

In the shadow of the wooden bridge that arched over the fresh water pond bordering the park, he'd pressed her to the soft, sweetly scented grass, torn at her dress, freed her flowing, midnight-colored hair from its pins.

And she'd screamed. After all Rosalie had meant to Austin, and all he'd meant to her, she had screamed.

The Half-Breed had appeared instantly, like a raging demon, and Austin remembered little after that, except grinding, ceaseless pain. He had run his saloon from a safe distance all this time, while fattening his bank balance with a few new enterprises, afraid to come home.

Well, he wasn't afraid anymore. With Rosalie dead two years—Austin had only recently learned that she'd perished bearing that savage's child—his life was not so precious now. If the Half-Breed killed him, as well he might, Austin would simply be in his rightful place at long last. With Rosalie.

The door of his bedroom opened so quietly that he barely heard it.

"Darnell."

He turned, smiling. "Joshua," he said cordially, "I was expecting you."

The Half-Breed towered in the doorway, and his jawline was hard and edged with white. His eyes were murderous as they assessed Austin. "I imagine you were," he drawled. "What brings you back to our fair town?"

Austin shrugged, reveling in the fact that he no longer feared this man. He hated him, that was true, but there wasn't a shred of fear anywhere inside him. "I have a business here, remember?"

"From what I've been told, you had a good thing going in San Francisco," observed the Half-Breed.

There was torment in the amethyst eyes of Caleb Tanner's celebrated bastard son, and Austin was pleased. "I was beginning to feel guilty, leaving the Shore House unattended for so long."

Joshua Tanner calmly closed the door. What was

that, writhing in his eyes? Grief for Rosalie, the beautiful Rosalie, the eternally lost? No, by God, it was something more. Austin's spirits soared.

"A drink?" he asked, opening a crystal decanter on his bureau.

Tanner shook his head. "You killed Alf Gunderson," he said bluntly. "Why?"

Austin did his best to look stricken. "I? Joshua, old friend, you imagine things! Sheriff Gunderson was found in Little Canton, after all. Obviously, his murder was a crime perpetrated by our esteemed yellow brothers."

"Sure it was."

Lifting his drink to his lips, Austin surveyed Rosalie's love with cultivated indignity. "Suppose I did? Just suppose, for one insane moment, that I did. What does it matter?"

"What does it *matter?*" rasped the Half-Breed, still poised just inside the door, like a vicious beast preparing to pounce. "Alf Gunderson was a man, Darnell. Not a hunk of seaweed. And you know damned well that the anti-Chinese element in this town used his death as an excuse to hang an innocent man."

Austin took a deliberately languorous sip from his glass. He knew, of course, about the Chink the hotheads had strung up in retaliation. To him, it was of no more moment than the squashing of a bug. *Two birds with one stone,* he thought jubilantly. *Austin, you always were efficient.*

"My sympathies about Rosalie and the . . . child," he said, aloud, after a long and calculated pause.

Rage moved in the savagely handsome face, but it was quickly suppressed. "Thank you," said the Half-Breed, with a certain barbed politeness. "When are you leaving?"

"I'm not," said Austin, raising his glass in an impudent salute. "After all, this is home."

"Is it?"

"Oh, yes. And Joshua?"

"What?"

"I don't care if you kill me, in case you're thinking of making a threat or two. I've already been a dead man for more than three years."

The Half-Breed rolled the orchid eyes that had so captivated Rosalie. "Jesus," he breathed. "You're insane."

Austin smiled warmly. "That makes me damned dangerous, doesn't it? There is nothing I won't do, no price I won't pay, to see you crawl, Tanner. And crawl you will, you bastard."

Joshua lifted one hand in blithe farewell. "Austin," he said, "I'm terrified."

And then the door was closing behind him and he was gone.

Austin turned and flung his glass against the panelled wall with such force that it shattered and rained tinkling shards of crystal onto the bed he'd meant to share with Rosalie.

Miranda suppressed a smile as she entered the parlor to greet her unexpected callers. How wonderfully disparate they were—Minnie Blode and Eloise Jennings!

"Tea?" asked the mistress of the house.

Eloise, who was perched on the edge of a brocade settee like an indignant black bird, blushed and smoothed the skirts of her mourning dress. "No, thank you," she said, in the tone of one who has just been invited to participate in a decadent pagan rite.

"Got any whiskey?" asked Minnie Blode, who was standing, her out-of-date hat comically awry. She looked as uncomfortable as Eloise, though probably for vastly different reasons.

Miranda turned her head slightly and bit her lower lip to keep from chuckling. "Yes. Yes, Mrs. Blode, I think I can provide that."

"Well, I never," said Eloise Jennings sharply.

You should, thought Miranda. "Do sit down, Mrs. Blode," she said, gesturing toward the sturdy chair her father had always favored. "I'll just get your refreshment and then we can talk."

When she returned, seconds later, with Minnie's whiskey, Miranda sat down in a chair upholstered to match the settee and reached out to fill a teacup for herself. *I wish I had your guts, Minnie,* she thought wryly. *Because this is definitely an occasion that calls for whiskey.*

"How's Brynne?" Minnie demanded, leaning forward slightly and squinting inelegantly at Miranda.

Miranda smiled warmly. "Brynne is just fine, considering the shocks she's had to endure lately. She was a little frightened to wake up in a strange house, but I was with her, fortunately, and once I'd explained, she was all right."

"It is highly improper," blustered Eloise, who had not thought to ask about her niece's condition, pursing her lips and jutting out her harsh chin.

I see what you mean, Drew, Miranda conceded silently. "I can assure you, Eloise," she broke in, politely but firmly, "that neither of my brothers has gone near your niece." *At least, not here.*

Eloise was clearly at a loss.

"I swear I feel about *that high,*" boomed Minnie, indicating an infinitesimal space with two work-roughened fingers. "That girl just doesn't deserve to be out of a job this way, but the truth is, it took more'n twenty years for Sam Prigg to speak up and I ain't of a mind to let him get away."

Miranda pretended an interest in her teacup, balanced on her knees, until she had her quivering mouth under control. "You're closing the dining hall?" she asked, when she dared speak.

Minnie nodded, "Yep." The artificial cherries perched atop her hat bobbed jauntily. "Sam don't want no wife of his slingin' hash for a bunch of bilge rats—"

"For *goodness* sake!" cried Eloise, flushing with outrage. "Must we discuss your romance, Mrs. Blode? I, for one, came here to talk about my niece."

Miranda drew a deep, preparatory breath. "Brynne is a charming girl," she said. "In fact, I'm so taken with her that I've invited her to be my companion."

"She cannot live in this house!" shouted Eloise.

Miranda sighed regretfully. "I totally agree, though, if one of my brothers has his way, she may become a member of the family."

Eloise looked apoplectic. Everyone in Port Propensity knew that she had high hopes for a union between Drew and her daughter, Letitia.

"I hope it's Joshua," said Minnie, with her usual blunt honesty. "That other feller is too wild for my taste."

"Andrew is simply high-spirited," put in Eloise, clearly insulted. "That is to be expected of a young man."

I love this, Miranda thought. "Drew is quite smitten with Brynne," she said, as though Eloise hadn't spoken. "And she might be just the settling influence he needs."

"Settling influence?" cursed Eloise Jennings, who was turning purple. "That little—"

Minnie bristled immediately. "Now you just watch what you say, woman," she warned. "Brynne's done no wrong but bein' too pretty. That's what riles you."

Here, here, cheered Miranda, in mannerly silence.

Eloise shot to her feet. "Walter and I will call for our niece within the hour. I will not have her—"

Miranda held up both hands in a polite request for silence. "I'm sorry. As I've told you, I asked Brynne to come and live with me, at the other house, by the park, you understand, and she has accepted. That way, the rules of propriety will be observed."

Eloise tapped one pointed, practical shoe in annoyance. "Miss Tanner, you are divorced. And even if you remove Brynne from this house, she will still be criticized."

It was then that Brynne walked in, looking like a

132

beautiful wraith in the soft blue morning gown Miranda had given her. Her cheeks were pallid and her eyes had a hollow quality that tore at the heart, but her chin was high, proud.

"I don't care if I'm criticized, Aunt Eloise," she announced. "I'd sooner be captured by drunken pirates than live with you."

Eloise's bright blue eyes were glazed with anger and some deep-seated, inexplicable hatred. "I hope you will recall those words, Brynne McFarren, when young Mr. Tanner recognizes you for the saucy tart you are and shows you the road!"

Brynne paled and stumbled back a step, as though she'd been struck. Her mouth moved, but no sound came out.

"Do you plan to marry Andrew Tanner," Eloise went on, her voice at once harsh and bitter and shrill. "Even knowing how that will hurt your cousin?"

Brynne swallowed visibly, and her eyes pleaded with a livid Minnie not to intervene. She seemed stronger when Miranda reached out to clasp her hand. "I have no plans to marry Drew or anyone else," she said evenly. "And I would not deliberately hurt Letitia for anything. She is the only real family I have."

"Your uncle and I have tried—"

"To get rid of me," Brynne finished bravely. "At first, that really bothered me, but now I don't care. Kindly don't give my welfare or my reputation another thought, Mrs. Jennings."

Eloise bridled like a skinny black horse and snorted, "You saucy little thing, your father would—"

Brynne sighed, closed her eyes for a moment. "My father would have welcomed Letitia as a daughter, had she been the one left alone. Good day."

"Good day!" snapped Eloise Jennings, and then she stormed out of the Tanner parlor and was gone.

"I guess you told her," said Minnie, flushed with hearty admiration.

But Brynne simply sank into the seat her aunt had just vacated, covered her face with both hands, and wept as though she would die of loneliness and grief.

Miranda glared at the empty parlor doorway, wishing she could go after Eloise Jennings and snatch her bald-headed. *You ice-hearted witch,* she thought bitterly. *I've known dogs with more family loyalty.*

Minnie took a more practical approach. She perched on the arm of the settee and drew Brynne close in a rough gesture of caring and comfort. "Don't be cryin' for that'un," she said. "Tears is wasted on such likes as her."

Brynne sniffled and drew a deep breath, and her eyes were shining as they came to Minnie's face. "I—I heard that you and Mr. Prigg are getting married," she said, with a somewhat shaky smile.

Minnie looked as though she might break down and cry herself. "Sunday, in Seattle," she said. "Sam has a daughter there."

Brynne patted the woman's hand gently. "I'm so happy for you, Mrs. Blode."

"You'll be all right, won't you, girl?" Minnie asked gruffly. "You'll come to me and Sam if you need someplace to go? We'll be right here in Port Propensity, once we're done honeymoonin'."

Brynne nodded hurriedly. "I've got a new job now, Mrs. Blode. A—And a home. I'm going to be Miss Tanner's companion—"

"Miranda," corrected Miss Tanner.

Brynne flashed the guileless smile that had so bewitched both of Miranda's brothers. "Miranda," she repeated firmly. "It certainly doesn't sound like much work, being a companion. Imagine being paid to read aloud and write letters!"

Minnie laughed, but her eyes came sharply to Miranda's face and asked a silent question.

Yes, Miranda answered, without speaking. *I'll look after her.*

Apparently satisfied, Minnie Blode said awkward farewells and left.

"She was so kind to me," Brynne said wistfully, as though it was a marvel that anyone could feel affection for her. Then, lifting her chin, she met Miranda's eyes and smiled bravely. "Are we going to move today?"

Miranda shook her head. "How Ling and her mother are still getting the other house ready. Brynne, your first duty as my companion is to accompany me to Seattle for a visit. We'll shop and maybe even attend Minnie's wedding."

Brynne's face was instantly alight. "Seattle," she breathed, in wonder.

Miranda smiled. "We'll stay a month, I think."

"A month?" Brynne echoed, awed.

"Yes," said Miranda briskly. "A month at least. Joshua has a house there. We'll open that, shop, give a few parties, enjoy some entertainments at the Opera House. Of course, you'll need proper clothes, part of your salary, naturally. I'll expect you to look nice."

Brynne's hands came together in a soundless clap of delight. "I think I'm going to like being a companion," she said.

Miranda folded her hands in her lap and framed her words carefully in her mind before she spoke them. "Brynne, you do realize that you could be more than a companion at any time, that you could be Drew's wife?"

Brynne lowered her eyes. "I couldn't do that, Miss— Miranda. I don't love Drew."

"Your feelings could change," offered Miranda, cautiously.

"No."

"Such finality. Brynne, Drew is an excellent catch, you know. Despite his status as a younger son, he'll have access to tremendous wealth the moment he marries."

Brynne's gaze lifted, steady and dark with some

singular misery, to Miranda's face. "I don't love him," she repeated. "He's so funny and so sweet and so handsome that I truly wish I did, but I—I couldn't pretend."

"Other women do."

Brynne swallowed. "That would be cruel. Drew deserves someone who loves him alone, really loves him."

"And your heart is taken."

Brynne stood up, turned her back. "Yes," she said, in a small, anguished voice.

Miranda shared Brynne's pain, and she rose from her chair to place gentle hands on her shoulders. "Joshua?"

Brynne whirled, suddenly, and searched Miranda's face with stricken, wary eyes. "Did he—"

"He didn't have to tell me," Miranda said softly. "I know him too well. What worries me is that *you* might not know him."

The gray eyes widened. "Is he terrible?"

Miranda laughed, in spite of the ache in her heart. "No. He's the finest man I've ever known, as a matter of fact. But, Brynne, he's been through so much, he's been hurt so badly."

Brynne nodded distractedly. "There is so *much* pain inside him," she whispered. "So much that there isn't room for any other feeling."

Miranda tried to smile and failed miserably. For the moment, there was nothing more to say.

Drew slid back in his chair, glaring, his wineglass still in his hand. *"Seattle?"* he demanded, incredulously. Damn, it was irritating enough that Brynne was cloistered away in her room. He'd looked forward all day to having her dine with him. But now Miranda was saying that she intended to take her to Seattle.

"I think it's an excellent idea," said Joshua, his own dinner sitting untouched before him.

Drew spared one scorching scowl for his brother and

turned his wrath on Miranda. "Why, Miranda? Isn't moving to the other house enough?"

Miranda sighed. "Drew, she'll be safe in Seattle."

"She would be safe *here*," Drew argued.

Miranda and Joshua exchanged one of their damnable, indecipherable looks. "No," said Miranda. "Besides, she's been through a great deal and it's time she had a little joy in her life."

"Joy!" scoffed Drew, bitterly. His jaw was clenched so tight that the whole side of his face ached. "Damn it, Miranda, if you drag her to one of your beloved parties and she meets somebody else, I'll never forgive you!"

Joshua sighed. "As usual, Drew, you're thinking of yourself. Think of Brynne for a moment. Think about what she wants, what she needs."

"She needs a husband!" snapped Drew. "She needs somebody to look after her."

An odd smile curved Joshua's taut lips. "That one, I think, can look after herself. Give her time, Drew. Distance."

"Time and distance," mocked Drew, knowing that he was beaten. "Damn it, I want her close!"

"You'll smother her," said Miranda, with gentle finality.

Drew set his wineglass down with a thump and stared at his sister. "And you think it's better to take her away," he accused. "You're looking forward to it, aren't you, Miranda? You plan to dress her up like some kind of pretty doll and then sit back and watch all those pimply clerks and lecherous timber barons fall over their tongues!"

Miranda rolled her eyes. "For heaven's sake, Drew, the child owns three or four dresses. Is your jealousy so virulent that you would deny her pretty clothes? As for the men, no power on earth could keep them from noticing Brynne, whether she was single or married." Her glance flickered briefly, eloquently, to Joshua. "That, I fear, is the price of loving a beautiful woman."

Joshua took a consuming interest in the contents of his wineglass. "Amen," he said, in an undertone.

The room was so quiet, so dark. Brynne lay very still in the large, sturdy bed, her hands cupped behind her head, watching moonlight and shadows mingle in patchy, shifting patterns on the ceiling. Tomorrow, with Miranda, she would leave for Seattle.

There would be parties, plays, new clothes, new friends. Brynne told herself that she wasn't at all certain she could bear the delight of it.

In truth, it was the idea of leaving Joshua Tanner that she found unbearable.

Restless, she turned onto her side, sighed, and studied the glossy, whispering leaves of the tall cottonwood tree rising just outside the window. Surely, with so many things to do and see and consider, there would be little time to miss Joshua.

An ache, knotted and hard in a far corner of Brynne's heart, contradicted this hope. If she lived to be a hundred, she would never forget him, never forget the scent of his hair and skin, the touch of his hands, the wondrous, primitive sensations his lips stirred in her when they claimed her own or hungrily devoured her breasts. She'd been spoiled for any other man.

Brynne moaned softly in protest. If only she could find those things with Drew, her life would be so uncomplicated! She closed her eyes tight and tried hard to love Drew, but the best emotion she could manage was camaraderie.

The door of the bedroom opened so quietly that she thought she'd imagined the sound. When it closed again, she sat up, her heart pounding in her throat.

Joshua stood at the foot of her bed, clothed in shadow, but she could feel his eyes touching her, imploring her somehow. Still, there was resistance in his bearing, too. It was as though she had drawn him to her against his will.

"Brynne," he said, in a hoarse whisper that conveyed both need and anger, hunger and rebellion.

Brynne knew that she should send him away, but she could not move or even speak. She simply stared at him, waiting.

After what seemed an eternity, he turned, as though to leave. Brynne closed her eyes and allowed the strange forces within her to restrain him.

With a desperate, angry moan, he rounded the bed and sat down on its edge. His hands came, hard and strong, to Brynne's shoulders.

"What are you doing to me?" he demanded, in a low, beleaguered tone.

Brynne could not speak, but her hands rose, of their own accord, to the nape of his neck. She caught the rich, clean scent of his hair as he bent toward her, his lips searching for and finally claiming hers. Her mouth parted willingly for the sweet, searing invasion of his tongue.

Joshua's hard, forbidding frame shuddered against her as he stretched out on the bed, fully clothed, never breaking the deep, wounding kiss. Brynne's back arched reflexively as one of his hands sought and then closed over a flannel-covered breast. His mouth left hers, at last, and he nipped, with gentle teeth, at the pulsing button pleading to be bared to him.

Brynne groaned in her need and pulled at the nightgown she wore with one frantic hand, desperate to be free of it. Her entire being was focused on one shameful, undeniable need—the need to be naked for this man's taking.

Joshua rose, knelt astraddle of Brynne's small, quivering frame, and rent the nightgown with one swift motion of his hands. His eyes glittered with savage passion in the silvery glow of the moonlight, silently charting the course of his possession.

"Brynne," he said, in a raw whisper. "I . . ."

She lifted a finger to his lips, to trace them, to silence

him, and took profound pleasure in the way he shuddered at her touch. "He who hesitates . . ." she teased, in a soft voice.

"Is lost," conceded Joshua, and the set of his jawline was angry for a moment, even forbidding.

There was a long interval in which, it seemed to Brynne, the whole world paused. She knew that powerful, opposing forces were warring inside Joshua Tanner and shamelessly hoped that he would not give in to those bidding him to turn away from her.

Finally, his hands came to close over her ripe, waiting breasts, to knead them gently, to chafe her pouting nipples until they throbbed. Then, as though savoring the conquering, he drew his fingertips down over Brynne's burning rib cage to her waist, back up again.

Brynne clasped her hands behind his neck in wanton demand and pulled him to her breast, writhing all the while beneath him. His tongue traced the circumference of one rosy nipple, sending shafts of sweet torment throughout her body, causing her to plead with him in ragged, shameless words.

Joshua laughed, low in his throat, but then his mouth closed, warm, around the aching button and he suckled as though taking some long denied, vital nourishment from her. Brynne knew, in that dizzying moment of indescribable pleasure, that she would always be able to sway this man by simply baring a breast to him, nursing him as a woman would nurse a child.

But was she swaying him? Dear Lord, she would agree to anything to keep him from drawing away. When he'd devoured the one breast, she shamelessly offered the other. As he drew on it, Brynne entwined her fingers in his hair and held him very close.

After a time, the suckling became less frantic, but no less delicious. He drank languidly of her sweetness, he nibbled, he flicked, he teased.

Then, abruptly, he broke away.

A treacherous, wounding void encompassed Brynne and she reached out, whispered his name.

Again, a low, gruff laugh escaped him. He undressed swiftly and then he was beside her again, his long frame gentle and warm against her. In a smooth, rolling motion, he sat up, pulling Brynne with him.

She stood before him, naked and proud, and shivered not with the cold but with the need of his loving.

"Witch," he rasped, sitting on the side of the bed, looking up at her in wonder and fury and hungry desire. His hands moved possessively, tenderly, on the soft flesh at the rounding of her hips and the sensation was so moving that Brynne let her head fall backward in stricken surrender and closed her eyes.

Joshua's lips seared Brynne's stomach like some kind of gentle fire as he tasted the soft flesh there and beneath. All breath left her as he revealed the rosebud hidden in silk and then claimed it hungrily.

Just when Brynne's world was about to splinter into glimmering, molten bits, he ceased his fierce sampling and drew her gently downward, onto him.

The entry was slow, sensual, exquisite. Sitting astraddle of his lap, facing him, Brynne groaned and let her head fall back again, reveling as he lowered his mouth to one of her breasts to slake his fathomless hunger at the nipple.

Instinctively, Brynne began to raise and lower her hips. Her reward was a desperate, ragged moan from the lips feasting upon her bounty, followed by a desolate, "Oh . . . God . . . *Brynne* . . ."

It was easy to push him backward, as big as he was, so that he lay prone and surrendering beneath her. She accelerated the ancient motion of her hips, reveling in the breathless pleas this brought from him.

When Joshua began to return her thrusts, however, the feeling of heady power shifted, became one of shivering, soaring need. Brynne was pleading herself then, in a desperate whisper, as his powerful body repeatedly bucked beneath her, driving her, filling her, completely dislodging all rational thought from her mind.

Their savage triumph came in one glorious moment and devastated them both. Had it not been for the quick masculine hand that rose to stifle Brynne's cry of release, the whole town would probably have known how well Joshua Tanner had loved her.

Chapter Nine

WHEN, AT LAST, BRYNNE SLEPT, JOSHUA DRESSED AND silently left the room. The hall was empty, but he hurried to his own door, all the same, having neither the breath nor the patience to answer questions.

Inside his room, Joshua lit the lamp at his bedside and turned slowly to look up at the portrait of Rosalie. He whispered her name, in a vain effort to conjure her, but she eluded him.

His throat raw, Joshua thought of the warm, living, beautiful woman he'd just left and knew that he loved her, that he would always love her.

He closed his eyes, desperately willing himself not to care for Brynne McFarren, not to need her, but the effort was hopeless. In fact, it was all he could do not to stride back to her room, wrench her out of the bed, carry her here, and ravish her all over again.

Still reeling, physically and emotionally, from the violent force of his release, Joshua opened his eyes. His spirit contorted within him as he approached the portrait and briskly took it down from the wall.

"Good-bye, Rosalie," he said, in a tormented whisper.

Joshua's vision was blurred as he slid the portrait

behind his bureau and stumbled to the bed, where he collapsed like a warrior felled in battle. Eventually, he gathered the strength to extinguish the lamp.

The mystical part of his spirit felt the essence of a joyous farewell frolic in the dark room, ebbing and flowing like some unseen tide.

How long had Rosalie been waiting, beyond his earthly blindness, for him to free her?

"I'm sorry," he said, and he was. He had not meant to restrain her with his grief.

As if in answer, he felt Rosalie's spirit brush briefly, sweetly, across his own, and then she was finally and irrevocably gone, except for her memory. Like Rosalie, he was free.

Staunchly, Joshua Tanner set about putting his thoughts and feelings into some kind of manageable order. He loved Brynne McFarren, but it was, judging by the events of that night, a good thing she was going away for a while.

He thought of Drew and frowned. He would have to hide his feelings for Brynne, for a time, until his younger brother had gotten over his infatuation with her.

Joshua's mind moved next to Austin Darnell. Whatever happened, Darnell mustn't know that the Half-Breed's one assailable weakness was a bright-eyed, saucy little Scot named Brynne McFarren.

Brynne awakened at dawn, that morning of July fourteenth, and could not get back to sleep no matter how hard she tried. Had she just dreamed those marvelous things that had happened during the night, or had they been real?

In the silence of the house, she heard one door open and then close, and then another.

On impulse, Brynne thrust back her covers and scrambled out of bed. It was then that she realized that her nightgown was torn from neckline to hem, and had to be held together at the front. Clutching it close, she opened her bedroom door and peered out into the hallway.

In the shadowy, gray light of the breaking day, she saw both Joshua and Drew walking toward the stairs and fixed all the forces within herself on the center of Joshua's hard, impervious back.

And as though she had reached out and stopped him, he paused, turned slightly, looked at her. As Drew went downstairs, unaware of the exchange, Joshua's lips moved in a silent, half-amused "good-bye."

Brynne ached to run to him, but something in his bearing forbade it. After all the glories of their sharing, he was dismissing her, rebuffing her. She had, evidently, served her purpose.

In more pain than Brynne McFarren had thought one frail human being could bear, she turned away and softly closed the door. "Fool," she berated herself, in a ragged whisper, as tears of despair coursed down her face.

After a time of total weakness, during which Brynne could do no more than lean against the door and weep, she drew a deep breath and tried to take herself in hand. What, after all, had she expected? A marriage proposal? Sweet, eternal devotion?

The fact was that, not once, not even in the height of his passion, had Joshua Tanner used the word "love." No doubt, Miss Brynne McFarren was nothing more to him than an impetuous amusement.

Brynne lifted her chin and wiped her eyes dry with the sleeve of her crumpled, ripped nightgown. She had danced and now she must pay the piper. It was as simple as that. All the same, Joshua Tanner needn't think that she was a round-heels, ready to fall to her back at a nod from him!

Before, there had been a certain dread intermingled with Brynne's delight over the long visit in Seattle. Now, she thanked God for the chance to go, to escape

Port Propensity before her senses overwhelmed her reason and had her groveling at the Half-Breed's feet like a trollop.

With fierce motions that caused her muscles to ache as fiercely as her soul, Brynne washed and dressed and brushed her hair to a high, crackling shine. Instead of pinning the mane up, as she normally did, she let it fall, loose and shimmering, around her shoulders and calico-clad breasts.

She stepped back, to assess herself in the vanity mirror, and decided that she would pin her hair up after all; wearing it down gave her a saucy, sensuous look that was a painful reminder of her sins. Hell or high water, Brynne thought, as she braided her hair into a single, gleaming plait, she would be a lady from now on.

She was winding the plait into a sophisticated coronet when Miranda tapped at the door joining their two rooms and then entered, without waiting for an invitation.

Brynne was very careful to avoid the wise, dark eyes. "Good morning," she said primly, wishing that she had hidden her sundered nightgown, rather than tossing it onto the bed.

Miranda sighed. "Did you sleep well?" she asked, in a pleasant tone that was, nonetheless, edged with something more.

Brynne only nodded, unable to speak, but her back stiffened when Miranda sat down on the edge of the bed and the springs squeaked.

There was an awkward, hellish silence, during which Brynne was certain that her knees would give out, and then, at last, she turned to face this woman who had been such a good friend to her. If Miranda had noticed the ruined nightgown lying inches from her hand, she was gracious enough not to let on.

She laughed softly at the sight of Brynne's face. "Relax, little one. I'm a woman, too, you know."

Brynne was still too stricken to speak.

146

"We should have left yesterday," observed Miranda. "I'll never forgive myself if you're pregnant."

Brynne felt sudden and florid color pounding in her face. Had she been able to will instant death for herself, she would have done it.

"Pregnant?" she echoed, hoping to sound shocked, even outraged, at the implication.

"Spare me, Brynne," said Miranda, with terse impatience. "I have ears."

Brynne lowered her head, ashamed and, now, alarmed. She hadn't even considered the fact that Joshua Tanner's seed might be growing within her. Dear Lord, what would she do if there was a baby?

Miranda's blue silk robe rustled prettily as she stood up. "Brynne, look at me," she ordered.

Miserably, Brynne obeyed.

"I am certainly no one to stand in judgment," said Miranda, in brisk yet gentle tones. "And I don't think any less of you for what's happened. But, Brynne, this is a deadly game you're playing. Your life and several others could be ruined by it."

"I know," whispered Brynne. And then she turned away and made a lengthy project of folding and packing the garments How Ling had washed and pressed for her.

She flinched a little as Miranda left the room, closing the door eloquently behind her.

"Damn your miserable hide!" Miranda hissed, scurrying furiously along behind Joshua as he strode toward the stables in the first, dazzling light of day. The hem of her good silk robe was clinging, dampened by the dewy grass, to her ankles.

Joshua stopped so suddenly that she nearly collided with him, and, when he turned to face his angry sister, his eyes were flashing with a sort of tormented mockery. "You've been alone too long, Miranda," he rasped. "Listening at doors!"

Miranda wanted to scream, she was so furious, but

she kept her voice to a scorching whisper. "I didn't *have* to listen at any door, Joshua Tanner! And if you hadn't worked Drew like a draft horse all day yesterday, he would have heard what happened, too!"

"So?"

"So the situation is bad enough around here without you creeping into his beloved's bedroom and availing yourself of her charms!"

"Did it ever occur to you that I might love Brynne?"

Miranda felt her lip curl in disdain. "Love!" she mocked bitterly. "You were repaying John McFarren through her. That is a cruel vengeance, Joshua!"

Joshua's face contorted, relaxed again. "That's what you think? That I was using her?"

"You're damned right that's what I think! To strike out at John McFarren—Lord in heaven, Joshua, the man is *dead*—and to hurt Drew in the bargain."

He sighed, raised his eyes to search the cloudless sky. The muscles in his bronzed neck corded ominously. "I don't blame Brynne for what her father did, Miranda," he said, in deadly tones. "And I'm not some monster just waiting for a chance to ruin Drew's life."

"It would kill him if he knew!"

Maddeningly, Joshua shrugged. When his eyes came back to Miranda's face, however, they were dark with pain. "He's a kid, Miranda. By the time Brynne's been in Seattle a week, he'll be laying some poor lumberjack's lonely wife."

Never, in all the years Miranda had known this brother of hers, had she wanted so badly to slap him senseless. It was the shifting ache in his eyes that stopped her.

"This is not one of Drew's passing flirtations, Joshua. He *loves* that girl."

"Then God help us all," Joshua replied. And then he turned, imperiously, and strode into the stable.

Miranda was still standing, stricken, in the dooryard when he rode out on Chinook.

The great black beast danced impatiently beneath

him as he restrained it to look down at his sister and mutter, "Drew is still in the house. Tell him his wages will be adversely affected if he's late."

Miranda suppressed a consuming urge to fling herself at horse and man, fists flying. "Joshua Tanner—" she said.

Impudently, he lifted one hand in a gesture of farewell and grinned. "Behave yourself in Seattle," he said, and then he blithely rode away.

Shaking with impotent rage, Miranda wrenched her silk robe tightly around herself and stormed into the house. She met Drew in the kitchen, where How Ling and her mother were working.

He raised his eyebrows in amused disapproval at the sight of Miranda's robe. "Out walking?" he teased, summarily taking a bite from a piece of toasted bread.

To her own surprise as much as Drew's, Miranda raised her hand and slapped her brother soundly across the face. Before he could react in any way, she was hurrying on, out of the kitchen, through the diningroom, into the hallway.

She swore, under her breath, all the way up the stairs.

Brynne stood still on the shifting, creaking wharf, her eyes warm on Letitia's sad face. Behind her, the sternwheeler *Marriott* was a rumbling, whistling hive of activity. "I'll only be gone a month," she reminded her cousin, almost shouting to be heard.

Letitia brightened. "Perhaps by the time you get back I'll have bosoms."

Despite her battered heart and everything else that tormented her, Brynne laughed. There were bright, blinding tears in her eyes when she hugged Letitia. "I'll bring you a present," she promised.

"You've left me one," Letitia retorted. "Drew Tanner."

Brynne frowned. "What about Harold?"

"Howard," corrected Letitia, raising her voice unabashedly over the noise of the steamboat. "He has sinus trouble!"

Miranda, having arranged passage and seen to the proper loading of her many trunks and valises, appeared at Brynne's side. "Who has sinus trouble?" she demanded, and even though she was smiling, there was a certain strained tautness about her mouth.

"Howard Macumber!" Letitia cried.

"Of the Macumber noses," added Brynne dryly, more anxious than ever to be gone.

In one final parry of touching good will, Letitia embraced Brynne. "Is it all right?" she whispered mischievously. "Will you hate me if I seduce Drew?"

"Don't you dare!" shouted Brynne, so forcefully that even the deckhands on board the *Marriott* turned from their labors to look.

A pretty pout moved in Letitia's innocent face. "How piggish, Brynne. *You* don't want him—"

"I'm not worried about him!" retorted Brynne, making no effort at all to keep her voice down. Before she could make her point, however, Miranda took her arm and briskly led her toward the steamer's boarding ramp.

"What was that all about?" the older woman asked, as the steamer chugged its way out of Port Propensity's sun-dappled harbor.

Brynne fixed her eyes on the Tanner shipyard, off in the distance, and imagined Joshua working there, shirtless in the morning sun. The resultant ache in her midsection was almost more than she could bear. "Letitia means to seduce Drew," she answered, in miserable distraction.

"So?" asked Miranda, with kindly, studied casualness.

"He'll break her heart," she mourned, but it wasn't Letitia's heart she was thinking of—at least, not entirely—and they both knew it.

"Perhaps it would be a good thing if Drew fell in love with Letitia," observed Miranda, who, like Brynne, had fixed her gaze on the naked timbers of the ships in the Tanner Yard.

"It would be wonderful," replied Brynne, grateful for the rising, salty wind that seemed to be awakening her from a long and fitful sleep. "Do you think—"

"No," said Miranda sadly.

And the subject was closed.

Seattle was a boisterous boom town, flung, haphazard, onto the side of a hill. There were mills on the waterfront, with shrieking saws, and, even in the broad light of day, the infamous Skid Road, with its brothels and shoddy saloons, was alive with activity. Wagons and horses seemed to race over the plank streets and the strident *clang-clang* of the horse-drawn trolley cars added to the din.

Brynne was overwhelmed.

"Have you ever been to Seattle before?" asked Miranda, having dispatched a young boy to secure a carriage.

Brynne shook her head, speechless with wonder. On the wharves beside the just docked steamer, men shouted to each other as they tied great ropes around pilings. The scents of kelp and saltwater and kerosene rose on the warm air and transparent jellyfish wafted through the sparkling water.

"My, my," said Miranda, her gentle, mobile lips curved into a smile. "Then there is much for you to see."

And there was. After they left the steamer and were helped into a hired carriage, they were plunged into the very core of that wonderful, shifting, ceaseless madness.

Chinamen sprinted along the walkways, baskets full of fresh fish suspended from bars balanced on their thin shoulders. Indians trudged by, in their buckskins and bare red feet, looking oddly detached from the clamor around them. Prostitutes from the Skid Road swung past, in their garish, flamboyant clothes, as much at home as the ladies who skirted them, carrying parasols and wicker market baskets.

And the shops! There were so many of them, and they displayed wares Brynne couldn't even have imagined behind their glass windows.

The carriage began to ascend the steep hill, skirting the massive tree stumps that grew in the road, and Brynne closed her eyes, quite overcome.

Miranda laughed out loud. "Welcome to the big city, Miss Brynne McFarren," she said.

Brynne laughed, too, in her delight, and opened her eyes to peer out at the multitude of wood-frame houses beyond the carriage windows. So many people living in one place—it was incredible.

"I don't see how anyone sleeps for all this noise," she said, with as much sophistication as she could manage.

Miranda sat back in the cushioned carriage seat across from Brynne's, looking every inch the lady in her smart, cream-colored traveling suit and elegant feathered hat. "The house is some distance from the city," she said, smiling. "And we have no neighbors, so it's quite peaceful."

Brynne had barely recovered a ladylike demeanor when the carriage turned onto a cobbled, tree-lined lane. Presently, the vehicle was guided into a circular driveway and came to a stop in front of a grand, red brick house with green shutters on its glistening glass windows. Two nervous maids, dressed in crisp black and sporting tiny, ruffled white hats, fidgeted on the tiered marble porch, waiting.

The door of the carriage opened with a creak, and the driver extended a hand to help an unruffled Miranda Tanner down. Brynne drew a deep breath, closed her eyes momentarily in preparation, and was squired out of the carriage like a titled lady visiting a palace.

Miranda calmly paid the gawking driver, with bills plucked from her beaded handbag, and asked him to go back to the wharf for the baggage. He obeyed with such eagerness that Brynne stared after him, open-mouthed.

She blushed when Miranda tugged at her arm.

One of the maids rushed up and curtseyed, to Brynne's fresh amazement. She was young, and not very pretty, due to an obvious bout, at some point, with smallpox, but her tiny, quick eyes were kind as they assessed Miranda Tanner's companion.

"Howdy-do," chirped the girl.

Miranda chuckled. "Placenta, this is Brynne McFarren. We'll be staying about a month, I think."

"Yes, ma'am," said the young woman with a nod, her ruffled hat bobbing in the hot breeze.

"We'll have lemonade in the garden, please," said Miranda, by way of dismissal, and then she was dragging Brynne along a flagstone walk that rounded the gracious two-story house and stopped in a shaded area lush with lilacs and blooming roses and beds of zinnias and bright petunias.

"Placenta?" marveled Brynne, who was, after all, a doctor's daughter.

Miranda laughed and removed her gloves and her hat and the tailored jacket of her traveling suit, dropping all into an ornate, white wrought-iron chair at a matching round table. "Isn't that a wonder? It seems Placenta's mother was awake during the delivery and thought the word too beautiful to go unremembered."

"Didn't the doctor explain?"

"It was of no use, I imagine. We usually call her 'Placie,' though Drew has been known to use a more . . . colloquial version of her name."

"He would," sighed Brynne, falling into one of the other chairs at the elegant table. "Oh, Miranda, if this house were mine, I would live in it always and never, never leave."

Miranda chuckled softly and folded her fine, ringless hands on the table. "Not even to attend a party or be fitted for a brand-new dress?"

Brynne smiled, reveling in the rich scent of the lilacs and the more subtle perfume of the roses. Bees droned their mid-summer song in the hazy heat and the sky was royal blue and it was all too beautiful to be borne by a mere human. "Perhaps," she relented. "For a pink satin with lace on the bodice."

Miranda laughed and shook her head.

A moment later, Placie brought two tall glasses brimming with ice-cold lemonade and set them on the table. She was a part of the magic, too. "Will there be anything else, Miss Miranda?"

Miranda considered, arching one dark, elegant eyebrow. "Something to eat, I think. Are you hungry, Brynne?"

Brynne realized, in amazement, that she was. The steamboat ride had lasted several hours, and it was now well past dinner time. Shyly, she nodded.

"I'm starved, too," agreed Miranda thoughtfully. "Perhaps a fruit cup, or some sandwiches—"

Placie was eager to serve; clearly, she adored her employer. "Cook went to market just this morning," she chimed. "We have bananas and oranges and peaches . . ."

Bananas and oranges. Brynne, who was always happy to have a pear or a speckled apple, marveled at such exotic offerings.

"That will do just fine," said Miranda calmly. "But please tell Cook that we won't be needing supper. My friend and I mean to do the town tonight."

Placie nodded and hurried away.

"Close your mouth, Brynne," said Miranda.

Blushing, Brynne obeyed.

"After we eat, I'll show you to your room. I think it would be wise if you took a short nap this afternoon, since we might be out rather late."

The last thing Brynne wanted to do was sleep. There was always the chance that she might awaken and find that she'd dreamed all this. But she wouldn't have argued with Miranda Tanner for the world. When the crystal bowls brimming with delicately sliced, sumptuous fruits arrived, she ate graciously, patterning her manners after Miranda's.

Her room was a cool, airy place, on the second floor of that spotless, uncluttered house. The bed was made of glistening brass, and it was graced with a pink eyelet counterpane trimmed with shiny satin. The curtains were of eyelet, too, and they covered windows looking out over the rushing excitement that was Seattle.

There was a white dresser with a mirror, a matching wardrobe and a folding screen made of rose-colored silk. The floor was wooden and polished to a high shine, with soft, nubby white rugs placed here and there. All in all, it was the most splendid room Brynne had ever seen.

She opened the gilded white doors of the wardrobe and peered inside, imagining how her clothes would look hanging there. Something shimmered in a dark corner, and Brynne reached for it, puzzled.

The item was a locket, and it was cool and elegant in Brynne's palm. After a time, her fingers trembling inexplicably, she opened its golden, heart-shaped face and drew in a sharp breath. There was a tiny daguerreotype of Joshua in one side of the locket, and a painted miniature of a stunningly beautiful, dark-haired woman in the other.

Profoundly stricken on some half-conscious level, Brynne stood still, staring at the costly locket. She started when a voice shrilled beside her.

"That's poor Mrs. Tanner," announced Placie, who had entered the room in complete silence, it seemed, though she was burdened with a huge crockery pitcher and a matching basin. "I declare, Clarissa and I nigh went crazy looking for that necklace. Where did you find it?"

Brynne's closed throat opened as Placie set the pitcher and basin on top of the dresser. "I—In the wardrobe."

"Mercy me," marveled Placie. "We scoured that thing, hoping it was there. This is strange."

"Yes," managed Brynne. "She was beautiful, wasn't she?"

"Like to take your breath right away," agreed Placie cheerfully. "She was nice, too. Never shouted at me or Lissy. This house hasn't been the same without Mrs. Tanner."

"What was her name?" asked Brynne, sinking to the edge of the bed because her trembling knees would no longer support her. "Her first name, I mean?"

"Rosalie," said Placie, dropping the locket into her apron pocket and then pouring warm water from the pitcher into the basin. "You can trust me to give this necklace to Miss Miranda the minute I get downstairs," she added, after a moment.

Brynne knew that the locket would, indeed, be given to Miranda. "Thank you," she said, somewhat distractedly.

Placie turned and assessed Brynne's blue calico dress with kindly resignation. "If you'll take that poor, bedraggled thing off, I'll try and do something with it."

The refreshing practicality of Placie's statement dispelled Brynne's odd mood, at least partially, and she smiled. "It's quite hopeless, I'm afraid."

Placie laughed. "Never you mind, Miss Brynne McFarren. *Brynne*—now that's a name you don't hear every day of the week. Miss Miranda will outfit you proper."

"You like Miranda, don't you?"

"I do indeed," replied the loquacious Placie. "There isn't a mean bone in that woman's body."

Brynne averted her eyes. "What about her brothers? Do you like them?"

Placie ruminated. "Drew likes giving orders and he pinches once in a while, but Joshua's all right."

Brynne calmly removed her shoes. "He must have loved his wife very much."

"There was some as said he worshiped her. I know I never heard them argue, and oh, the clothes he bought for that woman, the jewelry. Sapphires to match her eyes, he'd say . . ."

Brynne closed her eyes.

"You're a little peaked, Miss Brynne."

"Just Brynne, please. I'm no one special."

"I'll go and let you rest now," said Placie, in a pleased voice. "I didn't mean to talk your ear off."

Brynne did not open her eyes again until she had heard the door close. And Placie had been gone a very long time before she had the strength to stand up, strip to her drawers and camisole, and approach the basin waiting on the dresser.

The washing cooled her, calmed her screaming nerves a bit, enabled her to reach the bed before collapsing.

She understood the indefinable, ceaseless pain she'd sensed in Joshua Tanner. At last, she understood. A dry, desolate sob tore at Brynne's throat and, again, she closed her eyes tight.

But the knowledge that Joshua had had a wife, a wife he had obviously adored, followed her into the darkness. And it brought along a grief the like of which Brynne McFarren had never known.

Eventually, lulled by the lilac-scented breeze billowing the curtains and the genteel, mid-afternoon silence of that wonderful house, Brynne slept.

She dreamed that Rosalie Tanner stood at the foot of the bed, tugging mischievously at Brynne's bare ankle. Her rich, raven-black hair billowed around her shoulders and her eyes were a startling sapphire blue and her full lips were curved into a smile. She nodded her head and faded away, like so much wafting, ethereal smoke.

After that, Brynne dreamed that Joshua was with her, freeing her breasts of the camisole, stroking them, drawing the rosy tips to hard wanting with his fingers. She felt him remove the gauzy drawers, find the aching nubbin. She even felt him fill her, become an inexorable part of her.

And he moved upon her, this dream-Joshua, bringing her skillfully, sweetly, inescapably to a fulfillment so shattering that she whimpered in the throes of it.

Her breath tearing at her lungs, her legs apart to

157

welcome him, Brynne awakened to find that she was alone.

Her body still quivering with false satisfaction, she buried her face in a satin-covered pillow and wept. She'd lost Joshua Tanner long before she had even met him, but she would know no peace without him.

Joshua didn't need the wounded looks on the faces of his crew to tell him that he was in a foul mood. God help him, he couldn't keep his mind on anything for thinking about Brynne McFarren.

Wrenching off the bandanna tied around his forehead, to keep the sweat out of his eyes, he glared up at the sky, consulting the sun. She was in Seattle by now, and probably settled in the house.

Joshua's teeth ground as he permitted himself to imagine the stir she'd cause, once Miranda's dressmakers and milliners were through with her. Within twenty-four hours, there wouldn't be an unmarried man in all of Seattle who wasn't lusting after her.

You're thinking like Drew, the Half-Breed chided himself, but the insight didn't help. He'd kill the son of a bitch that touched her. He drew a deep breath. In his mind, he bared her plump, upright breasts and feasted on them, reveling in the whimpering pleas that she would utter. The vision prompted an unfortunate physical response and he bellowed a curse in frustration.

Sam Prigg looked up from the warped boards he was prying from the *Rosalie's* deck and laughed raucously.

"Shut up, you old reprobate!" barked the Half-Breed.

"Seattle ain't far," drawled the old man, unruffled. "Looks like maybe you'll be at my weddin' after all."

Joshua swore again, hoarsely, and turned away in a belated and largely hopeless attempt to hide his embarrassing condition.

Sam chuckled as he went on with his work. "I'm lookin' forward to my honeymoon," he said, and then he roared with laughter.

Chapter Ten

CORRINE TEMPLE PACED THE SIMPLY FURNISHED PARLOR of Joshua's Tacoma house in unfettered annoyance. Where was that man, anyway? He'd promised to come back from Port Propensity as soon as he'd dealt with Drew and "a few other problems" and already he'd been gone for nine days!

If that wasn't bad enough, the arrogant bastard hadn't even taken the trouble to send a wire or write a letter explaining the delay.

Simmering, Corrine collapsed inelegantly into a chair facing the ivory fireplace. If only she dared contact Joshua herself, if only she could board a steamer for that precious town of his and confront him. She'd tell that damned Indian a thing or two.

A rueful laugh rose in her throat. *Who are you trying to fool, Corrine Temple?* she asked herself. *If Joshua Tanner gave you the nod, you'd crawl to Port Propensity and wrap yourself around his ankles.*

Abruptly, Corrine bounded out of the chair and studied her reflection in the glistening mirror over the mantlepiece. She was beautiful, damn it, with her lush mane of auburn hair and her wide, blue-green eyes. Unlike most redheads, she wasn't plagued by freckles;

159

her alabaster skin was flawless, glowing. Her teeth were as white and even as the Half-Breed's own, and she knew how to please a man, any man.

And in addition to all this, she was patient with Joshua's endless business dealings. Didn't she wait, without complaint, while he met with officers of the Tacoma branch of his bank? Did she say so much as a word when they missed a dinner or a party because he insisted on actually working in the shipyard on Commencement Bay, instead of simply overseeing the operation? So why the hell was he treating her this way?

The possibility that had dogged Corrine ever since the man had brought her to this small but elegant house, that had probably dogged the half dozen women who had preceded her, rose in her mercurial mind and demanded to be recognized.

Joshua might not be in Port Propensity at all. He never dallied with the women in that town or even permitted whatever mistress he happened to be keeping to venture there. He could well be in Seattle, beginning a new romantic alliance.

If that was the case, Corrine's days were numbered. Everybody knew that the Half-Breed kept one mistress at a time.

"Damn!" she spat.

"Miss Temple?"

Corrine whirled, startled, to see the elderly housekeeper standing near the windows. The drapes were open and, through the glass, she could see a crimson and gold sunset rioting on the busy waters of Commencement Bay. "Yes?"

"This came for you," said the even-tempered old woman, who had reigned in the pleasant house, year after year, while the likes of Corrine Temple came and went. Implacable in her long tenure, she held out a letter.

Corrine snatched the missive and ripped it open, letting the envelope waft, forgotten, to the floor. The handwriting was Joshua's and the message, scrawled in bold, slanted letters, was singularly wounding.

I'm sorry. It's over. Good-bye. J.T.

Corrine read the note again and again. She couldn't believe he'd dismissed her so tersely. And, to make matters worse, the bastard had included a sizable bank draft to accelerate her departure.

"Miss?" prodded the ancient housekeeper sweetly, even though she knew damned well what was happening.

Seething, Corrine crumpled the letter in one hand and consigned it to the floor. Then, blood pounding in her classic cheekbones, she stomped one expensively shod foot in rage and fixed a murderous gaze on the housekeeper. "I'm going to Seattle," she announced coldly. "Kindly pack my things!"

Maude Simpson was unruffled. "Will you be returning?" she asked, her eyes slipping briefly to the letter on the rug and then coming back to Corrine's fury-flushed face.

Corrine thrust out her chin. "Yes!" she said. Maybe the others had been content with a figurative pat on the bustle and a bank draft, but Corrine Temple wasn't.

"Very well," sang Mrs. Simpson, in the tone of one who knew a hopeless pursuit when she saw one.

Brynne awakened late, that Wednesday morning, to find Placie standing at the foot of the bed, staring at her.

"Did you sleep good?" asked the girl.

Brynne chuckled ruefully. She'd slept like a dead person, she'd been so tired. Who would have thought that dinner in a hotel dining room and a play at the Opera House could wear a person out like that? "Yes," she said. "I certainly did. And for too long, it seems."

Placie smiled and bustled around to the side of the bed, carrying a wicker breakfast tray. "Miss Miranda said to let you sleep awhile, so we did. Now she wants you to eat and get downstairs right away."

Rarely had Brynne McFarren been served a meal in bed, and never had she experienced such a luxury when she wasn't ill. She was agape as she struggled into a sitting position to accept the tray. "Is she angry?"

"With that one, you'd know it if she was," Placie assured her, giggling. "I've seen Miss Miranda stand toe-to-toe with the Half-Breed himself and give back as good as she got!"

Brynne was glad for the covered dishes on the tray, now resting neatly across her lap. They gave her something to look at. "I thought you liked Mr. Tanner, Placie," she mused, helping herself to a glass of orange juice.

"I do."

"Then why call him by that awful name?" Brynne wanted to know, her eyes still carefully avoiding Placie's.

"Everybody calls him that, Brynne. It's an insult from some, but it's respectful from others."

Brynne nodded in a deceptively idle fashion and put down her juice to sample a steaming muffin speckled with sweet purple berries of some sort. "He does inspire a certain awe, doesn't he?"

Placie laughed, folding her arms and leaning back against Brynne's dresser. "Some would say it's terror he inspires. I think it's a shame when a man that handsome gets his heart broke."

"Yes," agreed Brynne, in a wooden voice, her appetite suddenly gone. "Placie, I'm not very hungry after all. Could you please take this food away? And tell Miss Miranda that I'll be down as soon as I've dressed?"

"Cook will fuss something awful," complained Placie, taking the tray reluctantly.

Chagrined, Brynne reached out, took the tray back, and began, dismally, to eat. She didn't taste a morsel.

Miranda was in the garden, half an hour later, when Brynne made her appearance. She looked up from the

162

letter she was writing at the wrought-iron table and smiled. "Good morning."

Brynne blushed a little and intertwined nervous fingers in the folds of her gray cotton skirt. "I'm so sorry that I overslept."

"Nonsense. You were exhausted. Did you enjoy last night?"

Reassured, Brynne sank into a chair across from her employer. "It was marvelous, Miranda. There was so much to see and do, I hardly knew where to look!"

Miranda laughed. "I thought your eyes would fall out when we were watching the play. You know, Brynne, you could probably be on the stage yourself if you wanted to."

Quickly, Brynne shook her head and averted her eyes. Just the thought of all those people staring at her was incomprehensible.

"What would you like to do?" Miranda asked gently, with sincere interest. "Marry and have children? Teach, perhaps?"

Brynne's eyes were glowing as they came shyly to Miranda's face. "I would like to be loved," she said, with soft certainty.

"That's all?"

"It's enough, when you consider all the things that would probably come with it—babies, a house, a garden . . ."

"Mercy, Brynne, how plebian. A *garden?*"

Brynne drew a deep, delighted breath and permitted herself to dream. The scents of lilacs and roses added a distinct reality to the pictures moving in her mind. "I'd have flowers, but vegetables, too. And the earth would feel warm when I put my fingers into it—"

"Good heavens!" gasped Miranda, with feigned indignation, "I've hired a farmer!"

Brynne pulled her head out of the clouds and studied Miranda intrepidly. "Why *did* you hire me, Miranda? You don't need a companion."

"Don't I? Port Propensity is a dull town, dear heart, in case you haven't noticed. I have no friends there. How would *you* like to depend on two bull-headed, opinionated brothers for intelligent conversation?"

"You don't have to live there," challenged Brynne. "And you've survived all this time without me to talk to."

Miranda rolled her beautiful, dark eyes comically. "Please. Don't remind me how long I've survived."

Gently insistent, Brynne leaned forward in her chair. "This is charity, isn't it? Either that, or you're doing it all for Drew."

"You're partially right," admitted Miranda calmly. "I love my brother, but I'm the first to confess that he can be something less than subtle. While you're here, he'll have a chance to think with his head, instead of his heart, and you won't be pursued to death. Besides, Brynne McFarren, I like you and I honestly enjoy your company."

Brynne felt the stubborn pride of all her ancestors rising up inside her, overflowing. "I don't need charity," she said.

"Charity, is it?" asked Miranda, with mild amusement. "We'll just see if you still think this is charity when you've kept up with *me* for a week or two, you obdurate little Scot!"

Brynne couldn't help laughing. "I can keep up," she vowed, lifting her chin.

"Good," said Miranda briskly, putting down her pen to seal the ink bottle and gather the blue vellum pages of her letter. "We'll start with my favorite dressmaker. When we've finished there, we'll have luncheon downtown. After that, we'll have plenty of time to choose some hats and shoes and pay a few social calls. When all of that is done—"

"I want a raise in salary," interrupted Brynne, her eyes sparkling.

"Poppycock," retorted Miranda, in lively rebellion. "You're overpaid as it is."

With that, she swept up her writing materials and went off to tell Cook's husband that the carriage would be needed in short order.

Keeping up with Miranda Tanner proved to be an exhausting task, indeed, even for Brynne, who had traipsed all over the hills at home, looking after her father's sheep.

Admittedly, however, being fitted for a lot of new clothes—all of which were, in Brynne's opinion, rather grand for a companion—proved to be a great deal more fun than herding sheep. After the fourth or fifth swatch of luxurious fabric had been matched to a design in the dressmaker's style book, Brynne lost count of the gowns Miranda was so blithely ordering for her. And besides dresses, there were to be silken, lace-edged underthings, too, along with nightgowns and wrappers and cloaks.

The seamstress seemed to be laboring under the delusion that the young lady required a trousseau, and neither Miranda nor Brynne bothered to correct her.

After securing a promise that the first of the garments ordered would be delivered within a few days, Miranda dragged Brynne to the milliner's shop in the next street and purchased a bewildering array of hats and bonnets for her companion.

By dinnertime, Brynne was too overwhelmed to eat. However, fearing to offend either Miranda or the mustached waiter in the busy downtown dining room they visited, she ordered barley soup.

"The dressmaker thought I was getting married," she confided, as Miranda ate heartily of the fried chicken she had ordered for herself.

Miranda said nothing and, though the fact that she was chewing had to be taken into consideration, Brynne was unsettled by her silence.

"Are you dressing me up for Drew?" she demanded.

Miranda nearly choked, then dabbed delicately at her mouth with a blue-and-white checked napkin.

"Brynne McFarren, what an outrageous question! I thought we'd settled this."

Brynne blushed. "Those clothes are simply too fine for a companion!"

Miranda made a mischievous face. "Not for *my* companion they're not," she retorted. "Brynne, stop being such a Dreary O'Leary—it's my money."

Once again stymied, for the moment, at least, Brynne swallowed her misgivings and managed a faltering smile. "Has anyone ever told you, Miranda Tanner, that you are impossible?"

"I?" echoed Miranda, in lofty tones. "Perish the thought. Hurry up with that gruel, or whatever it is, because we've still got to get shoes and call on the Allens and the Radleys."

Buying the shoes proved to be every bit as arduous and exacting a project as selecting the hats and dresses had been. To Brynne's carefully hidden and very profound relief, the Allens were not at home.

The Radleys, however, who were possessed of a noxious and pimple-ridden son with impudent eyes, prevailed upon Miranda and Brynne to share their supper.

Mr. Radley was a shipping executive with investments in the railroad, and his home was every bit as grand as the Tanner house, if too showy and cluttered for Brynne's taste. Mrs. Radley was a thin, pleasant woman, full of questions, and their son, who bore the outlandish name of Noble, was a leering bore.

"You could marry Noble," Miranda teased, when they were, at last, back in the carriage and on their way home.

"So could you," retorted Brynne, with a saucy toss of her head.

"He has lots of money," sang Miranda, her eyes dancing in the shadowy, half light of the carriage.

Brynne shivered in distaste. "If I wanted to marry for money," she said, when she had recovered some decorum, "I would be chasing Drew."

"Not Joshua?" ventured Miranda, raising one eyebrow.

Brynne lowered her eyes and shook her head. "He still belongs to Rosalie, I think."

There was a short silence and, when Miranda spoke, she spoke softly, and with resignation. "He loved her very much."

"She was beautiful," said Brynne, feeling defeated and tired and old before her time. "I—I saw her portrait in the locket I found—"

"I know. Placie told me that when she returned it to me."

"Will you give it to Joshua?"

Miranda considered sadly. Finally, she shook her head. "I don't think so. Her things upset him. He found a scarf that had belonged to Rosalie under a carriage seat once, a few months after she died, and he didn't do anything but brood for days."

"Placie said she was kind—Rosalie, I mean."

Miranda nodded. "We all loved her."

Brynne looked out the carriage window and studied the crescent moon in the dark, star-dappled sky. "Do you miss being married, Miranda?" she dared, desperate to change the subject.

A warm laugh bubbled up from Miranda's throat. "No more than I miss the scarlet fever I had when I was eleven. Alec was a waster, and if I never see him again, it will be too soon."

"But you're young, beautiful . . ."

"Thank you. I am also free, and I fully intend to stay that way. Tired?"

"Exhausted," sighed Brynne.

Miranda laughed. "Good. After we play three or four hands of canasta, you can go to bed."

Brynne sighed again. "This companion business is more difficult than I thought," she said, with resignation.

Miranda chuckled. "I warned you."

As it happened, there were no games of cards played

that night, for the house was in a stir when they arrived. There was a strange carriage sitting out front, and an imperious, redheaded woman was ordering the driver to carry in her trunks.

A long sigh and a very unladylike word escaped Miranda at the sight. When Cook's husband had stopped the carriage and helped its two passengers to alight, the visitor turned and smiled.

"Miranda!" she sang, drawing the word out in a way that was at once cordial and condescending.

"Corrine," replied Miranda, with tart politeness. "Won't you come in?"

In the oil-lit foyer, Corrine's beauty was clearly visible. Brynne felt a peculiar sort of dread gather in the pit of her stomach as she took in the bright, blue-green eyes, the cinnamon-colored hair, the perfect skin.

Corrine's gown and short cape were made of whispering, emerald green silk of the finest quality, and her gaze shriveled something deep within Brynne as the woman assessed her. "I don't believe we've met."

"Corrine Temple," Miranda said quickly, "may I present my companion, Miss Brynne McFarren?"

Corrine's full, rouged lips pursed for a moment, in pretty consideration. "McFarren," she repeated thoughtfully. "Now, where have I—"

Miranda caught Brynne's elbow just then, and her smile trembled oddly on her mouth. "Brynne, dear, I've got the most ferocious headache. Would you mind asking Cook for some powders?"

Uneasy and eager to quit the sudden oppression of that tasteful foyer, Brynne nodded and hurried away to comply.

Miranda folded her arms and glared inhospitably at her caller. "Get out, Corrine," she said bluntly. "Joshua isn't here."

Corrine was watching the arched doorway, through

which Brynne had just disappeared. "McFarren," she said again. "Who is she, Miranda?"

"She is my companion, as I told you, as if that were any of your business."

"Well, I don't like her."

"I'm devastated, Corrine. Heavens, I'll dismiss the wretch immediately."

The caustic barb brought Corrine's disturbing contemplation to an end and drew her piercing, aquamarine gaze back to Miranda's face. "If that fresh-faced snippet is a servant, I'll eat my new French silk. Have I been replaced?"

Miranda laughed, though the headache she'd used as an excuse to get Brynne out of this woman's firing range was becoming a gnawing reality. "I wouldn't know, dear. Shouldn't that question be put to my brother?"

Corrine's flawless complexion colored instantly, explaining rather a lot. "She's a bit young for Joshua," mused the beautiful concubine, after a few moments of recovery. "He prefers a certain experience, you know."

"I'm sure you've met that qualification," said Miranda, rising to the occasion. And then she caught Corrine by the arm and propelled her out of the foyer and onto the marble porch. "Good night, Miss Temple, and thank you so much for coming to call!"

The driver of the hired carriage shrugged philosophically and began lifting Corrine's many trunks back inside the vehicle.

To Miranda's vast relief, the lady allowed herself to be handed back into the carriage, albeit with a menacing glare and a muttered curse.

"Good night!" chimed Miranda, smiling and waving in cheerful farewell. All the while, she was mentally composing an ear-blistering lecture to be delivered the instant she saw Joshua again.

She turned slowly, closed the heavy door, and leaned

against it. Brynne was standing a few feet away, holding a glass of rather foggy water and looking stricken and young and out of her depth.

"My headache powders, I hope?" said Miranda, more to break the silence than to claim the medicine.

Brynne extended the glass. "Cook was gone to bed," she said miserably. "I found the powders myself. I hope I stirred them in properly . . ."

"Thank you," sighed Miranda, closing her eyes and taking a great draught of the nasty water.

"Miranda?"

"What, dear?"

"Why does everyone repeat 'McFarren' to themselves when they hear it, as though it were a curse or something?"

Miranda set the glass aside, on the foyer table. "What do you mean?" she hedged, knowing full well what Brynne meant. Somebody was going to have to tell the girl, but Miranda was damned if she would. The task belonged to Joshua.

Brynne swallowed and, when she spoke, her voice was hollow. "Ever since I came to Port Propensity with Evan, people have been taking note of my name."

"I hadn't noticed," lied Miranda, hating herself for the deception but still unable to explain. How long would it be, she wondered, until Corrine remembered?

Brynne sighed in frustration. "I suppose we still have to play canasta," she said, resolved to an unpleasant fate.

Relieved, Miranda chuckled warmly. "I'll beat you at cards another time," she said. "Just go to bed before you fall over in a quivering heap of pink lawn and gray cotton."

Brynne's face positively glowed with relief. "Good night!" she said quickly, and then she turned on one heel and fled.

If Miranda hadn't been so very frightened for her, she would have laughed aloud.

* * *

The Shore House was doing a brisk business, for a Wednesday night, and Austin Darnell was pleased. It wasn't the money that mattered—he had enough of that to last him for a lot longer than he planned to live—but the noise. Silence left a man with too much time to think, to remember.

Idly, he weaved his way from one table to another, greeting his customers. The girls were busy in their rooms along the mezzanine and there was a lot of good-natured, boisterous betting going on at the faro tables. The piano player was in as fine a form as one could expect, in a backwater town such as that one, and the four bartenders were hard put to keep up with the trade.

Nonetheless, one of them came discreetly to Austin's side, as he was laughing at one of Judge Hickman's abominable jokes, and tugged at the sleeve of his finely tailored, dove-gray suitcoat. "Excuse me, Mr. Darnell," the man whispered. "We've got a little trouble."

Austin lifted one eyebrow in eloquent question.

"It's that Tanner kid," the bartender confided, in a stage whisper. "He's raisin' hell upstairs and he's drunker'n three sailors on shore leave. If he was anybody else, we'd just throw him out, but . . ."

Austin shook his head. "No. I'll handle it." He was about to ask which girl the kid was with when a bouncer signaled him circumspectly from the top of the stairs. "Thank you," he said to the bartender, striding away.

When he reached the mezzanine, Jumbo O'Hoolihan was waiting nervously. "He's with Celeste, Mr. Darnell. We didn't know what to do—"

"Which one is Celeste?" snapped Austin, annoyed.

Jumbo grinned, revealing the most unfortunate set of teeth Austin had ever seen. "That's the one what tried to be a blonde and ended up with pink hair, Boss."

Room four, thought Austin, striding along the mezzanine and tapping discreetly at the proper door.

171

The answer was a feminine shriek, followed by, "Don't you dare do that again, Drew Tanner!"

Austin rolled his eyes and opened the door. If this kid had been anybody but the Half-Breed's baby brother, he'd already be skidding face first down the driveway.

Drew had the hysterical Celeste down on the floor, while he knelt astraddle of her. Both he and the woman were fully clad, but Drew had a handful of Celeste's hair in one hand and a pair of scissors in the other.

Much of Celeste's garish mane had already been snipped away, as evidenced by the tufts of pink hair lying all over the room, and what remained was riding her head in uneven shingles.

"He's baldin' me!" screamed Celeste.

Austin suppressed a laugh. "Drew," he said reasonably.

Drew looked up, weaving a little, squinted, and then grinned. "Hello, Austin. How ya been?"

Calmly, Austin approached, squatted down on his haunches, and removed the scissors from Drew's hand. "I've been just fine. How about you?"

Celeste saw her chance and scooted out from under Drew Tanner to make her escape, side-scrambling like a crab.

As Drew stood, so did Austin.

"Hey," Drew complained petulantly, as Celeste fled the room, leaving the door to gape open behind her.

"I didn't like her hair, either," said Austin, always the diplomat.

Drew's face contorted comically. Lord, the lad was drunk. "Pink. I'll be a sonnavabitch if it isn't pink . . ."

"How about a cup of coffee," offered Austin, laying one hand on Drew's shoulder. "We'll talk."

While Drew considered this suggestion, Jumbo loomed in the doorway in silent question. Austin held up two fingers and the bouncer nodded and lumbered away.

It took a long time to sober Drew Tanner up, and a lot of coffee, but it was worth it.

"You weren't mad because Celeste has pink hair, now were you?" Austin asked quietly, cautiously.

Drew shook his head. "She went away," he said.

"Who?"

"Brynne. Brynne McFarren. Damn it, Miranda took her to Seattle and . . ."

McFarren. The gruesome details of Rosalie's death loomed in Austin's mind, triggered by the name, but he hid his reaction with infinite care. "I see. Well, she'll be back one day soon, won't she?"

Before Drew could answer that, another man filled the doorway of Celeste's room and Austin knew without looking that it wasn't Jumbo.

"Isn't this cozy?" drawled the Half-Breed, in a voice that made Drew flinch visibly in his chair at the little table where Celeste got to know her customers before calmly turning them inside out.

Austin sat back in his chair, across from Drew's, and smiled. "Joshua. Good evening."

The Half-Breed's fierce, violet eyes were on his brother, and his hands were white where they gripped the framework of the door. Austin was wondering whether even Jumbo, for all his brawn, could handle this furious giant, when Drew rose unsteadily to his feet and held up both his hands, palms outward, in a gesture of peace.

"It's all *right,* Joshua. I'm all right. We're all all right—"

"That's what you think," rasped the Half-Breed.

Austin smiled again. "Drew was just telling me about his girl, Joshua. Relax."

Instead of relaxing, the Half-Breed tensed in a way that was, to Austin, intriguing. "Which one?" Joshua quipped, but it was too late and he knew it.

"Brynne McFarren," said Austin. "Didn't you say that was her name, Drew?"

Drew looked besotted and slightly green around the gills. "Yes," he said, with some difficulty.

The Half-Breed looked positively rigid. In what seemed like an instant, however, he broke his ominous pose in the doorway, strode across the room, and caught Drew by the back of his collar. The kid was almost to the threshold before his feet touched the floor.

"Go home," Joshua snapped. Drew scowled, brushed the pink hair from his trouser legs, and walked out with remarkable dignity.

Austin bit his lower lip to keep from grinning—after all, there was a limit to what the Half-Breed would take without retaliating. "Don't be too hard on the boy, Joshua," he said, in the friendly tones of a concerned mediator. "After all, he's in love." *And you are, too. I'd bet my last bottle, Tanner, that you are, too.*

The Half-Breed's crippling hands clenched into fists and then relaxed at his sides. "He's just drunk," he offered, from the doorway.

Austin drummed his long, tapered fingers idly on the tabletop. "McFarren," he mused, watching his old enemy with complacency. "That's an interesting coincidence, Joshua. Tell me—is she pretty?"

Tanner's lips curled in a laughable attempt at scorn. "She's a kid."

"Does she know you mean to kill her father?"

The Half-Breed drew a deep, rasping breath in an obvious try for patience. "I can't, much as I'd like to. He's already dead."

Austin stood up, calmly slid his hands into his trouser pockets. "Good," he said, in blithe tones. "I hope it was painful."

Joshua was turning to leave. "Good night, Austin," he snapped.

"The sins of the fathers—" Austin began, in a voice meant to stop the Half-Breed cold.

Sure enough, Tanner stood still, his hands suddenly

174

gripping the doorframe again, his massive, muscular back rigid.

Austin finished the altered quote in a quiet, calculated way. "Shall be visited on the daughter."

Now, Joshua turned. The paraphrase had definitely struck its mark. "That's very clever, Austin. Is it a threat?"

"It's a promise."

"You know, of course, that I'll kill you if you go near her."

The smirk came easily to Austin's face. "Of course. But it will be too late then, won't it? The debt will have been paid."

"It isn't her debt to pay," argued the Half-Breed, calmly. "She has no idea what happened."

Austin pretended an interest in the buffed, neatly filed nails on his right hand. "Perhaps you should explain," he said.

Chapter Eleven

DREW'S EXPRESSION WAS AT ONCE SHEEPISH AND DEFIANT when Joshua bolted out through the swinging doors of the Shore House to join his younger brother and Sam Prigg.

"I thought I told you to go home," Joshua snarled, facing Drew in the light from the doorway of the saloon as Sam unhitched the horses from the rail.

Drew scowled, standing his ground. "I'm not a kid anymore, Josh, I'm a man."

Joshua made a gruff, disdainful sound. "Keep talking, Drew. Keep pushing. Right now, I'd like nothing better than to turn you inside out."

"Josh," interceded Sam, with hoarse diplomacy. "Go easy."

"Go easy?" rasped Joshua, jerking the reins Sam offered into his hand. Chinook nickered and danced in protest. "Damn it, Drew, do you realize what you've done? Do you know how dangerous Austin Darnell is?"

Drew shrugged stupidly, but the light was beginning to dawn in his eyes, all the same. "Brynne . . . her father . . ."

"That's right," growled Joshua, mounting Chinook's

bare back and glowering down at his brother. "In Austin's mind, Brynne is as much to blame for what happened as her father would have been."

"That's crazy," protested Drew, lamely, as Sam nudged him to take the reins of his own horse.

"Austin's crazy," snapped Joshua. "So help me God, Drew, if he hurts Brynne because of you . . ."

There was a long, wretched pause, during which too many things were said without words. Drew was pale as he looked up at his brother.

"What do you care?" he hissed fiercely. "You hated McFarren, too." Drew fell silent, again searching his brother's face. "My God, you *want* her. You want Brynne!"

"Kid always was quick-witted," observed Sam wryly, mounting his horse.

"Shut up," snarled the Half-Breed, his attention fixed on his brother.

"You," breathed Drew, his face turning a waxen gray. "It was *you*."

"Drew—"

A raw, sob of mingled rage and pain tore itself from Drew's throat. "You bastard, you half-breed, sneaking, back-stabbing *bastard* . . ."

Joshua had taken note of the interest the scene was stirring in Austin's customers as they came and went. "We'll talk about this at home," he said, with finality, and then he reined Chinook into the darkness and prodded the animal to a dead run.

The ride home didn't take long enough. Joshua was settling Chinook in his stall when Drew rode in, followed closely by Sam Prigg.

An agile rider, Drew slid off his pinto gelding before it had come to a complete stop and dropped the reins to storm, a devil drenched in moonlight, into the stables. His hands were clenched at his sides and his eyes glittered with hatred as he faced his brother.

Eyes averted, Sam Prigg saw to Drew's horse and his own.

177

"Why?" whispered Drew, his face contorted in the flickering light of the one kerosene lamp Joshua had lit.

Joshua folded his arms and met his brother's gaze directly. "Why what? Why do I care for Brynne?"

Drew's seraphic lips curled with contempt and genuine pain. Clearly, he was in no condition to discuss the situation rationally. "Why did you make love to her?"

Joshua drew a deep breath, polished the lie carefully before he offered it. "I haven't touched her," he said, for Brynne's sake as much as Drew's.

Drew reeled a little, but his fists relaxed. "She said, she told me somebody had—"

"Well, it wasn't me."

For a few moments, there was no sound in the stables other than the routine shifting and snorting of the horses and the squeak of leather as Sam removed a saddle.

Joshua watched Drew's face closely during this brief interval. It had been his experience that people believed what they needed to believe, despite any evidence to the contrary. His theory was borne out when Drew tilted his head to one side and grinned.

"Damn and creation, was I drunk," he said. And then he turned and blithely walked off in the direction of the house, whistling.

"Sometimes I'd like to kill that kid," said Joshua, in low, harsh tones.

Sam came out of the shadows and sat down heavily on a bale of hay. "Seems to me you just had a chance to do that," the old man observed. "Why did you lie, Josh?"

"Who says I lied?" snapped Joshua, turning away from his friend to rearrange a row of bridles hanging neatly on the stable wall.

"*I* say you lied."

"You don't know anything."

"I know I left my tools outside the captain's cabin on

178

the *Rosalie,* and I know that last Sunday mornin' I went back to find 'em."

Joshua stopped his needless rearranging, his hands in midair, and lowered his head. *"Damn."*

"Don't worry about it. I ain't gonna tell Drew or nobody else. But you best marry that'un, Josh, 'cause there ain't many like her."

Joshua sighed, still unable to turn around and face his friend. He hoped his silence would stem the tide of Sam's oration.

"My first wife sure wasn't like her. Used to lay there like a scarecrow, grittin' her teeth and waitin' for it to be done with."

Despite everything, Joshua laughed hoarsely at the picture Sam was painting. Finally, he turned around, his hands on his hips, his head tilted to one side. "What the hell were you doing Sunday, Sam, peering through a knothole?"

To his credit, Sam blushed profusely. His wandering eye gave him a fierce look in the dim light. "Didn't need to look," he bristled. "The way that little'un was carryin' on, there was no question as she liked it. Don't you get her pregnant, Josh. She ain't for toyin', like them women you been takin' up with these last couple of years."

Pregnant. The word hit Joshua Tanner like a well-aimed brick. Until this moment, he had not even considered that hideous possibility, and he shuddered in the face of it.

Sam stood up quickly. "I'm sorry now, Josh. I'm real sorry. I wasn't thinkin', I just meant—"

"I know what you meant!" snapped Joshua, brushing past Sam Prigg to stand under the night sky and consume great gulps of fresh air.

Sam was at his side in an instant. "It ain't always like it was for your missus, Josh."

Again, involuntarily, Joshua shuddered. He closed his eyes and saw Rosalie's face, waxen and still. Forever still.

Sam caught anxiously at his arm. "Josh."

Joshua opened his eyes. "I need a drink," he said gruffly. "How about you?"

"Don't mind if I do," said Sam Prigg.

Drew's head was muddled, and he knew that it would hurt like hell in the morning. Pausing at the door of his bedroom, he thought of Celeste and her pink hair and laughed.

There were other things he should be thinking about besides that whore and her pale fuschia locks, he knew, but his thoughts were skittering around in his head like mice in the bottom of a cracker barrel, and he couldn't seem to capture even one of them.

He glanced toward Joshua's door, for no consciously conceived reason, and remembered. A vivid image of Brynne surrendering to his half-brother loomed in his mind and the resultant pain was so savage that he hurled one fist at the wall in reaction.

There was an explosive ache in his hand, and then fire seemed to streak up his arm and into his shoulder. Drew groaned and leaned against his bedroom door until his knees were solid enough to support him again.

He tried to move his fingers and the pain rose to a gut-wrenching crescendo. Drew closed his eyes and pulled in a deep breath, and cursed himself for an idiot.

After a second or two, he got used to the pounding pain and his attention was drawn, inexplicably, back to Joshua's room. He stumbled down the hallway and, with his left hand, opened the door.

The room was dark, except for the moonlight shafting in through one window, but Drew's eyes adjusted rapidly. *He didn't touch her. He said he didn't touch her.* The words pounded in his mind, a desperate litany, just as the pain pounded in his rapidly swelling right hand.

Drew braced himself against the churning nausea in the pit of his stomach. What was he doing in the Half-Breed's room, anyway? What did he hope to find?

180

His eyes scanned the wall facing Joshua's bed, slid away, lurched back. The portrait was gone. Rosalie's portrait was gone! In that instant, Drew knew that Joshua had lied. The woman that could take Rosalie's place had finally come along, and that woman was Brynne McFarren.

Something deep inside Drew contorted. *"No!"* he bellowed, reeling on his feet like a drunken madman. "No, goddamn it, *no!*"

The room swayed dangerously as the blood left Drew's head to throb in his broken hand. He staggered and then fell. "No," he sobbed.

And then Joshua was there. "What the . . ."

There was the strike of a match, accompanied by the inevitable smell of sulphur—Sam Prigg, damn him, was lighting a lamp, revealing Drew in his misery and his humiliation.

Drew sat up, and the effort was costly. He wouldn't have had the strength if it weren't for his hatred.

"The portrait," he rasped. "Where in hell is the portrait?"

Joshua was sitting on his heels now, examining Drew's hand. His eyes smoothly avoided his half-brother's as they sliced to Sam Prigg. "Get a doctor," he muttered.

Drew's hand felt ten times its normal size, and the pain was excruciating. "I'll . . . kill . . . you," he choked out. "I swear it, Joshua. I'll kill you—"

"Shut up," breathed Joshua. "How in God's name did you manage to break your hand?"

"You bastard, I'll—"

Joshua sighed and rose to his feet, pulling his half-brother with him. "I've heard it all, Drew. Bastard. Half-Breed. Those words don't hurt anymore, so save your breath."

Drew would have struggled free if he'd had the strength, but he didn't. He had no choice but to let Brynne's lover help him out into the hall, through the doorway and into his own room.

It was dark, and the floor was littered with books and discarded clothes. Joshua was cursing in irritation by the time he got the half-conscious Drew to the bed.

Drew collapsed onto the mattress. "Don't light the . . ."

Light flared in the room. "Damn," Joshua breathed. "How can you live in this wreckage?"

Aching in every fiber of his being, Drew flung his left arm over his eyes and laughed. It was a hoarse, sobbing sound, tinged with madness, but he didn't care. "You always did like things neat and orderly, didn't you, Joshua."

"Christ," muttered Joshua. Drew sensed that he wanted to leave but couldn't quite bring himself to do it. He was bound by some strange code of honor.

"Was she good?"

"What the hell are you talking about, Drew?"

At last, Drew was able to look up at his brother, who was towering beside the bed. "You know damned well what I'm talking about. Brynne—was she good?"

"How would you like me to break your other hand?"

"Was she?"

Joshua looked like a rumbling volcano preparing for a full-fledged eruption. "I'm going to give you the benefit of the doubt and assume you're delirious. I told you—"

"You lied."

"Did I?"

"Yes. You took the portrait down."

Joshua sighed, pushed three books and a sweater off the seat of a chair, and sat down. "Your logic escapes me, Drew. Because I took Rosalie's portrait down, I also seduced Brynne?"

The man was so reasonable, so rational. It took firm resolve not to accept his lies, and Drew was running short of resolve.

"Something made you take it down," he insisted.

Joshua swore.

"And you—you care for Brynne. You admitted that.

182

Why is she different, Joshua? Why could she get you to stop worshiping at Rosalie's altar when all—all the others couldn't?" Drew's hand ached so badly now that he had to swallow a groan. "W—Was it because you knew I love her?"

"Believe it or not, Drew," drawled the Half-Breed, "I wasn't created to make your life difficult."

"But you love Brynne McFarren."

"Yes."

"And you took her to bed."

The answering silence was all too eloquent.

A raw, dry sob tore itself from Drew's throat. "I hate you, J—Joshua. Oh God how I h—hate you."

"I know," said the Half-Breed, with weary resignation.

"No, you don't," moaned Drew, half crazy now, with the pain that shifted in his spirit and burned in his hand like fire. "Like father, like son. You're j—just like Papa—"

"Thank you."

Drew wanted to lie still, but he was writhing. "Don't thank me . . . whelp. You're a whelp off a filthy Indian bitch—"

Joshua stood up suddenly and turned away. "Stop it, Drew," he said raggedly.

But Drew couldn't stop. It was as though his mother was standing beside him again, urging him on, teaching him to hate, squelching every inclination to admire his half-brother. "Were you born on a teepee floor?"

The Half-Breed's shoulders tensed ominously, but he only lowered his head, as though Drew had struck him.

The pain was worse, so much worse. "I loved you," he said grudgingly.

The Half-Breed laughed, low in his throat, and it was a raw, broken, contemptuous sound. "Sure."

"I did," Drew insisted. "You were my brother. You could do anything. . . ."

At that, the Half-Breed turned to face Drew, and

there was pain shadowing his purple eyes that matched or even surpassed his brother's. "You're out of your head."

Before Drew could reply, the bedroom door jolted open and Dr. Barnett rushed in, with Sam Prigg on his heels.

"Good God," boomed the pompous, elderly physician, peering at Drew over the rims of his spectacles. "What happened to you, young fella?"

Drew turned his eyes to Joshua, without answering. He watched as his brother crossed the room, walked out, closed the door quietly behind him.

Sam Prigg was glaring at the doctor. "Don't go blamin' Josh, neither," he said defensively. "This here was the kid's own doin'."

"Shut your gabber and hold him down, Sam," grumbled the doctor, setting aside his bag and frowning at Drew's hand. "Afraid this is gonna hurt some, Son."

"Now, wait a—" Drew began, as Sam's hand pressed down hard on his shoulder.

"Gotta set it," grumbled Prigg, his breath warm and foul with whiskey.

"Hold him," breathed the doctor, and then, after drawing a deep, reluctant breath, he wrenched deftly at Drew's broken hand.

Drew's scream rose from his midsection and rattled against the ceiling, the sky, the far borders of the universe itself, and it was not a random cry, but a name: Joshua.

"I'm here," replied an even voice, from the foot of the bed.

"It isn't right yet," said the doctor irritably.

Drew twisted under Sam Prigg's restraining hands, frightened and sick. "No, oh, God, Joshua. Don't let them—"

"Wait," said Joshua. And then he was gripping Drew's shoulders, instead of Sam. However inescapable, his grasp was gentle and, though Drew could not see his face clearly, he sensed compassion in his brother's bearing, heard it in his voice. "Take a deep breath, Drew. Try to relax. I'll keep talking to you, and you listen, and before you know it, this will be over and done with. All right?"

Drew swallowed hard, nodded his head. "All right. Talk, for God's sake. . . ."

Joshua talked. He talked about many things, and nothing at all. And when the terrible pain came again, in a searing rush, Drew didn't scream.

It was done. Joshua stumbled blindly out of his brother's room, down the stairs, through the house. Outside, behind the stone springhouse, he wretched until his stomach was empty.

Miranda Tanner sat bolt upright in bed, her heart wedged into her throat. Drew. Something was terribly wrong with Drew.

She was out of bed and scrambling into her robe before she realized that she wasn't in the Port Propensity house, but in Seattle. And Drew wasn't just down the hall.

Trembling, Miranda removed her robe and sank dismally to the side of the bed. He hadn't called for her anyway, but for Joshua. She could only hope that the Half-Breed had heard—and cared.

At dawn, Joshua washed and changed his clothes and left his bedroom. Drew was sleeping soundly, his injured hand neatly splinted.

Ironic, the Half-Breed thought, *that he slept and I didn't*. And then he closed the door and strode down the hallway, to the stairs.

He had been working at his desk for almost two hours when How Ling crept in, eyes downcast, with the telegraph message.

Joshua unfolded the hand-copied note swiftly and grinned at its contents. *What happened to Drew? Miranda.*

"The man want to know if you make answer," ventured How Ling, in a voice barely above a whisper.

Joshua reached for a pencil and a scrap of paper and scrawled his reply. "Give him this, please."

Miranda was pacing the foyer when the messenger finally arrived, in the latter hours of that glowering, gray-skied morning, and she wrenched open the door the moment he turned the bellknob.

"Message for—"

Miranda snatched the paper from his hand and unfolded it. *Drew broke his hand. He'll live. Joshua.*

"Will there be a reply, ma'am?" asked the messenger, probably anxious to get back on his bicycle and ride away before the heavens opened up with a proper Puget Sound deluge.

"One word," said Miranda, taking a dollar from the pocket of her lavender morning gown and extending it to the young man.

"'Thanks'?" he guessed, grinning.

"'Corrine,'" replied Miranda, closing the door. "And keep the change!"

Brynne was just coming down the stairs when Miranda entered the main hallway, on her way to thank Cook's husband for venturing out so early to send the first wire.

"Good morning, Miss Layabed!"

Brynne's eyes were puffy and she still looked sleep-rumpled and a little confused. "Is it late?"

"Yes," said Miranda, in pleasant but matter-of-fact tones. "It's going to be a nasty day, though, so we'll stay at home."

Brynne looked so relieved at this news that Miranda laughed as she went on about her business.

The air was hot and heavy and, as Brynne stood at the open kitchen door, looking out, the first huge droplets of rain began to fall. The scents of sweet grass and dampened dust mingled pleasantly.

Behind Brynne, Placie and Clarissa were busy at the table, polishing all manner of silverware, while Cook, a portly, jocular woman, pared vegetables at the sink.

Miranda was closeted away somewhere, with a book, but Brynne hadn't been able to concentrate on the printed word. She was too restless to sit still, too uneasy and uncomfortable to fix her attention on any task so placid as reading.

Besides, her throat was raw and her nose was stuffy and she felt as though she were constantly on the verge of a sneeze.

"Close that door," ordered Cook briskly, "before that rain gets in here and warps my floor. I've got some tea brewing."

Brynne wondered distractedly what warped floors and brewing tea had to do with each other and obediently closed the door. Her chest began to ache as she sat down at the table and reached for a polishing cloth and a silver candlestick.

"Stop that!" snapped Placie.

Defiantly, Brynne drew the candlestick and cloth close to her and began to polish in earnest. "I'm a servant, too, Placie," she said, in an odd, thick voice.

Clarissa, a short, plump girl with the ingenuous face of a schoolgirl, giggled behind one hand. The lightning flashing outside cast blue glints onto the blonde curls springing out all over her head. "A servant," she repeated, with glee.

"I am," insisted Brynne, lifting her chin. "Just the same as you or Placie or Cook."

"If you say so," said Placie, her eyes dancing. "Only Miss Miranda don't take any of *us* out riding in her carriage and you don't see us getting decked out in fine clothes, neither."

Brynne swallowed and searched Placie's face and then Clarissa's. She found no rancor—only smug amusement. "I am a companion," she maintained, albeit not so certainly as before.

Placie laughed right out loud.

Annoyed and confused, Brynne wiped furiously at the elegant candlestick in her hand. "See?" she asserted. "I am working. I am employed in this household, just as all of you are."

Clarissa stopped polishing an ornate fork to look Brynne over with fresh speculation. "Which one wants you, Miss Brynne? Is it Drew, or the Half-Breed himself?"

Brynne blushed, outraged and shaken. "You think I'm being *kept?*"

"Aren't you?" quizzed Placie, companionably enough.

"No!" cried Brynne, leaping to her feet and flinging down her polishing cloth and waving the candlestick like a weapon.

"Must be Drew," ruminated Clarissa, as though Brynne hadn't spoken at all. "The Half-Breed sets his ladies up in private houses, and there's no fancy business about who or what they are."

Brynne sank slowly back into her chair, staring. All her angry protests died at the back of her throat. "That woman that was here last night—Corrine—"

Placie set aside a gleaming teapot to work industriously on a serving platter. "Now there's a passion pot," she confided blithely. "She's been here with Mr. Tanner a couple of times. Last month, he was working at the desk Miss Miranda uses, in the parlor, and snap my corset stays if that woman wasn't crouching under it. When I came in to announce dinner, they were—"

"Placenta!" snapped Cook, her many chins trembling.

"Well, they were. She was, anyway. Sounded like she was killing him."

Brynne felt her eyes widen. She leaned forward in her chair, ignoring Cook's umbrage, and though her mouth was open, she couldn't manage a word.

"Broad daylight, too," said Placie, putting a dramatic cap on the shocking story.

"One more word and you'll be cleaning moss out of the birdbath!" threatened Cook, lifting her paring knife like a battle lance.

Placie lowered her head and scoured furiously at the platter, stealing the occasional look at Brynne. Clarissa followed her fellow worker's lead and kept her observations to herself.

Brynne sat perfectly still in her chair, not even pretending to polish the candlestick she held. In her mind, she was seeing Joshua, hearing Joshua, grasping all too well what purpose Corrine Temple had had in hiding underneath his desk.

What a fool she'd been, actually thinking that she was special to Joshua Tanner! Their two encounters had not been at all special—at least, not to him.

Brynne wanted to scream and cry and throw things, but she didn't. Instead, she ordered her right hand to raise the polishing cloth to the candlestick gripped in her left. Eventually, her muscles obeyed her.

Drew sat up in bed and studied his splinted hand. The pain had ebbed to a bearable level, and, as he considered his situation, he was not unaware of its advantages.

No one could expect him to plane ship timbers or carry hot pitch, after all, when his right hand was clearly broken, now could they? Drew smiled.

There was a timid knock, just then, at the door of his bedroom.

"Come in," he said, in cheerful tones.

How Ling slipped into the room, her almond-shaped eyes carefully fixed on the tray she carried. She set her burden in Drew's lap and leaped backward, as though he might strike at her.

He laughed. "It's all right, How Ling. I'm in no condition to grope and plunder." He lifted a piece of toasted bread in his good hand and took a bite. "Where's Joshua?"

How Ling retreated another step, out of reach. Her fingers kept interlacing with each other and then relaxing. "He go to Little Canton. There is trouble."

Drew looked at the contents of the tray and wondered why the hell he'd been served breakfast—bacon and eggs and orange juice—when it had to be well past noon. "What kind of trouble?"

"Committee make many papers. Papers say Chinese must go."

"Go where?" asked Drew, who was not, for the moment, in a political sort of mood.

How Ling shrugged. "They not care. Just go."

"Are you scared?"

The girl considered and then nodded and her eyes still would not link up with Drew's. "Mr. Tanner say we not worry."

Drew summarily lifted his fork and broke the yoke of a fried egg. "Mr. Tanner," he scoffed. "He can't fight the whole white race, How Ling. Not even the Half-Breed is equal to a feat like that."

Exhibiting the first display of real spirit Drew had ever seen in her, How Ling thrust out her hands and tossed her head. "White man want us build railroads. Now done, so go. *Swim* back to Kwantung Province!"

Drew laughed. "They don't expect you to do that, How Ling. But, after all, this is the white man's country."

"White man is thief!" challenged How Ling, her black hair falling around her shoulders and shimmering even in the storm-strained sunlight. "He steal country from the Half-Breed's people!"

Drew sighed, took another bite of toasted bread. "If you can't hold onto what's yours, other people take it," he said. And he frowned as an alternate application of those very words rose in his mind. He imagined Brynne writhing in his brother's arms and all the food on his tray suddenly had the appeal of so much soggy sawdust.

How Ling was not only looking directly at him now,

but almost smirking. There was fire in her slanted eyes, and the hint of a smile lurked on her lips. "Yes," she said. "Stronger people take."

Drew scowled. Damn it, did she know how badly he wanted Brynne? Did she know that Joshua had gotten to her first? "If your people are smart," he said, "they'll pack up and leave before there's trouble."

"We not go away," she said firmly. "We stay."

"We'll see," snapped Drew.

"Yes," agreed How Ling, with dignity. "You not eat?"

Drew thrust the tray at her. "Take it away."

Quietly, How Ling obeyed.

Joshua strode into Walter Jennings's modest hotel lobby and approached the desk. He laid the printed flier down on the open pages of the registration book and secured it with a resounding crash of one fist.

Slowly, his adam's apple bobbing in his skinny neck, Jennings looked up from the receipts he'd been tallying. "Hello, Joshua," he said, with an admirable show of cordial surprise. He was careful, Joshua noticed, not to look down at the flier.

Joshua suppressed an urge to grasp the squirrelly innkeeper by the back of the neck and press his nose to the desk until the cartilage snapped.

"What the hell do you think you're doing?"

At last, Jennings read the flier he'd probably composed himself. He'd probably engineered China Joe's murder, too, but there was no proving that.

"Just looking after the working man's interests," he said, obsequiously. "Long as the Chinese move on by the first of November, there won't be any trouble."

"Where do they go, Jennings? To some other town where men like you will be waiting to drive them out again?"

"Now, Joshua—"

Joshua reached for the flier, crumpled it in one lethal

hand. "Call this off, Jennings," he warned, in a vicious undertone, "while you still can."

The innkeeper's mouth dropped open, and Joshua deftly stuffed the wadded flier past the man's teeth to the back of his throat.

"They stay," he said, and then he turned and strode out onto the rainy street.

Chapter Twelve

IT TOOK A LONG TIME TO DRESS, AND DREW MANAGED IT IN painful, awkward stages. The effort made his stomach queasy and caused sweat to bead on his upper lip and tickle between his shoulder blades.

He had no money, having spent his wages on that pink-haired whore at the Shore House, and that was a problem. Once he reached Seattle, he would be able to cajole all the cash he needed from Miranda, but the breadth of Puget Sound lay between him and his sister, and steamer fare would have to be paid before he could close the gap.

Drew considered the money Joshua kept in the drawer of his desk. Surely he wouldn't miss only a few dollars—

Carefully, his hand protesting savagely at any disturbance, Drew made his way down the stairway and across the hall, to Joshua's study. After one defiant glance at the portrait of his father over the fireplace, he tried the desk drawer.

It was locked.

Drew swore, looking around the room in distracted irritation. Here he was, a member of one of the richest families in the territory and he couldn't raise steamer fare!

It was then that someone turned the bellknob on the front porch. Mostly because he had to do something, even if it was a menial task that should have fallen to How Ling or her mother, Drew strode out of the study and opened the door.

Flossie Randall was standing on the porch, her blue eyes wide, her lips pursed. There was something furtive in her manner, and she kept glancing back toward the driveway, where her horse and buggy waited in the drizzling rain.

"The doc said you got hurt," she whispered.

Drew smiled his most fetching smile and held up his wounded hand as evidence.

"Ooooo," crooned Flossie, who wanted, he'd bet, to minister to things far removed from his hand. "Does it hurt?"

Drew nodded bravely. "If I could just get out of town," he muttered, with valiant despondency, "I'd be safe again."

Flossie's eyes widened further. "Safe?" she echoed.

Drew leaned forward. "My brother, you know," he confided.

Flossie blushed, and the tiny black curls framing her face bobbed with appropriate outrage. "The Half-Breed did that?"

He sighed a martyr's sigh, closed his eyes as if tormented by the very memory of his suffering, and nodded.

"Haven't you got any money?" Flossie demanded, in a shrill burst of practicality.

Drew affected a pitiable shudder. "He took that," he said, hoping that the laughter inside him wasn't visible in his eyes.

Flossie bent her head and began to rummage through her handbag. Then, like a rescuing angel, she held out a handful of crisp currency.

"I couldn't," breathed Drew, stepping back, trying to look stricken. "Not from—from you."

Sweet mischief danced in Flossie's eyes, and she licked her lips. "If we hurry, you can catch the steamer. I've got my buggy." Her blue gaze dropped to Drew's midsection and slid sensuously back to his face.

"Would you drive, Drew?"

And so it was that Drew Tanner not only had a ride to the wharf but enjoyed the trip.

By twilight, the rain had stopped. Brynne went out to the garden to sit at the wrought-iron table and consider her sorry plight. Never mind that the seat of the chair made her dress soggy. There was so much cold misery in her spirit that she hardly noticed.

If she did what Corrine had done, would Joshua love her? She blushed at the thought of herself hiding beneath a desk, doing something so unconventional, so scandalous. Merciful heavens, she hadn't even known that women did such things.

"Brynne?"

Miranda's voice made her start and blush all the harder, for fear that her thoughts might be written clearly in her face. "H-Hello," she stammered, dropping her eyes.

"What on earth are you doing out here? Do you want to catch your death?"

The gentle irritation lacing Miranda's words was, somehow, comforting. Brynne sniffled, covered her face with both hands, and then began weeping in earnest.

Instantly, Miranda was beside her chair, laying a warm, sisterly hand on Brynne's trembling shoulder. "Good heavens, sweetheart, what is it?"

Brynne howled.

"You miss Joshua, don't you?" guessed Miranda, softly.

It was close enough. Brynne nodded, her face still

hidden, and sobbed wretchedly. All at once, everything was hurting—her father's needless death, being so far from Joshua, knowing that she hadn't mattered to him, that simple ignorance would keep her from pleasing him the way women like Corrine did.

Miranda drew her companion gently to her feet and led her inside the house, where it was warm. The sneezing began as they climbed the stairs.

"My Lord," clucked Miranda. "It's a hot bath for you, young lady, and a good night's sleep."

After Placie and Clarissa had brought a tub and steaming water to Brynne's room and the bath had been accomplished, Brynne scrambled into a flannel robe that had been warmed before a downstairs fireplace, tied the belt, and fell into bed.

Within an hour, her throat had progressed from slightly raw to downright sore, and her nose felt as though it had grown to bulbous proportions.

"You look like an old sot from down on the sawdust," observed Placie, with affection.

Brynne was a country girl, essentially, but she knew that the phrase "down on the sawdust" referred to that notorious mecca of sin, the Skid Road. She put out her tongue at Placie.

"Cook's making you a mustard plaster," announced Placie, undaunted. "You'll be in fine fettle by morning, if you don't die of the stench."

Brynne groaned. "It's just a cold."

"Tell that to Cook," retorted Placie cheerfully. "Even the Half-Breed doesn't argue with that woman."

Cook appeared moments later with a sodden, noxious piece of flannel, which she insisted on placing under Brynne's robe, on her bare bosom. "Don't you go taking that off, either," the woman warned, with conviction. "If you do, I'll turn you over my knee, Miss McFarren, and have no doubt of it."

Brynne nodded obediently, her eyes wide. When Cook had quit the room, however, she reached up to remove the offending mustard plaster.

"Wouldn't do that if I were you," sang Placie. "One time Lissy got into the brown sugar and, time Cook was done with her, she couldn't sit down for a full day."

Brynne considered Cook's bulk and unassailable status in the household and lowered her hands. "It stinks," she complained. "And it's burning me."

"Means it's working," said Placie, without sympathy. And then she waltzed out, leaving Brynne to recover in irate solitude.

She'd been alone for half an hour or so, feeling patently sorry for herself, when the bedroom door creaked cautiously open and Drew Tanner himself appeared in the gap, grinning.

"Hello, sugarplum," he said.

Brynne was both relieved and embarrassed. She looked, as Placie had so aptly put it, like an old Skid Road sot, but Drew was a welcome diversion.

He approached the bed, casting comical, stealthy looks back over his shoulder as he crept nearer. "Good Lord," he breathed, when he finally reached the bedside. "What happened to your nose? And that *smell*—"

"Stop it," Brynne bristled, the splint on his right hand catching her eye. "You're hurt!"

He bowed. "And here for sympathy, which, it would seem, you're in no position to give."

Brynne laughed rawly and with an obvious nasal twang. "Poor, poor Drew!" she crooned theatrically. "Does it hurth?"

Drew's eyes were twinkling, even though there were shadows of pain shifting behind the merriment. "No, it doesn't hurth. What stinks?"

"Musthard plasther," said Brynne.

"I'd like to kiss you, Brynne McFarren."

"Donth you dare!"

Drew laughed. And then, bracing himself against the mattress with his good hand, he bent and brushed Brynne's lips with his own until they parted for him.

She awaited the tickle, deep in her womb, that she'd

felt when Joshua kissed her, but it didn't come. *It's probably because of my cold,* she thought.

"Andrew," interceded Miranda acidly, from the doorway.

Drew stiffened and pulled his lips from Brynne's, after a few leisurely nibbles. "Ummmm," he said, in a throaty voice.

Brynne wrenched the covers up over her head and didn't come out until she knew that both Miranda and Drew were gone.

After several hours, Cook came in and mercifully removed the mustard plaster. She pressed a cup of hot, creamy, sweet rum into Brynne's hands.

"Drink every drop of that," she ordered, and, for all her gruff manner, Brynne knew that Cook was enjoying the role of nurse.

The concoction was delicious, and Brynne consumed it immediately. It made her sleep and dream scrumptious, naughty things about Joshua Tanner.

Once, in the depths of the night, it seemed that she awakened and he was there, kneeling beside her bed, opening her flannel robe, cupping one sleep-warmed breast in his hand. The dream was so real that she even caught the fresh, ocean-air scent of his skin and hair.

It's the rum, thought Brynne, as the familiar hand slid down her stomach to the silken vee at the place where her thighs met. "Ummm," she whispered, as a sweet, swirling fire was fanned within her.

His fingers plied the aching nubbin, drawing, caressing, teasing.

Brynne gave herself up to the dream, closing her eyes, tilting her head back, moaning softly with pleasure. She felt a rush of cool air as the covers were tossed back—how real the dream was—and then he was consuming her greedily, this imaginary Joshua, bringing her swiftly to a sweet, shuddering release. She whimpered and knotted frantic fingers in his hair as he softly kissed the quivering bit of flesh back to swollen wanting.

In the morning, Brynne was still too sick to get out of bed. She stared up at the ceiling, remembering her sinful dream, and waited for Cook to appear with some new medicinal torture.

The door of her room opened slowly, and a familiar frame loomed there. Joshua's amethyst eyes swept from one end of Brynne's flannel-robed figure to the other, and his aristocratic lips curved into an impudent grin. Just before he closed the door again, he winked and made a low, growling sound in his throat.

Cheeks pounding with crimson color, Brynne gave a strangled cry of angry embarrassment and forced herself to look down at her crumpled robe. Joshua's night visit had not been a dream at all, but a scandalous reality. And he was amused!

Wanting to die, Brynne once again tugged her covers up over her head. She would hide from the world, that's what she would do, and no one, not Drew or Placie or Miranda or even Cook could persuade her to show her face in public again.

Perhaps an hour had passed when she heard the bedroom door open once more. Stubbornly, she burrowed down deeper between the sheets and stiffened. If it was Placie with breakfast, let her wait. Brynne McFarren was never going to eat again.

Only she was hungry.

"Brynne." The voice was low, a sort of rumbling vibrato, and it was unmistakable. "Come out of there."

"No," said Brynne, with staunch determination. "You leave this room, Joshua Tanner, before I scream."

"Scream," he said blithely, and there was a sort of shrug in his voice. "I'm not going anywhere."

The humor in his tones infuriated Brynne and, with sudden disregard for her decision to hide for the rest of her life, she flung back her covers and glared at the insolent giant towering at the foot of her bed. "You rounder!" she said hoarsely, her throat still sore, her nose still clogged.

"You liked me last night," he said, in a mock-wounded voice underlaid with suppressed laughter.

"You don't juth go around—you don't juth go around *nibbling* on people!"

His arms folded across his chest, he threw back his magnificent head and laughed. "You were juth irresistible," he teased, when his mirth had subsided a little.

Brynne could feel a slow blush rise all the way from her toes to the roots of her hair. She would cheerfully have killed Joshua Tanner, in that moment, but her rebellious body was, at the same time, remembering his touch. "Leaf me alone!"

"I'd like to," he said expansively, flinging his hands out wide in a gesture of hopeless resignation tempered with that insolent twist of his lips and the violet mischief in his eyes. "But you're so delicious, Pippin."

Brynne longed to fling something at him, but there was nothing at hand, save her feather pillows. "Wath Corrine busy?"

There was a change in his face, but it wasn't the one Brynne had hoped, unconsciously, to see. Instead of shame and remorse, blatant amusement played in his features. "So you've met Corrine," he said, folding his arms again. "I hope she didn't catch your cold."

A tremor of primitive, jealous rage jolted through Brynne's small frame, but she sat perfectly still. "No doubt thath would be inconvenient."

He tilted his head to one side and studied Brynne as though she were a wretched specimen. "I'm sure it would," he agreed ponderously. "How can she find a new lover if she's got a nose like yours?"

Brynne gulped. "A new lover?"

The violet eyes danced. "Brynne, Brynne," he scolded. "Don't tell me you thought that I was going to go on—er—keeping company with Corrine."

Brynne interlaced her trembling fingers and pretended a great interest in them. "She *ith* beautiful," she mourned, distractedly.

Joshua laughed. "She ith history," he said. He came

200

to the side of the bed then and calmly sat down on its edge. Brynne cursed the feelings that raged through her as the springs creaked under his weight, trembled involuntarily when his hand came up to caress her cheek. "Brynne, we have to talk about your father soon."

Remembering the foreclosure, the nightmare of finding John McFarren dead by his own hand—and, indirectly, this man's hand—Brynne stiffened. "Talk," she croaked.

He shook his dark head, and the scent of his hair undermined Brynne's resolve to resent him. "Not now. You're sick. But one day very soon."

Brynne would have cried if she hadn't known it would have disastrous effects on her already ridiculous nose. "You want to explain the foreclosure," she mumbled.

Joshua was instantly alert, and his hand dropped from her cheek. "What foreclosure?" he asked, frowning.

What an actor he was! He actually looked confused. Brynne turned away from him and scrambled out of bed on the opposite side, stomping to the wardrobe. There, she ferreted through her satchel until she found the papers that had driven her father to that deepest of all despairs. Keeping her distance, she flung the document over the bed.

Joshua, still sitting down, gathered the papers and glanced at the heading. Then, frowning, he skipped to the last page to read the signature. His eyes moved slowly to Brynne's face.

"You knew he hanged himself," she breathed, trembling. "Thath why."

"Brynne—"

She was crying now, and without shame. She was so filled with fury and pain that there was no room in her for anything else. "He wath honest! He would have paid you!"

Joshua rose slowly to his full and formidable height,

the papers still in his hand. "Brynne, we don't—I didn't—"

"Ith your bank—your signature!"

"No," he said, suddenly thrusting the documents toward her. "It *isn't* my signature."

"It seth 'Joshua Tanner'!" insisted Brynne, sniffling.

"Look at the initials beside it—they belong to a man who works for me. Brynne, it was all done by proxy. I didn't know."

Brynne resisted, but she believed him. The look in his eyes and the set of his jaw were visible evidence that he was telling the truth. And that only made it worse. Dear God, the man destroyed people without ever knowing that he'd done it! He allowed clerks and minions to shatter men like John McFarren with the stroke of a pen. "When the wool wath sold," she insisted bitterly. "He would have paid you."

Some kind of awesome upheaval seemed to be taking place inside Joshua Tanner. His jawline hardened ominously and his eyes were like consuming lavender flames. "He could never have paid me for what he did," he rumbled, in a low, deadly voice. "My wife. My child. How could he have paid me for them, Brynne?"

Brynne's mouth dropped open. "Your—"

But Joshua was turning away. The foreclosure papers billowed in the air and wafted downward as he flung them aside, and the floor seemed to shake under their minuscule weight. At the door, the giant paused and looked back, his throat working dangerously, his eyes fierce. "John McFarren was a butcher," he bit out, and then he opened the door and stormed away, leaving it to gape open behind him.

Confused and stricken, Brynne stumbled back to her bed and collapsed. Joshua Tanner's hatred was palpable, a raging entity loosed in the room.

My wife. My child. Butcher. In anguish, Brynne tried to shut out the echoing words, but it was no use. Dear God, what did he mean? John McFarren had been a good doctor, a gentle man—

Brynne twisted the edge of the pink eyelet coverlet on her bed in despairing realization. John McFarren had also fled his practice and his home, virtually on the spur of the moment, and he'd awakened almost every night after that, screaming the same phrase: *the bairn*.

God in heaven, had Joshua's child been the "bairn" of his nightmares? Had he killed not only the baby, but Rosalie, too?

It was impossible, wasn't it?

"Oh, *no*," Brynne whispered, shaking her head back and forth frantically. "No—"

And when Placie strolled in, minutes later, carrying a breakfast tray, Brynne was still shaking her head, still rasping a tormented denial.

"Brynne? Brynne!" Placie set the tray aside with a reverberating thump and grasped Brynne's shoulders in strong, thin hands. "My God—"

"No," said Brynne.

Placie cried out in her alarm, and the sound brought both Miranda and Drew, posthaste.

Brynne could not seem to stop the motion of her head or the one word that kept rolling off her tongue.

Drew thrust Placie aside roughly to wrap his uninjured arm around Brynne's shoulders. "What . . . *Brynne!*"

"He told her," breathed Miranda, standing on the other side of the bed. "Oh, my God, he told her."

Despite her distracted state Brynne was mute now, though she still could not stop shaking her head. She saw the contortion of Drew's features, the murderous look in his eyes, the thinning of his lips.

He was on his feet and striding out of the room in another moment.

Joshua was in the garden, one foot braced on a marble bench, and Drew saw the muscles tighten in that impervious back as he approached.

"Why, Joshua?" he rasped.

His brother did not turn, did not speak. The only

sound in the garden was the buzzing of bees and the breath grating in and out of Drew's lungs. The sweet scents of Miranda's lilacs and roses mingled to lend their own soft irony to the situation.

Drew's broken hand began to throb. All the same, he longed to batter Joshua's rock-hard back until the bastard caved in.

Finally, after a long time, Joshua turned his head. His booted foot was still resting on the bench, and he hooked his thumbs in the pockets of the black vest he wore over a white linen shirt. "She doesn't know it all," he said, betraying no emotion of any kind by his tone or the expression on his face.

Drew swallowed convulsively. "My God, Joshua, how could you do it? Brynne wasn't to blame for what happened!"

"Is she all right?"

Drew shuddered in the effort to control his anger. "How nice of you to ask, Joshua. She's in pieces!"

A kind of anguished contempt replaced the unreadable expression Joshua had worn only a moment before. "Not that one. She's made out of rawhide and vinegar."

"You *bastard.*"

Joshua smiled a bitter smile—a smile that belied the fathomless pain reflected in his eyes. "She's yours, Drew," he rasped. "All yours."

With that, Joshua sighed, slid his foot off the bench, and walked away, toward the front of the house.

After a moment of mute surprise, Drew scrambled after him. "Joshua, wait . . ."

Joshua was untying the dapple-gray stud he'd hired at a livery stable after getting off the steamer late the day before. The motions of his hands and arms were powerful and frightening as he wrenched the reins free of the hitching post.

"Joshua," Drew repeated.

The Half-Breed paused, the reins in his hands, and smiled that hideous, tortured smile again. "What?"

"I love her. I'll be good to her."

Joshua nodded and swung up onto the gray's bare back. "Take her away, Drew, out of Austin's reach."

Drew swallowed, wondering why he felt like such a loser when he'd just won the most important battle of his life. Even as he measured these thoughts, the Half-Breed's gaze lifted to the window of Brynne's room. "Tell her that the farm is hers," he said, and then he was reining the horse toward the street, riding away.

Drew felt hollow inside as he watched his brother ride out of sight.

Resilient even in the times when she most wanted to fold up and stop living, Brynne McFarren recovered from both her cold and the brutal exchange with Joshua in plenty of time to attend Minnie Blode's wedding.

Since some of her new dresses had already been delivered, she was spared appearing in calico or that infernal pink and white gingham. Taking Miranda's advice, she chose a linen dress and jacket of soft, robin's egg blue for the occasion.

The church was a crude structure, doubling as a schoolhouse during the week, but it was brimming with summer sunlight and happiness when Brynne entered it, circumspectly, that Sunday afternoon, her arm linked with Drew's.

Minnie and Sam, all dressed up in new finery, were happiness personified. They gloried in the attention of their many friends, now filling the church to capacity, and repeated their vows in forceful, certain voices.

Brynne envied them, half-heartedly, wondering when and if such a day would come for her. Unlike Sam's daughter and many of the other women witnessing the ceremony, she did not cry—there were no tears inside Brynne McFarren, and there was no laughter, either. It was as though every emotion had been scraped away or wrapped in batting, leaving her to feel nothing at all.

Midway through the service, Drew squeezed

Brynne's hand and grinned reassuringly when she turned to look at him.

She was about to summon up an answering smile when her attention was caught by the unmistakable aspect of the man standing at the end of the rough-hewn pew, one shoulder braced casually against the wall.

As though he felt her gaze, Joshua Tanner looked in Brynne's direction and nodded dispassionately. He might have been acknowledging a stranger or minor acquaintance, rather than a woman he had made love to.

Suddenly, Brynne wasn't hollow anymore. She was filled with churning pain, pain that bore no relation at all to the things he'd said about her father.

I hate you, she thought fiercely, as he idly shifted his attention back to the bride and groom at the front of the church.

Silent though they were, the words seemed to strike Joshua Tanner like a blow. He stiffened, sliced another look at Brynne—this time, a menacing one—and left the church. Brynne felt his absence as keenly as she would have felt the thrust of a knife.

When the ceremony was over, there was a reception at one of Seattle's modest hotels. Dreading yet another confrontation with the Half-Breed, Brynne attended simply because she loved Minnie Prigg with all her heart.

Drew was silent during the buggy ride down to the hotel—Brynne knew he'd seen her staring at Joshua and resented the silent exchange between them, however hostile it had been, but she didn't care.

As the Tanner buggy came to a stop in front of the Union Hotel, however, a cry of joy escaped Brynne. There, among all the wagons and buggies and horses, was a red painted vehicle marked, E. PIERPONT, DAGUER-REOTYPIST. LIKENESSES TAKEN.

Evan! Evan was there. Without waiting for any help

from Drew, Brynne scrambled out of the buggy, lifted her skirts, and ran inelegantly down the sidewalk.

Sure enough, Evan was inside the busy dining room, setting up his equipment to take pictures of Minnie and Sam Prigg.

Delighted at the very sight of her friend, Brynne thrust herself into his arms. He laughed and hugged her without hesitation. "What are you doing here? I thought you were—" his gentle eyes went briefly to Minnie, who was laughing like a schoolgirl and clinging to her proud groom's sturdy arm. "Oh. You're out of a job, then."

Brynne shook her head quickly, aware of Drew's silent and not wholly approving presence behind her. "I'm working for Miss Miranda Tanner, as her companion. Just look at the fine dress she bought for me!"

Evan was not looking at the pretty blue gown, however; his eyes were sharp on Drew Tanner's face. "A companion, is it?" he rumbled, his voice rife with suspicion. "Just what does this job require of you, Brynne?"

Brynne felt warm color surge into her face. She didn't dare look at Drew, but she could feel his patent annoyance in every tissue and fiber of her being. "It's honest work, Evan," she said. "You know I wouldn't—"

Evan was glaring at Drew. "It isn't you I'm worried about, love. It isn't you, indeed."

"You know my sister, Mr. Pierpont," Drew put in finally, his voice at once cold and diplomatic. "Miranda guards Brynne's virtue with all the ferocity of a Viking warrior."

Evan's face relaxed; he even managed a gruff, if somewhat dispirited, laugh. "Yes, I'd trust Miranda Tanner to look after my girl here."

There was an awkward silence, which Drew promptly remedied by going off in search of two cups of wedding punch.

"You can still go to Olympia," Evan reminded Brynne, out of the side of his mouth. "I'll be going there as soon as I've finished photographing all those lumberjacks up at Number Three."

"Number Three?"

Evan nodded, draping the black cloth over his camera. "It's one of Joshua Tanner's outfits. I couldn't take you there, of course, you being a woman, but I could sure fetch you on my way back through Seattle."

Brynne's mind was racing as Drew returned with two cups full of pink fruit punch. Maybe she *should* go to Olympia, where she wouldn't be a burden on Miranda Tanner, where she wouldn't encounter Joshua, where she wouldn't stir false hopes in an ever more attentive Drew.

"When are you leaving for the camp?" she asked, as one of Drew's friends pulled him aside to confer with him.

Evan was busy focusing and doing all manner of other mysterious things. "Tonight about sundown. Gotta be there first thing. But I won't take a woman to that place, so don't even ask. I'll stop by Miss Miranda's place in a couple of days."

"Good," said Brynne, thoughtfully, turning to look at Drew's well-tailored suit and to speculate.

Chapter Thirteen

ONCE THE DECISION HAD BEEN MADE, BRYNNE HAD TO act upon it. She could not wait several days for Evan to come back from the lumber camp, no matter how sensible it might be to do so. And if a woman could not go to that rough and boisterously masculine place, then she would not go as a woman.

After Drew had driven her back home, Brynne pleaded a sudden headache and scurried up the stairs before he could protest. Her heart in her throat, she peeked into one bedroom and then another and another, until she found the one that exuded the scent of Drew's cologne.

It was a messy, cluttered place. *I'm seeing the inside of your soul, Drew Tanner,* Brynne thought, as she rifled through the jumble.

Clutching the items she needed under one arm, she looked up and down the hallway and then darted across to her own room.

There, behind the changing screen, she removed her new blue dress and wrenched the trousers she'd purloined from Drew's room up over her hips. They fit tightly, given the difference in their two shapes, but they were comfortable, too. The flannel shirt was a bit too large, but that was fine. Coupled with the heavy jacket she'd found in the back of young Mr. Tanner's wardrobe, it would do much to hide her womanly bosom.

A cautious rap at the door caused Brynne to divest herself of the masculine garb with stomach-wrenching haste.

"Yes?" she called, in a shaky voice, peering around one end of the screen.

"Are you all right, dear?" chimed Miranda, without opening the door. "Drew told me—"

"Just a slight headache," lied Brynne, hating herself for deceiving this fine and generous woman. "I just need to rest for a little while."

"I'll see that you're left alone," replied Miranda, and then, apparently, she went away.

Brynne ached with remorse, but she knew that everyone, Miranda included, would be better off if her plan succeeded. At twilight, when Placie and her inevitable dinner tray had been turned away and everyone was occupied in the dining room, Brynne crept down the back stairs to the kitchen, looking like a very small man, except for her hair, which was a problem she had not yet solved.

But the fates must have been with her, for, on the pegs lining the wall of the back pantry hung, among other things, Cook's husband's worn, sweat-stained leather hat.

Thou shalt not steal, said the voice of Brynne McFarren's Scottish upbringing, as she stuffed her hair up inside the hat and drew it down, so that the floppy brim shadowed her face.

Just this once, she countered.

Then, almost as an afterthought, she found a scrap of paper in Cook's "junk" drawer, scrawled a hasty note on it, and risked discovery by dashing upstairs to leave the message on her bed.

After that, she crept out into the fading light of day and started the long walk down to Seattle proper.

She lurked near the Union Hotel, where she had encountered Evan earlier in the day, trying to ignore the openly curious glances of passersby, until she had seen the photographer load the last of his equipment into the wagon. Then, not creeping but swaggering, like a person who had every right to climb into the back of that red wagon, she did so.

It soon became apparent that the Number Three camp was much farther away than she'd guessed. The chemicals Evan used in his trade reeked, and the rolling shift of the wagon made her queasy. Still, they traveled.

Things slid about and rattled as the vehicle ascended and ascended, endlessly, as though climbing all the way to the sky. At last, however, it came to a stop.

The door at the back of the wagon creaked open, admitted a gust of cool, fresh, pine-scented air and a shaft of silvery moonlight. Overcome by the turbulence of the ride and the noxious smell of the chemicals she'd been shut up with, Brynne threw prudence to the winds and bolted out of the wagon, past a very surprised Evan, to vomit unceremoniously into the dirt.

"Mother of God!" roared Evan. "Who are you?"

Brynne was ignobly occupied and could not answer.

"Who—" Evan blustered, coming around to squint at her as she lifted her head, at last, and drew in a great gulp of clean air. *"Saints in heaven—"*

"I need water!" cried Brynne.

Angrily, Evan fetched a canteen from the wagon and thrust it into her hands.

After she'd rinsed the dreadful taste from her mouth and summarily spat, Brynne did her best to smile. "I could be your helper," she said hopefully, spreading her hands.

"I ought to turn you over my knee!" shouted Evan, storming back toward the wagon and thus forcing Brynne to follow in his wake. "It would be a favor to your poor dead father and all mankind in the bargain!"

Brynne fell back a step. "You won't take me back to Seattle, will you?"

Evan swore roundly. "I *can't* take you back. Number Three is right over that rise there and I've got photographs to take as soon as the sun's up!"

"Then there's no problem," said Brynne, with blithe relief.

"No problem?" boomed Evan Pierpont, with unusual force. "A hundred men work in that camp and you're likely going to be the first woman they've seen in two weeks and you stand there telling me there's *no problem?!*"

"They won't know I'm a woman, Evan! Look at my clothes!"

Evan looked. "Trousers!" he sputtered, aghast. *"Trousers?!"*

Brynne laughed. "They feel good, Evan. Women ought to wear them instead of dresses."

Even in the moonlight, Evan looked purple. For one terrible moment, Brynne thought he was going to make good on his threat and drag her over his knee.

"Don't you see?" she pleaded, retreating another step. "Everyone will think I'm a man."

Evan shook his head in outraged wonder. "I've never seen a man fill out a pair of trousers like *that,* and I'll wager these lumberjacks haven't either. You're staying inside that wagon the whole time we're here, Miss Brynne McFarren, and that's the last of it."

"I can't do that! Evan, I can't breathe in there!"

"Damn, damn, and double damn!" bellowed Evan, in frustration. "The man that marries you, miss, will get nothing else done for keeping you in line!"

Brynne bit her lower lip. "I won't talk, Evan," she offered desperately. "They'll be none the wiser if I don't talk. Please don't shut me up in that wagon."

Evan had turned away, and he was gazing up at the star-spattered sky, for all the world as though he expected God to write advice there.

Joshua opened the bedroom door without making a sound and strode through the shadows to the bed. He didn't know whether a look at Brynne McFarren's sleeping face would strengthen his resolve to forget her or destroy it entirely, but he didn't care. He had to see her.

The bed was not only empty, but neatly made.

Swearing hoarsely, Joshua found a match in his vest pocket and struck it, lighting the kerosene lamp on the bedside table. There was a note on the fussy pink counterpane, and he grabbed it, read the words written on the solitary page, and swore again.

Miranda, I'm safe with my friend. Please don't worry about me, and don't think I'm ungrateful. I can't be a trial to you anymore. Brynne.

Joshua wanted to rage and shout and throw things, but he forced himself to think calmly, precisely. Her friend. Now who would that be?

Unbidden, an image of Brynne falling over the tongue of a wagon at the Independence Day picnic rose up in his mind. And the wagon had belonged to Evan Pierpont, the traveling photographer.

Joshua recalled seeing the man at Sam and Minnie's wedding reception, when he'd gone into the hotel, briefly, to offer congratulations to the bride and groom.

Brynne had been there, looking cheerful and very much at home beside Drew, and Joshua had been eager to leave. Of course, he hadn't thought to ask where the photographer was going next. He wouldn't have cared.

Suddenly, because all his practiced instincts indicated that this was the friend of Brynne had referred to in her damnable note, the knowledge was crucial to his sanity.

Twenty minutes later, a grumbling, sleepy Sam Prigg opened the door of his hotel room and peered into the shadowy hallway. "Joshua? Damn it, this is no night to be pesterin' a man—"

It wasn't, and Joshua knew that Sam would bitch

about it for months whenever he could get anyone to listen.

"Where was the photographer going?" he demanded, in terse, callous tones.

Sam's wandering eye glinted murderously. "The what?"

"Evan Pierpont. Where was he heading when he left here?"

"How the hell should I know?" growled Sam, scratching his head and shifting from one foot to the other. "He don't keep me posted on his whereabouts."

"He's takin' portraits of the men up at Number Three," allowed Minnie irritably, from somewhere in the dark depths of the room.

Sam raised his bushy eyebrows in comical challenge. "You happy now, Joshua, or did you want to come in and chat awhile?"

Joshua laughed at the sarcasm and Sam's red and white striped nightshirt and turned away. "Good night," he called back, pointedly.

Moments later, on the dark street, he studied the spindly bay mare he'd gotten at the livery stable that afternoon and wished he'd brought Chinook from Port Propensity.

Hell and damnation. He hadn't expected to go chasing off to Number Three in the middle of the night. He'd come to Seattle only to see Sam and Minnie married.

Now, all the livery stables were closed and he had no time to search out and rouse their owners. The horses he kept in town were no better than the nag quivering before him now. They were too old for anything but pulling the occasional carriage or buggy.

Resigned, Joshua Tanner mounted the bay and reined it toward the mountains.

The rain came, in a pounding torrent, about an hour before sunrise. Brynne was forced from her pallet in the open air back to the smelly interior of the wagon, while Evan stoically took shelter beneath it.

With the sun came an impossibly blue sky—the storm had passed on.

Evan was not in a good mood as he rehitched the wagon and drove it over the hill to Number Three camp, and he said nothing, other than to inform a subdued Brynne that, as far as anyone they might meet in the next few days was concerned, her name was George.

Number Three was a busy place, a tent-and-shack city with streets of gummy mud. Men were filing in and out of a long, ramshackle building, which Brynne accurately pegged as the cookhouse, while other men loaded saws and heavy chains into wagons. Oxen, used to draw timber to the skid road, which would carry logs down the mountain, to the water, brayed in the freshly washed air.

An engine, shaped much like a large, black bottle, chortled and smoked on its wheeled base, spewing puffs of snow-white steam, and, as it picked up momentum, it added greatly to the general din.

"What is that?" puzzled Brynne, her bottom jostling somewhat painfully on the hard wagonseat.

Evan tossed a menacing glance in her direction and grumbled, "An engine."

"I *know* it's an engine," said Brynne stiffly. "What does it do?"

Evan sighed as he guided his patient team through the thick, grasping mud, sparing not one more glance for the strange, noisy machine. "It's called a 'donkey.' After the choke setters hook chains around the big timbers, the donkey engine pulls them out of the woods."

"To the skid road?"

"There's a dry chute here at Number Three," allowed Evan, grudgingly. "Goes all the way to the Sound."

Brynne imagined massive trees hurtling down the mountainside at breakneck speed and shuddered. "Why do they have oxen if they have an engine? And why do they call this place 'Number Three'?"

"Aren't you full of questions this morning? Engines break down, and the Tanners must have half a dozen camps like this one. I guess the Half-Breed didn't care to go naming each one."

The Half-Breed. Drat it all, she'd gone hours without thinking about him and Evan had to bring him up in conversation. "I would name them," Brynne said loftily, "if they were mine."

"Well, they aren't yours, are they, George?" snapped Evan, reining in the horses and pulling up the handbrake in simultaneous motions. "Now you mind that you don't wander off somewhere and wind up on the business end of a falling tree. Stay away from the steam-engine and all these timber rats in the bargain."

Brynne lifted her chin and jumped, with what she hoped was masculine off-handedness, to the ground. The impact made the balls of her feet ache piercingly, and it was all she could do not to cry out.

Naturally, the daguerreotypist was a novelty—it being a regular working day and all—and the lumberjacks were drawn toward his wagon by their own vain need to appear in as many photographs as possible.

Trying to ignore them and, at the same time, appear to be Evan's assistant, Brynne trudged valiantly back and forth between the wagon and the point her "employer" had chosen for a group portrait, lugging equipment. At every step, the deep mud pulled at her high-button shoes—if Drew's trousers and shirt came close to fitting her, his boots certainly hadn't—and it was almost as though the sticky stuff would wrench them right off her feet.

Finally, when Evan had his cameras and plates and all the assorted paraphernalia of his complicated trade at hand, he grouped the self-conscious men who ran the donkey engine around that rumbling metal beast and prepared to immortalize the scene.

Afraid of being ordered back to the wagon, Brynne drew her stolen hat down hard, so that any man in the camp would have had to stoop for a good look at her face, folded her arms, and stood back just far enough to escape Evan's immediate notice.

After more than half an hour of changing the men's poses, blustering about, and generally being obnoxiously officious, Evan was satisfied with the first round of photography and prepared to move on to the next. The men who operated the donkey engine, shyly eager at first, were bored and irritable by the time they were released to do their day's work.

One of them looked off into the distance, as Evan was bullying the bullwhacker and his eight yoke of oxen into place, and whistled shrilly through his teeth. Within a moment, Brynne realized that he had given some sort of signal—it seemed that every man in the camp had stopped whatever he happened to be doing to follow the first man's gaze.

Brynne turned, curious, to look. A bedraggled bay horse was picking its way gingerly through the thick mud and, on its back rode the rain-drenched, blatantly furious Joshua Tanner.

"Jumpin' jiggers," breathed a man standing a few feet away from Brynne. "If it ain't the Half-Breed himself."

"Looks mad enough to fight bear with a switch," observed someone else. "And will you look at that sorry horse?"

A few nervous chuckles rippled through the gathering crowd, but they were quickly suppressed as the Half-Breed rode into earshot.

Brynne stood rigid, the floppy leather hat still hiding most of her face, her arms folded, her breath burning its way in and out of her lungs, her stomach spinning as though she were walking a high fence blindfolded. *He won't recognize me,* she assured herself, as Joshua drew nearer, his dark hair plastered to his face, his orchid eyes murderous as they swept and reswept the company of men.

Brynne felt a measure of relief when the lethal gaze came to an abrupt stop at Evan and his camera. Evan was her friend, and nothing could make him betray her.

So intent was Brynne on watching the Half-Breed dismount and stride toward Evan that she didn't notice how rapidly the crowd around her was thinning out.

Evan listened in silence to whatever the Half-Breed was saying, apparently unperturbed. The same could not be said of Joshua, who was gesturing a wild accompaniment to the words Brynne was too far away to hear.

Suddenly, unbelievably, Evan turned and gestured toward her. The slow, ominous turn of the Half-Breed's head chilled her to the bone.

It was then that Brynne grasped the fact that she was no longer hidden in a group of men, as she had been moments before, but facing that harsh purple gaze all by herself. Sheer panic thawed her frozen knees and enabled her to whirl about and run through the muddy streets of the lumber camp, past the cookhouse, where there were, incredibly, four flapjacks nailed to the door, past the tool shed, past a horde of grinning men.

The Half-Breed caught up to her, grasped her arm, and wrenched her around with such force that the leather hat hiding her hair sailed off into the mud. As Brynne's golden-brown mane spilled down around her face and the shoulders of Drew's flannel shirt, her captor nodded affably to the lookers-on.

"Family problems, boys," he said, with maddening resignation, his grip tight on Brynne's arm. Almost idly, then, he brought his eyes back to her flushed face. "Come along, dear," he chimed, for all the world like a long-suffering husband. And then, in a gesture that made Brynne McFarren sputter with rage, he released his hold on her arm and grasped the front of her trousers at the waistline.

The men looking on guffawed as he turned and calmly dragged his captive down the muddy camp road at a pace that forced Brynne to double trot ungracefully just to keep from falling.

Delighted, the entire work force of Number Three camp followed along, calling out the occasional affable suggestion. Brynne was too furious to speak, and she knew that any attempt to break this man's hold on her trousers would be not only hopeless, but foolhardy.

Reaching the sad bay horse again, Joshua flung Brynne bodily up onto its back and glared at her, silently daring her to move.

Brynne was about to tell the legendary Half-Breed just exactly what she thought of his strong-arm tactics when the bay horse unwittingly acted in her defense. With the calm stupidity she suspected was native to this particular beast, it lifted one foreleg and laid the hoof firmly atop Joshua Tanner's left foot.

More in irritation than in pain, Joshua shoved at the horse. It was steadfast, and, except for a stubborn stiffening of its forelegs, it did not move at all.

He rasped a word intended to intimidate the creature, but it simply nickered companionably and stood where it was.

Brynne smiled and slid off the animal's back to stand facing the mighty Joshua Tanner. She looked at his face, which was rigid with anger, she looked at the hoof planted heavily on his boot, she looked at his other foot.

Then, having given the situation due consideration, she drew back her own foot and kicked the Half-Breed soundly in the shin.

He howled in wounded outrage and stumbled backward, landing in the mud. The lumberjacks, safe in the anonymity of their numbers, laughed uproariously.

But Brynne was only to know a brief moment of

triumph, for, when Joshua fell, the bay had stepped back, startled, and freed him.

The Half-Breed rose, with imperious dignity, from the mud. His jawline looked hard as steel and his lips were edged with white and his eyes were a hot, fierce shade of orchid.

Brynne commanded her trembling legs to run, but they would not or could not obey. The ferocious light in that scathing purple gaze held her fast.

After a veritable eternity, Brynne managed to take one faltering step in retreat. The moment she moved, the Half-Breed grasped her and flung her roughly and unceremoniously over one shoulder. She hung there, helpless, while the crowd of lumberjacks cheered.

Clearly, they were staying on the winning side.

Closing her eyes in profound embarrassment, Brynne hammered at the Half-Breed's back with her fists and squirmed rebelliously on his shoulder. "Put me down," she pleaded, in a mortified whisper. "Oh, Joshua, *please* put me down."

He said nothing, nor did he free her. Instead, he strode through that applauding, laughing horde of lumberjacks, Brynne jostling helplessly on his shoulder. She opened her eyes and saw that he was carrying her toward a tent.

"Joshua Tanner," she warned, in a frantic rasp.

The canvas flap of the tent brushed her arm and hip as they passed inside, and a musty smell rose to fill Brynne's nostrils. She gasped as Joshua thrust her down from his shoulder and onto a pile of empty burlap sacks.

Wide-eyed and afraid to rise from her undignified seat on the rough bags, Brynne stared at the man standing before her. She knew, even though she couldn't see his features, that Joshua Tanner was seething. Any second now, he would surely throttle her with his bare hands and her cries for help would go unheeded because he was, after all, the Half-Breed.

Brynne gulped, resigned to her fate. "I'm sorry I kicked you," she lied.

It was then that, incredibly, Joshua thrust back his head and roared with hoarse, weary laughter, his hands resting on his hips.

Brynne had had enough masculine amusement directed at her for one day, thank you very much, and her pride was stung. She leaped to her feet and raised both fists to pound furiously at his granite-like chest, little cries of rage tearing like sobs from her raw throat.

The heels of Brynne's palms were throbbing by the time he grasped her wrists and stayed the attack with effortless grace. He pulled her toward him and, despite her almost hysterical anger, she felt her traitorous body responding to the lean, compelling pressure of his chest and hips and thighs. Against her will, she uttered one soft, despairing whimper.

The sound had a peculiar affect on Joshua. He drew her closer still, bent his magnificent head, and claimed her lips with his own. At the same time, his hands released her wrists and slid slowly down her sides to her hips. He cupped the round firmness of her bottom and pressed her to him.

Brynne felt the hard demand of his manhood and, to her chagrin, she also felt the aching expansion of her secret place as it yearned for his conquering.

The kiss broke at last, and she could sense his gaze traveling over her, even though she couldn't see his face very clearly. She shuddered as he began unbuttoning her baggy flannel shirt and her breasts pulsed in wanton anticipation of nourishing him.

"Joshua," she whispered. "We can't . . . they'll know . . ."

He laughed gruffly, his thumb and forefinger sliding beneath her muslin camisole to pluck with gentle insistence at one distended nipple. Searing lances of desire quivered in every part of Brynne's body. "They already know, Pippin," he said.

Brynne trembled as wanton hungers and the need to rebel warred within her. It did no good to remind herself of their fundamental differences or of the humiliating scene he'd just made in front of a hundred men. She could think of nothing but the sweet glories of joining her body with his.

Easily, he lifted her, his hands on her waist, until her feet were far from the floor of the tent and her breasts were on a level with his face. The war was lost as his lips closed, warm and moist, over one throbbing, muslin-covered nipple. Brynne herself tore her camisole, with one hand, so that she could be bared to him.

When Joshua had taken satisfaction at one breast, he idly sampled the other, showing no signs of tiring, even though he still held Brynne high off the ground.

Finally, however, with a low groan, he lowered her slowly to her feet, so that her soft, pliant curves chafed his hard frame in passing.

Brynne offered no protest as he lowered her to the bed of scratchy burlap sacks and removed her shirt and torn camisole with deft hands. Her borrowed trousers and drawers met the same delicious fate.

Brynne bit her lower lip to keep from crying out with pleasure and urgency as he entered her. The coupling was an angry one, swift and fierce, but it was no less rapturous for Brynne than their other, more tender encounters. The animal needs within her, heightened by his hard, furious thrusts, drove her quickly to a searing release.

Only a moment later, Joshua trembled upon her, lunged deep, and shuddered violently. A low growl echoed in the dark, musty tent.

"Woman," he breathed, in a tone that was at once accusatory and tender, "*damn* you for what you do to me."

Brynne blushed, still trembling herself, still joined with this impossible, magnificent, contradictory man. "For what *I* do to *you?*"

Joshua swore and rose to his knees in a graceful,

rolling motion. In the half light, Brynne saw that he was righting his clothes.

She blushed again, to think he'd taken her in the middle of a lumber camp, in broad daylight, and not even bothered to disrobe. Suddenly, she felt cheap and wounded and badly used.

"You had no right," she whispered miserably.

"Speaking of rights," rumbled the Half-Breed, flinging her discarded shirt and trousers and drawers at her, "what in the hell are you doing up here?"

Brynne kept her eyes down as she wriggled into her clothes. "I don't have to account to you, Joshua Tanner," she muttered.

His hand was rough as it caught under her chin and lifted. "This time you do, spitfire. This is my camp and those are my men out there."

Color pounded in Brynne's cheeks as she imagined how the lumberjacks must be speculating about what the Half-Breed and his woman were doing in the tent. Probably, they would leer at her when she came out. "They'll laugh," she said aloud, in distracted misery, her eyes averted from Joshua's face despite his grasp on her chin.

"They wouldn't dare. But they'll talk about this for years, thanks to you."

Brynne broke his hold on her chin with an angry thrust of her arm. "Thanks to me? It wasn't my idea to come in here and . . . it wasn't my idea to come in here!"

Joshua laughed. "You little she-wolf. If I had any sense at all, I'd blister your delectable little bustle."

"You'd just better not, Joshua Tanner! You'll rue the day you lay a hand on me!"

She saw his head move in a slow, resigned nod. "Pippin, I rue the day I *met* you."

"Thank you very much!"

"Don't mention it. And don't ever, *ever* come up here again, Brynne. It's dangerous." Almost as an afterthought, he gripped her shoulders. "Now, do whatever you have to do, because we're leaving for Seattle as soon as I've talked with a few people."

"We're not going anywhere!" gasped Brynne, her fingers trembling as she tried to button her shirt.

Joshua, kneeling, thrust her hands aside with gentle impatience and took over the task for her. "I'm taking you down off the mountain today and that's that."

"Evan won't let you!" Brynne snapped. "He doesn't approve of you!"

"That may well be, Pippin, but the fact remains that he thinks taking you back to Seattle is a grand idea." He'd buttoned the shirt to the very last button then, but his hands lingered gently on Brynne's tingling neck.

The knowledge that she would surrender to him all over again, at the slightest provocation, caused her to tremble with mingled rage and shame. The hopelessness of it all brought tears to her eyes.

Joshua's thumbs rose to her face, gently drying it. "Brynne, I—"

She sniffled, wanting to twist away from him but unable to move. "All those men out there are probably saying I'm your woman," she said in despair.

"The Half-Breed's woman," he said, as though tasting the words and, indeed, the prospect itself.

Brynne's mouth fell open for a moment. "You call yourself 'the Half-Breed'?"

His powerful shoulders moved in a shadow-ridden shrug. "Why should I be different?"

"Doesn't it hurt, when they say that?"

Joshua shook his head, and the unspoken lie was visible in the motion.

Brynne swallowed, so desperate to change the subject that she blurted out the first concern that came to mind. "What did my father do, Joshua, that would make you call him a butcher?"

Joshua's hands fell away from her, leaving an aching void on the flesh they had just caressed. "Not here, Brynne. We can't talk about it here."

"Where, then?" pressed Brynne, scrambling to her

feet. A wild, twisting dread was writhing now, in the pit of her stomach, and she felt as though she wouldn't be able to breathe until he'd answered her question.

"I don't know," he said grimly. And then he stood up, some private despair visible in the broad set of his shoulders, turned, and left the tent.

Chapter Fourteen

Brynne scrambled to her feet and scurried after the Half-Breed. Leaving the tent and facing all those leering men would be hard enough without having to do it alone.

Joshua's strides were long as he walked away, and Brynne, to her outrage, nearly had to run to keep up with him. Though most of the men had now gone further up the mountain to work, she could feel the amused gazes of those remaining in every pore.

"Are you hungry?" snapped the Half-Breed, almost as though she were a bothersome child getting underfoot.

"Yes!" hissed Brynne, more because she sensed he was hoping that she wasn't than because she felt a need for food.

He took her elbow in a grip that bordered on pain and half-dragged, half-thrust her toward the cookhouse. The flapjacks were still nailed to its door, though they were sliding precariously.

Brynne's curiosity got the better of her defiance and her pride, and she wrinkled her nose. "Why—"

Joshua's fierce orchid gaze lingered only briefly on

the impaled flapjacks. "It means the men don't like the food. Still hungry?"

Brynne was pondering the question when he tossed her through the doorway. Here, as at Minnie Blode's, the floor was shredded to a spongy mash by the loggers' calked boots, and there were long, rough-hewn tables everywhere.

Unlike Minnie's place, the shadowy interior smelled of sweat and dust and rancid grease. The cook, a skinny little man with an unkempt beard, stood at the stove, simultaneously stirring the contents of a kettle and scratching one armpit.

Brynne whirled and scrambled past a grimly amused Joshua Tanner and stood, gasping, on the step. Even the occasional lewd assessment of a passing lumberman was easier to endure than the inside of that cookhouse.

While Joshua harangued the cook in colorful terms, giving him two hours to clean the place up or leave camp, Brynne recovered her composure. Beyond a yoke of oxen and a wagon loaded with tools, Evan Pierpont was herding another group of men into a pose.

She stormed toward her betrayer, her head held high, her hands swinging at her sides. Reaching him, she came to a threatening stop, not at his shoulder or behind him, but directly in front of the camera.

Evan came out from under the drape scowling. "What the . . . I've got pictures to take . . ."

"You told him!" Brynne accused, freshly stunned and outraged at the notion. "You told Joshua Tanner that I was here!"

Evan stood his ground, raised plump hands to his thickening hips. "He asked," the photographer said mildly.

"I thought you were my friend!"

"I am," said Evan. "And that's why I pointed you out. Now, get out of my way, please. I've got work to do."

Blushing, Brynne stepped aside.

Evan was draping himself and the camera again. "Watch out for the lice," he said.

Brynne swallowed hard. "Lice?"

Evan was focusing. "Lice," he repeated. "If you get them, we'll have to dip you in kerosene."

Brynne suddenly itched from head to toe. Then, with an indignant toss of her head, she put the feeling that the noxious little bugs were crawling all over her down to fancy and marched away, toward Evan's wagon. She would wait there until she had decided what to do.

Surreptitiously, his face hidden beneath the draping, Evan Pierpont watched as the girl fled. Lord, the way she looked in those trousers made a man's blood churn in his veins. No wonder the Half-Breed wanted her.

Evan thought of that glowering giant hauling Brynne off over one shoulder. God knew what they'd done in that tent, though the general idea certainly wasn't hard to grasp. He smiled to himself.

Whatever else the Half-Breed might be, he was no liar. He'd told Evan that he loved Brynne McFarren, that he bore no grudge against her for her father's mistake, that he would protect her always. That was good enough for Evan.

He fixed his attention on the preening choke setters gathered before his camera and sincerely hoped that, this time, the Half-Breed hadn't bitten off more than he could chew.

Miranda was in no mood, that rain-washed morning, to exchange barbs with Corrine Temple. Brynne was gone and so was Joshua and when Drew made the obvious deduction, all hell would break loose.

All the same, Miranda Tanner was nothing if not a cordial hostess, so she went to the parlor to at least greet her guest. Corrine was standing at the desk, looking somewhat somber in a gray dress and cloak, her eyes fixed on the paperwork Joshua always left behind him like a trail. She started as Miranda made her presence known.

"Good morning."

Corrine's blue-green eyes looked wounded and hollow as they rose to Miranda's face. "Where is he?" she asked, without preamble.

Miranda lifted her chin. "Joshua?" she stalled, trying to look puzzled.

"You know damned well it's Joshua I want to see," snapped Corrine. "Where is he? With Brynne McFarren?"

I pray that he is, thought Miranda. "I don't know, Corrine. When I got up this morning, he was gone."

"What about the girl?"

Miranda hated to lie, even to someone like Corrine, who had no business questioning Brynne's whereabouts anyway, but this time she managed it. "Brynne has been ill. She's still in bed."

Corrine looked relieved, and her sudden smile was pretty, if somewhat vicious. "I see. I've remembered who she is, Miranda. Her father was the doctor that—"

Just then, Drew came bolting into the parlor, shoving his way past Miranda and sneezing inelegantly before he turned to face his sister and demanded, "Where is she? She's with Joshua, isn't she?"

Miranda closed her eyes and swore silently. When she opened them, she saw that Corrine was glaring at her and so was Drew.

"Where is Brynne?" repeated Drew, furiously.

Miranda noted his watery eyes and reddish nose with wry amusement. He'd caught Brynne's cold, probably by kissing her. "I don't know," she said, in all honesty.

"Damn!" Drew roared, and then he was overcome by a rather comical, if germy, spate of sneezes and coughs.

"You lied to me!" cried Corrine, her lower lip thrust out.

"He took her back to Port Propensity!" barked

Drew, before he succumbed to another bout of coughing.

Miranda had her doubts about that, but it seemed fortuitous that both Corrine and Drew seemed to subscribe to the theory. If they both charged off to investigate, Joshua would have time to find Brynne, bring her back, and work out some sort of plausible story. "I suppose," she began, with an uncertainty calculated to further their suspicions. "Yes, I suppose that might have happened."

Barely ten minutes had passed before Drew and Corrine were on their way to Port Propensity. Just to be on the safe side, Miranda found Cook's husband and sent him off to the telegraph office to dispatch a warning to Joshua.

Brynne tried her best to ignore Joshua Tanner as he strode confidently toward the wagon, where she sat, with as much decorum as possible, on the high wooden seat.

Reaching her, he extended a hunk of stale-looking bread. "Sorry, Pippin. It was the cleanest thing I could find."

Starving, Brynne snatched the morsel from his hand and angrily began to eat it. It was probably fortunate, she thought, that she was too upset to taste anything.

The wagon shifted and creaked as Joshua climbed deftly up the side and sat down beside a recalcitrant, sullen Brynne. Now that Evan had turned traitor, there was no one near to take her part, no one to stand between her and the Half-Breed.

"Brynne."

She chewed industriously, refusing to turn and meet the fierce lavender eyes, refusing to acknowledge his presence at all.

He laughed. "You need a bath," he announced.

Incensed, Brynne pivoted to glare at him and found herself trapped by a searing orchid gaze. Her bread scrambled into her throat, flailing there, blocking anything she might have said.

One of Joshua's hands came up to rest tenderly on her passion-tangled hair. "There's a cabin just over the hill," he began hoarsely, his eyes pulling at her lips somehow, causing them to part. "We could talk there."

He didn't have talking in mind, but Brynne couldn't gather enough wind to say so. If she drew a breath now, she knew, she would certainly choke on the bread she'd just swallowed.

Just as though she'd agreed to the plan, Joshua Tanner vaulted easily to the ground and lifted an unprotesting Brynne after him. People were staring again as he pulled her, by one hand, toward the fragrant, lush woods bordering the camp.

They must have traveled a hundred yards or so before Brynne tossed aside the crust of her bread and dug in her heels in stubborn rebellion.

"I'm not going anywhere with you, Joshua Tanner," she announced.

Dapples of tree-strained sunlight danced on his soiled, rumpled shirt front as he folded his arms and looked down at her. "You could always scream," he suggested affably, as though it were a shared dilemma.

Brynne bent her head and kicked furiously at a fern growing in the brown-and-green, needle-carpeted path. All around them, birds sang in blithe accompaniment to her quandary. In the distance, she could hear the chortling chug of the donkey engine, the profane shouts of the workers, the bray of oxen. And then there was a cry and the very earth itself shook beneath her feet. A loud, rumbling, scraping sound echoed up and down the mountain.

Without thinking, Brynne grasped at Joshua's arms and held on for dear life. "What is that?"

He laughed and drew her close. His embrace was as tender as the deep amusement in his voice. "It was a tree, Brynne," he said. "Going down the dry chute."

231

Brynne felt foolish, but she was still a little shaky, too. Suddenly, she was very conscious of her small size in relation to a very large and dangerous world. "Oh," she said, suppressing an urge to sink against this towering man in shameful weakness.

His lavender eyes were gentle on her face, and they sparkled as he bent and lifted her easily into his arms. "What is it about you, Pippin," he whispered gruffly, "that makes me forget all my good intentions?"

Brynne had no desire, at that point, to stand on her own two feet. "I didn't know you'd ever had a good intention, Joshua Tanner."

He laughed. "Touché, Pippin."

The cabin was some distance away, secreted away in a copse of towering pines. Grass grew, lush and impossibly green, around its log walls, and trillium and wild tiger lilies rioted everywhere.

The one-room interior was surprisingly clean—a bed stood in one corner, neatly made, and there were no cobwebs hanging from the ceiling. A small black stove gleamed in the corner opposite the bed, and there was even a table with a blue-and-white checkered cloth draped over it.

"Who lives here?" Brynne wanted to know, as Joshua finally set her on her feet.

"I do," he answered, moving past her to take kindling and wood shavings from a brass bin beside the stove and lay a fire.

Brynne was startled. "But you live—"

He laughed again. "The Half-Breed has many lodges," he said. "Seattle, Tacoma, Port Propensity, here. It boggles the mind, doesn't it?"

"You come here when you want to be alone," guessed Brynne, feeling at once stricken and pleased.

He nodded and reached for a sizable copper tub that was hanging from a peg on the cabin wall. "You, believe it or not, are my first guest."

Brynne tilted her head to one side, studying him, and

he laughed at the skepticism in her face when he turned, the tub still in his hands.

"You don't believe me!" he accused.

Brynne squared her shoulders and tried to look as though she didn't feel jealous of previous guests. "You must have lots of women."

"One."

Brynne blushed miserably. "Corrine?"

"Guess again."

She tossed her head in wretched defiance. "I wouldn't know any of the others."

Joshua shook his magnificent head in good-natured bewilderment and walked past her. "I'll get the water for your bath, Miss Brynne McFarren. Don't go away."

Brynne stumbled to the quilted bed, sat down on its edge, and then bolted to her feet again, as though it had burned her bottom. Heavens, first she'd spread herself like a harlot in the tent in camp, and now here she was alone with Joshua Tanner in the depths of the woods! Had she no scruples?

She sighed and sat down again, with resignation. Not where the Half-Breed was concerned, she didn't. Her blood was already racing in anticipation of the marvelous delights the day would probably hold.

A mischievous smile curved her lips as she heard Joshua nearing the cabin with the tubful of water, doubtless taken from some icy mountain spring. Perhaps she wasn't the only one who was vulnerable to the passions of the flesh.

He nearly dropped the brimming tub when he came in and saw her sitting far back on the bed, her shoulders to the wall, with one breast bared in singular invitation.

Joshua's face contorted as he set the tub carefully on top of the stove to heat and turned to survey Brynne. She felt sweet, soaring triumph as she watched his immediate and obvious response.

With a groan, Joshua came to her, stretched his powerful frame out on the bed so that he was lying sideways across her lap. She lifted gentle hands to his hair as he succumbed to a witchery as old as time itself.

It was dark outside, and no crickets sang in the grass, for another storm was brewing. Brynne sleeping peacefully on his bare shoulder, Joshua Tanner didn't care if the whole world was washed away in a roaring downpour.

They'd made love all day, bathed each other, and made love again. His throat closed as he remembered every touch, every kiss, every caress.

God, the little imp had turned him inside out, time and again, and, just when he thought she'd exhausted her fathomless imagination, she wanted to try something new. Now, lying still at last, he was glad they didn't have to leave because he doubted he had the strength to walk across the room.

Brynne stirred beside him and he thought of what he would have to tell her. He shuddered. Things might never be the same between them again, once she knew, but he loved her too much to risk letting her hear the story from the wrong person.

Joshua closed his eyes. He'd loved Rosalie so thoroughly, so completely, so desperately. He hadn't thought it possible to care so deeply again, but he did. He loved Brynne McFarren.

Suddenly, she yawned and opened those marvelous gray eyes. Her hands moved in a slow, torturously pleasurable circle on his hard, naked stomach.

The things she'd learned—indeed, the things they'd learned together—were bright in her eyes. She moved her lips over the course her hand had just charted.

Quickly, gently, Joshua caught her head in his hands just in time to prevent the game from going further. Lord, if *that* happened again, he would be too drained to tell her, and he had to do it now, while he was filled with purpose.

"Brynne," he pleaded. "Listen to me."

She smiled mischievously, her hand sliding beneath the blanket to offer delicious torment. "I'm listening."

Joshua freed himself. "I mean it," he said, as sternly as he could. But it was so hard to even breathe, let alone talk.

Brynne's other hand moved over his thigh to tease, caress, command.

"Brynne—*Brynne!*"

The hand tightened, tugged. "What?"

Joshua Tanner groaned, fire consuming the white-hot blood in his veins, and slid down to lie flat on his back. It was hopeless.

The covers moved, and he felt Brynne's warm, soft flesh brush his side as she slid languidly downward. "Wench," he rasped.

"Is this what your women do?" she asked, in an impish, quilt-muffled voice.

Joshua cried out hoarsely in answer and arched his back.

Brynne McFarren sat up in bed, her arms wrapped around her knees. Joshua slept soundly beside her, his naked back gleaming bronze even in the darkness.

She sighed. If the men in the lumber camp had speculated about the goings-on in that tent, they must be in a perfect dither over their departure for the cabin.

Setting back on her pillow, Brynne smiled. They would say she was the Half-Breed's woman, and they would be right. Her smile faded slowly.

For how long would she enjoy that questionable status? How many nights had Corrine and the others—for Brynne was certain that there had been others—shared with him?

She shivered and closed her eyes. She couldn't hope to be Joshua's wife. He had never said he loved her, after all. And he had offered no promises for the future, either.

Tears burned in Brynne's eyes, tightly closed though

235

they were. When the Half-Breed grew tired of her, thrust her aside, she would suffer for a while and then go on with her life, however difficult that might prove to be.

In the meantime, she would love Joshua Tanner as fully and as well as she knew how. Having made this decision, Brynne McFarren slept again.

When she awakened, the gray light of a struggling dawn was at the windows and she was alone. Brynne sat up in bed, her heart pounding behind her ribcage. Had Joshua left her behind? In a panic, she scrambled out from under the covers and began tugging on her drawers and the trousers and shirt she'd stolen from Drew. Color ached in her cheeks as she imagined presenting herself to a knowing, scornful Evan, tainted merchandise no longer of use to the Half-Breed.

"Damn," she whispered, sitting down again to jerk her high-button shoes on over her scratchy black stockings.

The cabin door creaked open as she was washing her face at the basin of clean, tepid water Joshua had left on a sidetable. Her hair in damp tendrils around her face, hope throbbing in every pulsepoint, Brynne turned.

"Good morning," drawled the Half-Breed, his eyes sifting leisurely over Brynne and then searing their way back to her face.

Brynne's relief was so great that she swallowed hard and swayed a little. This evidence of weakness stung her pride and caused her to thrust out her dripping chin. Before she could speak, Joshua laid a cloth-wrapped bundle on the table in the center of the room and came to her, grinning. He took a towel from the wooden bar above the basin and gently dried her face.

His purple eyes assessed her with mingled speculation and amusement. "Regrets?" he asked, in a voice so low that Brynne was never certain whether she'd actually heard the word or simply divined it, somehow, from his manner.

Regrets. Looking up at him, in the hush of that early mountain morning, she knew that she would have plenty of regrets one day—enough to last a lifetime. For now, however, there was no room for such a wasteful emotion; for now she was filled with the warm satisfaction of his skillful loving. Throat aching, she shook her head.

Joshua bent to kiss her lightly. "All hail the mighty hunter," he said, in a gruff voice tinged with humor. "I have challenged Charlie the Cook and prevailed."

Hunger gnawed at Brynne's midsection—after all, she had had nothing to eat the day before besides the hurried breakfast Evan had thrown together over their campfire and that hunk of stale bread later on. Food had been the furthest thing from her mind when the rest of the world was sitting down to supper.

Still, she remembered the condition of that cook-house, with the flapjacks nailed to its door, and she glanced warily at the bundle on the table, her nose wrinkling. "What is it?" she asked.

Joshua laughed and swatted her playfully on the backside. "Yours is not to wonder what, Pippin. Yours is but to eat. The ride down the mountain is a long, hard one, and the last thing I need is a hungry woman whining every inch of the way."

Insulted, Brynne stuck out her chin and pushed past the giant to unwrap the food he'd wrested from Charlie the Cook. "I never whine," she said loftily.

He rounded the table, in a silent motion, to face her, and cool, reserved respect glimmered in his orchid eyes. "I can believe that. Doesn't anything in the world scare you, Pippin?"

Brynne felt the flesh on her face pinken slightly, and she averted her eyes, pretending a deep interest in the cold chicken and hard-crusted bread that would be their breakfast. *Losing you scares me,* she thought, but her words belied everything she was feeling.

"What good is being scared?" she asked.

Joshua waited until she'd sat down at the table and

then sat down himself, watching her in a way that only added to the strange uneasiness she'd been feeling ever since she woke up.

They both ate hungrily, and neither spoke.

When they'd eaten, however, Joshua searched her face, looked away, forced his gaze back to her. "Brynne—"

It took all her courage to raise her chin and meet his eyes squarely. "Yes?"

Joshua's chair scraped along the wooden floor as he stood up suddenly and turned away. He was looking out one of the cabin's two front windows, his shoulders taut in the gathering light of day. "I loved my wife," he said, after a long, wretched silence. "I loved her very much."

Brynne busied trembling hands by gathering up the scraps of their food. The Half-Breed's pain seemed to fill the cabin, like some invisible entity. "I know," she said softly.

He lowered his head slightly, his hair glinting like polished ebony in the light from the window. There was another silence, this one even more oppressive than the first, and it was all Brynne could do not to cross the room in a hurry and try to comfort this proud, stricken savage of a man.

All her instincts gathered into one restraining force, Brynne sat still, her hands folded in her lap, and waited.

Finally, Joshua turned, slowly, until she could see him in profile. His voice was soft with an anguish that tore at Brynne's heart. "Rosalie was pregnant," he began. "I was away when she went into labor. I—I thought she'd be safe with Miranda—"

Brynne closed her eyes and bit her lower lip, bracing herself. In her mind, she saw her father waking, wild-eyed, from a nightmare, heard him crying out in horror. Aching, every sense straining to know what Joshua wanted to say and yet, at the same time, resisting the information, Brynne waited.

But suddenly there was a quickening in Joshua Tanner. Brynne felt it herself and opened her eyes.

Every muscle in his body seemed taut with alertness, and he crossed the room in long strides to yank an ominous-looking rifle down from the wall over the bed. "Stay where you are," he ordered, in hoarse tones.

Brynne shivered. She couldn't have moved if she'd wanted to. "What—"

There were horses outside—she could hear them nickering in the early morning chill, hear the creak of saddle leather and the jingle of bridle bits. Added to this was the gruff meter of men's voices.

"Joshua—"

He was loading the rifle with brisk, practiced motions, and his jawline looked hard. He did not spare so much as a look for Brynne, but only muttered, "Be quiet."

"Tanner!" roared a man's voice, from the cabin's wildflower-strewn dooryard.

Carrying the rifle, Joshua went to stand just to the side of the closed door. With his free hand, he gestured for Brynne to move out of the center of the room. "Yo!" he yelled back, as Brynne marshaled her weak knees into action and scrambled over to perch on the edge of the love-rumpled cot.

"Come out," called the strange voice, and, for all its loud volume, it was oddly refined. "Bring the girl!"

Joshua said nothing.

Leather creaked as one man dismounted. The voice was nearer when it spoke again, and evenly, almost cordially modulated. "Damn it, Joshua, don't be so inhospitable. We've been riding in the rain all night. The least you could do is offer us some coffee or something."

Joshua was still silent. His glance swung, briefly, in unmistakable warning, to Brynne. Then he cocked the rifle.

"You've got McFarren's daughter in there," the man

went on calmly, causing icy fingers to play scales on Brynne's rigid backbone. "I want her."

Joshua let his forehead rest against the cabin wall, drew a deep, visible breath. "She isn't here, Austin."

"You're a liar," came the companionable retort, from just the other side of the bolted door. "Send her out and we'll go."

"I said she isn't here."

"And I say she is. So did Sam Prigg and about half the men over at Number Three."

Brynne saw Joshua's sun-bronzed hand tighten on the rifle and felt profound, breath-stealing fear. Who were these men, and why did they want her? Had they hurt Sam Prigg?

"Look out the window, Joshua," Austin urged, in that same terrifyingly cordial voice. "We've got your sister. And we know the girl is with you."

Brynne's blood seemed to fill her veins to the bursting point as Joshua slipped to the window, looked out, and swore. "If you've laid a hand on her, Darnell, I'll pull your liver out through your nostrils."

"Give us the girl."

"Go to hell."

"I'll kill Miranda, Josh. Right here, right now. And I've learned some tricks that will make it truly unpleasant for her."

Soundlessly, as bemused as a sleepwalker, Brynne got to her feet and was looking out the window before Joshua pierced her with a menacing glare.

Miranda sat proudly, sidesaddle, atop a dancing pinto mare, her hands bound, her dark hair tangled and falling from its pins, her skirts billowing in the soft morning breeze. Brynne gasped as Joshua gripped her wrist and flung her backward, away from the window, onto the floor.

She got as far as her knees before he stopped her with a scorching look. "Why do you want me?" she choked out, to the invisible Austin.

Joshua swore under his breath, and the look he

hurled in Brynne's direction made her wonder whether she would be safer outside the cabin than in.

Austin laughed, for all the world like a gentleman exchanging light repartee with good friends. "She's not in there, eh? You always were a bad liar, Joshua." He paused, then went on. "Listen to reason, my friend. We have your sister. You've probably had a very entertaining night. Why not call it good? What, after all, is one pretty little roll in the straw compared to your own flesh and blood?"

Joshua drew a deep, measured breath. "Send Miranda in here, and I'll come out."

"I don't want you, Josh. At least, not now. Right now, I want that butcher's kid."

"You'll have to kill me first."

"No, I won't. I can kill Miranda, remember?"

"You don't want to do that," replied Joshua, with admirable calm, his attention mercifully diverted from Brynne, who was, by then, inching toward the rear part of the cabin. "There won't be any place to hide if you do."

Brynne was only half hearing the conversation now. She'd reached the bed and was studying the shuttered window above it. Joshua was too bone-stubborn to turn her over to the riders outside in exchange for Miranda, even though he had to know that they were in earnest.

Terrified, Brynne knew only one thing for certain, that she couldn't let Miranda die because of Austin's grudge against her father and herself, whatever it was. In a lightning motion, she leaped onto the bed, pushed open the window and the shutters beyond, and was hurtling through the opening before Joshua could reach her.

She landed in a heap in the damp, fragrant grass and righted herself quickly. She was rounding the corner of the cabin to face the riders and the mysterious Austin at the same moment that Joshua kicked open the door and came out.

Austin, a remarkably handsome man with light

brown hair and fresh, well-cut clothes, spared only a second to stare at Brynne, but that second was enough, for within it, Joshua got hold of him and wrenched him into a lethal choke hold.

With his right hand, the Half-Breed yanked a thin, glistening knife from its place inside the startled Austin's coat and raised it to the vulnerable place just below the man's right ear. His eyes glittered with cold fury as they swept the half-dozen gaping riders surrounding Miranda.

"My sister, if you please," he said, in a rasping, demonic voice.

Miranda grinned, assessed her captors briefly, and saw, as Brynne did, that they weren't about to risk Austin Darnell's life by trying to detain her. She slid, with consummate dignity, from her perch on the pinto's back and walked elegantly toward the cabin.

Joshua's purple gaze moved over the riders in dismissal, though he still held Darnell, still pressed the point of the knife to his flesh. "Ride out!" he shouted.

"What about Mr. Darnell?" dared one man.

The Half-Breed's massive, muscle-corded shoulders moved in a deceptively idle shrug. "If we get back to Seattle without any trouble, so does he. Ride, before I gut him."

The men turned, slowly, and disappeared into the thick woods. When they were gone, Joshua ignored Brynne and Miranda and flung the thwarted Austin off the cabin's small porch into the grass.

Chapter Fifteen

CONTEMPT AND HATRED PLAYED IN JOSHUA'S FACE AS HE studied the man sprawled on the ground. "You'd better thank God there are women here," he said.

Miranda stepped up to her brother and extended her bound hands. "Yes, Joshua, I'm all right," she said, with a wry twist of her mouth. "Thank you so much for asking."

The Half-Breed's eyes caught briefly, dangerously, on a stunned Brynne, who was still cowering at the corner of the cabin, before coming unreadably to his sister's face. Without a word, he untied her hands and approached Austin Darnell with the length of rope that had bound Miranda.

"Now, Josh, just a—" sputtered Darnell, struggling part way to his feet.

With a well-aimed boot, Joshua caught him in the middle of the chest and sent him sprawling again. Easily, he gripped one of the man's wrists and wrenched it around behind him with such force that Darnell grimaced and willingly offered the other wrist to be bound to the first.

"There's some twine in the cupboard," allowed the

Half-Breed tersely, without looking up from his flushed, humiliated captive. "Get it."

Miranda obeyed with cool dispatch, and then watched calmly as her brother bound Austin Darnell's elegantly booted feet. Brynne leaned against the splintery wall of the cabin, gaping.

The pit of her stomach swirled within her when, at last, the Half-Breed was satisfied that Austin couldn't escape. In that moment, he straightened and fixed a scathing gaze on Brynne.

"Uh-oh!" sang Miranda, folding her arms.

"Didn't I tell you," the Half-Breed began, in a deadly whisper, his eyes riveted on Brynne, "to stay put and keep quiet?"

Brynne managed a half-hearted, quirky smile, for all her inward trembling. "What are you so upset about?" she asked, holding her hands out wide in a gesture meant to remind him that all's well that ends well. "If it hadn't been for me, you wouldn't have got the jump on this rascal and Miranda wouldn't be free!"

Joshua's face was so hard, so impervious. It was difficult to believe that this was the same man who had taken pleasure at her breasts in the night, who had whispered gentle pleas, who had moved upon her in graceful, urgent passion. He was an angry stranger now, and he didn't seem at all grateful for Brynne's grand sacrifice.

"You could have been killed," he said coldly, advancing one step toward her.

Brynne backed away, stumbled, landed on her rump in the verdant grass. "Now, Joshua . . ."

He was approaching rapidly now, in long, fierce strides. Desperate, Brynne turned, planning to scramble away.

But Joshua caught the back of her trousers, at the waistline, in one inescapable hand, and wrenched her to her feet. She was gasping with surprise and no small measure of fear when he swung her around in a wide arc and propelled her toward the cabin.

She uttered a strangled cry of alarm and fury as he thrust her past an unprotesting Miranda to send her sprawling through the cabin doorway.

Brynne was just getting to her feet when he picked up the rifle, handed it to his sister, and indicated Austin Darnell with a sharp nod of his head. "If he moves," rumbled the Half-Breed, "shoot him."

Blithely, as though called upon to perform such tasks every day of the week, Miranda took the gun and aimed it squarely at Austin Darnell's head.

Joshua kicked the door shut behind him with one heel and glared at Brynne. "Woman," he said, in an evenly governed voice. "When I tell you to stay put, you will stay put. And when I tell you to keep quiet, *God help* you if you don't."

Brynne was terrified, but her fierce Scottish pride was in full play. "No man gives me orders," she said, standing her ground.

Joshua's powerful hands came to rest on his hips and he searched the ceiling for a moment, his throat working with suppressed fury, his jawline trimmed in white. When his eyes came back to Brynne's flushed face, they were calmly lethal. He studied her briefly and then closed the gap between them in one lunging stride.

Brynne howled in stunned outrage as he gripped her wrist in an iron grasp, sat down on the edge of the bed, and flung her, face down, across his lap. She struggled valiantly, but he subdued her with maddening ease by scissoring her thighs between his muscular legs.

After that, his words were punctuated by hard, stinging blows to her upended posterior. "I've—never —struck—a woman—in my life—but you—*by God*— are the exception!"

Brynne wanted to scratch his eyes out, to kill him, but her struggles were in vain. She had no choice but to endure the outrage, but she didn't have to endure it in silence. She screamed the whole time, at top volume.

* * *

Miranda smiled at the man looking up the rifle barrel as Brynne's shrieks echoed through the clean morning air.

"Good God," breathed Austin, frowning in a gentlemanly fashion. "It sounds like he's killing her."

Miranda only nodded.

Austin maneuvered himself into a sitting position. "Aren't you going to rush in and rescue her?"

"Rescue her? If I were strong enough, I'd have spanked her myself. Now, shut up, you bastard, before I blast you to nasty little bits."

An intelligent sort, Austin fell into a spell of silent reflection.

The ride down the mountain promised to be every whit as arduous as Joshua had predicted. As she rode beside Miranda, uncomfortable on the plodding horse borrowed from the rumuda at the lumber camp, Brynne had plenty of time to consider her own impetuous nature.

There was no need to think about her throbbing derriere, for every motion of the horse beneath her was a stinging reminder.

Miranda, as at home on horseback as she would have been in the seat of her fine carriage, pretended an interest in the two men riding just ahead—her half-brother and the captured Austin Darnell. Brynne couldn't help admiring the woman—even after what must have been a dreadful night, and that followed by the scuffle at Joshua's cabin, she was every inch the lady.

"How did you end up with that gang, Miranda?"

Miranda's eyes shifted to Brynne's face. The usual warmth was there, along with relief, but there was anger, too. "I was having tea in the garden when Austin and his friends came to call."

"And they just . . . just grabbed you?"

"Something like that."

"Why didn't you scream? Drew would have helped you."

Miranda tilted back her head and studied the glowering sky. "Drew had gone chasing off to Port Propensity, looking for you. Brynne, why did you leave like that?"

Brynne had known the question was inevitable, and she'd considered her answer. "I thought it would be better if I wasn't in your way."

"I see."

"Did the men hurt you, Miranda?"

Miranda smiled. "I've had better nights. However, Austin is smart enough to know what would happen to him if he touched me."

They were leaving the narrow, rutted, path of a road now—Joshua had decided that it would be wiser not to use it, just in case Austin's men decided to try anything. They would, instead, follow the dry chute down the mountain. "Who is he—this Austin man—and why did he want to abduct me?"

Miranda tensed her shoulders, drew in a deep breath, and relaxed again. "I think it's Joshua's place to explain that, not mine."

"Will they send him to prison?"

Miranda considered only briefly. "Unfortunately, no. He's a rich, powerful man and he'll be released within the day. Right now, however, he's valuable; as long as we have him, his men will keep their distance."

Brynne shuddered involuntarily. She was dirty and hungry and her bottom stung. What new glories would the day hold? "I'm sorry, Miranda, for getting you into this."

The dry chute was in sight now; it was a deep, wood-lined trench dug right into the side of the mountain and, even as they approached, their horses dancing skittishly, a massive timber roared past, shaking the earth as it went. Miranda waited for the din to subside before she answered.

"There are few things I wouldn't forgive you for, Brynne. I know you didn't mean for any of this to happen, so forget it."

"But . . ."

Miranda's eyes darkened with weary purpose. "Just don't hurt either of my brothers, Brynne. That I wouldn't overlook."

Brynne ached to think of all the things Miranda must be thinking about her. After all, hadn't it been all too obvious that she had spent the night with Joshua, alone, in that isolated cabin? "I wouldn't do that, Miranda."

"Maybe not purposely," said Miranda, in a voice made of dignity, good breeding, and steel. "You know, I suppose, that they both want you, that they had serious differences even before you came into their lives?"

Brynne nodded. "Yes. They hate each other, don't they?"

"It would be more accurate to say that Drew hates Joshua."

"I—I tried to get away, Miranda. I didn't want to hurt Drew, and I know I can never have Joshua. But somehow he found out that I'd gone to the lumber camp with Evan Pierpont and he came to get me."

Miranda's dark eyes assessed Brynne dispassionately. "It's too late to run from Joshua now, Brynne. There isn't any place that's far enough. He's in love with you."

Miserably, Brynne shook her head. "No. He just— he just wants me. For the moment, I'm his woman."

"And you're willing to settle for that?"

Another timber came raging down the mountain, through the dry chute, and, even though they were at least a hundred yards from the chasm, the noise was deafening. "What else can I do?" Brynne asked, in a tremulous, choked voice, once she could be sure of being heard. "He doesn't love me."

Miranda's mouth fell open. After a moment, however, she recovered herself. "Men don't always say what they feel, Brynne, especially men like Joshua."

Brynne cursed the tears smarting in her eyes. Why couldn't she hate that impossible man? Good heavens, he'd sullied her, even assaulted her, after a fashion, and here she was mourning the transitory nature of their alliance! "Joshua was telling me—just before you came this morning—how very much he'd loved Rosalie. He loves her still, Miranda, and I don't think he'll ever stop."

Miranda sighed. "Why do you think he can't stay away from you, Brynne? Believe me, it isn't just your favors. As indelicate as it may be to say so, Joshua isn't exactly destitute for feminine attention."

Remembering the impossibly beautiful Corrine Temple, Brynne winced. "I'm only one of many, Miranda."

Suddenly, startlingly, Miranda laughed. "You? One of many? Why, that's delightful, Brynne. Just how many women do you think would dress up in a man's clothes and go traipsing off to a lumber camp?"

Brynne blushed and lifted one hand to dash away her tears. There was no defense for her behavior—it was shameful, scandalous, unheard-of. "I'm sorry," she said lamely, after a long time.

Miranda smiled knowingly. "I imagine you are. But, ten to one, you'll be in trouble again before the rest of us catch our breath."

Brynne glared at the imperious, dark-haired man riding just ahead, with Austin Darnell. Fresh outrage filled her. "He *beat* me," she marveled. "He threw me over his knee like a child and he—"

Miranda feigned horror and shock. "No!" she cried, pursing her lips and rounding her magical, dark eyes and raising one hand to her throat.

Brynne ducked her head, embarrassed. "You heard," she muttered, stricken.

"And so did everyone else within ten miles," agreed Miranda. "Just don't expect any sympathy from me on that score, Brynne McFarren. I don't think men should spank women, and I'm pretty sure Joshua would agree, but you had that one coming."

Having no answer, Brynne kept her peace.

Midway down the mountain, Joshua lifted one arm in a signal that he had deigned to stop. Brynne was tired and her backside was sore, but she was angered by his easy, presumptive command. Letting her horse's reins fall to the ground, she slid gingerly from its back and folded her arms as the Half-Breed strode toward her.

Miranda, for all her disapproval, took a protective stance beside Brynne. Her eyes met Joshua's scathing lavender gaze intrepidly. "Do you think they're following us?"

Joshua's towering frame seemed charged with some indefinable emotion. He glanced toward the woods, his eyes catching only briefly on Brynne's furious face, and shook his head. "We'll get to Seattle without any trouble. After that, anything could happen."

High overhead, dark clouds collided silently in the brooding sky. Brynne felt the first sprinkles of warm rain touch her upturned face. "Why did those men want me, Joshua?"

Miranda walked nonchalantly away, toward Austin Darnell, who, though he had been allowed to dismount, was still bound securely at the wrists.

Joshua sighed. "That's a long, complicated story, Brynne, and we don't have time for conversation right now. Suffice it to say that Austin blames you for something your father did."

"What? Joshua, I know it has to do with your—your wife and baby, but how would that concern him?"

"He was in love with Rosalie."

The rain was coming down harder now, in pelting droplets. Joshua ignored it, even as it drenched his dark hair and the shoulders of his bedraggled shirt. Just for a moment, he let all the pain he'd been hiding since Brynne met him show in his eyes.

Then, before Brynne could press a single word past her constricted throat, he turned and strode away. The horses were allowed to rest for a few minutes and drink at a stream nearby, and then the journey resumed.

It was twilight when the four riders reached the base of the mountain and neared Seattle.

Brynne and Miranda were summarily ordered to go home, while Joshua and Austin went on into the city itself to pay a call on the sheriff.

At the Tanner house, the women turned their horses over to a gaping stablehand—Cook's husband—in weary silence. As if to lend reassurance, Miranda linked her arm through Brynne's as they walked toward the house itself.

Clucking with motherly disapproval, Cook took in Brynne's unconventional garb and Miranda's dishevelment and sent Placie and Clarissa scrambling to heat bathwater.

When Miranda had finished her ablutions, Brynne helped empty the tub and then refill it. Placie hovered in the downstairs dressing room even as Brynne stepped behind the screen to take off Drew's clothes.

"You been on the mountain with the Half-Breed all this time!" babbled Placie, delighted. "Glory be, Drew and Miss Temple aren't going to like that!"

"Go away, Placie," Brynne muttered, coming out from behind the screen, wrapped in a towel, and stepping into the tubful of hot water.

Placie stood fast, though she did have the good grace to turn her back so that Brynne could toss the towel aside and sink into the steaming bath. "You scared us all to death, Brynne McFarren, disappearing like that! And then Miss Miranda was gone, too! I declare, Cook's been crying and fussing and wringing her hands the whole time—"

Brynne closed her eyes and sank gratefully to her chin in the spacious tub. "We're both all right, Placie," she said.

Placie turned, her arms folded, her eyes sparkling. "What was it like, Brynne, being alone with the Half-Breed and wearing trousers?"

"Wearing trousers has its advantages," said Brynne evasively, taking up a sponge and scented soap. "And what makes you think I've been with Joshua?"

"The look in your eyes, maybe. And you've got a sort of a—well—a *glow*. You've been under some man's covers, Brynne McFarren, and don't you try telling me you haven't. I'd wager my Sunday dress it was Mr. Tanner himself."

Deliberately, Brynne widened her eyes. "He made violent love to me, Placie," she said, with appropriate drama. "He tore my clothes off and he . . ."

Color surged into Placie's avid face. At a loss, for once in her life, she whirled and fled the dressing room in embarrassment.

If she hadn't been so bone-tired and sore, Brynne would have laughed out loud. Once she had washed her hair and gotten the mountain grime off her body, she dried herself, bundled up in the flannel wrapper someone had provided, and stumbled out into the kitchen.

Joshua was sitting at the table, idly turning a matchbox in one hand. He surveyed Brynne with a coldness that chilled her in spite of the warm robe she wore.

"Sit down and eat," he said.

Brynne's eyes fell on the plateful of warm food Cook had evidently set out for her. Lord, how she wanted to defy this domineering man and walk away, but she was wretchedly hungry.

Carefully, she sat down, took up a fork, and began consuming the roast beef, the mashed potatoes and gravy, the boiled asparagus. All this time, the Half-Breed was watching her in stony silence.

When her hunger had been eased, Brynne slid the plate away and moved to stand up.

"Don't," warned Joshua, in a voice of scratchy gravel.

Brynne colored slightly and sank back into her chair. The only rebellion she dared display was the refusal to meet his eyes. "What do you want?" she whispered.

There was a silence, and, when Joshua Tanner finally spoke, his tones were gruff with weariness and anger and something indefinable. "What do I want?" he echoed sardonically. "I want to turn back the calendar, to the Fourth of July. That done, I want to be anywhere except Port Propensity. China sounds good."

"That way you wouldn't know me."

"Exactly. But I do know you, don't I? You are the bane of my existence, but I know you and there is no changing that."

Brynne met his eyes with deliberate, caustic spirit. "Now that is a brilliant deduction," she said. "You're not only a gifted lover, you're *smart*, too."

Joshua closed his eyes, but only momentarily. It was as though he was waging some fierce, inward struggle. "I'm sorry I ever touched you, if that means anything."

Brynne was hurt, though she did her best to hide the fact. "I've had second thoughts myself," she said.

A sudden and furious gust of rain pounded at the kitchen windows, and the few kerosene lamps Cook had lit flickered eerily. "Have you?" asked Joshua, raising one dark eyebrow in grim amusement. "I could take you here if I wanted to, right now, and we both know it."

Brynne felt a warm flush rise from her stomach to her face. "You needn't boast, you arrogant—"

"I'm not boasting. You're as attracted to me as I am to you, and I don't see any point in pretending otherwise. God help me, Brynne, I'm obsessed with you. One minute I decide to keep my distance and then, the *next* damned minute, I'm in bed with you."

Brynne said nothing, but her hands were entwined in her lap so tightly that the knuckles ached.

"I even told Drew that he could have you," Joshua went on, in that low, even voice. "I went back to Port

Propensity, intending to forget you ever existed. And the second, the *second*, Brynne, that I knew he was on his way to Seattle to court you, I couldn't stay away. I walked away from my business, from everything, because I couldn't stand the thought of my brother or anyone else touching you."

"Why are you telling me this?"

He sighed, searched the murky ceiling briefly. "I guess I was hoping you would let go of me, Brynne."

Brynne was shattered by his words, and tears of stark misery burned in her eyes. Her throat ached, and her stomach was spinning within her. How brief it had been, her tempestuous time as the Half-Breed's woman. "Let go?" she whispered.

Suddenly, his hand came across the table to clasp both of hers in a warm, work-hardened grip. "I don't think you understand what I'm saying, Pippin," he told her, in gentler tones. "I—"

Brynne wrenched free of him and leaped to her feet, shame pulsing in her cheeks and tearing at her broken heart. "I understand, all right, *Mr.* Tanner! Well, you needn't think that I'll cling to your ankles and weep when you go! You're free. Go where you want to, do whatever . . ."

Joshua smiled ruefully, not bothering to stand. "How I wish I could do just that—leave, never look back. Brynne, I need you. I want you."

By now, Brynne was totally confused. Tears of weariness and pain slid down her cheeks as she collapsed into her chair again. He needed. He wanted. But would he ever love?

She sighed and covered her face with both hands. If only she could turn back the calendar, too. To the time before her father had died, before she'd met Joshua Tanner. Oh, to be back on that isolated sheep farm, totally innocent and minding her own business. A shuddering sob escaped her.

"Don't cry," Joshua pleaded, in a ragged voice. "Please, Brynne."

"I want to go home!" she cried, in weary hysteria, her shoulders moving in rhythm with her grief.

"To the farm? You could, you know—it's yours."

Brynne lowered her hands slowly to stare at Joshua Tanner. She could not deal with the strange torment she read in his face, so she concentrated on the raven-black hue of his hair, the impossible orchid of his eyes, the breadth of his shoulders. "Mine?" she asked, in a wooden voice.

"Yours," he replied evenly. "The papers are being drawn up now."

Brynne stiffened. "Is this my payment for being your woman?"

He laughed, but there was no humor in the sound. "It was a mistake in the first place—the foreclosure, I mean. So the farm belongs to you."

Brynne was on her feet in an instant, grateful for the wild, shuddering rage within her because it displaced some of her pain, some of her shame. "Now that my father is dead, you're trying to undo the damage! Well, you take that farm, Mr. All Powerful Joshua Tanner and you—"

Joshua bounded out of his chair, his face contorted, suddenly, with a rage that equaled or even surpassed Brynne's. *"Damage?"* he bellowed. "Damn it all to hell, woman, don't you stand there and talk to me about *damage!* If that drunken butcher hadn't killed himself, I would have done it for him!"

Brynne trembled, jolted to her soul by the horrible sincerity in his words. "He died because of you!"

"A fair exchange if I've ever heard one!" roared Joshua.

"Stop it, both of you!" interceded a pale Miranda, from the dining room doorway. "Joshua, leave this room, this instant. We've all had all the drama we need for one day. And as for you, Brynne McFarren, I'm giving you exactly five seconds to get up those stairs and into bed."

Brynne and Joshua exchanged murderous looks, but

neither of them spoke. Joshua strode to the outside door, jerked it open, and stormed out, leaving it to gape open to the night.

Brynne watched him go, cast one despairing look at Miranda, and scurried up the back stairway. Once in bed, she cried wretchedly for half an hour and then lapsed into a dreamless, heavy sleep.

For all her weariness and her aching muscles and her still smarting backside, she awakened early the next morning. Knowing that Joshua Tanner was nowhere in that spacious house—she could feel his absence like a void—she brushed her hair and washed and, after putting on shoes and a sprigged cambric dress, marched resolutely down the stairs to face the day.

The sun was in hiding, she saw, as she stood at the parlor windows, looking out over Miranda's garden, and rain was battering the colorful flowerbeds and dancing on the marble benches and the wrought-iron table outside.

"Well," growled a furious masculine voice, from the parlor doorway, so startling Brynne that she flinched.

Drew's hazel eyes flashed with anger as he approached her. He thrust his uninjured hand into the pocket of his tweed trousers, as though fearing that he might double it into a fist and strike her.

She met his gaze, watched in fearful wonder as the hazel glitter in his eyes turned to a dark jade color. "Hello, Drew," she managed, with much effort.

" 'Hello, Drew,' " he mocked bitterly. "Is that all you have to say?"

Brynne felt responding anger rise within her. "What should I say, Drew?"

He paused, almost as though she had brandished some lethal weapon, and the change in his face was startling. Where there had been deadly fury, Brynne saw pain. Even the shade of his eyes was affected; it shifted from jade to a tawny gold to a soft hazel. "I love you," he rasped.

Brynne stiffened. "No."

His jawline tightened, and she caught the familiar scent of his cologne as he drew nearer. "No? Why 'no,' Brynne? Because you've been rolling around in the Half-Breed's bed?"

Fury jolted through Brynne—without thinking, she raised one hand and slapped Drew Tanner as hard as she could.

Drew's eyes were jade green again as they scraped her face. "Do you possibly think," he began, in a deadly, rumbling voice, "that Joshua could or would forget his precious Rosalie for you? For anybody? My God, Brynne, wake up before it's too late! He's *using* you."

"I know," she whispered brokenly, slowly lowering her hand.

"You *know?* Then why in God's name . . ."

Brynne shook her head miserably. How could she answer that question for Drew when she didn't know the answer herself?

Drew's hand caught under her chin, and he forced her to look at him. "Marry me, Brynne. Now, today. If there's a child, we'll say it's mine."

"Why would you do that?"

"Because, God help me, I love you. I'll have you any way I can get you—including on your way out of my brother's bed!"

"How romantic," broke in a caustic, feminine voice, from across the room.

Both Drew and Brynne whirled to see Corrine Temple standing in the arched doorway of the parlor, looking rain-dampened and discouraged in an emerald green dress and trailing cloak. She sighed and tugged with ladylike grace at her spotless kid gloves.

"Accept Drew's offer, Brynne, dear," she urged. "Believe me, the Half-Breed's devotion is a transitory thing."

Brynne wanted to run, to hide, not only from this

257

knowing woman, but from Drew, also. The trouble was that her knees suddenly seemed to be made of mush and she couldn't summon the strength to solidify them.

Drew caught her arm quickly, guided her to the nearest chair, but his eyes were on Corrine Temple. "Get out, Corrine. Now."

"I'm only trying to help!"

"Well, you're not," snapped Drew.

Corrine hovered in the doorway. "So this is John McFarren's wonderful daughter—my, my."

"Corrine," warned Drew, in a voice Brynne would have been afraid to ignore, a voice she had never heard him use before.

"You know why Joshua is availing himself of your sweet charms, don't you, dear?" Corrine went on, just as though Drew hadn't spoken. "He's repaying an old and ugly debt."

Drew's good hand tightened into a fist, and he would have descended on Corrine if Brynne hadn't caught at his wrist and held on with all her strength. "No, Drew," she whispered, "please. Let her finish."

"Thank you," said Corrine sweetly, her eyes touching on Drew's taut, fury-reddened face and then slipping back to Brynne. "I guess I'd want revenge, too, if I were Joshua," she went on, with cultivated reluctance. "What happened was really so dreadful, you know."

Drew wrenched free of Brynne suddenly and stormed toward Corrine as though he meant to kill her where she stood. "Shut up," he growled. "In the name of God, Corrine, shut up!"

Corrine was dodging him, and the horrible thing she wanted to say came at Brynne in a babbling, wounding rush. "Your father was drunk—he couldn't get the baby into the right position—Rosalie was dying—he cut the child into pieces!"

Brynne screamed and bolted to her feet, and then the parlor faded into blackness.

Chapter Sixteen

EVERY MUSCLE AND TISSUE AND FIBER IN JOSHUA TANner's prone body ached. He caught the scents of kelp and sweat and rotted rope and opened his eyes. It was dark, and his hands and feet were tied.

With a rumbling groan, he tried to sit up and failed. The floor seemed to shift and roll beneath him, and, after a moment, he heard the lapping of waves and realized where he was.

Muttering a curse, he again attempted to sit up. This time, he succeeded.

All around him, in the darkness, rats scurried on whispering feet, their eyes glinting scarlet in the gloom. He drew a deep breath and began to work at the rawhide strip binding his wrists behind him.

While engaged in this largely hopeless pursuit, Joshua permitted himself to remember the events that had brought him to the hold of a filthy ship bound for God knew where. There had been the row with Brynne, in the kitchen, the night before—it had taken place the night before, hadn't it? That made today July twenty-second.

Wednesday, he thought. *It is Wednesday.* And then

he laughed at himself for caring what damned day of the week it was, anyway.

After Miranda had broken up the battle, he'd gone to the stables, chosen a horse, ridden down to Seattle, to the Skid Road. There, he'd visited one saloon and then another, desperate to get as drunk as he possibly could. Apparently, he'd succeeded. With a sigh, Joshua ceased struggling with the rawhide—it was tearing into his flesh and getting tighter all the time—and let his head rest against the pile of crates behind him. It must have happened in that last place, the one where the whore had offered him unspeakable pleasures for a bargain price.

He hadn't accepted—much as he enjoyed unspeakable pleasures, he wanted only Brynne McFarren—and the whore had been shrilly annoyed at his refusal. She must have put a few drops of chloral into his drink, because he remembered nothing after that. Nothing at all.

Joshua laughed out loud. How many times had he warned Drew to stay away from the Skid Road and places like it, where a man could be crimped and find himself working for his passage to somewhere he hadn't meant to go? God knew when the opportunity to jump ship would present itself.

While Joshua was considering the irony of it all, a hatch creaked open, admitting some light and the clean scent of rain. He saw a familiar form climb deftly down the ladder, knew before the lantern the visitor carried was lit that he was in a hell of a lot more trouble than he'd guessed.

He nodded cordially to the man towering over him. "Austin," he said.

Austin laughed. "How do you like the rawhide, Injun? We learned that little trick from your people, you know."

Joshua said nothing. He simply studied Austin's face, which was illuminated by the glow of the lantern and the gray light coming down from the hatch.

"Another hour or two and it'll feel like your hands are being sawed off," observed Austin.

Still, Joshua kept his peace.

With a sigh, Austin set the lantern aside and sat down on a crate. "And now to get down to issues," he said pleasantly. "Namely, Brynne McFarren. You know, Joshua, I don't think I'll kill her after all. She's too pretty for that. Since you are—forgive me—tied up, so to speak, I'll wire my men from the next port and have her fetched. Yes, that's it. And, when I get back to Seattle, I'll take her to bed and—"

"Shut up."

"Joshua, you disappoint me. You know very well that I don't have to 'shut up,' as you so crudely put it." He sighed and shook his head and appeared to be weighing the matter. "She's a sweet thing, isn't she? All curves and sauce and spirit. A man with that one in his bed might not miss Rosalie quite so desperately."

Joshua closed his eyes and swallowed hard.

"Tell me, Joshua, what does she like?"

Bile burned in Joshua's throat, and his voice was a razor-sharp rasp. "Men. That lets you out, Austin."

Austin's rage was palpable in the stinking hold of that ship, but he spoke evenly. "Brynne probably thinks you're dead, you know. After I get through with her, she'll almost certainly turn to Drew."

With monumental effort, Joshua kept his tones cool, even. "How did you get Sam Prigg to tell you we were on the mountain?"

Austin chuckled. "It was really so easy, Joshua. He was grumbling that you'd interrupted his honeymoon to find out where the photographer went and one of my people heard him. Miranda was in an awful state, poor darling, when I dropped by to give her my regards, and the maids were babbling about a note. Of course, I guessed the rest."

"Why did you bring my sister?"

"Insurance, Joshua. Also, I was afraid she might

guess what was going on and think of some way to warn you. She's abominably clever, you know."

"You weren't in jail long."

Austin shrugged at this observation. "An hour. Two at the most. After all, Joshua, it was my word against yours."

"Now what?"

"We dock in Portland this afternoon—briefly. I'll be leaving the ship there, I suppose, since I've decided to go back and court the fair Brynne. You, my friend, will perhaps survive a few months at sea. Won't you?"

"You'd better pray that I don't."

"Don't tempt me, Joshua. Killing you would be easy."

"Then why don't you do it?"

"That's simple. I want you to crawl first. I want you to know what I'm doing to your woman." Again, Austin's face contorted. "I promise you, Joshua, that she isn't going to enjoy it. Does that make you feel better?"

A howl of rage tore at the back of Joshua's throat, but he would not let it pass.

Austin went blithely on. "American women are spoiled, you know. Their delicate sensibilities have to be considered to such a tiresome extent. Don't worry, though. If you ever see Brynne again, which you probably won't, she'll be well taught."

Joshua spat.

Almost idly, Austin Darnell rose to his feet and took up the lamp again. "That isn't all I have planned, of course. I know you'd think me remiss if I left that little disagreement we had over Rosalie a few years ago go unavenged."

"We can't have that," snapped Joshua. "Tell me, though, Austin. What do you have planned?"

Austin only smiled. Then, after extinguishing the lamp, he climbed, whistling, up the ladder to the deck, where he neatly closed the hatch.

Fifteen minutes later, four seamen, each of whom

smelled worse than the hold itself, came to fetch Joshua.

It was raining, and, his hands still bound, though his feet, of course, had been freed, Joshua lifted his face to the sky. The fresh air did much to clear his fog-ridden brain.

As his escorts thrust him in the direction of the main mast, Joshua looked around. They were already at sea, and sailing at a good clip down the coast. Sure enough, they were bound for Portland.

"The shirt," said Austin, as one man cut the shrinking rawhide from Joshua's wrists and two more immediately grasped his arms. Since there was no escaping the inevitable, he offered no resistance at all.

He felt the garment tear away from his body. The salty spray felt good on his naked back.

The two men restraining Joshua flung him up against the mast, stretched his arms around it, bound him again. He lifted his head and waited.

Bobby O'Keefe watched in stricken silence as Darnell took the whip and uncoiled it. He knew the man tied to the mast—Mother of God, it was the Half-Breed himself—but he didn't dare try to stop Mr. Darnell now or he'd wind up feeling the bite of that crippling leather snake himself.

Still, he'd worked for the Half-Breed. He was a good man, and fair, and once, when Bobby had gotten into a bit of trouble on the Skid Road, Joshua Tanner had gotten him out of it again.

Darnell drew back the whip and, in that moment, Bobby O'Keefe caught the Half-Breed's eye. Tanner recognized him, shook his head in a silent warning.

Bobby closed his eyes as the whip whistled through the salty, rain-misted air and made sharp contact. Sick inside, he awaited the inevitable scream of pain.

But there was no scream. Bobby opened his eyes and watched helplessly as the Half-Breed's back was laid open, again and again. Tanner was in agony—sweat poured off his face and his jawline was so taut that the muscles stood out, clearly visible. But the man would not cry out.

Finally, when the Half-Breed's knees buckled and he went down, still tied to the mast, his back bleeding crimson, the captain wrested the whip out of Darnell's hands and flung it overboard.

"Christ, you tryin' to kill the man?" he snarled, ordering Joshua untied with a harsh nod of his head.

Darnell's face was twisted. He looked, to Bobby O'Keefe, like a madman. "He didn't scream," the ship owner breathed. "Goddamn it, the bastard didn't scream!"

"He's near dead," said one of the sailors, as Joshua Tanner folded, unconscious, and lay prone on the slippery deck.

"Jesus God," muttered the captain.

Bobby looked once more at the Half-Breed's shredded back and stumbled away to brace himself against the ship's rail and vomit over the side.

In Portland, Tanner was carried down the wharf on a litter, despite of the bellowed, maniacal protests of Austin Darnell.

And Bobby O'Keefe jumped ship.

It was all Miranda could do not to pace back and forth along the steamboat landing and wring her hands. The *Marriott* was late.

Beside her, as oblivious as his sister to the bustling profanity of Seattle's waterfront, Drew looked up at the polished blue sky and frowned. When his eyes came to Miranda's face, they were jade-green with a worry that probably matched her own. "It's been four days, Miranda," he stewed, quite unnecessarily. "My God, you'd think after *four days* she'd be coming around—"

Miranda squared her shoulders as she caught sight of the familiar steamer rounding a bend and paddling into Elliott Bay. She stared at the vessel, as though she might accelerate its approach by an act of will. "Four days isn't a very long time, Drew," she said, without looking at her brother.

Only it was. It was a very long time for a vivacious, spirited girl like Brynne to hide inside herself. Lord, in all those minutes and hours and days the child had hardly slept or eaten, and she hadn't spoken at all. It was as though she was engrossed in a continuous drama whose players were invisible to everyone but herself.

Inwardly, Miranda sighed. Would that Brynne's mental state, frightening as it was, could be all she had to worry about. But there was Joshua.

Where was he? Miranda hadn't seen her brother or heard from him since the previous Tuesday, when he and Brynne had argued so heatedly in the kitchen. Nearly a week had passed; surely he'd had adequate time to sort out the complex things she knew he'd been feeling that night, time to come to grips with his anger and his passion.

The *Marriott* came into port, her whistle shrill in the shimmering heat of that July day, and several of her crewmen bounded over her side to the creaking wharf and began making her fast.

The boarding ramp was lowered with a resounding thump, and an assortment of passengers disembarked. Miranda found herself wishing that Joshua would come striding down the wharf, safe and sound and eternally practical. If anyone could reach Brynne, he could.

But he wouldn't appear, of course. She had already made discreet inquiries and learned that her brother was not in Port Propensity or Tacoma.

Drew was beginning to fidget at Miranda's side; he hadn't wanted to leave Brynne long enough even to perform this errand. "Where are they?" he muttered.

As if in answer, Letitia appeared, followed by a scowling, wary Minnie Prigg. Letitia smiled uncertainly, looking strikingly pretty in her soft blue traveling suit, and came toward Miranda and Drew in short, anxious strides.

Her handbag dangling from one wrist, Letitia impulsively took both Miranda's gloved hands in hers. "How," she faltered, her blue eyes glistening, "how is Brynne?"

Minnie was watching Drew suspiciously, as though she suspected him of laying plans to sell the McFarren girl into slavery. "What happened?" she demanded.

To keep the tenuous peace, Miranda delayed the answers to both questions long enough to ask a seething Drew to see to the baggage still on board the *Marriott*. When he had strode off to obey, she squeezed Letitia's hands and smiled at the angry concern in Minnie Prigg's face.

"Brynne isn't well, I'm afraid," she told them gently. "She's had a nasty shock."

Letitia's bright eyes widened with sincere worry. "Someone told her what happened to Mr. Tanner's wife and baby," she guessed, in a small, distracted voice.

Miranda nodded. "I blame myself. I should have explained—"

"Who did tell her?" demanded Minnie, casting one scathing look backward, toward the steamer, where Drew was claiming an assortment of trunks and valises. "Him?"

Quickly, Miranda shook her head. "No, Minnie, it wasn't Drew. This has been so very difficult for him. He wouldn't have hurt Brynne that way—" She'd been about to add that he loved the girl, but the look on Letitia's elfin face stopped her.

Drew was approaching now, carrying a worn valise in his good hand, squinting ominously in the dazzle of sunlight that winked on the blue water. "They'll send the rest along later," he said, when he reached the three women waiting at the base of the wharf.

Letitia's gaze fell to the splint on his right hand and she paled. Before she could ask the inevitable question, Drew smiled at her, somewhat grimly, and offered his arm.

"Madame Fortuna's potion is working," he said,

and, instantly, the girl's face was a glorious shade of crimson.

To keep from wondering what would become of Brynne McFarren and where Joshua had disappeared to, Miranda pondered the mysterious remark her younger brother had just made all during the carriage ride home.

Brynne was sitting in a wicker chair in the garden, exactly where Drew had so reluctantly left her less than half an hour before. Her hands were folded in her lap and her eyes were fixed, unseeing, on the stone bird-bath, where two plump robins were performing vigorous ablutions.

"Brynne?" ventured Letitia, forgetting Drew to approach her cousin.

There was no answer, of course, and, except for a taffy-colored tendril of hair at her right temple, lifted by a passing breeze, no motion.

Letitia rounded Brynne's chair to face her, drop to her knees on the mossy, stone floor of the garden, and take the still hands into her own. "Brynne, I'm here," she said, in broken, tremulous tones. "Brynne?"

Brynne did not respond.

Letitia swallowed, searched her cousin's face with stricken eyes. "It's too horrible to bear, isn't it?" she whispered. "Oh, Brynne, I know what you're feeling."

Suddenly, Brynne trembled violently. Miranda and Drew and Minnie watched in stunned silence as she lifted her arms, raw sobs ripping themselves from her throat, and flung herself into Letitia's embrace.

Miranda felt tears rise, stinging and hot, in her eyes. *We said all the wrong things*, she thought. *We said it didn't matter, we said she mustn't blame herself. We said everything but the blunt, naked truth: that it was horrible.*

And it had been. Miranda Tanner shuddered, in the warmth of that fragrant garden, just to recall it. She glanced at Drew and saw the rigid set of his jawline, his fine shoulders, his lips. He started toward Brynne, whether drawn by her pain or thrust forward by his own, Miranda didn't know, and then hesitated. Gently, Miranda caught his arm and led him away, and a disconcerted Minnie followed.

Letitia's voice was a soft, tender song of reason behind them as she comforted her cousin.

Drew scowled as he turned from the liquor cabinet in the cool parlor and extended drinks to both Minnie and Miranda before taking up his own.

"Why couldn't we reach her?" he asked, of no one in particular.

Miranda sighed. "Perhaps because we weren't willing to face what really happened ourselves, Drew," she said.

Minnie Prigg took a sip from her glass and savored it grimly for a moment, before adding her opinion. "Can't keep a secret like that for long. I wonder that old Doc McFarren didn't tell her himself."

"How could he, Minnie?" Miranda asked, as a headache pulsed behind her temples. "It hardly bears thinking about, let alone explaining. Dear Lord, the man's life must have been hell."

Drew was standing at the window overlooking the garden, and his concern for the shattered Brynne was almost palpable in the room. "Joshua should have told her," he said, in gruff, furious tones. "They certainly had plenty of time to talk."

Minnie Prigg was instantly alert. "Brynne and Joshua?" she mused, peering at Miranda over the rim of her double bourbon.

Miranda nodded and then quickly silenced Minnie with an eloquent shake of her head.

"Where the hell is he, anyway?" Drew thundered on, his back still turned, his gaze still fixed, apparently, on Brynne and Letitia. "My God, she's in pieces and he's probably off rolling around in the hay with one of his whores."

Miranda knew better, though she almost wished she could believe that her half-brother was with a woman.

That would be so much easier to deal with than other possibilities, such as Austin Darnell. "Drew," she protested, weakly.

At the gentle reprimand couched in his name, Drew turned. The words he said obviously cost him a vast and painful price. "Brynne needs him. Damn it, Miranda, where is he?"

"He ain't with no whore," said Minnie bluntly. "Not if he's been courtin' Brynne. Ain't the Half-Breed's way."

It wasn't Joshua's way—Minnie was right, however crudely she'd stated her case. Even his mistresses, brief though their tenure might be, enjoyed absolute fidelity while they held his quicksilver interest. And Brynne was, Miranda knew, so much more to him than a mistress.

Drew lifted his glass and tossed back its contents. His voice was hoarse when he spoke, and very unsteady. "I'm going to find our legendary brother, Miranda. Wherever he is, whatever he's doing, I'm going to find him. And when I do, he's going to be sorry he ever dallied with Brynne McFarren."

Minnie laughed, and the sound was midway between a guffaw and a hoot. "You little rooster," she said, with undisguised contempt. "If it comes down to cases, my money's on the Half-Breed. And anything you say to him better be politely put!"

Drew flushed and stormed out of the parlor. The epithet he shouted in parting would have stunned anyone but Minnie Prigg.

Miranda closed her eyes and slid deeper into her chair and wished she'd spent this particular summer in Tibet.

Giggling. Someone was giggling.

Joshua opened his eyes to see two young girls peering speculatively into his face. They paled and darted away like tropical fish, calling for their mother.

He was lying in a bed, on his stomach. But where?

He hadn't recognized the children, he didn't recognize the plain, sturdy bed or what little he could see of the room.

After drawing one deep, preparatory breath, Joshua moved to rise out of the bed. Pain raged across his back like a brush fire, and he dropped, with a guttural groan, back to the sheets.

"Lie still, now," ordered a masculine voice, from the foot of the bed. "Won't do to rip open all those wounds again."

His eyes closed against the scalding pain that lingered in every muscle from the nape of his neck to the base of his spine, Joshua bit back the screams that still raged, trapped, inside him. He remembered now, remembered being tied to the mast of one of Austin's ships, remembered the ceaseless, tearing bite of the lash.

"Who are you?" he demanded.

The man came to the side of the bed, drew up a ladder-back chair, and sat down. He was a massive man, built much as Joshua's father had been, and he had a thatch of unruly red hair and keen blue eyes. "I'm Captain Jack Dancer," he said. "And you?"

Joshua decided to withhold that particular bit of information, for the time being at least. "Why?" he countered.

"Why did Darnell whip you? Or why did I bring you here?"

"Both, I guess," answered Joshua, conscious, now, of a brutal, pulse-metered ache in his lungs. Christ, was he coming down with pnuemonia, on top of everything else?

"I figure you probably know better than I do why Darnell would want to lay your back open. I only went along with it because he said you raped his daughter."

"He doesn't have a daughter."

Jack Dancer averted his eyes. "Well, I believed him. And having two little girls myself—"

The gigglers, no doubt. In spite of everything, Joshua smiled. Would he ever have a daughter? He hoped that

270

he would, and that she would look exactly like Brynne. "No hard feelings," he managed. "This is your house, I presume?"

"It is," admitted Jack Dancer staunchly. "Needed to bring you somewheres before you up and died. Course, I'm out a ship now, since Darnell decided to sail without me. Tell me your name, son, and I'll see word gets to your family."

"Tanner," said Joshua, after a long, strength-gathering pause. "My name is Joshua Tanner."

Dancer's blue eyes widened. "Good God! You ain't the—"

Before Joshua could answer, the earth opened up and swallowed him whole, or, at least, it seemed so to him. After a while, it released him again and he floated in a dark universe dappled with cold, distant stars.

Filled with furious purpose, Drew looked in on Brynne, who was, thanks to the efforts of Letitia Jennings, sleeping soundly in her bed, and then left the house.

Rounding a high hedge, the horse he'd saddled minutes before, in the stables, trotting companionably along behind him, he nearly collided with a messenger.

"Your name Tanner?" demanded the boy, trying to wipe his sweating brow and right his bicycle at the same time.

Drew nodded, and the messenger thrust a piece of crumpled paper at him.

The telegram was headed with a street address, and its message was brief and to the point. *Mr. J. Tanner here. Wounded. Pnuemonia. Jack Dancer.*

Wounded. The word tugged at something Drew had kept hidden deep within himself for most of his life, causing it to stir painfully. In a daze, he pried a coin from his trouser pocket and thrust it at the boy. "Thanks."

"Any answer?"

Tell him not to die, thought Drew. *Tell him I don't*

271

want him to die. "No," he said, after a long pause. "No, there's no answer."

Twenty minutes later, having helped himself to Cook's entire food budget for the month and the healthy store of cash Miranda always kept in her bureau drawer, Drew set out for Portland, Oregon.

Brynne sat up in bed and sniffled. Letitia was curled up in a chair nearby, reading by the light of an elegant globe lamp. "What time is it?"

Letitia closed the book, laid it aside, came to sit on the side of Brynne's bed. "It's late, Brynne. Go back to sleep, please."

"Why aren't you asleep?" stalled Brynne, who had no desire to go back to the terrible nightmares that had so troubled her during her fitful rest.

"I wanted to look after you, goose. Are you feeling better now?"

Brynne nodded, but, at the same time, betraying tears gathered in her eyes.

Letitia took Brynne's hand in a warm, firm grasp. "It's over, darling. It's done. And there is no point in letting it torment you."

Brynne's lower lip trembled. "No wonder Joshua called my father a butcher. He was right. Oh, dear God, Letitia, he was right!"

"No," Letitia countered, shaking her head.

"But the baby—"

"It wasn't a living child, Brynne. Your father knew that."

Sobs were shaking inside Brynne, clamoring to get past her pride and her determination to be strong. "How do you know, Letitia? How do you know that the baby didn't feel the scalpel?"

Letitia's hands came to Brynne's shoulders with surprising strength. "Stop that," she ordered. "Brynne McFarren, you stop torturing yourself! I know it was a stone baby because my mother was there, helping Uncle John."

Brynne swallowed, stared at her cousin. "A stone baby?" she echoed.

Letitia nodded, bit her lip, went on. "Mama said the baby died inside Mrs. Tanner weeks before the birth. She kept it a secret because she thought it would be too hard for the—for her husband to know."

A dreadful realization was moving through Brynne, tearing at her, making her tremble. *"They never told him.* Letitia, they never told Joshua that the baby would have been stillborn, did they?"

Letitia looked puzzled and more than a little alarmed. "I don't know, Brynne," she said softly. "It was all so awful—Mrs. Tanner died and then your father ran away and Joshua was saying such terrible, terrible things about him. I think Mama must have been afraid to approach him."

Brynne threw back her covers and hurtled out of bed, her knees trembling, her stomach threatening gross rebellion. "Don't you see, Letitia! Joshua thinks that baby was alive! Oh, dear God, he *thinks it was alive."*

Letitia rose to her feet, her face grim and stern, one index finger wagging in warning. "You get back into that bed, Brynne McFarren. Right now."

"I've got to tell him!"

"You can't tell him anything—he isn't here. Now get back into bed!"

Temporarily defeated, Brynne sank back onto the tumble of crisp sheets and satiny blankets. "Where is he?"

Letitia shrugged. "I don't know, Brynne. Drew's gone off looking for him, though, so stop worrying."

Stop worrying. Brynne began to cry.

Letitia sat down again, pulled her cousin into a gentle embrace. "You love him, don't you?" she whispered miserably. "Oh, Brynne, not him! Not the Half-Breed."

"Don't call him that!" sobbed Brynne furiously. "His name is Joshua!"

"His name is Trouble," retorted Letitia. "Sleep now, Brynne, please."

"Sleep! Oh, Letitia, you don't know how he's hurting, how he's *been* hurting since Rosalie and the baby—"

Letitia sighed and pressed Brynne gently back onto the pillows. Then, calmly, she poured a dose of laudanum the doctor had left into a spoon. "Take this," she said.

Irritably, Brynne obeyed. The first dose was followed by a second, and, within minutes, she was sleeping and the nightmares were all around her.

Dawn was spilling into Portland like golden medicine into a bowl when, at last, the swift clippership *Sealth* dropped anchor, far out on the water. The tide was too low to allow her to dock.

Impatient to reach Joshua, Drew bribed two crewmen to row him ashore in a skiff.

An energetic timber town, much like Seattle, Portland was just shaking herself awake when Drew scrambled out of the boat and climbed the ladder to the wharf, his splinted hand braced against his middle.

Without looking back at the sleek *Sealth*, he strode toward the center of town, consulted the crumpled telegraph message for perhaps the hundredth time, and stopped a scurrying Chinaman to ask directions.

Jack Dancer's house was easy to find, and he reached it within five minutes.

A sturdy structure of red brick, the Dancer house had glistening windows, pristine white shutters, a porch trimmed with gingerbread scrollwork. Obviously the owners were prosperous.

Drew did not consider the early hour, he simply reached for the brass doorknocker and tapped it hard against its gleaming base. A wan looking woman wearing a crisp black dress and a small, ruffled white cap came to the door, and her eyes were wary as they assessed his stubble of a beard, his travel-rumpled clothes, his broken hand. "Yes?"

Quickly, before she could decide that he was an unsavory element in search of a handout, he stated his name and his business.

Cook was shaking her head and grumbling over a crumpled copy of the *Seattle Times* when Miranda wandered into the kitchen that morning, two days after Drew had left to search for Joshua, and poured herself a cup of coffee.

"What is it?"

Cook paled. "Says here that a ship caught fire at sea. Austin Darnell was aboard, and there weren't any survivors."

Joshua. Had Joshua been aboard that ship, too, as Austin's prisoner? Miranda's stomach clenched spasmodically. She searched Cook's face and saw the same wretched thought written there.

Chapter Seventeen

IT WAS VERY LATE WHEN DREW RETURNED AND, NO DOUBT drawn by the light burning in the parlor, he joined Miranda there. He looked gaunt, spent somehow, and much older than his nineteen years. His clothes were a total mess and there was a preparation going on in his weary hazel eyes that made his sister ache with dread.

"He's dead," he mumbled. "Joshua is dead."

Ever since learning that Austin's ship had burned—was it only that morning that Cook had shared the news?—Miranda had been preparing herself for this moment. She'd known, somehow, that Joshua had not just gone off somewhere to lick his wounds, that he'd met with serious trouble.

She clasped the arms of her chair in trembling, white-knuckled hands, and a quivering whimper of naked grief escaped her. Oh, God, not him. Not Joshua.

"No," she said, giving voice to something within her that firmly denied Joshua's death.

Drew came to stand in front of her—she noticed that the bandages on his hand were dirty—and then dropped to his heels, so that he could look up into her face. "Miranda, I'm sorry. I know you loved him."

Miranda fought down the strong thing within her that would not believe Joshua was gone. Wishful thinking—it had to be wishful thinking. "He was on board Austin's ship, wasn't he?"

Drew hesitated and then nodded quickly. "Yes."

The tears came then, hot, copious, un-Mirandalike tears. Drew rose far enough to kiss her forehead, then rounded the chair and walked across the spacious parlor. She could hear the melodic clink of crystal as he poured brandy.

"How is Brynne?" he asked softly, facing Miranda again, extending the glass.

Miranda took a deep sip from the brandy before answering, and still her voice was shakey and suppressed sobs set its cadence. "Thanks to Letitia, she's recovering nicely. But this—this is going to . . ." The words fell away as she lifted tear-blurred eyes to her brother's face.

He sighed. "It's all right, Miranda. I'm not stupid. I know about Brynne and Joshua. I know they were lovers. I don't think we should tell her—not yet, anyway."

"But the body, the funeral, Drew."

"Miranda, there isn't any body."

Wild hope sprang up in Miranda's heart and filled her throat so that she could barely speak. Maybe, just maybe, that insistent thing within her was right—

Drew scowled at the obvious hope in her face. "He's *dead*, Miranda," he said firmly. And then he sank into a chair and drew it closer to hers. "About Brynne—"

Miranda swallowed, closed her eyes for a moment. "She will be destroyed, Drew."

"No. I won't let that happen."

"She loved him!"

"She *thought* she loved him," countered Drew, lifting his glass in a distracted toast, his eyes darkening to a dusty jade hue and fixed on something far away.

"As Joshua's brother, I feel a certain responsibility to . . . step in, shall we say?"

Brynne stood silently at the front window of Miranda's small, simply furnished house, looking out. It was the last day of October and a skiff of snow was wafting down from the sky to dust the grass and glisten, like feathery eiderdown, on the needles of the pine trees. Soon, it would be dark, and most all of Port Propensity's children would venture out to do their Halloween mischief.

For now, though, they were inside warm houses, having their supper. The public park, visible from the front windows, looked deserted and sad in the gathering twilight, and snow mounded gracefully on the rails of the wooden bridge.

Brynne's heart ached within her as she looked at the place where the gypsy's wagon had been, that long ago day of the Independence Day picnic. She thought she'd accepted Joshua's death, but it had a way of creeping up on her, unawares, and startling her with a fresh intensity of pain.

The gypsy had predicted her love for Joshua Tanner, with surprising accuracy. *But you didn't say he'd die*, mourned Brynne. *You didn't say Joshua would die.*

At the back of the house, Cook and Placie, temporarily transported from Seattle, were busy preparing spiced cider and candied apples for the inevitable Halloween callers. Brynne considered joining them, but the truth was that she simply hadn't the spirit to share in their merriment. She laid a gentle hand to her stomach, thought again of Joshua Tanner, and was about to turn away from the window when she saw Letitia open the front gate and come scurrying up the snowy walk, clutching something and looking patently determined.

Despite the singular anguish that had dogged her for months now, Brynne smiled. Madame Fortuna had been right about more than one thing—it wasn't even Christmas yet, and Letitia had bosoms.

She hurried to the door to admit her cousin.

"It's cold out there!" accused Letitia, shivering as Brynne pressed the door shut against an icy wind.

"Come and stand by the fire," ordered Brynne, as her cousin handed her a copy of *The Ladies' Companion* and removed her snow-dampened bonnet and matching cape.

"What's this?" Brynne frowned, scanning the cover of the well-worn magazine.

Letitia kissed Brynne's cheek and then waltzed over to stand at the hearth. "It contains our fates, Brynne McFarren."

Brynne rolled her eyes. Letitia had the voluptuous body of a woman, but she was still a little girl in so many ways. "How can a magazine . . ."

Letitia bridled, rubbing her hands together, in the heat of the fireplace, to warm them. "At the stroke of midnight, we'll know who we're going to marry."

Brynne thought of Joshua, lying dead at the bottom of the sea, and ached. "I have no intention of getting married," she said stiffly.

Letitia tossed a meaningful glance at Brynne's still flat stomach—besides Miranda and one doctor in Seattle, she was the only person in the world who knew about the part of himself Joshua had left behind. "You are so stubborn!"

Brynne sighed. Why couldn't anyone—most particularly Drew Tanner—seem to understand? She had loved Joshua; she loved him still. She could not simply turn away from that and fall willingly into some other man's bed, not even if it meant making life much easier for herself and the baby. Marrying anyone else, however convenient, would be whoring.

Of course, there had been a marked cooling of Drew's ardor in the past few weeks, to Brynne's relief, and she noticed that his gaze was often drawn, almost unwillingly, to Letitia.

Now, Letitia came and wrenched the magazine summarily from Brynne's hand, irritated and impatient. Petulantly, she flipped through the pages until she came to a piece bearing the heading, "Who Will Be My Husband?"

Brynne made a rude sound.

Letitia didn't seem to notice, and her color was high. "I do hope you have an extra white nightgown, and some hand mirrors," she mused, her pretty lips pursed with concentration.

"My goodness," breathed Brynne.

Flashing blue eyes came to scorch her face. "Brynne McFarren, you're dreary. You're downright *dismal!* Joshua is gone and you'd be well-advised to marry someone, wouldn't you? Besides, what harm can there be in a simple game?"

What, indeed. Brynne shrugged, mostly to keep the peace, and, at midnight, when their stomachs were full of spicy cider, candied apples, and popped corn, Letitia and Placie garbed themselves in flowing white nightgowns and prevailed upon a grumbling Brynne to do the same.

Their hair hanging free—for the magazine dictated that it must—the three young women made their way to the top of the cellar stairs. Shivering with delight and because the floor was achingly cold under bare feet, Placie handed out the mirrors.

"Here's how it works," whispered Letitia, her eyes sparkling. "You back down the cellar stairs, holding up the mirror. When you reach the bottom step, you should see the face of the man you're going to marry in the looking glass."

Brynne folded her arms and frowned cynically. "More likely, we'll crack our tailbones. Jiggers, you two don't seriously believe—"

"Oh, shut up," snapped Letitia, lifting her chin. "Who goes first?"

"It was your idea," Brynne reminded her archly. "You do it, and for heaven's sake, don't fall."

Letitia drew a deep breath and closed her wonderful blue eyes for a moment, in delicious preparation. Brynne knew that she was hoping to see Drew Tanner's face in her mirror.

"Ready?" whispered Placie, barely able to contain her excitement.

Letitia nodded and began backing cautiously down the cellar stairs, into the gloom. Placie peered after her.

"What do you think she'll see, Brynne?"

"Stars," retorted Brynne acerbically. "She's bound to fall on her backside."

Before Placie could reply to that, there was a sudden and thunderous knocking at the front door. Brynne frowned as she turned, still clad only in the white nightgown Letitia had insisted she wear, and rushed to answer the door before the whole house was roused.

Turning the knob, she peered around the edge of the door, her flannel-clad form hidden. "Yes?"

The young man standing on the front porch was covered with snow—enormous flakes of it were floating down from the sky by then—and, even though Brynne couldn't make out the stranger's face in the darkness, she was alarmed by the unbridled annoyance she sensed in his manner.

"Is this the Tanner house?" he demanded.

Brynne nodded, wondering if she should slam and bolt the door. She couldn't quite bring herself to do that, mostly because something mysterious was quickening in the pit of her stomach. "This is Miss Miranda Tanner's residence," she said, politely.

"Then why hasn't anyone come for him?" shouted the young man, his arms moving in the shadows as he wedged his hands into the pockets of his coat.

Brynne shivered as the snowy wind rounded the half-closed door and stung her flesh through the nightgown. The odd feeling in the pit of her stomach intensified. "Come for whom?" she whispered.

"For Mr. Tanner! He's almost well, and . . ."

Brynne closed her eyes. He was talking about Drew —surely, he was talking about Drew. But Drew wasn't sick or hurt, and why would anyone have to go and fetch him when he was right in Port Propensity? "I don't understand."

"I don't understand, either!" yelled the stranger, seething. "There's been money coming regular, and one feller visits now and then, but—"

Brynne's knees threatened to buckle. Just in time, she remembered that it was Halloween. That was it, this man was playing a cruel prank. "How dare you come to this house in the middle of the night and try to make us believe . . ."

Just then, Miranda appeared, wearing a blue silk wrapper and carrying a lantern in one hand and a derringer in the other. "What is your name?" she demanded imperiously, of the stranger, "and what do you want?"

"My name is Bobby O'Keefe, ma'am," came the furious retort. "And I'm wondering what kind of family Joshua Tanner has that they'd let him mend far from home like that!"

"My brother is dead," said Miranda.

"Then how could he write this?" Bobby O'Keefe shot back, thrusting a crumpled, damp piece of paper into Brynne's hands.

Trembling, wanting to turn away from this vicious joke and yet unable to stop hoping, Brynne unfolded the paper and read it by the light of Miranda's lantern.

Pippin, Congratulations on your marriage. Drew is a fortunate man. You needn't avoid me anymore, because I have no intention of making trouble for you. Best wishes, Joshua.

A cry of mingled protest and hope was torn from Brynne's throat. She watched Miranda's face as she, too, read the note.

"He's alive," breathed the Half-Breed's sister. "Oh, thank God, Joshua is *alive*."

Brynne trembled. "It's a prank, Miranda," she whispered, in a small and wretched voice. "Don't you see that it's a . . ."

Miranda shook her head. Slowly, she lowered the derringer to her side and stepped back in a tacit invitation for Bobby O'Keefe to enter the house. "I know my own brother's handwriting, Brynne," she said. "And Joshua himself wrote this letter."

Brynne McFarren fainted.

It was morning when Brynne awakened, and the snow had not stopped falling. Joshua was alive. The knowledge sent her bounding out of bed, scrambling for her clothes.

She had to go to him; there was so much to say.

In the distance, a whistle shrilled. November first. Today, the Chinese would be expelled, according to the fliers that had been circulating in Port Propensity for weeks and weeks.

Brynne dressed rapidly. As tragic and infuriating as the knowledge was, there was nothing she could do to stop the madness. Besides, nothing truly mattered but the fact that Joshua was alive somewhere.

As she brushed her hair, in long, fierce strokes, Brynne looked at the sleeping Letitia, still cuddled in the big bed. She wondered if the silly little imp had actually seen a man's face in her hand mirror the night before, at the base of the cellar stairs.

With an imagination like Letitia's, anything was possible. She wanted to marry Drew so badly that her mind had probably conjured his image in the looking glass.

Drew. The realization struck Brynne with painful, searing force. Drew had known, all along, that Joshua was alive. He'd been sending money and even visiting, according to Bobby O'Keefe. And, apparently, he

283

hadn't only deceived Miranda and Brynne herself, but Joshua, too. Joshua thought she'd married his brother.

Brynne closed her eyes and fought down a screaming rage. To think Drew had lied like that, let his own sister suffer needless grief! If he'd been standing before her then, she would have killed him without a second thought.

Sternly, Brynne caught herself. There was no time to plot vengeance now. She had to go to Joshua, tell him that she most certainly wasn't married, tell him that the child Rosalie had borne him had never suffered as he'd thought.

The one thing she could not tell him was that he'd fathered another child. The knowledge would no doubt stir his honor and cause him to offer a marriage proposal, and, much as Brynne McFarren longed to be the Half-Breed's wife, she wasn't about to trap him like that.

But she could think of all these things later. *Joshua was alive.*

Miranda was up and fully dressed when Brynne went downstairs, and there was a mischievous light dancing behind the relief and weariness in her dark eyes. The house was toasty warm and the scent of bacon frying was everywhere.

The two women embraced, drew apart to smile at each other with tear-polished eyes.

"I didn't dream it, did I, Miranda?" Brynne whispered.

Miranda could only shake her head.

"We've got to go to him," Brynne hurried on. "Now, today."

Miranda found her voice, and that look of prankish delight flared again in her eyes. "One minute, companion. I refuse to go anywhere until I've had my morning coffee."

"I'll get it for you, then," Brynne cried, rushing, in her eagerness to be done with such mundane matters and go to Joshua. She was breathless and smiling when she pushed open the kitchen door.

And he was there.

Joshua Tanner was standing in the mirage of shimmering heat in front of Cook's gleaming black stove.

Brynne's throat closed over all the things she'd meant to say when she encountered him—she could do nothing but stare, drinking in the sight of him.

He nodded cordially, like a brother greeting a sister. "Mrs. Tanner," he said, and there was a bite in the words.

He looked so thin. Brynne felt tears sting her eyes as Placie and Cook slipped past, to hurry out. Still, she could not speak.

Joshua turned away, to refill the empty coffee mug in his hand. How gaunt and vulnerable and defeated he looked. Brynne shuddered to think of all the dreadful things he must have been through.

At last, he was facing her again, his lavender eyes lingering sadly at her lips, her breasts, her slightly thickened waistline. The room seemed to buckle crazily, and then he was moving toward her, setting his mug down on the table with an angry thump.

Reaching her, he stood very close. Brynne sensed the battle being waged within him and then saw it played out in his wan features. With an involuntary groan, he lifted his hands, undid the buttons of her sedate blue woolen dress, tugged down on her camisole, so that her full breasts were bared to him.

She shivered as she felt his finger circling one dusky nipple, rousing it to offer him that singular nourishment that she so loved to give. She whispered his name raggedly as he bent his head to sip at her.

But, suddenly, he made a growling, angry sound and his mouth left her nipple, the teeth scraping it harshly as he drew back. His hands were hard on her shoulders and his eyes were flashing with orchid ferocity when Brynne dared to meet them.

"So this is the kind of wife my brother has," he drawled.

Outrage and frustrated need made Brynne thrust out her chin. She felt color rise over her bared and still pulsing breasts to pound in her face. "I am no man's wife, Joshua Tanner!"

Joshua paled, and his fierce purple eyes seemed to tear at her face. *"What?"*

"I know Drew told you that he and I were married. It's a lie," she said proudly, angrily. "And furthermore, Joshua Tanner, I should scratch your eyes out for ever thinking that I would love you the way I have and then marry your brother!"

Something murderous moved in the handsome, tormented face, and the look in his eyes tore great, hurting pieces from Brynne's spirit. "He told me—my God—*my God,* I believed him—"

"We thought you were dead, Joshua," Brynne broke in, her voice surprisingly firm and steady in her own ears. "Drew told us you were."

A violent tremor moved through the Half-Breed's towering frame, and his hands tightened on Brynne's shoulders. His throat worked, but he said nothing.

In that instant, Brynne was terrified. There was murder gathering in this man like a storm. If she didn't find a way to calm him, to stop him, he would find his brother and kill him. While Brynne felt the same need to avenge herself on Drew, she knew that Joshua would hang for the killing and they would be parted again—this time, forever.

She took one of his hands from her shoulder and placed it so that it cupped her breast. Reflexively, roughly at first, he caressed her, stirring primitive needs within her.

"You once boasted that you could take me even in a kitchen," she reminded him, watching with both relief and wanton pleasure as the riotous fury in his face subsided a little. "Are you as good as your word, Joshua?"

He laughed, and it was a low, rumbling, weary sound. "We can't delay breakfast," he said. "What would the others think?"

Brynne pressed him into a chair—for all his size, it was easy to do—and bent over him, so that the nipple of her right breast brushed his lips.

Joshua groaned, caught the offered nubbin hungrily, and suckled. Brynne's womb quickened within her, so great was the passion he stirred, and she moaned aloud, not caring if the whole town heard.

Joshua released the hardened nipple to laugh, then came slowly to his feet. Gently, his hands on Brynne's shoulders, warm beneath the fabric of her dress, he drew her close and kissed her with unrestrained hunger. She could feel the hard shaft of his manhood pressing against her, and she longed to sheath it in her own receiving warmth. His tongue explored the depths of her mouth, a gentle invader compelling her on to aching passion. Finally, his hands slid from beneath her dress and he lifted his mouth from hers to possess her with his eyes. "The bacon is burning," he said.

"I don't care," replied Brynne. And then she clasped his hand and pulled him into the dark, fragrant privacy of Cook's pantry. There, she bolted the door.

Joshua laughed, and the sound was rich and warm in the pleasant gloom. "God, how I've missed you, Brynne McFarren. How I've wanted you . . ."

Brynne knelt. His groan was half a protest and half a plea. He was still shuddering, minutes later, when he lifted her to her feet, covered her lips with his own, kissed her so deeply that the world seemed to fall away beneath her.

Gently, almost desperately, he lowered her to the floor. Just the weight of him, pressed against her, made her cry for the joy of knowing he was here, alive, wanting her. "Oh, Joshua," she whispered brokenly. "Love me. Take me . . ."

A soft, hoarse laugh came from his throat. "Oh, no, Pippin. I'll have my vengeance first."

Brynne writhed, aching to receive him, but she knew there was no point in hurrying him. The Half-Breed made love at his own pace, just as he did everything else.

The coming minutes were glorious, they sundered Brynne's mind and spirit and sent them soaring in diverse directions. His fingers, his lips—he was touching her in so many places that she lost count.

When, at last, he entered her, the first of several shattering releases rocked her. He made no attempt to stifle her cries. Instead he seemed to revel in them, and found ways to amplify them with devilish skill.

When the highest peak had been reached, they lay breathless, legs entwined, waiting in a daze for their spirits to settle back into their exhausted bodies.

How Ling was frightened. Her uncles and the others in Little Canton seemed unconcerned that November first, the deadline day, had finally arrived.

Lum Su operated his thriving laundry as though it was just another day, cheerfully starching white men's shirts and pressing their trousers. Kwan So packed fresh fish to sell from house to house, and How Ling's own mother prepared to go and clean Drew Tanner's home.

"Mother," How Ling protested, in the clipped, swift dialect of Kwantung Province. "We cannot go out and work today. It is too dangerous. The whites want us to leave."

How May responded in the same language, for it was the only one she knew, though she did understand a smattering of English. "They cannot drive us out. Where would we go? And we have done nothing wrong."

How Ling listened distractedly to the noises of the pigs living beneath their shack of a house. "They don't care where we go, Mother. And it doesn't matter that we have done no wrong. They don't want us here."

"We will do our work," said How May staunchly, in a tone that brooked no argument.

How Ling wanted to weep in her frustration and her fear. Why was it that her mother and the others could not believe what was about to happen? They thought they had rights, because so many were citizens. They thought there would be no trouble, or that, if there was, the government of the territory would help them.

How foolish they were! Their only hope had been Joshua Tanner, the Half-Breed, and he was dead.

"You heard the whistle," How Ling protested. It was her desperation that caused her to do the unthinkable and defy an elder.

"That was only for the shipyard workers and the others," came the dismissive retort.

"No," argued How Ling bravely. "No, Mother. It is Sunday. The white men don't work today. Only we work." This last was added bitterly, and it stirred genuine anger in How May's normally placid face.

"You will be silent!"

In despair, How Ling bit back the other words that wanted to follow those she had already said. It was no use—no use at all.

Brynne stood up, slowly, and began righting her clothes. Beyond the pantry door, Placie and Letitia were chatting jubilantly, though their words were indiscernible.

Joshua laughed as he, too, prepared himself to meet the world. "What are you thinking, Pippin?" he asked.

"That they'll know."

"And?"

"And I don't care."

He laughed again, and she felt his hands come to rest tenderly on her face. "Have you no shame, woman?"

Brynne lifted her chin. "No. Not where you're concerned, Joshua Tanner."

Joshua nibbled deliciously at her earlobe, traced the

length of her neck with warm lips. "Do you realize that we could probably live in here for months?"

"The food would be gone in a week," said Brynne, the ever practical Scot.

Joshua's hand closed eloquently, possessively, over her right breast. "Maybe yours would," he drawled.

Brynne thought of the baby growing within her and smiled over her secret. What would he say if he knew that someone small and vulnerable was about to come and take nourishment at the breasts he so enjoyed?

It was then that she remembered another baby—Rosalie's. Joshua's.

She drew in a deep breath.

Instantly, Joshua's hands came to her shoulders. "What is it, Brynne?"

"I was thinking of what my father did."

He was silent, but Brynne could feel the old pain surging through him and into her.

"Joshua, the child didn't suffer."

He trembled, and his voice was a vicious rasp. "What are you saying?"

"It was dead, Joshua. It had been dead for weeks before Rosalie delivered it. She couldn't bring herself to tell you."

The silence in that dark pantry was pulsing, threatening.

Brynne raised her hands to Joshua's shadowed face, felt his mingled anguish and shock and hope in the taut planes of it. "I'm not trying to excuse my father, Joshua, and I'm not making this up just to make things easier for you. My Aunt Eloise was there, and she can verify everything."

Violently, Joshua broke free, turned away. "Why in God's name did they let me go on thinking that my child was butchered alive?" he rasped.

"Papa was afraid, Joshua. I know now that that's why we left in such a hurry, why he drank so much, why he had the nightmares. Why he finally—"

"Your aunt," Joshua whispered. "Why didn't your aunt tell me?"

"Joshua, she was afraid to. You were making threats. She was wrong to let you suffer, but I can understand her fear."

Brynne heard him fall heavily against the wall, and her throat constricted as deep, dry, sudden sobs shook him. She approached slowly, drew him into her arms, and held him.

"I love you," she told him, against her will and her better judgment. "I will always love you."

Joshua shuddered in her arms, but offered no spoken response. After a time, however, his raw grief abated, and Brynne sensed a quickening within him, a new strength.

"Drew and Miranda," he mused, after a long, healing time. "Brynne, did they know?"

"No, Joshua," Brynne assured him, her hands moving gently, warmly on his shoulders.

His taut body slackened, but then, a moment later, something primitive and frightening moved inside him. "Drew," he said, in a low voice that nonetheless seemed to shake the very foundations of the world.

Brynne grasped at him as he tore himself away from her and flipped the catch on the pantry door. "No . . . oh, Joshua, wait. . . ."

Joshua didn't seem to hear her. He was striding through the kitchen, toward the back door, oblivious to everything but one unspeakable purpose.

"Joshua!" Brynne screamed, ignoring the gaping Placie and Letitia, who were sitting at the table.

The glass in the kitchen door shook musically as he slammed it behind him.

"What on earth was going on in there?" demanded a wide-eyed Letitia, rising slowly to her feet. "Brynne—"

"Oh, shut up!" hissed Brynne, tearing a shawl from the peg beside the door and hurrying outside. A moment later, she was running through the dusting of powdery white snow, in pursuit of the Half-Breed.

Again, she screamed his name.

His long strides grew to a lope, and he did not look back. He was clearly bent on making his way through the trees and dense underbrush that separated this house from the one high on the hill. "Go inside!" he yelled.

Brynne ran faster, following the footprints in the snow when she lost him in the blackberry thicket behind the outhouse. "They'll hang you!" she shouted, into the icy, silent snowfall and the thick foliage.

"I don't care!" he bellowed, from somewhere well up the hillside. "Goddamn it, *go home!*"

"I won't go home, Joshua Tanner!" Brynne retorted, at the top of her lungs. "I won't! Maybe you don't care if you hang for murder, but I do!"

Silence.

"Joshua!"

Snow was gathering, clean and cold, on Brynne's eyelashes and her cheeks. Though she couldn't see Joshua, she knew that she'd halted him, that he was hesitating, listening.

"Do you want your baby to be as lonely as you were?" she called, closing her eyes, willing her heartbeat to slow to a bearable pace. "Do you want it to be a bastard?"

There was a rustling in the blackberry vines and hazelnut bushes, and snow shimmered to the ground as Joshua displaced them. His face was taut and pale as he approached.

"What baby?" he demanded, in a harsh whisper, taking her shoulders in a fierce grasp. "Brynne, *what baby?*"

She hadn't meant to tell him, at least, not like this. Tears streamed, warm, down Brynne's cold-reddened, aching face. "Our baby, Joshua. Yours and mine."

His eyes slid angrily, wildly, to her stomach, back to her face. "No. Oh, my God, *no.*"

Brynne wanted to die. This was just the reaction she'd feared, though she had, at times, convinced herself that he would want to marry her. "I'm sorry," she said, in a broken and hopeless voice.

Joshua swore savagely. "When?"

"April," confessed Brynne.

Chapter Eighteen

FURIOUSLY, JOSHUA THRUST HER AWAY FROM HIM. SHE nearly fell into the thorny, snow-laden blackberry bushes, but he grasped her again, just in time, and wrenched her against him. His face was hard, cruel, unforgiving.

"Damn you," he breathed. "Damn you for doing this to me, Brynne!"

Suddenly, Brynne's grief was overshadowed by her outrage. She raised her hand and slapped him brutally, all the force of her pain and her shame giving her strength. "I hate you," she breathed.

He released her and turned away, and Brynne sank to her knees in the snow. Covering her face with both hands, she wept wretchedly. Only when her tears were spent did she see that Joshua was gone.

There was a light sprinkling of snow on the stone marking Rosalie's grave, and Joshua did not bother to brush it away. She'd loved the snow.

He sighed and said her name and it held no magic. The woman filling his mind and spirit was Brynne McFarren, and she left no room, damn the wench, for anyone else.

Pain grasped at his midsection as he read the words etched into Rosalie's monument. Would he, one day, lay Brynne here, too? Would she, like Rosalie, be buried with his child in her arms?

It was then that he heard the shouting, coming from the park at the base of the hill, then that he remembered the date: November 1. It was the day set, months ago, for the forceable expulsion of Port Propensity's Chinese citizens.

Almost grateful that there was a battle to be fought, Joshua Tanner turned from his fears and Rosalie's grave and stormed toward the woods and the narrow path that led down to the park.

He pushed aside memories of Brynne McFarren flinging watermelon at him there, on the Fourth of July, and broke into an easy run. He would have all his life to think about her, to love her and fight with her—provided he lived through this one day.

Drew, carrying a rifle purloined from Joshua's gun cabinet in the big house on the hill, was not surprised when the Half-Breed came out of the woods lining the park and stormed toward the gathering of men. He'd known Joshua would come back one day and, despite the shiver of justified fear coiling in the pit of his stomach, he was glad.

The other men—Walter Jennings and the rest—looked as though they'd seen a ghost. They carried torches, even though it was daylight, and the pitch sputtered and snapped over their heads in the falling snow. The Chinese the mob had already managed to gather up were huddled together inside the circle of angry white men, shivering with fear and cold.

We're all afraid, Drew thought pragmatically. *Every last one of us, yellow or white.*

The Half-Breed elbowed his way easily into the circle, his eyes touching on Drew only briefly. Sam Prigg and half a dozen other men rallied behind the giant, looking as grimly determined as their leader.

Drew shuddered. Why couldn't that damned Indian ever link up with the fact that he couldn't fight the whole world? What were a handful of men—and the Half-Breed wasn't even armed—against an entire town?

"You're beat this time, Josh," ventured one of the men standing near Drew. "These yellow devils is leavin' town, whether you like it or not. We've got a schooner at the wharf right now, to take them away."

The Half-Breed stood taller than ever, it seemed to Drew, his booted feet set wide apart, his eyes flashing with purple malice as they assessed the mob. Again, Drew shuddered.

They'll kill him, he thought, with calm despair, just as he caught sight of Brynne and Miranda and Letitia standing a few yards away, bundled in shawls and cloaks, watching with wide, frightened eyes.

Drew sighed. He'd certainly made a hell of a mess of everything—Joshua's life, Brynne's, his own. He'd been so damned sure he loved Brynne, loved her enough to say Joshua was dead when he knew his brother was recovering from a near fatal beating and a subsequent bout of pneumonia.

But lately he'd been thinking about Letitia Jennings almost constantly. He heard the ingenuous ring of her laughter at the oddest times, could be moved to emotions he'd never thought possible by the curve of her small, perfect breasts and the aqua light in her eyes.

Good God, he loved her. Now, seeing her standing with Brynne and Miranda, watching him, he suddenly wanted her to see a very different Drew. Calmly, he took his place beside Joshua and thrust the rifle he carried into his brother's hands.

There was a startled look in Joshua's eyes, and some of the bone-numbing anger was displaced, for the moment, by an emotion Drew couldn't begin to read.

"When this is over . . ." warned the Half-Breed, in a low, dangerous voice.

"I know," Drew broke in philosophically.

Some of the Chinese women were weeping, holding their children in their arms. The sound stirred shame in Drew Tanner, caused him to stand just a little closer to his brother.

"Step aside, Joshua!" yelled Walter Jennings, with bravado. "We don't plan to hurt these people."

Joshua's rock-hard jaw convulsed slightly, relaxed again. "Go home, Jennings. Forget this."

"You can't fight us all, Tanner!" put in another man. "We'll get mean if need be."

Joshua cocked the rifle Drew had given him in defiant answer.

"They aren't worth dying for, Joshua," reasoned Jennings, in a tremulous voice. "For God's sake, get out of our way!"

"They're people," retorted Joshua, in an even voice. "Women, kids. I won't stand here and see them herded down the wharf like so many cattle."

Sam Prigg stepped forward, to stand at Joshua's left side. "You might just bring us down, Jennings. You got the guns fer it. But me and the Half-Breed and these other fellas is gonna take a goodly share of you sons a bitches with us. You're the one what said they weren't worth dyin' for. What be your choice?"

Drew was scared stupid, and his right hand, long since free of its splint, ached fiercely. Still, somehow, he found his voice, and it was the voice of a man. "You all know my brother. You can stand here and argue from now till the judgment and you won't move him. Why risk your lives?"

"Thought you stood with us, boy," observed a man standing beyond the ever thickening veil of silent snow. "And it seems to me that you'd have somethin' to gain if the Half-Breed was gone."

Drew could not look at Joshua—he knew too well what he would see if he did. Contempt. Disbelief. He thought of Letitia as he spoke. "He's my brother," he said. "If Joshua falls, I fall."

"This isn't going to keep me from tearing you apart

when this is over, you know," the Half-Breed reminded him, in an undertone. "Grand stand or no grand stand, your ass is grass."

Drew grinned, despite his fear and his shame and a thousand other unsettling emotions that had no names. "I always could outrun you, Big Brother," he replied.

Joshua chuckled.

The mob was getting nervous now. Men were shifting from one foot to the other, grumbling, looking around. In the huddled nest of Chinese, a baby squalled. *I've had better days myself, kid*, thought Drew.

"What's it going to be, Jennings?" demanded Joshua.

Letitia's father paled. Even though the Half-Breed and his friends were outnumbered, the odds of his surviving the first shots fired weren't good, and he clearly knew it. "They're taking white men's jobs, Tanner," he whined lamely.

"That may be true in other places," answered the Half-Breed, with quiet reason. "But it doesn't apply here, and you know it. The men who work for me get the same pay, no matter what color their hide is. I don't lay white men off and hire Indians and Chinese at half the wages."

"Our beef ain't with you," said a millworker, who seemed to be wavering between one faction and the other. "You're a good boss, Mr. Tanner."

The Half-Breed disagreed. "Most of these people are American citizens, with as much right to live in this territory as you or I. I'll die before I'll let you run them off."

"Why?" rasped Jennings, genuinely puzzled. "What the hell are they to you?"

"People," said the Half-Breed flatly. "And I'd take the same stand if they were trying to drive *you* out."

Several of the torch-bearing members of the mob casually shifted sides, coming to stand behind the Half-Breed. Bystanders joined him, too—one of them was the good-looking gambling man who had bought Austin Darnell's business after his death had been confirmed, and another was Bobby O'Keefe, who had been Joshua's friend during his recovery at Jack Dancer's house in Portland.

O'Keefe turned an acid look on Drew and then smiled cordially at the mob. "My money's on the Half-Breed," he said, in a clear voice. "Why don't you people go home and do your hating where it won't get you killed?"

Drew turned slightly, to glance at Letitia. She was watching O'Keefe now, and there was an unsettling gleam of admiration in her eyes. *Jesus*, thought Drew miserably. *She likes him.* His loins began to ache in rhythm with the ghosts of the fractures in his right hand.

The snow fell harder, faster, stinging Drew's hands and face, causing the flames on the torches to crackle and flicker and smoke. He was truly startled when a small hand clasped the crook of his elbow and he looked down to see Letitia standing defiantly at his side. "Are you going to shoot me, Papa?" she challenged, in a ringing voice. "If you shoot Drew and the others, you'll have to kill me, too."

Drew's heart soared within him, despite the awesome fear that Jennings might just be crazy enough to shoot his own daughter. And, for the first time, he understood Brynne's fierce loyalty to the Half-Breed, and he wasn't surprised to see that she'd taken her place at Joshua's side, her eyes as stormy as the winter sky.

"Kill us, Uncle Walter," she said, raising her chin, ignoring the angry shock in Joshua's face. "Why don't you just kill us all?"

Walter Jennings swore roundly, but he lowered his rifle. And, at his lead, so did the other men. Torches hissed as they were extinguished in the snow, pistols scraped leather as they were jammed into holsters.

As if by magic, the grumbling crowd began to

disperse. Drew knew for a certainty that there would be more trouble, but, for this one day, the crisis was past. Easily, he slid his arm around Letitia's shoulders.

The Half-Breed's rifle fell to the ground with an ominous clatter as he turned to his brother. "Now," he breathed, his eyes darkening with rage, his features taut. "About what happened."

Letitia scrambled out from under Drew's arm and stood in front of him, a small, soft, fierce barrier. "Don't you lay a hand on him, Joshua Tanner."

Joshua's eyes widened. "What the—"

"I won't let you hurt him," Letitia said, shaking free when Drew laid restraining hands on her shoulders. "I love Drew, and I won't let you touch him!"

The Half-Breed was stunned for a moment, but, then, to the amazement of everyone, he threw back his head and shouted with laughter. Brynne was flinging alarmed looks from Joshua to Letitia and back again, and she was gripping her man's arm with white-knuckled hands. "What's so funny?" she demanded, in a shaky voice.

"He's in love with a woman just like you," Joshua said, between bursts of hoarse, throaty amusement. "I couldn't have wished for a better vengeance!"

Brynne colored to the roots of her hair and kicked at Joshua's shin, only to be easily restrained.

Drew turned his small defender to face him, his hands gentle. "He's right, Letitia," he said. "I do love you."

The proud blue eyes shone with tears. "You wanted Brynne," she reminded him, accusingly. And then, incredibly, she turned and started toward Miranda's house at a furious pace, making her way through the thinning crowd of Chinese and the workers who had gathered either to support the Half-Breed or to do battle with him.

Drew bolted into a run. "Letitia, wait!" he called gruffly, slipping and almost falling into the snow-slickened grass. "Damn it, will you *wait?*"

Letitia walked faster, and Drew raced after her, oblivious to the laughter behind him.

Brynne felt warm, despite the snow and the chill of that November day. She'd been so caught up in Drew and Letitia's romantic drama that she didn't notice the departure of everyone else until it was too late. She was alone with the Half-Breed.

"Brynne," the giant began, in an awkward, little-boy voice. "I . . ."

Brynne leaped back as though his touch would burn her, her arms folded across her chest. "Don't you say another *word* to me, Joshua Tanner. You've said quite enough!"

"No, I haven't," he argued softly, and there was snow gathering in his rumpled ebony hair, on his eyebrows, on his wide shoulders. "Pippin, I love you."

Brynne felt wild hope swath through her like a river, but her practical Scottish nature quelled that quickly enough. "Bullfeathers," she said.

Joshua laughed. "Damn if you aren't just payment for every sin I've ever committed. Marry me, Brynne, or we'll both burn in hell for our lust."

Brynne thrust out her chin. "Marry *you*, is it? I'm not that desperate to give my child a name, mister!"

"Your child? You started it by yourself, did you?"

Brynne was stubbornly silent.

Joshua let out his breath. "Brynne, I've had months to think. Months to believe you were my brother's wife. For God's sake, have mercy on me, will you? I'm not declaring myself just because you're carrying my baby—"

"Then why?" snapped Brynne, furious and hopeful and totally confused. "I know you loved Rosalie!"

"I did," he said, with cool sincerity. "She was the breath in my lungs, the blood in my veins, the reason I could bear being the Half-Breed, being the bastard son. But she's gone now, God rest her, and you're here."

"How very convenient!"

"I need you, Brynne. And not just in bed, if that's what you're thinking. I need your sauce and your spirit and your laughter. I need the way you wrinkle your nose when you're puzzled and the way your eyes flash when somebody steps on your stupid Scottish pride." His fine lips curved into a grin that would have done Lucifer himself proud. "Marry me out of pity if you won't do it for love."

Brynne flushed and kicked at his shin, purposely missing this time. "You're impossible, Joshua Tanner!"

"But you love me?"

She laughed, in spite of herself. "You know I do, you rake."

Apparently unconcerned with the fact that they were standing in a public place, in the middle of a snow-storm, the Half-Breed dropped theatrically to one knee. "If you won't have me for a husband, woman, I swear I won't draw another sane breath."

"Get up!" pleaded Brynne, wildly embarrassed.

Joshua smiled, shrugged, remained on his knee.

"All right!" cried Brynne, flinging her arms out wide in joyous defeat. "All right, I'll marry you!"

"Today?" he pressed, tilting his head to one side.

"Today," agreed Brynne, and the angry scowl on her face was suddenly impossible to maintain.

The door of Brynne's bedroom swung open at one nudge from the toe of Joshua's boot, and she thought how odd and ironic life was—why, you could leave a room with no hope of having the man you loved and enter it next as his wife.

"I love you, Brynne Tanner," Joshua said, as he set her gently on her feet and lifted her chin for his kiss.

The way he was sipping at her lips made Brynne feel drunken, and she swayed a little in his embrace. Fire shot through her as he undid the buttons of her very best dress, a pretty, embroidered satin of ivory. With gentle fingers, he plucked at the nipples pouting beneath her camisole.

I am his wife, she thought, and the knowledge, coupled with the sweet plundering of her breasts, caused her to whimper with delight.

He slid one side of the silken camisole down to reveal her, to take sustenance at a nipple already hardened for his possession. An interlude of delicious torment followed, and Brynne Tanner moaned shamelessly with pleasure, not caring that there were wedding guests lingering below, in Miranda's parlor.

"I can't wait," Joshua confided raggedly, his breath warm on her breast. "God help me, this time I can't wait."

Brynne nodded as he sank into a chair, pulling her after him. She slipped from his grasp just long enough to undo his trousers and reveal him. He tilted his head back and moaned, his fingers tangled in her hair, as vulnerable now as his wife.

For a time, she pleasured him, reveling in the pulsing beauty of his surrender. Then, in motions designed to heighten his pleasure, she rose and slowly removed her clothes.

With a raspy cry of impatience and need, he wrenched her to him, turning her so that she was facing away from him. She moaned at the ancient delight of sheathing him, at the magical motion of his hands closing over her naked breasts.

Joshua lifted her, far enough that he had almost completely withdrawn, and then lowered her again. She relived the sweet force of his entry over and over, her eyes closed, her spirit soaring free of her body to drift in the snowy skies above the little house.

Never, for all their loving, had the sensations he aroused in her been so soul-rendingly ferocious. Brynne was certain that her flesh had been bonded to his, by the heat of their passion, and that they would be one forever.

Joshua began to move rapidly beneath her, and his words were hardly more than harsh, ragged breaths. "Oh . . . Brynne . . ." He stiffened suddenly beneath her, as his wife was flung heavenward on the treacherous force of her own fulfillment, and growled with fierce and echoing need, *"Brynne . . ."*

Brynne wafted slowly down from the sky, catching on smaller, yet wickedly piercing, releases as she went. She was almost delirious when she finally sank back against her husband's hard, heaving chest in sated exhaustion.

They sat, still joined, for some minutes, each unable to move. Then, however, the passions began to stir again.

Brynne stood up, drew her husband with her to the marriage bed. They were not so driven now, and the heat between them had time to build to a new intensity.

Brynne Tanner thought, as her husband sipped languidly at her breast, that she could ask nothing more of this life than the love of the man who was stretched out, naked, beside her.

But he ceased his suckling to search her face with mischievous orchid eyes. His hand moved over her flat, warm, satiny belly to the vee of silk beneath.

Brynne stretched and whimpered involuntarily as he found the nubbin hidden there and bared it with his fingers. It waited, pulsing, as his lips slid, like slow fire, over the rounding of her breasts, over her middle, and then past the part so anxious for surrender to the insides of her thighs, the tender backs of her knees, the curve of her calves.

Even when his warm mouth came tantalizingly back to its destination, he would not give the full satisfaction Brynne craved with all her heart and soul. Instead, he kissed and nibbled and caressed, delighting in the shameless pleas she uttered.

304

She thrust her legs out wide in desperate surrender, begging now. But her pleas fell away as he conquered her, displaced by a cry of lust and welcome.

April 22, 1886
Seattle, Washington Territory

Brynne Tanner smiled up into her husband's face as the infant girl snuggled close to her breast.

"Hey," protested the Half-Breed, looking less wan and frightened than he had during the rigors of his daughter's delivery. "That's *mine*."

Brynne laughed as the baby suckled in earnest, her tiny, perfect fingers moving like the brush of butterfly wings against her mother's flesh. "As you can see, she's intimidated."

Joshua shrugged. "Try reasoning with a woman. How do you feel, Pippin?"

"Warm, good, and sore."

Joshua chuckled hoarsely as he sat down on the side of their bed. Night was wet and angry at the windows, and Brynne knew that Cook and Placie were waiting anxiously in the hall to see the baby.

"My God," Joshua breathed. "I was scared."

Brynne reached out, touched his hand. "I know. Why do you think I denied myself the right of every woman giving birth?"

He frowned. "What right?"

Brynne laughed. "Next time, Joshua Tanner, you will kindly leave me alone with the doctor, so I can scream properly."

Joshua looked frightened again. "Does it hurt that much?"

"More." Brynne looked down at her daughter, Joshua's daughter, and she thought the love inside her could not be contained. "But you were worth it, Caroline Snowbird Tanner. You were worth it."

Joshua reached out with touching caution to feel the soft, dark down gleaming on Caroline's tiny head. "Maybe we shouldn't have any more babies. I mean . . ."

Brynne smiled at him with weary mischief. "All right. We'll abstain."

"Abstain?" he croaked, swallowing.

Brynne shrugged. "How else can we be sure of having only one child, Joshua?"

He laughed. "Let's have a dozen."

"At least," replied Brynne.

Miranda's trunks made a small mountain on the wharf, and she tried hard to hide the tears in her eyes as she kissed Brynne and Joshua and Caroline good-bye. It was only mid-afternoon, but Port Propensity's Fourth of July celebration was already beginning.

"Where in heaven's name are Drew and Letitia?" she demanded with false petulance, needing something to say.

Joshua grinned and tossed his magnificent head toward the carriage at the base of the wharf. "In there. And I wouldn't go and say good-bye if I were you."

Miranda laughed. "Good Lord, those two are worse than some other newlyweds I know. Would you believe that they were making love in the springhouse yesterday, when I went out to get eggs and cream?"

"That was us," said Joshua crisply, flinching in mock pain as Brynne elbowed him, hard, in the ribs.

Other passengers were boarding the steamer now, and the vessel's whistle sounded shrill, in the bright, blue-gold heat of that Independence Day. Drawn by the sound, Drew and Letitia deigned to come out of the carriage and bid a proper farewell to Miranda.

She kissed them both soundly, and cried as she held little Caroline in her arms just once more. The child was so very beautiful, she thought, with Joshua's raven black hair and Brynne's slate-gray eyes.

But it was time to go, time to stop looking after her brothers and make a new life for herself.

"Good-bye," she whispered wretchedly, kissing the baby's forehead and then thrusting her back into her papa's strong, waiting arms. "Good-bye."

With that, Miranda Tanner turned and raced toward the boarding ramp and up onto the deck. Not once did she look back.

Letitia linked her arm through Brynne's and the two women led the way back toward the carriage. "Do you think Madame Fortuna will be at the picnic again this year, Brynne? Perhaps we could ask her if there will be a man in Miranda's life soon."

Brynne laughed and shook her head.

Drew's wife looked suitably offended. "Madame Fortuna was right about a lot of things, may I remind you? Did I or did I not grow bosoms? Did you or did you not fall in love with a dark-haired man?"

Brynne sighed. "Letitia, you *ninny*. She knew you would develop. It was inevitable. And it was just luck that she described Joshua so well."

Letitia raised one delicate eyebrow. "Was it? How about Halloween night?"

To Brynne, Halloween night was the night she'd learned that Joshua was alive. She looked back, over one shoulder, to smile at him, to reassure herself that he was really there, carrying Caroline and talking business with Drew.

They reached the carriage and, as Joshua opened the door to help Brynne and Letitia inside and surrender a now fitful Caroline, Brynne finally answered. "What about Halloween, Letitia?"

Letitia reached out to claim Caroline and comfort her in able arms, glaring, all the while, at the child's mother. "I saw Drew's face in my mirror, that's what!"

Brynne laughed, sat back, and closed her eyes. Then,

because Caroline demanded it, she bared one breast and fed her baby.

Joshua left the picnic subtly, and made his way to the graveyard at the top of the hill. He stood, not at Rosalie's resting place, but at the one beside Brynne's mother's. He'd had John McFarren moved here because he believed that, even in death, a man should be near the woman he loved.

He studied the crudely carved, wooden marker, also transported from the McFarren farm, and felt aching love for the woman who had made it. For all John had taken away, he'd given back much.

Joshua raised his head and searched the blue, blue sky. He was aware, totally, of the woman standing behind him, but he pretended not to know she was there.

"Do you still hate him, Joshua?" Brynne whispered.

Joshua shook his head, without turning around, and said, "No."

She came to him, took his arm. "I love you."

He smiled down at her, kissed her quickly. "Where is my daughter?" he demanded, with mock fierceness.

"Drew and Letitia are holding her hostage," said Brynne, smiling. "They won't release her until we promise not to go back to Seattle tonight."

Joshua shook his head, wondering at the changes he'd seen in his brother over the past few months. Drew was not only a remarkably devoted husband to Letitia, but a definite asset to Tanner Enterprises, too. He was managing the Port Propensity operation with surprising deftness and skill. "I suppose we'll have to ransom her by promising to stay one more night," he said.

Brynne looked pleased, but she was tugging him back toward the merriment and general mayhem of the Independence Day picnic. "Let's go, Joshua," she pleaded. "Evan wants to take our portrait and they're about to let the greased pig go and . . ."

Joshua threw back his head and laughed, but he allowed himself to be led back to the picnic. He had, as it happened, a few plans of his own.

Brynne Tanner sighed with contentment as the sky darkened and the first Independence Day rockets burst there, spewing shimmers of silver and gold to rival the moon. She was full, to brimming, with happiness and fried chicken and cautiously eaten ice cream.

She frowned. From the blanket where she sat, her arms wrapped around her knees, she could see Drew and Letitia spooning beneath a willow tree beside the pond. She felt oddly lonely at the sight, for Placie had taken an exhausted Caroline home to the house on the hill, and Joshua had disappeared.

As someone set off a string of very loud firecrackers, the horses around the park nickered and danced in protest. Women began to shriek with playful fear.

It was then that Joshua loomed before her, suddenly, and she saw in the flickering light of the torches that he was carrying something in both hands. Something dripping and pulpy and red.

She leaped to her feet in delicious terror, backing away from Joshua and from the watermelon he held so threateningly. "Ooh," he breathed, with evil relish. "Pippin, I've got you now!"

Brynne shrieked and ran, stumbling, toward the table where other women were taking ammunition from hard, green rinds. Just as she reached this comical armory, however, she felt Joshua's watermelon strike the back of her head and slide, seedy and cold, down her neck and into her dress.

She screamed. "Joshua Tanner," she gasped, turning on him, glaring at him. "Look what you've done! I'm all dirty!"

He laughed and, in one fluid motion, swept her up into his arms. "I can fix that," he said, striding toward the pond at the park's edge.

Brynne trembled with horror and outrage. "No!" she

shrieked, as the realization of what he planned washed over her.

He stopped where the rental rowboats were docked, his face benign and full of humor in the light of the torches.

"You wouldn't," pleaded Brynne, as he considered his options. "Oh, Joshua, tell me you won't!"

He laughed, bent his head to sip teasingly, warmly, at the fullness of her lips. "Why shouldn't I?"

Brynne puzzled for a moment, then spouted, "Because I could catch pneumonia and die!"

Joshua lifted one eyebrow, debating. "In July?" he asked. "That pond is as warm as bathwater . . ." he paused, a wicked light gleaming in his orchid eyes. "That's what you need. A proper bath."

Brynne blushed, closed her eyes and gasped as one of his hands came boldly to caress her right breast. "And you plan to *help*, I suppose," she drawled.

"Of course," he said, his finger circling idly around her gingham-covered nipple. "As any good husband would."

Brynne laughed hoarsely and caught his hand, just to keep from offering herself to him then and there. "Damn you," she breathed.

No one noticed when the Tanners went home.

If you
enjoyed the
passion and adventure
of this book...

then you're sure to enjoy the Tapestry Home Subscription Service℠!

You'll receive two new Tapestry™ romance novels each month, as soon as they are published, delivered right to your door.

Examine your books for 15 days, free...

Return the coupon below, and we'll send you two Tapestry romances to examine for 15 days, free. If you're as thrilled with your books as we think you will be, just pay the enclosed invoice. Then every month, you'll receive two intriguing Tapestry love stories — and you'll never pay any postage, handling, or packing costs. If not delighted, simply return the books and owe nothing. There is no minimum number of books to buy, and you may cancel at any time.

Return the coupon today . . . and soon you'll enjoy all the love, passion and adventure of times gone by!

HISTORICAL *Tapestry* ROMANCES

Tapestry Home Subscription Service, Dept. RPSR 12
120 Brighton Road, Box 5020, Clifton, N.J. 07015

Yes, I'd like to receive 2 exciting Tapestry historical romances each month as soon as they are published. The books are mine to examine for 15 days, free. If I decide to keep the books, I will pay only $2.50 each, a total of $5.00. If not delighted, I can return them and owe nothing. There is never a charge for this convenient home delivery—no postage, handling, or any other hidden charges. **I understand there is no minimum number of books I must buy, and that I can cancel this arrangement at any time.**

☐ Mrs.   ☐ Miss   ☐ Ms.   ☐ Mr.

Name _____ (please print) _____

Address _____ Apt. # _____

City _____ State _____ Zip _____
(   )
Area Code   Telephone Number

Signature (if under 18, parent or guardian must sign) _____

This offer, limited to one per household, expires July 31, 1984. Terms and prices are subject to change. Your enrollment is subject to acceptance by Simon & Schuster Enterprises.
Tapestry™ is a trademark of Simon & Schuster, Inc.

Tapestry
HISTORICAL ROMANCES

Breathtaking New Tales

of love and adventure set against
history's most exciting time and
places. Featuring two novels by the
finest authors in the field of romantic fiction—<u>every month</u>.

Next Month From
Tapestry Romances

ALLIANCE OF LOVE
by Catherine Lyndell
JADE MOON
by Erica Mitchell

POCKET BOOKS